The Aesthetics of Space in Nineteenth-Century British Literature, 1843–1907

Edinburgh Critical Studies in Victorian Culture

Series Editor: Julian Wolfreys

Recent books in the series:

Rudyard Kipling's Fiction: Mapping Psychic Spaces
Lizzy Welby

The Decadent Image: The Poetry of Wilde, Symons and Dowson
Kostas Boyiopoulos

British India and Victorian Literary Culture
Máire ní Fhlathúin

Anthony Trollope's Late Style: Victorian Liberalism and Literary Form
Frederik Van Dam

Dark Paradise: Pacific Islands in the Nineteenth-Century British Imagination
Jenn Fuller

Twentieth-Century Victorian: Arthur Conan Doyle and the Strand Magazine, *1891–1930*
Jonathan Cranfield

The Lyric Poem and Aestheticism: Forms of Modernity
Marion Thain

Gender, Technology and the New Woman
Lena Wånggren

Self-Harm in New Woman Writing
Alexandra Gray

Suffragist Artists in Partnership: Gender, Word and Image
Lucy Ella Rose

Victorian Liberalism and Material Culture: Synergies of Thought and Place
Kevin A. Morrison

The Victorian Male Body
Joanne-Ella Parsons and Ruth Heholt

Nineteenth-Century Settler Emigration in British Literature and Art
Fariha Shaikh

The Pre-Raphaelites and Orientalism
Eleonora Sasso

The Late-Victorian Little Magazine
Koenraad Claes

Coastal Cultures of the Long Nineteenth Century
Matthew Ingleby and Matt P. M. Kerr

Dickens and Demolition: Literary Afterlives and Mid-Nineteenth-Century Urban Development
Joanna Hofer-Robinson

Artful Experiments: Ways of Knowing in Victorian Literature and Science
Philipp Erchinger

Victorian Poetry and the Poetics of the Literary Periodical
Caley Ehnes

The Victorian Actress in the Novel and on the Stage
Renata Kobetts Miller

Dickens's Clowns: Charles Dickens, Joseph Grimaldi and the Pantomime of Life
Jonathan Buckmaster

Italian Politics and Nineteenth-Century British Literature and Culture
Patricia Cove

Cultural Encounters with the Arabian Nights in Nineteenth-Century Britain
Melissa Dickson

Novel Institutions: Anachronism, Irish Novels and Nineteenth-Century Realism
Mary L. Mullen

The Fin-de-Siècle Scottish Revival: Romance, Decadence and Celtic Identity
Michael Shaw

Contested Liberalisms: Martineau, Dickens and the Victorian Press
Iain Crawford

Plotting Disability in the Nineteenth-Century Novel
Clare Walker Gore

The Aesthetics of Space in Nineteenth-Century British Literature, 1843–1907
Giles Whiteley

Forthcoming volumes:

Her Father's Name: Gender, Theatricality and Spiritualism in Florence Marryat's Fiction
Tatiana Kontou

The Sculptural Body in Victorian Literature: Encrypted Sexualities
Patricia Pulham

Olive Schreiner and the Politics of Print Culture, 1883–1920
Clare Gill

Victorian Auto/Biography: Problems in Genre and Subject
Amber Regis

Gissing, Shakespeare and the Life of Writing
Thomas Ue

The Persian Presence in Victorian Poetry
Reza Taher-Kermani

Women's Mobility in Henry James
Anna Despotopoulou

Michael Field's Revisionary Poetics
Jill Ehnenn

The Americanisation of W.T. Stead
Helena Goodwyn

Literary Illusions: Performance Magic and Victorian Literature
Christopher Pittard

The Ideas in Stories: Intellectual Content as Aesthetic Experience in Victorian Literature
Patrick Fessenbecker

Pastoral in Early-Victorian Fiction: Environment and Modernity
Mark Frost

Edmund Yates and Victorian Periodicals: Gossip, Celebrity, and Gendered Spaces
Kathryn Ledbetter

Literature, Architecture and Perversion: Building Sexual Culture in Europe, 1850–1930
Aina Marti

Oscar Wilde and the Radical Politics of the Fin de Siècle
Deaglán Ó Donghaile

Home and Identity in Nineteenth-Century Literary London
Lisa Robertson

Rereading Orphanhood: Texts, Inheritance, Kin
Diane Warren and Laura Peters

Plotting the News in the Victorian Novel
Jessica Valdez

Manufacturing Female Beauty in British Literature and Periodicals, 1850–1914
Michelle Smith

For a complete list of titles published visit the Edinburgh Critical Studies in Victorian Culture web page at www.edinburghuniversitypress.com/series/ECVC

Also Available:
Victoriographies – A Journal of Nineteenth-Century Writing, 1790–1914, edited by Diane Piccitto and Patricia Pulham
ISSN: 2044–2416
www.eupjournals.com/vic

The Aesthetics of Space in Nineteenth-Century British Literature, 1843–1907

Giles Whiteley

EDINBURGH
University Press

Edinburgh University Press is one of the leading university presses in the UK. We publish academic books and journals in our selected subject areas across the humanities and social sciences, combining cutting-edge scholarship with high editorial and production values to produce academic works of lasting importance. For more information visit our website: edinburghuniversitypress.com

Edinburgh University Press Ltd
The Tun – Holyrood Road, 12(2f) Jackson's Entry, Edinburgh EH8 8PJ

First published in hardback by Edinburgh University Press 2020

Typeset in 11/13 Adobe Sabon by
IDSUK (DataConnection) Ltd

A CIP record for this book is available from the British Library

ISBN 978 1 4744 4372 2 (hardback)
ISBN 978 1 4744 4373 9 (paperback)
ISBN 978 1 4744 4374 6 (webready PDF)
ISBN 978 1 4744 4375 3 (epub)

Contents

Illustrations

Series Editor's Preface

'Victorian' is a term, at once indicative of a strongly determined concept and an often notoriously vague notion, emptied of all meaningful content by the many journalistic misconceptions that persist about the inhabitants and cultures of the British Isles and Victoria's Empire in the nineteenth century. As such, it has become a by-word for the assumption of various, often contradictory habits of thought, belief, behaviour and perceptions. Victorian studies and studies in nineteenth-century literature and culture have, from their institutional inception, questioned narrowness of presumption, pushed at the limits of the nominal definition, and sought to question the very grounds on which the unreflective perception of the so-called Victorian has been built; and so they continue to do. Victorian and nineteenth-century studies of literature and culture maintain a breadth and diversity of interest, of focus and inquiry, in an interrogative and intellectually open-minded and challenging manner, which are equal to the exploration and inquisitiveness of its subjects. Many of the questions asked by scholars and researchers of the innumerable productions of nineteenth-century society actively put into suspension the clichés and stereotypes of 'Victorianism', whether the approach has been sustained by historical, scientific, philosophical, empirical, ideological or theoretical concerns; indeed, it would be incorrect to assume that each of these approaches to the idea of the Victorian has been, or has remained, in the main exclusive, sealed off from the interests and engagements of other approaches. A vital interdisciplinarity has been pursued and embraced, for the most part, even as there has been contest and debate amongst Victorianists, pursued with as much fervour as the affirmative exploration between different disciplines and differing epistemologies put to work in the service of reading the nineteenth century.

Edinburgh Critical Studies in Victorian Culture aims to take up both the debates and the inventive approaches and departures from convention that studies in the nineteenth century have witnessed for the last half century at least. Aiming to maintain a 'Victorian' (in the most positive sense of that motif) spirit of inquiry, the series' purpose is to continue and augment the cross-fertilisation of interdisciplinary approaches, and to offer, in addition, a number of timely and untimely revisions of Victorian literature, culture, history and identity. At the same time, the series will ask questions concerning what has been missed or improperly received, misread, or not read at all, in order to present a multi-faceted and heterogeneous kaleidoscope of representations. Drawing on the most provocative, thoughtful and original research, the series will seek to prod at the notion of the 'Victorian', and in so doing, principally through theoretically and epistemologically sophisticated close readings of the historicity of literature and culture in the nineteenth century, to offer the reader provocative insights into a world that is at once overly familiar, and irreducibly different, other and strange. Working from original sources, primary documents and recent interdisciplinary theoretical models, Edinburgh Critical Studies in Victorian Culture seeks not simply to push at the boundaries of research in the nineteenth century, but also to inaugurate the persistent erasure and provisional, strategic redrawing of those borders.

Julian Wolfreys

Acknowledgements

I am thankful for the support, both financial and collegial, which I have received from a number of sources while writing this book.

Many thanks to those colleagues with whom I have had the pleasure of discussing ideas that have eventually found their way into the book. In particular, thanks to Beyza Björkman Nylén, Elisabet Dellming, Dennis Denisoff, Bo Ekelund, Stefano Evangelista, Gül Bilge Han, Stefan Helgesson, Richard Hibbitt, John Miller, Wendy Nakanishi, Irina Rasmussen, Margaret Stetz, Jeremy Tambling and Magnus Ullén. Jeremy's influence, in particular, is palpable throughout this book even when not cited directly, a product of my seemingly endless rereading of his work on Dickens. Thanks also to my doctoral students Rayanne Eskandari and Jonathan Foster, and to the master's students who took courses on realism and aestheticism at Stockholm University for the lively discussions.

I have had the pleasure of presenting elements of my research a number of times over the past few years. Particular thanks are due to Bethan Carney, Holly Furneaux and Ben Winyard for the invitation to present a paper at 'Dickens and Fantasy', Senate House, London, October 2017, and to Joe Bristow, Charlotte Ribeyrol, Dennis and Stefano for the invitation to present a paper at 'Curiosity and Desire in *fin-de-siècle* Art and Literature', Clark Library, UCLA, May 2018. Thanks also to Virginia Langum for the invitation to present a paper at Umeå University, January 2018. I am grateful to all those who listened to those papers, and a number of others presented at Stockholm University, and for the useful discussions provoked.

Financial support for both archival research trips and the reproduction of images has been provided by the Faculty of Humanities at Stockholm University. I thank them for their generosity. I would like to thank Tower Hamlets Local History Archive and the Victoria and Albert Museum for permission to include reproductions in this book. At Brasenose College, I would like to thank Georgina Edwards for arranging for my visit to Pater's rooms.

An earlier version of parts of Chapter 4 have been previously published as 'Cosmopolitan Space: Political Topographies in Oscar Wilde's London,' *Victoriographies*, 7:2 (2017a): 124–42, and other parts in 'A Swine from Epicurus's Herd: The Culinary, Aesthetic, and Erotic in Wilde and Huysmans', in *Modernism and Food Studies: Politics, Aesthetics and the Avant-Garde*, ed. Jessica Martell, Adam Fajardo and Philip Keel Geheber (Gainesville: University Press of Florida, 2019), pp. 19–38. Elements of Chapter 2 have appeared in 'Dickens and Southey: *The Mystery of Edwin Drood* and *The Curse of Kehama*', *Dickens Quarterly*, 35:3 (2018): 262–6. I thank Edinburgh University Press, the University Press of Florida and Johns Hopkins University Press for permission to reproduce material here.

At Edinburgh University Press, I would like to thank Julian Wolfreys, Michelle Houston, James Dale, Ersev Ersoy, Rebecca Mackensie, Adela Rauchova and Fiona Sewell. Jules's keen interest in this project from the time of our first discussions, Michelle's help guiding the process from beginning to end, and Fiona's close attention to detail have been invaluable. Thanks also to the anonymous readers who have given insightful feedback on drafts of the book: needless to say, any remaining errors are my own.

Finally, a special word of thanks must go to my family, Cecilia, Samuel and Elias. Cecilia, in particular, has read drafts of the manuscript, and has taken a number of the photographs included in the book, as well as helping with the maps. This book is for her.

Luke Fildes's 'In the Court' is reproduced by permission of the Victoria and Albert Museum archives. Phil W. Smith's 'St. George's in the East from the London Docks' is reproduced by permission of the Tower Hamlets Local History archive. Gustave Doré's 'Opium Smoking – The Lascar's Room in "Edwin Drood"' and 'Over London by Rail' are reproduced from images made available by Gallica, the digital library of the Bibliothèque nationale de France.

Maps of Paris are based on Alexandre Vuillemin's 'Hachette Pocket Map of Paris' (1892). Maps of London are based on Charles Booth's 'Maps Descriptive of London Poverty' (1889). Maps of Rome are based on Heinrich Kiepert's maps of 'Roma Urbs ab Augusti Imp. Tempore' and 'Forum Romanum' (1903).

Abbreviations

AR Joris-Karl Huysmans, *À rebours*, ed. Rose Fortassier (Paris: Imprimerie nationale, 1981); *Against Nature*, trans. Robert Baldick (Harmondsworth: Penguin, 2003)

AS Henry James, *The American Scene*, ed. John F. Sears (Harmondsworth: Penguin, 2003)

BH Charles Dickens, *Bleak House*, ed. Nicola Bradbury (Harmondsworth: Penguin, 2003)

CNJ Henry James, *The Complete Notebooks*, ed. Leon Edel and Lyall H. Powers (Oxford: Oxford University Press, 1987)

CR Oscar Wilde, *Criticism: Historical Criticism, Intentions, The Soul of Man*, ed. Josephine M. Guy (Oxford: Oxford University Press, 2007)

CW John Ruskin, *The Complete Works of John Ruskin*, ed. E. T. Cook and Alexander Wedderburn, 39 vols (London: George Allen, 1903–12)

DG Oscar Wilde, *The Picture of Dorian Gray: The 1890 and 1891 Texts*, ed. Joseph Bristow (Oxford: Oxford University Press, 2005)

ED Charles Dickens, *The Mystery of Edwin Drood*, ed. David Paroissien (Harmondsworth: Penguin, 2002)

GL Walter Pater, *Gaston de Latour*, ed. Gerald Monsman (Oxford: Oxford University Press, 2019)

IH Henry James, *Italian Hours*, ed. John Auchard (Harmondsworth: Penguin, 1995)

IP Walter Pater, *Imaginary Portraits*, ed. Lene Østermark-Johansen (Oxford: Oxford University Press, 2019)

LCD Charles Dickens, *The Pilgrim Edition of the Letters of Charles Dickens*, ed. Madeline House et al., 12 vols (Oxford: Clarendon Press, 1965–2002)

LHJ Henry James, *The Letters of Henry James*, ed. Leon Edel, 4 vols (Cambridge, MA: Harvard University Press, 1974–84)

LOW Oscar Wilde, *The Complete Letters of Oscar Wilde*, ed. Merlin Holland and Rupert Hart-Davis (London: Fourth Estate, 2000)
LWP Walter Pater, *The Letters of Walter Pater*, ed. Lawrence Evans (Oxford: Oxford University Press, 1970)
MD Virginia Woolf, *Mrs Dalloway*, ed. David Bradshaw (Oxford: Oxford University Press, 2009)
ME Walter Pater, *Marius the Epicurean: His Sensations and Ideas*, 2 vols (London: Macmillan, 1910)
MS Walter Pater, *Miscellaneous Studies* (London: Macmillan, 1910)
PS Henri Lefebvre, *The Production of Space*, trans. Donald Nicholson-Smith (London: Blackwell, 1991)
PW Walter Benjamin, *The Arcades Project*, trans. Howard Eiland and Kevin McLaughlin (Cambridge, MA: Harvard University Press, 1999)
RTP Marcel Proust, *À la recherche du temps perdu*, ed. Jean-Yves Tadié, 4 vols (Paris: Gallimard, 1987–9); *In Search of Lost Time*, ed. Christopher Prendergast, 6 vols (Harmondsworth: Penguin, 2003)
SE Sigmund Freud, *The Standard Edition of the Complete Psychological Works of Sigmund Freud*, trans. James Strachey, 24 vols (London: Vintage, 2001)
SF Oscar Wilde, *The Short Fiction*, ed. Ian Small (Oxford: Oxford University Press, 2018)
SHR Walter Pater, *Studies in the History of the Renaissance*, ed. Donald L. Hill (Berkeley: University of California Press, 1980)
SW Walter Benjamin, *Selected Writings*, ed. Michael William Jennings, Howard Eiland and Gary Smith, 4 vols (Cambridge, MA: Harvard University Press, 1996–2003)
U James Joyce, *Ulysses*, ed. Jeri Johnson (Oxford: Oxford University Press, 2008)
UT Charles Dickens, *'The Uncommercial Traveller' and Other Papers, 1859–70*, ed. Michael Slater and John Drew (London: Dent, 2000)

For ease of reference, I give citations by book/part, chapter and page number.

References to Wilde's plays are by act and line number to Peter Raby's edition, *The Importance of Being Earnest and Other Plays* (Oxford: Oxford University Press, 2008). References to Wilde's poetry are by line number to the texts in *Poems and Poems in Prose*, ed. Bobby Fong and Karl Beckson (Oxford: Oxford University Press, 2000).

References to Charles Baudelaire's *Les fleurs du mal* are by line number to the bilingual edition translated by James McGowan, *The Flowers of Evil* (Oxford: Oxford University Press, 2008).

Citations from the Bible are of the King James Version. Definitions and etymologies are taken from the *Oxford English Dictionary*.

A Note on Translations

I have given citations of foreign-language literary works referring to the original and then the English translation, silently modifying wording of the translation as needed. Where I cite no English translations, as in the art criticism of Huysmans and Zola, translations are my own. In the case of secondary criticism originally in other languages, I have simply given the page number of English translations.

Prologue

Joris-Karl Huysmans, or 'After Dickens'

Chapter 9 of Joris-Karl Huysmans's (1848–1907) *À rebours* [*Against Nature*] (1884) sees the aesthete protagonist des Esseintes overwhelmed by a fit of Baudelairean spleen. Attempting to 'cool his brain with some of the solanaceae of literature [*solanées de l'art*]', he turns to the work of Charles Dickens (1812–70), 'so charmingly adapted for convalescents and invalids' (*AR* 9.177; 109). Des Esseintes turns to literature for 'effects', opening Dickens in the hope of changing his mood. Art is *productive* and its effects bodily, convalescent, '*effets hygiéniques*' (11.201; 132). To des Esseintes's surprise, however, the novelist produces the 'opposite effect' to that expected, and he reacts against Dickens's characters, with their 'all-concealing draperies [*vêtues jusqu'au cou*]':

> By the virtue of the law of contrasts, he jumped from one extreme to the other, recalled scenes of full-blooded, earthy passion [*des scènes vibrantes et corsées*], and thought of common amorous practice such as the hybrid kiss, or the columbine kiss as ecclesiastical modesty calls it, where the tongue penetrates the lips [*ils pénètrent entre les lèvres*]. (9.177; 109)[1]

Dickens's realism is accused of romanticism, his 'chaste lovers' and 'puritanical heroines' only partially hidden by the modesty of their clothing. Desire has been marginalised, masked like the bodies in euphemisms of 'ecclesiastical modesty'. Dickens is accused of being fearful of penetration, whether sexual or into the heart of things.[2] Consequently, des Esseintes puts Dickens aside, and with him 'all thoughts of straight-laced Albion [*la bégueule Angleterre*]' (*AR* 9.177; 109). Cultures clash: French decadence is pitted against a prudish Britain, with Dickens's name metonymic not only for London but for the nation itself.

This engagement with Dickens, seemingly an incidental flourish meant to take aim at conservative British culture, is more important than might be initially suspected. It reminds us that Huysmans is writing 'after Dickens', and that later nineteenth-century literature is haunted by the spectre of Dickens's work. In one sense, to write 'after Dickens' means after realism, and in this context, it should come as no surprise that *À rebours* is often regarded as the moment when Huysmans, who had hitherto been associated with and identified himself with naturalism, broke with Émile Zola (1840–1902) (Baldick 1955: 78–91; Laver 1954: 59–73; Livi 1972: 25–37). As Robert Baldick puts it, 'no longer blinded by the Master's dazzling descriptive talent', Huysmans opened his 'eyes [. . .] to the psychological poverty' of Zola's novels (1955: 79). In a similar move, this particular passage of *À rebours* characterises the idea of writing after Dickens as a reaction against his *ressentiment*: Huysmans charges Dickens with suffocating his subjects, constructing a reality sanitised from difference.[3] Realism is accused of evading reality, so that Dickens's novels become understood as a reaction against life. This seemingly incidental or marginal episode in chapter 9 of *À rebours* suggests a flaw in the realist project.

Given these stakes, it is hardly a surprise to discover that des Esseintes is unable to put Dickens aside for long. His spectre resurfaces in chapter 11, a return betraying a repetition compulsion, suggesting both the desire to work through the problem of realism and that we will never fully be able to write 'after Dickens'. Again, the context is convalescence, but this time the encounter produces markedly different effects. Des Esseintes takes the train from his countryside retreat to Paris, dreaming of London:

> The work of Dickens, which he had recently read in the hope of soothing his nerves, [. . .] slowly began to act upon him in an unexpected way, evoking visions of English life which he had contemplated for hours on end. Then, little by little, an idea insinuated itself into his mind – the idea of turning dream into reality, of travelling to England in the flesh as well as in the spirit, of checking the accuracy of his visions [*de rêves vérifiés*]; and this idea was allied with a longing to experience new sensations [*éprouver des impressions*] and thus afford some relief to a mind dizzy with hunger and drunk with fantasy. (*AR* 11.201–2; 132)

Des Esseintes does not have the idea of travelling to London; it is not *his* idea. Rather, the idea 'insinuates' itself into his thoughts; it comes from elsewhere, like a thought of the outside, *la pensée du dehors* (Foucault 2000b), experienced as an affect. A few years earlier, Walter Pater (1839–94), speaking of Giovanni Boccaccio (1313–75) in his *Studies in the History of the Renaissance* (1873), had noted how 'real passions' could come to 'insinuate' themselves into the spectator through aesthetic reflection (*SHR* 134). In this 'insinuation', the subject remains unaware, lost in an aesthetic contemplation that operates simultaneously in two directions, producing the world as an aesthetic object and the contemplating subject as the work of art. Dream is turned into reality, valued only insofar as it affords the opportunity of verifying the accuracy of one's impressions. It is art that gives meaning to the world, and like Pater, what des Esseintes desires is 'to experience new sensations' (*AR* 11.202; 132; compare *SHR* 189).

Writing after Dickens, Huysmans's novel offers a snapshot of a late nineteenth-century 'aesthetics of space'. In the pages which follow, Huysmans approaches one nineteenth-century city space through another one; writing after realism, he reads the city 'after Dickens', so Paris is approached through a literary London, creating an aesthetics of these spaces which refigure both alike. Take the weather: thinking of Dickens, we are told that 'the abominably foggy and rainy' climate had 'fostered' des Esseintes's thoughts (*AR* 11.202; 132). The weather had been 'atrocious for the past week', creating a landscape of 'sooty rivers', 'watery mist' and 'muddy puddles [*fangeux des flaques*]' (*AR* 11.200; 130, 131), generically 'Dickensian' phrasing.[4]

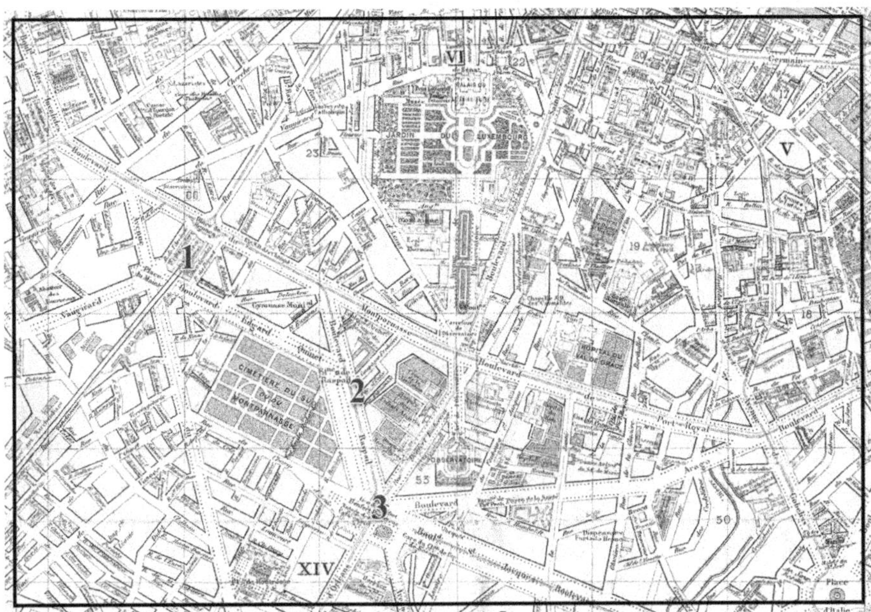

Figure i XIVe arrondissement: Observatoire

1. Gare Montparnasse; 2. Boulevard d'Enfer, renamed 1887; 3. Barrière d'Enfer

These meteorological conditions reinforce 'the memories of what [des Esseintes] had read' (*AR* 11.202; 132). The text of Dickens, once put aside, returns, but otherwise. The tempestuous skies are '*flots d'encre*' (11.200; 130), not so much a pathetic fallacy as a textual phenomenon, floods of Dickensian ink producing an aesthetics of this space proleptically.

Arriving in Paris at the Gare Montparnasse in the 14th arrondissement, built in 1840 and expanded in 1858, des Esseintes finds himself on the Boulevard d'Enfer (11.202; 133). This Road of Hell lay on the present site of Boulevard Raspail, renamed in 1887, three years after the publication of *À rebours*. It ran north–south through the 6th, 7th and 14th arrondissements; at the southern end lay the Barrière d'Enfer, the Gate of Hell, referred to by Victor Hugo in *Les Misérables* (1862) (1951: 5.1.18.1242; 1982: 384), located in Place d'Enfer, now Place Denfert-Rochereau.[5] The connotations are obviously hellish, but the location also speaks to a revolutionary spirit that encoded the real Boulevard d'Enfer, where the infamous Maison de Port-Libre was located, housing prisoners before their execution during the Reign of Terror. The space recalls the trace of the political, of revolutionary space and of space as revolutionary, a phenomenon that we will meet throughout this book, consistently politicising the aesthetics of space.

From the Boulevard d'Enfer, des Esseintes hails a cab. He travels north over the Seine to Rue de Rivoli, one of Paris's most significant commercial streets, benefitting from Haussmannisation in the 1850s. Windows, water and waste dominate the imagery. 'The cab lumbered off, its wheels throwing up showers of shit [*crotte*]', and 'the roadway was nothing but swamp [*marécage*]' (11.202; 133).[6] The imagery suggests that the nineteenth-century cosmopolitan metropolis was founded on unstable ground, like a house built on sand (Matthew 7: 24–7). Such associations recall Venice, the city that prompted John Ruskin's (1819–1900) important meditation on the aesthetic qualities of space, and which will prove important to the argument of this book. In Huysmans's text, the city seems to be emerging from the swamp, suggesting perhaps Dickens's London of *Great Expectations* (1860–1), where the chiasmus of 'Mudbank, mist, swamp and work; work, swamp, mist and mudbank' (2003e: 28.229) swamps the reader in the text. Dickens yokes 'swamping' to 'work' in both directions, suggesting capitalism as something which cannot be escaped and which drowns its subjects.

It is in the midst of this swampy Paris, so reminiscent of Dickens's London, that des Esseintes watches the omnibuses sweeping past, and sees how 'women holding their umbrellas low and their skirts high flattened themselves against the shop windows to avoid being splashed' (*AR* 11.202; 133). Viewed through des Esseintes's eyes, this mundane street scene becomes a quintessential question of the aesthetic. It appears staged, choreographed, imaged in a kind of suspended moment, arresting the flow of time in a chronotope that petrifies it in the instant, a movement doubly impossible since the nineteenth-century city is precisely the domain of speed. Huysmans's antithesis suggests an eroticism (the hitching up of the hem of the skirt) at the same time as foreclosing it (covering the exposed leg with the umbrella). Pressed against the window, the women become part of the display of the windows of the arcades, commodified objects on view, like works of art.[7] They are subject to des Esseintes's male gaze, performing the ballet of umbrella and skirt precisely since they know that they are always being watched (Lacan 1998b: 80–2). Des Esseintes himself is situated at a privileged remove from the street scene, watching the women from behind the glass of the cab, which 'quickly streaked with trickles of water' (*AR* 11.202; 133). Such a remove isolates the spectator from the scene outside, where life is performed, the city becoming an aesthetic spectacle. The incident, in which des Esseintes gazes at the scene from a detached distance, recalls the train journey he had taken from the countryside into Paris, described a few paragraphs earlier. There, des Esseintes had first begun to dream of London, and the windows afford a striking simile: 'Through the rainswept windows the countryside flashing past looked blurred and dingy, as if he were seeing it through an aquarium full of murky water' (11.201; 131). Such jarring juxtapositions already speak through an alienated language, defamiliarising reality, speaking to the *Entfremdung* of the observer.

Further remarkable similes attend des Esseintes's cab journey. The noise of the rain sounds 'like sacks of peas being emptied out over his head' and 'clots of mud spurted up from all the sides of the cab like sparks from a firework [*feu d'artifice*]' (*AR* 11.202; 133). The French term carries the trace of the thematic of artifice and taken in context, Huysmans's European readers may have recalled James McNeill Whistler's (1834–1903) infamous painting of a muddy, murky fireworks display in *Nocturne in Black and Gold: The Falling Rocket* (1877). It was this work which Ruskin had attacked in letter 79 of *Fors Clavigera* (1871–84), leading Whistler to sue him for libel. The ensuing court case was an event with major significance for the direction of contemporary European art, to which Huysmans alludes in *Certains* (1889) (2006: 368). There, he speaks appreciatively of the *Nocturne*, making clear where his sympathies lie, describing 'fireworks exploding with blood-stained streaks' (2006: 369), exploring a violence in the text.

Huysmans was impressed by Whistler, seeing in his work something of a kindred spirit, and both the American painter and the movement of impressionism are key artistic inter-texts informing the tradition of writing the aesthetics of space. Huysmans had seen Whistler's exhibitions at the Salons of 1882 and 1884, the year *À rebours* was published. In his review, he reserves particular praise for the *Portrait of Lady Meux* (1881), described as 'phantasmic [*fantomatique*]', at once a 'realistic, intimate painting, but already treading into the beyond [*l'au-delà*] in a dream' (2006: 368).[8] It is this kind of conjunction, in which a discourse of realism begins to slide into something 'aesthetic', which this book investigates. In these passages, Huysmans images Whistler's aesthetic as dream space, a topic which Walter Benjamin (1892–1940) discusses, alongside the phenomenon of intoxication, as an experience proper to the 'spacetime' of the nineteenth century (*PW* 389; K1,4). Commenting on the *Portrait of Lady Meux*, Huysmans makes a similar link, associating Whistler and 'the visions of de Quincey, those leaky rivers [*fuites de rivières*], those fluid dreams [*rêves fluides*] born of opium' (2006: 369), which comes unbidden to his mind. Huysmans suggests that art directs the subject 'inevitably', and in making the association with Thomas de Quincey's (1785–1859) *Confessions of an English Opium-Eater* (1821), he links the dream space of the nineteenth-century city with opium, just as the late Dickens had in *The Mystery of Edwin Drood* (1869–70). Huysmans reads Whistler though de Quincey, and to the extent that these pages of *À rebours*, reading Paris through Dickens, recall this earlier appreciation of Whistler, both in terms of the aestheticisation of space, and at the lexical level of verbal echoes, the passage sees Huysmans read the text of Paris at once through three prior aesthetic prisms (Dickens, Whistler, de Quincey), all of which are simultaneously being called to reread each other.

For des Esseintes, 'the appalling weather struck him as an instalment of English life paid to him on account in Paris' (*AR* 11.203; 133), a fittingly economic lexicon. He images 'a picture of London as an immense, sprawling, rain-drenched [*pluvieux, colossal, immense*] metropolis, stinking of soot and hot iron, smoking tirelessly in the fog' (11.203; 133–4). From this panoramic view, obscured by the ubiquitous smoke and fog, but also impossible to take in precisely owing to its immensity – a city without limits, without measure, sublime and monstrous (Kant 2000: 131–4) – des Esseintes zooms in, allowing Huysmans to gain spatial tension and a sense of depth.[9] Des Esseintes 'could see in imagination a line of dockyards stretching away into the distance, full of cranes, capstans, and bales of merchandise, and swarming [*grouillant*] with men' (*AR* 11.203; 134). Huysmans's writing is itself Dickensian, deploying rhyme, alliteration and isocolon ('perte de vue, pleins de grues'). The zooming trajectory moves topographically according to distributions of size and power in the means of production and the products – from the machines and objects through to people, who are 'swarming', connoting a becoming-animal (Deleuze and Guattari 2004b: 270–1). We are situated on the 'dark, slimy waters of an imaginary Thames, in the midst of a forest of masts [*une futaie de mats*]' (*AR* 11.203; 134). This specific metaphor dates to the seventeenth century; it is a literary figure, produced through textual repetition, and occurs twice in reference to London in the works of Dickens: in *The Old Curiosity Shop* (1840–1) (2000a: 5.47) and in *Martin Chuzzlewit* (1842–4) (1999: 9.134).[10] The forest gives height, but immediately gives way to an image of depth: des Esseintes sees the Metropolitan Railway, the first of its kind in the world, introduced to London in 1863. Or rather, the underground is felt rather than seen, and the trains 'rumbled [*roulaient*] along, occasionally emitting ghastly screams [*cris affreux*] or vomiting floods of smoke' (11.203; 134), personified, so that the underground figures as demonic, another kind of Boulevard d'Enfer, running just beneath the surface of things. Travelling on the underground with Leslie Stephens (1832–1904) in March 1869, Henry James (1843–1916) described it as 'a marvellous phenomenon – ploughing along in a vast circle thro' the bowels of London' (*LHJ* 1: 91), associating the earth with the body. In des Esseintes's imaginary, it signifies the trauma, the wounding, which underwrites modernity. Fittingly, in this context, we find that, back on street level, the world is shrouded in 'an eternal twilight [*un éternel crépuscule*]', in language implying Charles Baudelaire (1821–67) more than Dickens.[11] For Baudelaire, twilight constitutes 'the witching hour [*l'heure bizarre*], the uncertain light' which illuminates the modernity of the city (2006: 401). In this sense, Huysmans's reading of Paris through Dickensian London is itself aesthetically informed by Baudelaire's treatment of another version of Paris. No nineteenth-century metropolitan space is wholly discrete – other traces 'insinuate' themselves into any aesthetics of space.

In the dusk, des Esseintes sees 'an endless stream of traffic [*des flots de voitures*]' flowing 'between two columns of earnest, silent Londoners [*des colonnes de gens, silencieux, affairés*], their eyes fixed ahead and elbows glued to their sides' (*AR* 11.203; 134). Another antithesis, the adjectives seem to have swapped their attendant nouns, so that the stream, an image of nature, describes the inanimate world, and the columns, an image of architecture and man-made order, describe the people. It is an analogy that Dickens had used in *Nicholas Nickleby* (1838–9), where the crowd is comprised of 'streams of people apparently without end' (2003g: 32.390), with Dickens, in his turn, echoing the Romanticism of William Wordsworth (1770–1850), who sees an 'endless stream of men, and moving things' (7.157) in the London of *The Prelude* (1850). The trace of the prior text *insists* here (Lacan 2007a: 412–41), with the repetition a form of automatism, so that this passage sees Huysmans reading Dickens reading Wordsworth reading . . .

It is in this ellipsis, in this metonymy of texts, that we see precisely an aesthetics of space: in the literary tradition which this book begins to delineate, charting the ways in which mid-to-late nineteenth-century 'aesthetic' writers began to write space after realism and after Ruskin, the 'real' city is only ever engaged with as always already mediated through prior aesthetic representations. This intertextual fabric comprises the substance of a 'representational space' (*PS* 42), in the language of the philosopher Henri Lefebvre (1901–91). But Huysmans's aesthetics of space differs from the representational spaces of realism in particular insofar as it is always bound up with a certain 'aesthetic effect'. Such effects are not the signifiers of 'realism', or of 'reality' as such, but rather signify to the reader that these literary spaces must be approached first and foremost in the spirit of art.

In speaking of aesthetic effects and of the aesthetics of space, it might seem easy to dismiss the politics of this kind of writing, in the sense in which figures such as Theodor Adorno (1903–69) have dismissed aestheticism.[12] This would be reductive, however, for as this book will show, politics is an indispensable trace at work in the aesthetics of space. This political dimension is both present in the text and productive, put to work, by the authors, whether consciously or unconsciously. Indeed, here in *À rebours*, at a moment which we might least expect to discover the spectre of Karl Marx (1818–83), we find that Huysmans's simile is Marxist in the most rigorous sense: what is at stake in the aestheticisation is in part precisely the alienation of man. In this 'endless stream of traffic' (*AR* 11.203; 134), the proletariat march on 'silent' and 'work-like', those columns which prop up the economic superstructures of the city, and Huysmans's antithesis highlights the question of alienation, making what is 'most unnatural, [. . .] most natural in being so', as Dickens puts it in *Dombey and Son* (1848) (2002a: 47.700). The image is revealed

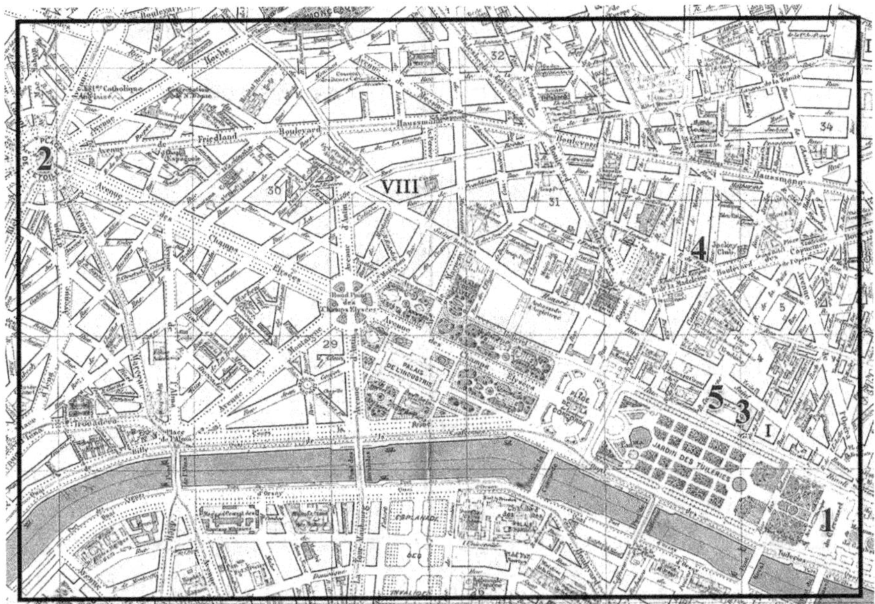

Figure ii Ie arrondissement: Louvre

1. Place du Carrousel; 2. Arc de Triomphe; 3. Librairie Galignani, 224 Rue de Rivoli; 4. Galerie Georges Petit, 8 Rue de Séze; 5. The Bodega

as resting on a logic which is ultimately economic, and 'des Esseintes shuddered with delight [*frissonait délicieusement*] at feeling himself lost in this terrifying world of commerce, immersed in this isolating fog, involved in this incessant activity' (*AR* 11.203; 134). The loss of the self here is a voiding of the subject in a moment at once erotic and thanatic, with the 'endless stream of traffic' foreshadowing in this sense the concluding lines of Franz Kafka's (1883–1924) 'Das Urteil' [The Judgment] (1912).[13] In Huysmans's hands, the simile images London as the capitalist- machine, a move as Deleuzian as Carlylean. What is at stake is the circulation of the city, a complex libidinal economy, a question of flows.

By this point, des Esseintes is somewhere near the Place du Carrousel in the 1st arrondissement, where the guillotine stood from 1792 to 1793. Seeing that it is dark, with the *crépuscule* of Dickens's London having seemingly magically produced its effects on the Parisian scene without anything having been explicitly registered in 'reality', des Esseintes notes that 'the gas lamps were flickering in the fog, each surrounded by its dirty little halo' (*AR* 11.203; 134). An almost oxymoronic conjunction of the spiritual and the sordid, the image is perhaps inspired by the 'halo' effect of a dirty London described in *Barnaby Rudge* (1840–1) (2003c:

3.33), or by Baudelaire's 'lost halo' of *Le Spleen de Paris* (1869) (1961: 299–300; 2010: 88).[14] The London fog is the quintessential Dickensian image of the metropolis, most readily conjuring up the cities mapped in *Bleak House* (1852–3) and *Our Mutual Friend* (1864–5), and by the time that Huysmans wrote *À rebours*, it had become a way of seeing London, particularly influential on Oscar Wilde (1854–1900). Looking through the window of the cab, des Esseintes can make out only one landmark, the Arc de Triomphe du Carrousel (*AR* 11.203–4; 134), built 1806–8 to commemorate the victories of Napoleon I (1769–1821). The Arc figures as both an imperial folly and a simulacrum, designed by Charles Percier (1764–1838) and Pierre François Léonard Fontaine (1762–1853) in imitation of the Arch of Constantine in Rome (AD 312). The Arc images Paris as capital of the nineteenth century (*SW* 3: 32–49; Casanova 2004: 23–34), its 'triumph'. As simulacrum, the Arc also recalls its own imitation, Marble Arch in London, begun in 1827 to a design by John Nash (1752–1835), before being completed in 1833 to a reduced scale by Edward Blore (1787–1879). In this sense, Paris, the capital of the nineteenth century, is the space to which London responds, so that to view London in the nineteenth century means simultaneously seeing the trace of Paris.

Finally arriving on Rue de Rivoli (*AR* 11.204; 135), des Esseintes is dropped off outside Librairie Galignani, established in 1801 and moving to its present site (no. 224) in 1851. He is going to buy a guidebook to help him navigate London: either *Baedeker's* or *Murray's*. Such a book will allow him to map the city, mediating his relationship with space. In Lefebvrean terms, approaching the city with *Baedeker's* means that a concrete representation of space is allowed to produce a specific representational space (*PS* 38–9). In possessing such a text, des Esseintes seeks to avoid the fate of the ill-informed *fin-de-siècle* tourist, such as Lucy Honeychurch in E. M. Forster's (1879–1970) *A Room with a View* (1908), who finds herself stranded 'in Santa Croce with no Baedeker' (1986: 2.17), unable to accurately identify the beautiful without it. In the window of Galignani's, books are presented to the eye as delicacies,[15] and tempted, des Esseintes enters. In the bookshop, he finds himself a foreigner at home, already a tourist, with women 'unfolding maps and jabbering to each other in strange tongues [*des langues inconnues*]' (*AR* 11.204; 135). The reference is biblical (Isaiah 28: 11; 1 Corinthians 14: 18; Acts 2: 4), the glossolalia here registering a *fin-de-siècle* cosmopolitanism, which also indicates a threat to the single, national subject: strange tongues make one a stranger at home, lost in one's own language. He opens *Baedeker's*, presumably the 1866 edition of *Londres*, and, inspired by a discussion of London's art galleries, begins to muse on pre-Raphaelite pictures he had seen at international exhibitions. He names John Everett Millais's (1829–96) *The Eve of St Agnes* (1863), alongside the 'weirdly coloured pictures' by George Frederick Watts (1817–1904) (*AR* 11.207; 136), whose work Huysmans had seen the year before at an exhibition at the Galerie Georges Petit, 8 Rue de Séze. Dreaming of travel, des Esseintes thinks about travelling to see art, and then compares this art with the work of other artists – Gustave Moreau (1826–98), Michelangelo (1475–1564) and Raphael (1483–1520) – in an endless proliferation of texts and their boundaries: one text, *Baedeker's*, German but a book in French writing about England, sets off a metonymic slide of intertextual allusions (Romanticism, impressionism, pre-Raphaelitism, Renaissance art) which is only arrested by a shop assistant, 'surprised to see a customer day-dreaming at the table' (11.207; 136).

Des Esseintes returns to the cab, which is directed to the 'Bodega', a wine bar on the corner of Rue de Rivoli and Rue Castiglione, only 120 metres away. Passing the arcades on his right, des Esseintes notes how their 'brightly lit windows looked like a gigantic night-light burning cheerfully in the pestilent fog' (11.207; 136). The theme of the arcades is familiar today thanks to Benjamin's important study of nineteenth-century Paris, *Das Passagen-Werk* [*The Arcades Project*] (1927–40), which sees these shopping streets as 'the hollow mold from which the image of "modernity" was cast' (*PW* 546; S1a,6). Arcades such as the Passage des Panoramas, located in the 2nd arrondissement between Boulevard Montmartre and Rue Saint-Marc and built in 1800, were covered walkways allowing people to stroll between shop fronts, protected from the weather, and they proliferated across nineteenth-century Paris. The arcades mobilise desire, linking an aesthetic gaze with commodity fetishism. They become 'a world in miniature' (*SW* 3: 32). Moreover, Huysmans's image of 'night-lights' foregrounds the sense in which the arcades' aesthetic 'fascinated' the public, 'radiat[ing] through the Paris of the Empire like grottoes' (*PW* 564; T1a,8).

Arriving at the Bodega, des Esseintes finds it popular, 'packed to the doors' with English people. A series of figures are introduced in turn, the descriptions generic rather than specific. He sees 'pale, gangling clergymen', then 'laymen with bloated pork-butcher faces or bulldog muzzles', a 'tow-haired stick of a man' using a microscope to read the paper in the corner of the room, and in front of him, 'a sort of American naval officer, stout and stocky, swarthy and bottle-nosed, a cigar stuck in the hairy orifice of his mouth' (*AR* 11.208–9; 137–8).

Already, such characters give themselves to des Esseintes as somewhat 'Dickensian' in spirit, as a kind of caricature. While generic, they somehow evoke the 'pale, thin, cadaverous' clergyman of *Sketches by Boz* (1833) (1995: 2.25), Mr Gridley of *Bleak House*, who is characterised as a bulldog (*BH* 29.405), and Sam Weller of *The Pickwick Papers* (1836), whose eyes double as 'a pair o' patent double million magnifyin' gas microscopes of hextra power' (2003k: 34.464). In the Bodega, des Esseintes finds himself gradually becoming 'dulled by the monotonous chatter of these English people', a comment both on the characters as cliché and on the unromantic musicality of English diction. He 'drifted off into a daydream' (*AR* 11.209; 138), since dream space is proper to the aesthetics of the nineteenth-century city. Now, des Esseintes 'call[ed] to mind' some specific figures: first, Mr Wickfield from *David Copperfield* (1849–50), 'white hair and rich [*enflammé*] features', then Mr Tulkinghorn, 'phlegmatic, cunning, ruthless' (*AR* 11.209; 138).[16] Both are lawyers, the latter character murdered under a painting of Allegory in *Bleak House* (48.669), Dickens's novel of the Law, where the labyrinthine case of Jarndyce and Jarndyce allegorises London (Tambling 2009: 139–63). As such, the figures suggest a subtle but all-encompassing panopticism operating simultaneously in three different spheres: firstly, in the 'real' space of the tavern; secondly, through Dickens's texts and through the force of their 'realism', where their description also establishes a certain ideological approach to reality; and thirdly, in the way in which this disciplinarity structures des Esseintes's own dreams. Now, he finds that these figures 'stepped right out of [*se détachaient de*] his memory to take their place in the Bodega, complete with their mannerisms and gestures' (*AR* 11.209; 138). They 'detached' themselves: what is at stake is a question of the production of an effect where the subject des Esseintes no longer directs the process. Art is performed, embodying itself in space, so that these figures take their place in a Bodega already populated by Dickensian characters. It is only insofar as des Esseintes considers the customers of the Bodega already to be 'Dickensian' that Dickens's actual characters may step forth into these surroundings as though already at home.

Thinking of Dickens and 'the London of the novelist', des Esseintes considers it divided. On the one hand, London is the metaphorical home which is 'well lighted, well heated, and well appointed', populated by Little Dorrit, Dora Copperfield and Ruth from *Martin Chuzzlewit*: it is domestic, pure and innocent (*AR* 11.209; 138). For Huysmans, such characters embody the 'discrete interiors' of Dickens (2006: 243), as he puts it in an 1877 essay dealing with the American painter Mary Cassatt (1844–1926), at once suggesting their decorative function, and that the sphere of the domestic is proper to the 'hygienic' effects of Dickens's realism.[17] In *À rebours*, however, this domestic ideal is imaged as a 'cosy ark' 'sailing snugly through a deluge of soot and mire' (*AR* 11.209; 138).[18] The biblical analogy tellingly evokes the antediluvian, if not prelapsarian, which immediately serves to undercut the idealism.[19] Still, even he is not immune to the temptation to linger longer in 'this London of the imagination', 'settl[ing] down comfortably' in his thoughts (11.209; 138). Indeed, he is so lost in these fantasies that he mistakes 'the dismal hootings of the tugs by the bridge behind the Tuileries' (11.138; 209), the gardens located on the bank of the Seine to the south of the Bodega, for the sound of boats on the Thames. Huysmans is caught mapping London onto Paris, and both as dream space.

Des Esseintes's stomach is turned by a glass of Amontillado (11.138; 209–10), another example of the bodily effects of art. The name of the sherry had reminded him of Edgar Allan Poe's (1809–49) 'The Cask of Amontillado' (1846), a narrative of being buried alive, *unheimlich* in Freud's sense (*SE* 17: 244), but additionally uncanny here. 'The spine-chilling nightmare [. . .] took hold of his imagination', Huysmans writes, with des Esseintes again constructed as a passive subject of art. But 'behind the kind, ordinary faces of the American and English customers in the Bodega', des Esseintes 'fancied he could detect atrocious, uncontrollable thoughts, dark and odious designs' (*AR* 11.209–10; 138–9). The allusion figures for des Esseintes's desire for entombment, of course, but there is something else at work: Huysmans reads Poe not only into real life (the Bodega's actual customers), but simultaneously into Dickens. Poe's gothic and its thanatic connotations are revealed to be swarming beneath the surface of his realism. Coming immediately after the *heimlich*, cosy image of an ark protecting Dickens's feminine ideals from the dirty metropolis beyond, this incident reveals des Esseintes's paranoia. Linking to the question of Dickens's *ressentiment*, Huysmans contends that beneath the kindly exterior of these characters lurks another reality, 'the crawling and glistening indestructible life' (Žižek 2005: 114), siding with the death-drive (*Todestrieb*). Dickens is revealed to be at pains to evade the real through his '*effets hygiéniques*', with his realism revealed here to be disciplinary and regulative, a question of biopolitics.

Leaving the Bodega, des Esseintes discovers himself again in the Dickensian weather, 'swamped by the driving rain' (*AR* 11.210; 139). It is now night, and he looks 'along the arcades of the Rue de Rivoli, drowned in shadow and submerged in moisture, and imagined that he was standing in the dismal tunnel beneath the Thames' (11.210; 139). The image is one of drowning, less a fantasy of inter-uterine existence (*SE* 5: 399–401) than a thanatic wish to lose himself in the unconscious. The reference is to the Thames Tunnel, built by Marc Isambard Brunel (1769–1849) in 1825–43, connecting London's north and south banks between Wapping and Rotherhithe, and a landmark that warranted its own entry in *Baedeker's Londres*. A technological marvel of Victorian civil engineering, the tunnel went vastly over budget, a 'monument to British stupidity and dogged obstinacy', as one later American visitor put it (Kirwan 1870: 27). There, a sort of shanty bazaar lined the side of the pedestrian walkway, selling tourist tat, and attracting prostitutes, as well as calling 'into existence a distinct class known as "Tunnel Thieves"' (Kirwan 1870: 27). It is this space which Virginia Woolf (1882–1941) refers to in *The Voyage Out* (1915), where Rachel dreams of 'walking through a tunnel under the Thames', seeing 'little deformed women sitting in archways playing cards, while the bricks of which the wall was made oozed with damp, which collected into drops and slid down the wall' (2009b: 386).[20] For Woolf, the Thames Tunnel

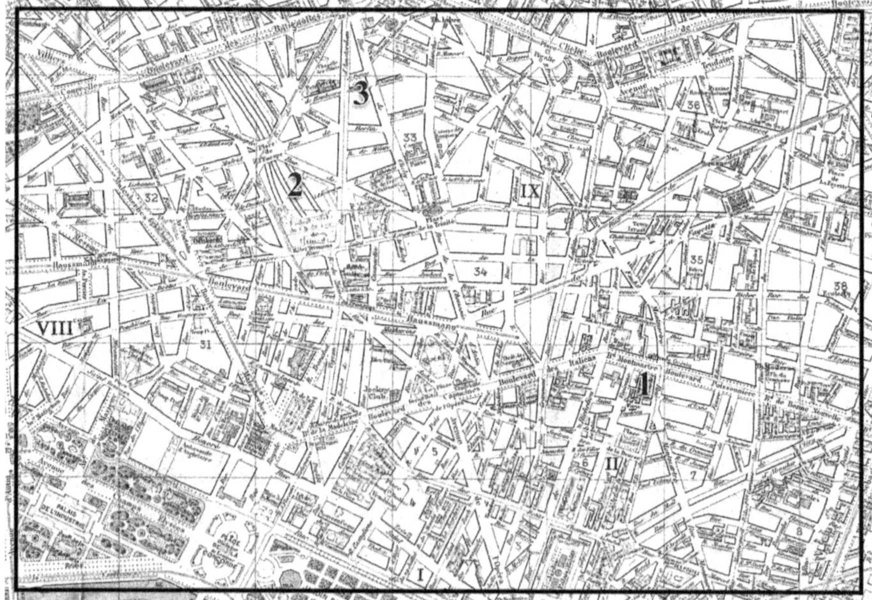

Figure iii VIIIe arrondissement: Élysée

1. Passage des Panoramas; 2. Gare Saint-Lazare; 3. Restaurant Austin, 24 Rue d'Amsterdam

becomes a nightmarish dream space. Huysmans's analogy is even more remarkable: reading the Rue de Rivoli through the Thames Tunnel, he evokes at once an entire socio-politics, where Parisian commodity culture and *haute couture* is founded on another, invisible economy of the lower classes that sustain it. Huysmans's image draws the analogy between these subterranean stalls and the arcades where nineteenth-century fashion was defined.

But if *À rebours* is on the one hand a 'breviary' of decadence, to use Arthur Symons's (1865–1945) famous phrase (1919: 265), a *Baedeker's* to living the aesthetic life, it is also a document of the relative failure of this very same ideal. Unsurprisingly, then, we see that des Esseintes finds that he cannot live wholly in the mind, and with his imagination arrested by hunger, he directs his cab to a tavern in the Rue d'Amsterdam by the Gare Saint-Lazare (*AR* 11.210; 139). The location is significant: opened in 1837, it had featured in Claude Monet's (1840–1926) series of paintings depicting the station, including *Le Pont de l'Europe*, first exhibited at the Third Impressionist Exhibition of 1877 at a moment marking a break point in the artist's career. Huysmans had noted as much in an essay of 1883, published the year before *À rebours*. There, he comments on how Monet's earlier impressionism amounted to little more than an 'egg badly hatched from realism' (2006: 271), but had developed recently a more visionary aesthetic of 'swarming [*fourmillantes*] colours' and 'reverberating things' (2006: 272). Zola would proclaim *Le Pont de l'Europe*, set at dawn, with the station lit ethereally by sunlight filtering through the steam of the trains, as the image of contemporaneity itself ('Là est aujourd'hui la peinture'), emblematic of a new aesthetic modernity. 'Our artists must find the poetry of the stations, as their predecessors found the poetry of forests and rivers' (1981: 100), Zola writes. By placing Huysmans's text in its cultural context, we see that des Esseintes's journey towards the Gare Saint-Lazare may well have been understood by his readers as one into the heart of modernity, a modernity which was itself defined by a new kind of aesthetics of space.

Des Esseintes travels approximately two kilometres north to Restaurant Austin (no. 24), which, although unnamed here in Huysmans's novel, had a long-standing reputation for English cuisine in the heart of Paris. In 1865, the Goncourt brothers, Edmond (1822–96) and Jules (1830–70), had praised the 'sincere and honest roast beef' served there, crowned by them the culinary equivalent of 'the reign of Louis-Philippe' (1956: 63). The building had also housed some famous literary tenants: Baudelaire took rooms above the Austin and, before him, Théodore de Banville (1823–91) lived there until the 1848 Revolution. Later, Banville had arranged to meet the English poet and translator John Payne (1842–1916), friend of Dante Gabriel Rossetti (1828–82) and associated with pre-Raphaelitism, at Austin's in June 1886, a meeting arranged by their mutual friend Stéphane Mallarmé (1842–98) (Mallarmé 1969: 43). With this unfulfilled liaison dating to just two years after the publication of *À rebours*, it suggests that Austin's was a meeting place for the English in Paris. Unsurprisingly in this context, we find that des Esseintes notes that the customers are English, 'islanders', and ones who are 'insulaires' (*AR* 11.210; 139). Watching two women eating (again, a question of the gaze), des Esseintes's appetite is piqued, desire as desire of the other (Lacan 1998b: 235), and he feasts on oxtail soup, smoked haddock, that 'honest' roast beef which the Goncourts had recommended, blue Stilton and rhubarb tart, washing it all down with English ale (*AR* 11.211; 139). If *À rebours* is 'the major work on an eating disorder ever written', as Naomi Schor has argued (2001: 91), we see in this passage that it is only through aesthetic identification that des Esseintes rediscovers his appetite. Regardless, eating at Austin's, in the heart of Paris, des Esseintes's meal is stereotypically English, making his body already something of a tourist.

Recuperating from his gastronomic exertions, des Esseintes considers the previous occasion he had ventured abroad, to Holland, his mind perhaps jogged by the name of the street (Rue d'Amsterdam). Before leaving for that trip, he had also been inspired by art, with Rembrandt van Rijn (1606–69), another figure whom Huysmans speaks of as 'fascinating' his viewer (2006: 77), taking the role of Dickens. Des Esseintes had imagined 'for his own private pleasure, ghettoes [*juiveries*] swarming with splendid figures', a visionary world of decadent carnival, of 'never-ending festivity' and 'riotous joviality' (*AR* 11.212; 141). The idea suggests a becoming-animal which is a becoming-intense (Deleuze and Guattari 2004b: 256–341) and a deterritorialisation of the self. It registers a thanatic desire in which the subject loses itself in the crowd, even if in the case of des Esseintes, as with Baudelaire's *flâneur*, this is an operation which is always undertaken from the vantage point of the margins, and where the spectacle can be consumed from a distance in the comfort of one's 'private pleasure'. Des Esseintes finds that Amsterdam had 'seduced [*séduit*] him', but only a certain aesthetics of this space, so that the experience 'proved a bitter disappointment' (*AR* 11.212; 141). Reality fell short of his own aesthetic vision that 'soared into a dream world of false trails and impossible ambitions' (11.212; 141). Des Esseintes realises, to use Pater's description of another painter, Antoine Watteau (1684–1721), that he was 'always a seeker after something in the world that is there in no satisfying measure' (*IP* 79).

With the time for departure approaching, des Esseintes finds that 'the food he had eaten was lying heavy on his stomach, and his whole body felt incapable of movement' (*AR* 11.215; 142). But this incapacity is taken for an omen:

> After all, what was the good of moving, when a fellow could travel so magnificently sitting in a chair? Wasn't he already in London, whose scents, atmosphere, citizens, food, and even cutlery, were all about him? What could he expect to find over there, save fresh disillusions [*désillusions*] such as he had suffered in Holland? (11.215; 142–3)

Feeling an 'immense aversion' now to travel, des Esseintes determines to abort his journey and return home. Having already experienced London through Dickens, he concludes that it 'would be madness to risk spoiling such unforgettable experiences by a clumsy change of locality' (11.216; 143). He returns to Fontenay, 'feeling all the physical weariness and moral fatigue of a man who has come home after a long and perilous journey' (11.216; 143).

Notes

1. Robert Baldick gives 'the tongue is brought into play' for 'ils pénètrent entre les lèvres', but this obscures the force of the verb in Huysmans's sentence.
2. The French 'lèvres' connotes both the lips and the labia.
3. In this sense, Huysmans's response to Dickens, diagnosing realism as *ressentiment*, and the context of convalescence, recalls Nietzsche's *Also sprach Zarathustra* (published in 1883, the year before *À rebours*), where Zarathustra recovers from a bout of nausea, produced by experiencing life as 'identical', and the abyssal thought of the eternal return of the same (2006: 173–9). On Nietzsche and *ressentiment*, see Deleuze 2006: 104–38.
4. Compare the 'foggy sea' of *Our Mutual Friend* (1997: 3.1.417), the mist of *Great Expectations* which obscures the far bank of the river in a 'watery lead colour' (2003e: 1.5.35), and finally the 'slimy' and 'muddy' swamps of Limehouse in *Bleak House* (*BH* 57.869).
5. For Huysmans's nineteenth-century English readers such as Oscar Wilde, who claimed *À rebours* as a model for Dorian's 'poisonous' yellow book

(*DG* 10.274; *LOW* 524), the name of the road may have had additional connotations. It recalls the Rue Saint-Thomas de l'Enfer which features in Thomas Carlyle's (1795–1881) *Sartor Resartus* (1833–4), where Teufelsdröckh experiences his 'Baphometic Fire-baptism' (2008: 128) – in reality (but the force of this commonplace is exactly what the tradition of the aesthetics of space calls into question), Leith Walk in Edinburgh, where Carlyle experienced his own spiritual epiphany. Huysmans knew *Sartor Resartus*, praising Carlyle as 'the historian who had the good faith to confess that, at bottom, there was no real history' (2006: 284), and quoting Teufelsdröckh approvingly on 'Symbols': 'SILENCE AND SECRECY. Altars might still be raised to them (were this an altar-building time) for universal worship' (2008: 165).

6. The latter term also recalls the Eden of *Martin Chuzzlewit*, that 'hideous swamp' 'choked with slime and matted growth' (1999: 23.360), based on Dickens's visit to Cairo, Illinois, described in *American Notes* (1842): 'A dismal swamp, on which the half-built houses rot away' (2003a: 2.4.190).
7. The idea of glass and the commodity has already been alluded to earlier in the chapter, when des Esseintes sits down 'before a glass-fronted bookcase in which a collection of silk socks was displayed in the form of a fan' (*AR* 11.200; 131) in contemplation of the most mundane of human vestures (socks) imitating a commodified aesthetic object (fan).
8. The idea of the *au-delà* will be pursued in a different context in Huysmans's *Là-Bas* [*The Damned*] (1891), where the idea of a spiritual 'beyond' that might transcend the materialism of naturalism is linked to 'the most extreme religious excesses' of the occult and Satanism (1985: 1.40; 2001: 14). In linking the spiritual in the *au-delà* to aesthetic (and erotic) 'excess', Huysmans's phrasing in both the essay on Whistler and *Là-Bas* anticipates Maurice Blanchot on the step (not) beyond (*le pas au-delà*) the pleasure principle (1992).
9. On the 'zooming' techniques and their significance in French decadent literature, see Przyboś 2002. Recall Michel de Certeau's epigraph to *The Practice of Everyday Life* (1984), commenting on the 'anonymity' of the subject when situated in the large city. In a certain tradition of realism, de Certeau argues, 'the increasingly sociological and anthropological perspective of inquiry privileges the anonymous and the everyday in which zoom lenses cut out metonymic details – parts taken for the whole' (2002: v).
10. The image seems to have been first used by Michael Drayton in *The Battle of Agincourt* (1627) (1753: 21), and became regular currency during the eighteenth century, notably used by Tobias Smollett in *The Expedition of Humphry Clinker* (1771) (2009: 92) and by Thomas Pennant in his popular *Account of London* (1790: 281). Dickens will also use the image in *American Notes*, there in reference to New York (2003a: 1.5.89).
11. See in particular Baudelaire's 'Le Crépuscule du soir' from 'Tableaux Parisiens'.

12. For Adorno's critique of Wilde, see 2004: 21, and for an influential development of the point, see Bürger 1984: 49–51.
13. Kafka's short story concludes with Georg Bendemann committing suicide, letting himself drop from a bridge into the river below while 'an absolutely unending stream of traffic [*unendlicher Verkehr*] flowed over the bridge' (2009: 28), and where the German for traffic, *Verkehr*, is also the word for intercourse. Kafka read Huysmans's *À rebours* with Max Brod in the early 1900s (Anderson 1992: 8).
14. For a reading of 'Perte d'auréole' emphasising its significance in terms of a post-Marxist reading of 'modernity', see Berman 1988: 156–60.
15. Every object's colour is attended by culinary adjectives: the books' covers 'butcher's-blue or cabbage-green'; the cloth 'dyed nut-brown, leek-green, lemon-yellow, or currant-red' (*AR* 11.204; 135). The analogy will be reversed a few pages later when Huysmans's narrator speaks of 'hams as brown as old violins, lobsters the colour of red lead' (*AR* 11.210; 139), so that, instead of inanimate objects being made attractive by association with food, food is unpalatable by association with inanimate objects. A focus on the culinary is common in Huysmans's work during the period, with his previous novel, *À vau-l'eau* [*Downstream*] (1882), narrating the existential crisis of the clerk Jean Fontalin, suffering from 'la monotonie de la nourriture', an endless quest for a satisfactory meal in a satisfactory restaurant (1882: 3.93; 2005: 44). See Whiteley 2019.
16. The reference is to *David Copperfield* (2004: 15.230), particularly germane to des Esseintes's situation, since Mr Wickfield's 'richness' is the product of 'port wine' (16.234). Huysmans must have read Dickens in the original, his French terms differing from those in the popular Hachette translations, against which I have checked them.
17. In this essay, Huysmans (2006: 243) adds three further Dickensian feminine paradigms: Esther Summerson of *Bleak House*, Florence Dombey, and Agnes Wickfield of *David Copperfield*.
18. This image of Dickens's 'cosy ark [*arche tiède*]' (*AR* 11.209; 138) recalls ironically des Esseintes's desire, expressed earlier in the novel, to retreat to his own 'snugly heated ark [*arche immobile et tiède*]' (*AR* 22; 72) away from the vulgar realities of the world. Such lexical echoes complicate Huysmans's treatment of Dickens in this passage, and, by extension, his response to Dickens's realism.
19. See Jameson 2002: 172–93 for an initial discussion of the problematic of realism as *ressentiment*.
20. Perhaps Woolf's own description of these 'deformed women' alludes somewhere to the Paris of Baudelaire and the 'monstres disloqués' of 'Les Petites Vieilles' (l. 5).

Introduction

The Spatial Turn

In des Esseintes's aborted journey to Dickens's London, Huysmans's *À rebours* offers a snapshot of a burgeoning tradition of later nineteenth-century writing which develops the idea of an aesthetics of space. Building upon and responding critically to a certain 'realist' literary tradition, this aesthetics of space attempts to find new ways to speak about how space is experienced by the nineteenth-century subject, and how such experiences are always already 'aesthetic' ones. It focuses on the potential of 'aesthetic effects', ones which act on the body, and which alter how that body engages with the spaces which it navigates. What is at stake for this new tradition is not simply an aesthetic *response* to space, but an aesthetic *approach* to it; not simply an aesthetic *appreciation* of space, but an adopting of aesthetic *intentions* towards it. Moreover, in this tradition, space is approached through its prior aesthetic representations, so that any aesthetics of space constitutes an intricate textual sensorium. In such a tradition, the idea of 'making *sense* of the text and experiencing it with one's *senses*' becomes blurred, as Kostas Boyiopoulos puts it in his study of *fin-de-siècle* Anglophone symbolist poetry (2015: 1). While this book is primarily interested in writers of prose rather than poetry, it maintains a similar interest in the sensuous and material aspects of the aesthetic. More specifically, it focuses not only on the way in which space affects the subject, but also on how this tradition represents these sensory experiences to the reader. Such an emphasis on the sensual makes these figures forerunners of the impressionist and modernist approaches to space. It is this tradition of the aesthetic literary treatment of space, one that passes from Ruskin, through Dickens, Pater, Wilde and James and on to modernism, which this book will begin to unpack, as a set of sketches towards a tradition.

After Realism

As we have seen, Huysmans is writing 'after Dickens' in *À rebours*, in an incident that plays around with various different ideas of what to write after Dickens means. One of the most obvious ways to understand the idea is to take it as a challenge or response to realism. Of course, precisely whether or not Dickens himself was a 'realist' or would have understood his work in this light is a difficult question, but as George Gissing (1857–1903) argued, 'had the word been in use', Dickens 'must necessarily have called himself a Realist' (1898: 75). The term was actually only coined in English in 1853 (Villanueva 1997: 6), meaning many of Dickens's most recognisably 'realist' works predated the designation. Nevertheless, and in spite of his criticism of the tendency of Victorian literature 'to be frightfully literal and catalogue-like – to make the thing, in short, a sort of sum' (Forster 1966: 2: 279), Dickens remains shackled to a model of verisimilitude which assumes the ontological priority of the thing. Even given the romantic, melodramatic aspects of his work, or the criticism of his realism on empiricist grounds by contemporaries such as George Henry Lewes (1817–78) and George Eliot (1819–80) (Bowen 2000: 16–19), it is clearly the case that the majority of Dickens's novels possess, or at least aspire to, 'formal realism' in Ian Watt's terms (2001: 32). The aim is to present a coherent and contextualised picture of a life or a number of lives, attentive to their everyday situation and grounded in a reality which is credible and true to empirical facts, but also one which edits that world judiciously, producing a version of reality that has been 'artistically constructed' (Villanueva 1997: 37).[1] Hence, even when Dickens introduces elements which stretch this credibility, as in the infamous incident of Krook's spontaneous combustion in *Bleak House*, an allegorical death speaking to a corruption 'inborn, inbred' (*BH* 32.519), and a plot point which Lewes attacked, Dickens was at pains to justify such creative liberties. As he put it in the novel's preface, 'everything' he wrote was 'substantially true, and within the truth' (*BH* 5).

For the majority of his career, Dickens's formal realism had been allied with a sharp social commentary and also the desire to encourage political change. It marries an attempt to capture a representation of the effects of city life with an attempt to know the causes. His impact was immense, and as the nineteenth century progressed, London became 'Dickensian', both literally and literarily. But as Nicholas Freeman puts it, Dickens's death in 1870 presented writers with a key decision: 'writing in a culture in which Dickens' works overshadowed their own, [. . .] would they decide to inhabit a "Dickensian" London, or would they instead seek new ways of representing [space] in fiction?' (2007: 19). This Dickensian London had profoundly impacted the cultural imagination of his peers, and as Philip Collins has shown, 'people were "doing"' the city of *Oliver*

Twist (1837–9) before the 1840s (1983: 118; quoted Freeman 2007: 20). In different ways, all of the writers that this book deals with are writing 'after Dickens': Ruskin, who appreciated Dickens but was also suspicious of that sentimentalism which threatened to undermine his politics; Pater in his attempts to sidestep the spectre of the Dickensian city; Wilde in his outright rejection of both the novelist and 'realism'; and James, a London-based novelist whose reading of New York is circumscribed throughout both by Dickens's treatment of an earlier America and by the inevitable comparisons which must be drawn between the nineteenth-century European city and the early twentieth-century American one. Indeed, as we shall see, even the 'late Dickens' of *The Mystery of Edwin Drood*, who will primarily concern us in Chapter 2, may be seen to be writing 'after Dickens', in response to his own dominant and dominating image of city space.

Still, what exactly was the 'Dickensian' city to which all these authors responded? Or more specifically, how did the city that later authors wrote differ from that constructed by Dickens? Such questions are of importance to understanding the complex mediations through which nineteenth-century literary representations of space developed in the years between the death of Dickens and modernism. There are, of course, no simple answers to such questions, both on spatial and on stylistic grounds. The ways in which spaces are represented in literature are to a large measure dependent upon specific local, cultural and geographical questions, so that a different city from London may not simply be written 'after Dickens', but may instead be written 'after Balzac'. In this sense, while the various different representations of space are necessarily in communication with one another, what it means to write nineteenth-century London is not the same as what it means to write nineteenth-century Paris, Venice or New York. Moreover, there were also a large number of different stylistic and philosophical ways in which authors went about tackling the problem of writing 'after Dickens'. In his study of post-Dickensian literary London, Freeman usefully divides the writers he considers into three basic categories: empiricists, impressionists and symbolists. This book is primarily interested in writers who work within the latter two categories, and particularly in a certain tradition of literary 'impressionism' which, reacting against Ruskin, passes through Pater to Wilde and James. For their part, the empiricists maintained 'a positivist belief that the city could be mapped and eventually understood by the process of painstaking investigation and analysis' (Freeman 2007: 26), in a gesture which builds on the politics of Dickens's formal realism in the naturalism of writers such as Gissing. Such a naturalism constitutes what Darió Villanueva calls 'genetic realism', predicated on 'the existence of a univocal reality which precedes the text' that the writer attempts to transcribe (1997: 15). As Symons put it, Zola's naturalism attempted to capture 'the exact representation of everything that visibly existed, exactly as it existed' (1919: 4). But while the naturalists 'fulfil[ed] the invaluable service of placing real characters in precise settings', the aesthetes came to consider it flawed, 'condemned to repeat itself over and over, and endlessly to go over the same ground' as Huysmans wrote in his 1903 preface to *À rebours* (*AR* 52; 205). By contrast to the empiricists, the impressionists were 'less ambitious in conceding that, if the city could be known, then it could be so only fleetingly, and from a wholly subjective position' (Freeman 2007: 26–7). The symbolists, such as Symons, on the other hand, 'offered a more mystical response' (Freeman 2007: 27), reading the city as a rebus or constellation, pregnant with transcendental meanings. In point of fact, all of the writers discussed in this book are precisely interested in the question of how best to represent reality, which is to say, in the problem of realism in literature. But regardless of these points of sympathetic convergence, it remains the case that, when read in the light of Dickens's achievements, it would be easy to overlook or minimise the spaces of aesthetic literature as insubstantial, lacking in reality. Moreover, it would be easy to read such diaphaneity as politically vacuous, which is to say, to read its so-called 'decadence' as an ethical 'problem'. The London of Wilde's *The Picture of Dorian Gray* (1890/1) begins to look a little thin and threadbare when compared to the complex, lived, vibrant spaces of Dickens's *Our Mutual Friend*, as though the city were nothing but an insubstantial pageant, scene dressing rather than a real space in which life is played out.

What then is the function of space in aesthetic literature? One potential answer lies in Julian Wolfreys's critique of the *fin-de-siècle* gothic of Wilde. Wolfreys characterises the writing of the city in the second half of the nineteenth century as one in which space assumes a 'function [. . .] as psychic context'. In comparison to Dickens's socially engaged response to space, Wilde 'tend[s] to employ stock images of the city', 'without necessarily allowing' them to 'transform' his texts (Wolfreys 1998: 209n.). While much is provisional in Wolfreys's phrasing, and he recognises the idea of writing '"after Dickens" as an imprecise phrase which gestures towards aesthetic redirection' rather than marking a definitive 'epistemic shift' (1998:

209–10 n.), the implication is that London is primarily psychogeographical in Wilde's writings. In dividing the city spaces of his fictions along a west/east axis, Wilde seems to oversimplify his representation of reality, so that psychological states (rational/irrational, conscious/unconscious, safe/dangerous) are mapped onto space, superimposed onto geographical locations, which are then made to symbolise these states. Such a schema reworks a long-standing representation of space, evoking 'the dichotomy between the shadows and the light, between diabolical and the divine', as Lefebvre puts it (*PS* 242). In a similar vein, Linda Dryden has contextualised Wilde's writing alongside contemporary newspaper reporting of the Ripper murders in 1888, which rested on establishing and mapping London as double, 'divided along its East/West axis' (2003: 36).[2] It is a tale of two cities, as Franco Moretti puts it, not of Paris and London as the two capitals of the nineteenth century, but of two separate Londons (1998: 77–140). The West End figured for the rich, and the East End for the poor, but the West End also and at the same time figured for a conservative, stable and ordered world, against a thanatic, 'labyrinthine' East End of unconscious desires and pleasures. With this in mind, Wolfreys rightly reminds us to be alert to the risk of conflating 'the symptoms' of the spaces revealed in aesthetic literature 'with a finitely knowable' or 'historical' space (1998: 12). What is at stake, at least in the case of Wilde, appears to be something akin to what Lefebvre calls 'a psychoanalysis of space' (*PS* 99).[3]

Of course, in reality, what is at stake is actually a certain way of reading spaces. As Alex Murray argues in *Landscapes of Decadence* (2016a), no space is by definition 'decadent', but decadence becomes a way of reading it. Indeed, this kind of way of reading space is not limited to the writers of aestheticism and decadence: in Thomas Hardy's (1840–1928) *The Woodlanders* (1886–7), for instance, the Darwinian struggle for existence is linked to 'the depraved crowds of a city slum', with the Wessex countryside clearly a landscape of decadence, in which 'the leaf was deformed, the curve was crippled, the taper was interrupted; the lichen ate the vigour of the stalk, and the ivy slowly strangled to death the promising sapling' (2009: 48). Likewise, one may recall Arthur Machen's (1863–1947) spaces, invested with gothic horror and a certain luxurious sense of degeneration. Such spaces become another version, a decadent one, of that tradition of 'dark' Romanticism, where the sublime is a moment not simply of registering a transcendental 'thrownness' (*Geworfenheit*), to use the Heideggerean language, but of what Ruskin will call the 'fall' of 'civilized' values.

Still, Wolfreys's argument regarding the psychoanalytic mapping of space in Wilde is germane to my argument in this book. While I argue that Wolfreys overstates the case and underestimates the political significance of Wilde's London, my analysis of the nineteenth-century aesthetics of space is certainly informed by psychoanalytic ideas. As Lefebvre puts it, space can be at once 'replete with places which are holy or damned, [. . .] rich in fantasies or phantasmagorias' and 'rational, state-dominated and bureaucratic' (*PS* 231). As a narrative move, however, the first thing to note is that Wilde's London appears to hark back to the early Dickens. Writing 'after Dickens', the 'stock' imagery Wolfreys alludes to is precisely 'Dickensian'. The west/east divide is something which the early Dickens uses as a plot point. As Moretti has shown, *Oliver Twist* may be read as a 'Newgate' novel, dividing the city latitudindally, 'where the metaphor of the labyrinth [. . .] returns time and again whenever the story approaches the dangerous classes of Fagin and company' (1998: 84). The same metaphor dominates Wilde's attempts to write London's slums, and we will have cause to discuss the figure of the 'labyrinth' in particular, and the use of 'stock' imagery in general, in more detail in the chapters that follow. But we should note from the outset that dividing the city into two neat parts is also bound to narrativity, a way of making sense of space that is also a way that produces a certain kind of narrative. As Moretti puts it, '*without a certain kind of space, a certain kind of story is simply impossible*' (1998: 100), and this specific narratological gesture reflects the new social realities that confronted the early nineteenth-century novelist. Faced with the difficulties in representing something so vast as the modern city, they sought to reduce the experience of chaos by remapping the city as a binary system (Moretti 1998: 107). Writing about London was a daunting prospect, with the city overwhelming, its population booming from around one million in 1800 to just under four and a half million by 1881, primarily because of immigration. London was a 'great and monstrous thing', as Daniel Defoe (1660–1731) puts it in *A Tour Through the Whole Island of Great Britain* (1724–7) (1986: 208), so that any attempt to represent it becomes a sublime experience of something without limits, 'formless' or deformed (Kant 2000: 151).[4] As Joseph Conrad (1857–1924) would later comment in his author's note to *The Secret Agent* (1907), set in the London of the late 1880s, the city 'presented itself [as] a monstrous town more populous than some continents' (2008b: 231).

The problem of representing such a 'monstrous' space relates to what Fredric Jameson famously calls an 'aesthetic of cognitive mapping' (1991: 51), his term for describing the pressing task for the subject when faced by the bewildering spatial logic of the postmodern city. Jameson's idea builds on the insights of Kevin Lynch (1960), who argues that in the modern city, the subject is unable to map either their own position in space or the urban totality. This displacement, this inability to effectively map or localise the self in space, is precisely a mark of 'alienation', what Marx calls the subject's estrangement (*Entfremdung*). While Jameson's point refers to the postmodern experience, we see in the gesture towards binary simplification of the early nineteenth-century novelist a similar kind of operation. And as such, in adopting a similar kind of binarity, Wilde seems to return to this earlier, simplified response to the city. More specifically, it suggests that Wilde's spaces are less 'real' than those of the later Dickens, who, from *Nicholas Nickleby* onwards, began to 'settle' the '*third space in the middle*' of London (Moretti 1998: 117), which is to say, populate it with characters and gradually make those characters the motors of his plots. In this sense, Arthur Clennam of *Our Mutual Friend* represents both spatially and literally a class in the middle, caught between the banker's speculations and the debtor's prison. When compared to the remarkable mediatory achievements of Dickens's last completed novel, Wilde's psychological troping of London seems regressive and politically effete: not a 'real' treatment of space, but one which is reductive, uninterested in social mediation.

But at the same time, there is something more to the aesthetic approach to space, and particularly city spaces, than has hitherto been said. One of the problems lies in precisely what one understands the category of the 'aesthetic' to be and how one defines the relationship between nineteenth-century realist and aesthetic literature. To consider the point, let us return to the problem of writing 'after Dickens'. Arguably, one of the principal strategic moves of aesthetic literature was to define itself against 'realism' and 'naturalism', in terms of both matter and form (Byerly 1997: 184–95). In this sense, while *Dorian Gray* contains 'a certain amount of intrusion of real life and its sordid aspects', as Pater noted in his review of the novel, it also documents Wilde's 'emphatic' protest 'against so-called "realism"' (Beckson 1998: 83, 84), the idea that realism was a 'prison-house' for the artist, as he put it in 'The Decay of Lying' (1891) (*CR* 88). The subject matter of realist literature, focusing on the 'everyday' and on a certain 'bourgeois' ideology and mentality, seems to be anathema to the project of aestheticism. As Huysmans put it, Zola's naturalism 'had no room – in theory at least – for exceptions'; 'in the pretext of being true to life', the naturalists created characters 'who came close as possible to the average person' (*AR* 52; 205). Aestheticism, on the other hand, focused on the idea of the exceptional in life and art. Likewise, the formal focus on a language that may suitably represent such a reality seemed to differ markedly between aesthetic and realist literature, where an ornate and markedly 'poetic' prose style replies to a sparser descriptive one.[5] These divisions are, as we have already pointed out, precarious, particularly given the ways in which British aesthetic and decadent literature acknowledged and welcomed the influence of the French Romanticism of Victor Hugo (1802–85) and Gustave Flaubert (1821–80), and the tradition developing out of them, passing through the Goncourt brothers, Théophile Gautier (1811–72), Baudelaire and Zola. In his influential study of realism, *Mimesis* (1946), Eric Auerbach (1892–1957) argues that French naturalism, in its focus on both the flowers of evil and style, already amounts almost to a kind of aestheticism (2003: 497–500). But regardless, the aesthetes certainly saw their project as philosophically differentiated from that of realism: the aim was not simply to represent life empirically, but to represent it aesthetically. In Pater's famous shift from Matthew Arnold's (1822–88) dictum that the aim of criticism should be 'to see the object as in itself it really is', towards a more phenomenological appreciation of the world, which would allow one 'to know one's impression as it really is' (*SHR* xix), the aesthetes aimed to 'treat life in the spirit of art' (1910a: 62), as Pater puts it in 'Wordsworth' (1874).

From one point of view, Pater's subtle reworking and rebuke of Arnold's critical functionalism may also be read as a kind of riposte to realism. Arnold's theory is 'realist' in its belief both that there is an empirical reality behind any work of art which it aims to represent, and that the critic should judiciously sort the cultural wheat from the chaff, evaluating good and bad, in what one might call a 'project of enlightenment' (his formal realism).[6] As such, and while there is much that separates Arnold from Dickens in terms of their politics, the critical 'insight' Arnold espouses is markedly Dickensian in spirit. The politics of Dickens's realism is most famously imaged in that moment in *Dombey and Son* when the narrator asks for 'a good spirit who would take the house-tops off, with a [. . .] potent and benignant hand' (2002a: 47.702). As Raymond Williams (1921–88) argues, this 'potent' hand is that of 'the novelist; it is Dickens seeing himself' (1973: 157), and its benign vision is allied with what Ruskin calls *theoria*, moral insight. It is this idea of *theoria*, which Ruskin differentiates from *aesthesis*, sensuous vision, in the second volume of *Modern Painters* (1846), which underwrites the analysis of this book. We will trace this tension in Ruskin's work as it relates to the ways in which space is represented, both as manifested in his later works, such as *The Stones of Venice* (1851–3), and in the writers that followed him, those who, either implicitly or explicitly, offered replies to this way of reading space.

Seeing through the housetops means seeing into the heart of real-life conflicts and conditions. And as Peter Brooks puts it, the 'gesture' of removing the housetops 'also suggests how centrally realist literature is attached to the visual, to looking at things, registering their presence in the world through sight' (2005: 3). Realism is all about the details, and about registering them visually. The realist novel, from the time of those early forerunners such as Defoe that fascinated Watt, to the nineteenth-century masters such as Stendahl (1783–1842), Honoré de Balzac (1799–1850) and Flaubert in France, and Dickens and Eliot in Britain, is concerned with how different kinds of spaces are inhabited. It recognises that lives are played out in space, and seeks to illuminate these spaces, be they the domestic interior or the wider cityscape, focusing on both the people that populate them and the things, the 'cultural bric-à-brac and decorative allusion', that mark what Fredric Jameson calls 'the *bourgeois cultural revolution*' (1986: 379, 373) through which the modern subject came to define themselves and their lives. These trinkets have fascinated in particular Roland Barthes (1915–80), who used their presence to develop his influential theory of the 'reality effect'. For Barthes, realism is characterised by the incidental, the superfluous, 'a kind of narrative *luxury*, lavish to the point of offering many "futile" details and thereby increasing the cost of narrative information' (1989: 141). Focusing on the barometer in the first of Flaubert's *Trois Contes* (1877), Barthes argues that such 'insignificant notation[s]' (1989: 142) do not serve to further the plot, but respond to what he calls 'the tyrannical constraints of [. . .] aesthetic verisimilitude' (1989: 144), a kind of '"realistic" imperative [. . .], as if the referent's exactitude [. . .] governed and alone justified its description' (1989: 146). This '*referential illusion*' produces a new kind of textual effect which is itself 'precisely *realism*': 'the very absence of the signified, to the advantage of the referent alone, [which] becomes the very signifier of realism' (1989: 148). For Barthes, realism is less a literary philosophy than an effect, a simulacrum to stand in for 'reality'.

Building on Barthes's argument, we might argue that later nineteenth-century literature takes such reality effects to an extreme: in the tradition of writing charted in this book, as opposed to the realist tradition of a Balzac or a Flaubert which concerns Barthes, we find that these kinds of circumstantial and superfluous details produce less an effect of 'reality' than one which might be primarily considered 'aesthetic'. For instance, Huysmans's description of the window of Galignani's is not a 'realistic' one but, in its aestheticisation of space, an invitation to the reader to approach space in the spirit of art. And it is important to note that while Barthes is particularly interested in the extraneous objects or things that populate the realist novel, the idea of 'reality effects' can be broadened to include anything that gives such a sense of reality, including, for instance, street names and similar spatial markers. Likewise, aesthetic effects are anything that connote a bodily sensation of beauty. Take the brief moment in *Dorian Gray* when Lord Henry is at Hyde Park's Speakers' Corner, listening to a preacher, and comments that 'London is very rich in curious effects' (*DG* 19.350).[7] The present book is interested in the ways in which these kinds of 'aesthetic effect' are bound up with the ways in which space is perceived and represented in nineteenth-century writing. Mallarmé's comments on his attempt to develop a symbolist style may stand as a description of the ways in which the Anglophone aesthetes, writing after Dickens and realism, sought to 'invent a language' that came 'from a very new poetics, [. . .] best define[d] in these words: *Paint not the thing, but the effect that it produces*' (1959: 137).

Barthes's argument is important, but must be challenged precisely on political grounds, for in his version of realism, it is as though the text were suspended in a kind of ideological vacuum. As Jameson has shown, the 'reality effect' of realism cannot be entirely divorced from a certain social realist tradition, even while it puts this tradition into question (1986: 373–83). The same is true of those 'aesthetic effects' charted in this book. Indeed, and in contrast to some of the more extreme statements with respect to the autonomy of art of figures such as Pater and especially Wilde, as well as some of the more privative critical interpretations of their works, this book argues that aestheticism cannot be divorced from the social and political world in which it was developed and conceived. Following Pater's lead in *Marius the Epicurean* (1885), it considers aestheticism as an engaged philosophy, guided by the 'maxim of *Life as the end of life*' (*ME* 1: 2.8.142). While both writers clearly believed that art should not be trammelled by 'moral' import, a point indeed crucial to Pater's reply to Ruskin's discussion of *theoria* and *aesthesis*, and while neither would have admitted that the beauty of art was determined, or should be limited, by social or ideological questions, both were keenly aware of the political contexts that underwrote the production of art and which allowed it to be appreciated. Likewise, aesthetic writers were also aware of the political forces that produce those spaces they sought to read aesthetically. As Kristen Ross puts it, 'space, as a social fact, as a social factor and as an instance of society, is always political' (2008: 9).

Reading Space: Theoretical Considerations

Based on the belief that 'aesthetic effects' always already carry the traces of the society in which they were conceived and the politics which informed them, the theoretical framework underwriting this study is indebted to a certain dialectical materialist tradition of the criticism of space. It situates itself within the critical discourse surrounding the writing and reading of the city in nineteenth-century literature and asks a simple question: how did British writers associated with the aesthetic movement respond to space? In order to answer this question, this book builds on work by Freeman (2007) and Murray (2016a), the former limiting his discussion to literary representations of a single city, London, but broadening it to consider authors who were not part of the aesthetic movement, the latter discussing a wider variety of different spatial 'landscapes'. The present study differs from both in the ways in which it sees the writers contributing to the tradition under consideration as writing not simply 'after Dickens', but also, and as importantly, 'after Ruskin'. Like Wolfreys, I use the idea of writing after Dickens and Ruskin strategically, as useful ways of indicating a shift in perspective, rather than considering the terms as designating an epistemic shift. The tradition of the aesthetics of space mapped in this book does not constitute a radical break with earlier traditions of writing space, be they those of the Enlightenment realists, the Romantics, or the crowning achievements of nineteenth-century French, British or Russian realism. I am well aware that all of these earlier movements show an interest in representing reality aesthetically, and all to some degree register an aesthetics of space. As we shall see, the tradition of the aesthetics of space capitalises productively on these debts, just as modernism owes its own debts to aestheticism.

Jameson has discussed the 'spatial turn', in which critics have come to consider questions of spatiality central to understanding the movement of 'modernity'. In a famous lecture from 1967 on 'Des espaces autres' [Different Spaces], Michel Foucault (1926–84) argues that if 'the great obsession of the nineteenth century was history: themes of development and arrest, themes of crisis and cycle, themes of accumulation of the past, a great overload of dead people', the twentieth century was 'the age of space' (2000a: 175).[8] Jameson argues, however, that the nineteenth century was itself also an age of space: the period of the Enlightenment had witnessed the emergence of 'a new form of space', that of *Alltag*, 'daily life' (1986: 374), which the realist novel itself played a part in producing. As Ross writes in her study of the emergence of 'social space' in the Communes of nineteenth-century Paris, 'everyday life is born in nineteenth-century Europe' (2008: 9). Building on Ross's work, but shifting the focus from poets such as Arthur Rimbaud (1854–91) to consider European 'aesthetic' writers more broadly, we might equally well suggest that the later nineteenth century, reacting against the realist novel, responded to the emergence of another related but distinct kind of spatiality: one which resisted precisely bourgeois, 'democratic' ideology in focusing on the momentary experience of the exceptional. What is key is the 'impressionistic' moment whereby space is appreciated by the subject not solely 'in itself', but through recognising those 'impressions' as they themselves are (*SHR* xix). Such an emphasis precisely divides *aesthesis* from *theoria* in Ruskinian terms (*CW* 11: 62). Indeed, the tradition of the aesthetics of space only becomes possible at this precise historical moment in the second half of the nineteenth century, and if the tension between *theoria* and *aesthesis* predates Ruskin and nineteenth-century realism, *Modern Painters* provided the critical resources for those who followed, allowing them to conceptualise these two different ways of approaching space. As such, the tradition of the aesthetics of space was precipitated by concurrent developments in nineteenth-century aesthetic theory and the socio-material conditions of modern space (and particularly metropolitan space, given that this kind of space was the dominant product of, and produced, this modernity), as a synthetic response to the conditions of a new kind of 'reality'.

Broadly speaking, the critical heritage dealing with literary representations of space can be divided into two distinct, though often interrelated discourses: critical realist and post-industrial (Tambling 2001: 2–3). The critical realist tradition begins, in earnest, during the middle of the nineteenth century with Friedrich Engels (1820–95) in *The Condition of the Working Class in England* (1844). This approach stretches through to twentieth-century criticism, most obviously in important works such as Raymond Williams's *The Country and the City* (1973): its focus is on capitalism, industry and questions of class. Dickens's journalism might be argued to constitute an early part of this tradition, and his realism, as well as that of works such as Elizabeth Gaskell's (1810–65) *Mary Barton* (1848), an aesthetic response to it. In French realism, it reaches its high point in Balzac's multivolume project *La Comédie humaine*, a history of Paris from the Restoration and July Monarchy, as Engels noted in a famous 1888 letter to the radical Margaret Harkness (1854–1923). Responding to her novel *City Girl* (1887), he added: 'Realism [. . .] implies, besides the truth of detail, the truthful reproduction of typical characters under typical circumstances' (Marx and Engels 2001: 166).

The post-industrial tradition, on the other hand, focuses less on the question of class struggle than on the psychic toll of modern space. Such a tradition is often said to begin with Georg Simmel's (1858–1919) important essay on *Die Großstädte und das Geistesleben* [*The Metropolis and Mental Life*] (1903), but we can see traces of it already in Ruskin in a work such as 'Fiction, Fair and Foul' (1880). This tradition includes Benjamin's *Das Passagen-Werk* and T. J. Clark's *The Painting of Modern Life* (1984), but also takes in the work of postmodern theorists such as Jean Baudrillard (1929–2007) on the 'hyperreal' (2004). As such, the post-industrial tradition is also deeply interested in the aesthetics of how such spaces have been read. Unsurprisingly, then, my analysis of the tradition of the aesthetics of space finds itself closer to the post-industrialist discourse than to the critical realist one. While the spaces discussed in this book are primarily 'real' ones, rooted in real lived experiences of certain nineteenth-century spaces, they are also literary constructs which differ necessarily from their models, so that when we speak of a 'real' London or Paris during the course of this book, the quotation marks already indicate a putting-into-question of the status of the 'real' that critical realism would baulk at. For such a tradition, the 'real' city is knowable through its social construction, and it is the task of criticism to map this city. But in charting the way in which the city is treated as a work of art, the aesthetics of space is less interested in the question of the represented than in the representation, the ways in which the experience of space is created as an aesthetic object. This study, in other words, is interested in the artist as painter of modern life, and if the tradition of the aesthetics of space in Anglophone literary traditions originates with writers all too aware of their status as writing after Dickens and after Ruskin, it is also built upon an awareness of Baudelaire. Indeed, Baudelaire's essay on 'Le Peintre de la vie moderne' [The Painter of Modern Life] (1863), focusing on the figure of the *flâneur*, the alienated observer of the crowd, has already been used as a model for reading the aesthetics of Parisian space by

Benjamin, but the British version of this aesthetics of space, linking writers such as Pater, Wilde and James, has not been fully mapped. This book is partly a response to this gap in the critical heritage.

The primary theoretical fulcrum of my analysis combines insights derived from Lefebvre and Benjamin, alongside others gleaned from psychoanalysis and poststructuralism. Sitting somewhere between the critical realist and post-industrial traditions, Lefebvre's basic argument is that space is not something that was simply 'there', but has instead been produced across time (*PS* 36–7). Moreover, space is produced by, and produces, social relations, so that, as David Harvey puts it, 'space and the political organization of space express social relationships but also react back upon them' (1973: 306). According to Lefebvre, history has witnessed the production of a series of different modes of spatiality, from natural or 'absolute' space, through the 'secular' space of the Middles Ages and the early modern period, to the 'abstract' space of the nineteenth and twentieth centuries. Lefebvre coins three distinct concepts to help understand the different ways in which any space may be produced and used: spatial practice, representations of space and representational spaces. The literary works which are the subject of this study produce representational spaces, space as '*lived* through its associated images and symbols'. This is 'space which the imagination seeks to change and appropriate. It overlays physical space, making symbolic use of its objects' (*PS* 39). We have already seen one such operation of 'overlaying' in the ways in which the early realist novel seeks to reduce the chaotic reality of the experience of space by dividing the city in half. But of course, the very fact that we are discussing a number of different representational spaces implies limits. As Lefebvre writes, considering de Quincey and Baudelaire, Hugo and Comte de Lautréamont (1846–70), 'the problem is that any search for space in literary texts will find it everywhere and in every guise: enclosed, described, projected, dreamt of, speculated about' (*PS* 15). Nevertheless, an aesthetic representation of space is to a degree mappable, both geographically onto a 'real' space, and socio-politically, and representational spaces are not blind to the forces that produce them. The text(ure) of this space is the dialectical precipitate of what Lefebvre calls a certain set of spatial practices, 'space as it is perceived [*perçu*]', which is to say, engaged with on a daily basis, as well as certain representations of space. The latter is 'conceptualised [*conçu*] space' which identifies 'what is lived and what is perceived with what is conceived', not least the dominant mode of production which produces it (*PS* 38; 48). Indeed, representations of space are often allied with state power. Such a representation of space is the theme of Jorge Luis Borges's (1899–1986) parable 'On Exactitude and Science' (1946), which tells of an ancient map 'whose size was that of the Empire, and which coincided point for point with it' (2004: 181). Mapping space, knowing its contours and limitations, produces knowledge but also exercises power, an imperial operation captured in the famous map of Conrad's *Heart of Darkness* (1899). Dramatising the ways in which 'many blank spaces on the earth' became filled in with 'farcical names' (2008a: 130) in the years following the initial Scramble for Africa (1881), the continent becomes 'a place of darkness' (2008a: 108).

These three key terms – spatial practice, representations of space and representational spaces – will recur throughout the analyses of this book, helping to show the ways in which representational spaces relate to the other ways in which space is produced. But if the aesthetics of space treats space in the spirit of art, it produces less a realist mapping than a representational space. 'Representational space is alive', Lefebvre remarks, and literary texts may 'speak' to the reader. They have 'an affective kernel or centre' and 'embrace [. . .] the loci of passion, of action and of lived situations' (*PS* 42). Affective and passionate, engaging with space implicates the body (*PS* 40), and as we shall see, this question of the body is one that divides Ruskin from those such as Pater who follow him.

In implicating the body, one of the effects of modern space is that 'it unleashes desire' (*PS* 97). Here Lefebvre's analysis can usefully be placed in dialogue with that of Benjamin. Left unfinished at Benjamin's death, *Das Passagen-Werk* collected a series of fragments on nineteenth-century life and the city, primarily focusing on Paris and its arcades. It centres on a reading of Baudelaire as an allegorist of the modern city, building on Benjamin's earlier work on baroque tragedy in *Ursprung des deutschen Trauerspiels* [*The Origin of German Tragic Drama*] (1928). In that work, dealing with the emergence of allegorical drama during the Thirty Years War (1618–48), Benjamin argues that allegory is the mode of writing that responds to historical trauma, etymologically a wound which cannot heal (Greek: *τραῦμα*). In such historical periods, allegory becomes the way in which writers can register a sense of a temporality that is *unzeitgemäße* or untimely. Whereas symbolism implies a direct and supposedly 'natural' relationship between signifier and signified, allegory, insofar as it is always metonymic, is catachrestic (Greek: *ἀλληγορία*, 'speaking otherwise'), registering a breakdown in the stable semiotic economy, a point at which meaning is fractured or broken. Benjamin argues that the nineteenth century registers another, different moment of trauma: that of modernity.

In his Exposé of 1935, Benjamin reads Baudelaire's 'Le Cygne' from *Les Fleurs du mal* [*The Flowers of Evil*] (1857) as symptomatic of nineteenth-century Paris. The poem's persona is seen walking the streets, noting how 'the old Paris is gone' (l. 7) following the renovations undertaken by Georges-Eugène Haussmann (1809–91). In response to a ballooning population that had doubled since 1815, much of old Paris was demolished under Haussmann's direction between 1853 and 1870, with new boulevards cut and widened. Haussmann's vision was a quintessential representation of space in Lefebvrean terms, which sought to make abstract space more 'visible', using modern communication routes to 'rationalise' space, exercising power. It ushered in a 'revolution of representation' (Ferguson 1997: 115–51). But as Benjamin argues, the result was that Haussmann 'estrange[d] the Parisians from their city'; they no longer felt at home, starting 'to become conscious of the inhuman character of the metropolis' (*SW* 3: 42). This is the kind of *unheimlichkeit* that Marx linked to alienation and identified as the quintessential experience of 'modernity'.[9] In' Le Cygne', this alienation produces melancholia, and figures Paris as ruin:

> Paris may change, but in my melancholy mood
> Nothing has budged! New palaces, blocks, scaffoldings,
> Old neighbourhoods, are allegorical for me,
> And my dear memories are heavier than stone. (ll. 29–32)

In linking allegory and melancholia, Benjamin's argument builds on Sigmund Freud (1856–1939), who differentiates melancholia from mourning, insofar as in the former, the object of cathexis is lost, so that the state cannot be 'worked through' (*SE* 14: 243–58). For Benjamin, the metonymy characteristic of allegory marks its melancholia, registering precisely the trauma of the lost object. Commenting on 'Le Cygne', Benjamin argues that 'the gaze of the allegorist, as it falls on the city, is the gaze of the alienated man. It is the gaze of the flâneur' (*SW* 3: 39), a point that links his engagement with Baudelaire to Dickens, another *flâneur* (Hollington 1981). Benjamin had read *Old Curiosity Shop* in October 1930,[10] discussing it with Adorno, who sees in Dickens's novels 'a fragment of the dispersed baroque that maintains a strange ghostly presence in the nineteenth century' (1992: 171). We will see the ghostly traces of this 'dispersed baroque' recur in the tradition of the aesthetics of space.

For Lefebvre, Romanticism may be understood as 'the transitional moment that separated abstract spatiality from a more unmediated perception' (*PS* 290), and it is in this context that we can perhaps best understand one of the most famous allegorical responses to the modern city of British literature. In much-discussed passages of book seven of *The Prelude*, Wordsworth records having heard as a child of how 'next-door neighbours' in London lived as 'Strangers, and knowing not each other's names' (7.117–88). Arriving in London for the first time, Wordsworth imagines viewing the city from a distance (7.249–53) in a kind of 'theoretical' gaze, in the sense in which Ruskin uses the term *theoria* – one which extrapolates from the chaotic reality, perceived from the vantage point of a kind of ideal subject, overseeing the whole and presenting the 'truth of space'. Yet modern space resists such a theoretical gaze, as Wordsworth makes clear: looking over the city from above, London is figured through a metonymy of the monumental, including both Wren's Monument, built in 1677 to commemorate the 1666 Fire of London, and 'Bedlam', Bethlem Hospital, noting its statues of 'Melancholy' and 'Raving Madness' (1676), designed by Caius Gabriel Cibber (1630–1700). Even monumental London is hard to read: Wren's Monument suggests the city's resistance to destruction or erasure, monumental space figuring the trace of an imperial will to power (*PS* 143), while Bedlam's statues read London otherwise, suggesting a resistance to being encompassed or known, the city figuring a site of madness and a space that makes its subject mad. From this elevated vantage point, Wordsworth then finds himself thrust down, in a zooming movement which we have already seen at work in Huysmans. This zooming movement registers not simply the movement of the eye, but a sense of alienation, so that it becomes hard, if not impossible, for the subject to know their place. Wordsworth finds himself 'amidst the hurry of crowds', his senses assaulted by 'colours, lights and forms, the Babel din / The endless stream of men, and moving things' (7.157–8), another image repeated in Huysmans. Such a visceral experience risks escaping the eye, which is to say, risks escaping a 'theoretical' comprehension in Ruskinian terms. The only one seemingly unmoved by the experience is the blind beggar who, precisely in his blindness, with 'his fixed face and sightless eyes' (7.622) becomes an 'emblem' or allegorical figure (7.619). Unsure where to focus, Wordsworth's vision is assailed by:

> Face after face - the string of dazzling wares,
> Shop after shop, with symbols, blazoned names,
> And all the tradesman's honours overhead:
> Here, fronts of houses, like a title-page
> With letters huge inscribed from top to toe;

Stationed above the door like guardian saints,
There, allegoric shapes, female or male,
Or physiognomies of real men. (7.174–80)

The metonymies of faces and names, the inscrutable primacy of signs and symbols that resist a direct reading, suggest that the city itself produces 'allegoric shapes' and can only be read as an allegorical text (Tambling 2009: 21). Wordsworth's experience of the crowd is one of trauma, and thus compares to Benjamin writing on Baudelaire. But what differentiates Wordsworth from Baudelaire, and from the British aesthetic writers that are the subject of this book, who are all influenced by both poets to various degrees, is precisely Wordsworth's resistance to this experience. As we shall see, the idea of allegory, of the figure of the *flâneur*, of the modern city as traumatising and its spaces as ruined, recur throughout this book, but in the tradition of the aesthetics of space, Ruskinian *theoria* is supplanted by *aesthesis* as the dominant mode of reading the city. In contrast to Wordsworth, writers such as Wilde and James are fascinated by the pleasure of the gaze and of the experience of the loss of the self in an aesthetics of space.

For Benjamin, reading the 'modern' city allegorically means reading it as a 'dream world', so that its space become a kind of 'phantasmagoria' (*SW* 3: 40). This is Marx's term for the commodity fetish, which '*congeal*[*s*] *labour-time*' (1990: 130), petrifying time in the thing. In *Das Passagen-Werk*, Benjamin associates 'dreamtime' with 'spacetime' (*PW* 389; K1,4), the latter term (*Zeitraum*) linking space and time dialectically, in a manner which echoes both the philosophy of Martin Heidegger (1889–1976), for whom *Ereignis* marks the spatial and temporal unity of Being and beings, and Mikhail Bakhtin's (1895–1975) concept of the chronotope. For Bakhtin, the chronotope refers to 'the intrinsic connectedness of temporal and spatial relationships' in which 'time [. . .] thickens, takes on flesh, becomes artistically visible; likewise, space becomes charged and responsive to the movements of time, plot and history' (Bakhtin 1981: 84). The aesthetics of space is precisely such a chronotope, making time visible in space and space in time, the beautiful moment or instant crystallised as an image that encapsulates space-time. But as 'dreamtime', Benjamin's idea also connotes the sense in which desire can be invested in space, akin to the process which psychoanalysis calls cathexis. For Baudelaire, 'le Cygne', a ghostly swan which is also a sign (its homophone, 'le signe'), and which he sees haunting Paris, is precisely the trace of desire in space.

Another way in which we can understand how desire is invested in space is through the work of the philosophers Gilles Deleuze (1925–95) and Félix Guattari (1930–92). In *L'anti-Œdipe* (1972) and *Mille plateaux* [*A Thousand Plateaus*] (1980), they build upon Marx's argument in *Das Kapital* (1867) regarding the two circuits of production: C-M-C, in which commodities are exchanged for money and then traded for other commodities, and M-C-M, in which money is transformed into commodities and then back into money again. For Marx, M-C-M is precisely 'the general formula of capital' (1990: 257), since this circuit involves investment and speculation: the same commodity is bought not with a view to its use value, but precisely on the basis of its exchange value – it is bought only to be sold on again. Money is put into circulation, invested with a view to return. Deleuze and Guattari rework Marx's idea alongside a theory of desire informed by psychoanalysis into the triad of territorialisation, deterritorialisation and reterritorialisation, and link it to the distinction they draw between two types of space: 'smooth' and 'striated' (2004b: 536–7). Space is 'originally' smooth, they argue, corresponding broadly to what Lefebvre calls absolute space (*PS* 234). For Deleuze and Guattari, space is not bounded, and it is only with the advent of humanity that space became subdivided into regions. They call this the process of 'striating' space, linked to the birth of agriculture, when the nomadic tribes settled down, becoming sedentary. For Deleuze and Guattari, this act of settling space territorialises it, dividing it up, leading to the idea of private property, and thus, by extension, capitalism (2004b: 473–4). Deterritorialisation is the process through which these territories change hands (historically, through acts of war),[11] the boundaries redrawn, after which space is reterritorialised in new formations. This process is akin to the circuits that Marx identified as the motors driving capitalist accumulation, and which Lefebvre sees as driving the production of new kinds of spatiality, beginning in the Middle Ages (*PS* 262–3). But Deleuze and Guattari also note that capitalism creates new possibilities for this process of deterriorialisation. In this sense, Freud was perspicacious in adopting the 'economic' model for his early understanding of psychic process, suggesting that the subject invests desire in the same way as capitalism does. Capital is virtual money, no longer linked to a real-world referent (such as the gold standard), but which has been deterritorialised, referring only to itself. It relies for its existence on economic circuits and flows, so that capitalism has as its goal a kind of limitless deterritorialisation, an endless process of the investment of desire in which speculation reproduces itself in an ever-increasing process. And as Lefebvre argues, the 'abstract' space of the nineteenth century is precisely engaged in this kind of deterritorialisation, linking 'the various *flows* involved: flows of energy and labour, of commodities and capital' (*PS* 347).[12] In this sense, the production of space is linked to capitalism in its modern form, as the production of abstract spaces.

What is at stake in Deleuze and Guattari's philosophy is a kind of 'libidinal economy', and recent work on the *fin de siècle* has shown the productive ways in which these kinds of ideas can help us read the circuits of desire which characterise the literature of the nineteenth century.[13] More specifically, the idea of deterritorialisation is a useful one in understanding both the ways in which space was produced during the period, and how this production of space was bound to capitalism. As we shall see, one example of the phenomenon in the nineteenth century may be seen in the railway, which deterrirorialises space in two related fashions. Firstly, railways literally ripped up existing spaces, a process memorably captured in *Dombey and Son*, where Dickens describes the demolition of Camden Town for the construction of the London and Birmingham railway, 1833–7, as a 'great earthquake' that 'rent the whole neighbourhood to its centre' (2002a: 6.78). But secondly, the railways also deterriorialise the space between those metropolitan centres that they connected. By linking these centres directly, those waysides in the countryside that used to be intrinsic to any journey between them become bypassed. Dickens's 'drowsy' Cloisterham of *The Mystery of Edwin Drood* is precisely such a marginalised space during the period of the novel. Space is now reterritorialised into a new form, whereby entire older communities become redundant and fall into ruin.

Towards a Tradition of an Aesthetics of Space

This book works towards establishing the idea that the second half of the nineteenth century witnessed the development of a tradition of writing an aesthetics of space. Like Ellen Eve Frank's work on 'literary architecture' (1979), including chapters on Ruskin, Pater and James, I use the word 'tradition' in the etymological sense, suggesting a mindset which was handed down through the writers under consideration, rather than implying that these writers consciously considered themselves a 'movement'. The book understands 'space' in broad terms to include the idea of extension, the idea of specific spaces such as the countryside or the city, and the idea of architecture and mapping as producing certain spaces. It differs in emphasis from those previous studies upon which it builds in three important ways: firstly, insofar as its analysis is not limited to a single city; secondly, in the focus it places upon 'aesthetic effects' and how prior representations of space, and the political histories of these spaces, are bound up in the aesthetics of space; and thirdly, and most crucially, in the emphasis it places upon Ruskin's distinction between *theoria* and *aesthesis* in understanding this tradition of British writing.

As we have seen, the aesthetics of the space of Huysmans's Paris implies Dickens's London. This point is important: in the context of the tradition of the aesthetics of space which this book addresses, no space is wholly discrete, so that other traces 'insinuate' themselves into any aesthetics of space. Ruskin's Venice and Pater's Rome imply London, Wilde's London implies Paris, and James's New York implies at once Venice, London and Paris. In this sense, this is not a study of the aesthetic production of a specific space. Rather, it looks at how nineteenth-century writers began to develop an idea of an aesthetics of space more broadly. Indeed, a number of previous studies have examined the ways in which most of the writers that this book discusses treat the city, and a number of readings of individual cities during the periods have been previously undertaken.[14] I build on this previous research, but seek to map a different kind of tradition, one which considers the extent to which the aesthetic representations of these individual spaces by these individual writers find themselves in dialogue with one another, and particularly with the aesthetic theory of Ruskin and with the post-realist awareness of writing 'after Dickens'. The present study aims to begin to sketch this narrative of the aesthetics of space, working towards delineating some of the contours of this tradition, in which what is of significance is the way in which writers approach space. In other words, while the historical conditions of these spaces are key to their specific aesthetic effects, what links them is not geographical but temperamental: an awareness of, but also a certain resistance to, the 'theoretical' gaze of the realist project.

These kinds of responses are ones grounded in the bodily experience of these spaces, registering the sensory impressions that affect the process of appreciation. As Moretti puts it, building on the geography of Claudio Cerreti, what is at stake 'is not just "extension" [. . .] but "intension" too: "the *quality* of a given space"' (2004: 96). But 'intensive' spaces are also clearly intertextual, in the sense that any aesthetic appreciation of a space is one which is mediated through prior aesthetic representations. With reference to the bodily nature of this experience, this book builds upon Wolfreys's insights regarding the ways in which Dickens marks a new form of writing the city, which, in its focus on the visual and aural, constitutes a kind of 'phenomenology of the urban' (2012: 7), anticipating less the work of Edmund Husserl (1859–1938) than that of Maurice Merleau-Ponty (1908–61). And if I agree with Moretti that 'space acts upon style' (1998: 43), I take the point somewhat differently from him, insofar as I am interested in the ways in which literary style seeks to represent or imitate the experience of a given space. Consider, briefly, Nicholas Nickleby's famous second entry into London:

> They rattled on through the noisy, bustling, crowded street of London, now displaying long double rows of brightly-burning lamps, dotted here and there with the chemists' glaring lights, and illuminated besides with the brilliant flood that streamed from the windows of the shops, where sparkling jewellery, silks and velvets of the richest colours, the most inviting delicacies, and most sumptuous articles of luxurious ornament, succeeded each other in rich and glittering profusion. Streams of people apparently without end poured on and on, jostling each other in the crowd and hurrying forward, scarcely seeming to notice the riches that surrounded them on every side; while vehicles of all shapes and makes, mingled up together in one moving mass, like running water, lent their ceaseless roar to swell the noise and tumult. (2003g: 32.390–1)

The passage is built out of only two sentences, the length of which, piling subordinate clause upon clause, gives a tangible density to the picture. But this density comes at a price, anticipating Wordsworth insofar as the sensory bounty simultaneously registers the overloading of the senses. The coach passes 'quickly-changing and ever-varying objects', a phrase which must be understood doubly, both as the world in process and as a comment on fashion in the city. London here is figured through its shops, foreign and opulent, with the city cosmopolitan, populated by 'emporiums of splendid dresses' and its 'tempting stores of everything', a phrase only partly hyperbolic. For Dickens, there is no want of 'objects in the crowd itself to give new point and purpose to the shifting scene'; it produces a plenitude which resists the attempts of the realist novelist to capture a stable image of the city, slipping past the controlled and controlling gaze. Nowhere in the nineteenth century other than the metropolis could one experience as much as swiftly, could one's eye alight on so much which gives itself to be read otherwise. The city is simultaneously conjunction and disjunction, as mirrored in Dickens's syntax: only in London can one find that 'life and death went hand in hand; wealth and poverty stood side by side; repletion and starvation laid them down together'. Dickens breaks the paragraph, interjecting simply, 'But it was London' (2003g: 32.391), offering all the explanation that may be possible.

The tradition of the aesthetics of space is further defined by the ways in which, writing after realism, it recognises that any experience of space is one which is mediated both by that space's prior aesthetic representations, and by representations of other spaces which inform the subject's response to it. Passages such as the one from *Nicholas Nickleby* offered a stylistic model for writing nineteenth-century space, one which all of the writers dealt with in this book, coming after Dickens, internalised to some degree. Moreover, such passages are precisely the kinds of aesthetic traces that underwrite the ways in which later writers, including the late Dickens, come to appreciate these kinds of spaces. Of course, the idea that a writer's approach to space may be inflected by the trace of prior textual representations is not itself a new phenomenon, but the sense in which space is necessarily read by these writers as a kind of intertextual phenomenon is important: the point is that the tradition of the aesthetics of space recognises that there is no *theoria* without *aesthesis*.

This focus on the textual materiality of the aesthetics of space builds on more recent work on Dickens. Jeremy Tambling argues that Dickens's prose style constitutes a kind of 'poetry of the city' in which he silently cites others and autocites himself, a process that makes his language, 'in spite of its familiarity, strange' (2015: 6). For our purposes, what is at stake is precisely the sense in which a space comes to be appreciated 'for the first time' (*ED* 23.261) only when mediated through the words or images of another. It makes the experience of the aesthetics of space not only representative of a chronotope but also anachronistic (Tambling 2010: 14–15), with the later experience read through the earlier one, and where one space may be read through another. It means that Ruskin reads Venice through Lord Byron (1788–1824), Pater reads Amiens through Ruskin, Wilde reads London through Dickens, and so forth. Indeed, reading a space through prior aesthetic traces – traces of the text which mark the history of the space and imply 'spacetime' – is precisely a question of investment and desire. It marks the sense in which the space is always already inscribed by fantasy. Wolfreys, in a reading informed by Jacques Derrida's (1930–2004) deconstruction, develops the idea of 'architexture' to refer to the ways in which the trace of the text always inflects any given approach to a space, and associates it with the spatiality of the nineteenth-century city. For Wolfreys, Dickens's 'language registers the endlessly signifying processes of iterability and *différance* which is the city, and which mark the city as being structured like the unconscious (or like a language)' (1998: 149). Wolfreys's point, however, does not simply speak for the city: all spaces may be said to be inscribed by *différance*, and more broadly, as Lefebvre argues, the interrelationship between the spaces of the town and countryside 'constitute a *texture*' (*PS* 235). But insofar as such spaces are 'structured like the unconscious', Wolfreys's phrasing also invokes the psychoanalytic theory of Jacques Lacan (1901–81) (1998a: 48), whose insights regarding the idea of the 'insistence' of the letter would become important to Tambling's later analysis of Dickens. Indeed, 'insistence' will also prove significant in the analyses of this book, helping us understand why later writers recycle 'stock' imagery, and explain the ways in which the tradition of the aesthetics of space mobilises repetition, on both the thematic and stylistic level, in order to imply both an awareness of coming 'late' and the idea of the death-drive.[15]

Most significantly, it is a combined sense of writing after Dickens and Ruskin that creates the nineteenth-century British tradition of the aesthetics of space. Stuart Eagles (2011) has considered the idea of coming 'after Ruskin', but his focus is primarily political and social rather than aesthetic. For the purposes of this study, 'after Ruskin' implies in particular an awareness of his distinction between *theoria* and *aesthesis*, drawn in *Modern Painters*. This distinction is between two ways of looking at art, and by extension, space, ones which Ruskin then sees at work in landscape painting, and particularly in Joseph Mallord William Turner (1775–1851), but which in its turn informs his own reading of space in *The Stones of Venice*. Ruskin associates the moral insight of *theoria* with Christianity; as Peter Fuller puts it, his 'system depended upon the idea that nature was in some sense a garden made by God, for man' (1988: 5). For this reason we find that Ruskin promotes *theoria* at the expense of a simple 'bodily', sensory engagement with space, *aesthesis*. As previously noted, *theoria* may be allied with the realist project in its desire to see beyond the surface, linking *Modern Painters* to Dickens's realism of seeing through the housetops, but this comparison is also to oversimplify both Ruskin and realism. As Jameson has recently argued, realism is a complex phenomenon, and may be understood as antinomical. The genre's pretence towards representing reality, Jameson argues, is founded on an 'irrevocable antagonism' (2013: 11). On the one hand, there is 'the narrative impulse', which gives structure, order, sequence and causality, bound to chronological time (15–26);

on the other, 'affect, or the body's present' (27–44). The latter is registered in the urban phenomenology of Dickens, but also in the sense in which such a present eludes presence, standing apart from chronological time, another anachronism, as in the phenomenology of the intensive aesthetic 'instant' of Pater. Jameson's insights are useful, and if the success of formal realism lies precisely in the juxtaposition of these antinomies, an aesthetics of space shifts the balance firmly towards affect as the primary way in which space is represented.

Of course, neither Ruskin nor Dickens would have been wholly comfortable with the comparison I am making between *theoria* and the 'realist' gaze. In a famous letter to Charles Eliot Norton (1827–1908), written from Venice and reflecting on Dickens's death, 9 June 1870, Ruskin sought to differentiate himself from the novelist on political grounds:

> Dickens was a pure modernist – a leader of the steam-whistle party par excellence – and he had no understanding of any power of antiquity except a sort of jackdaw sentiment for cathedral towers. [. . .] His hero is essentially the ironmaster; in spite of *Hard Times*, he has advanced by his influence every principle that makes them harder - the love of excitement, in all classes, and the fury of business competition. (*CW* 37: 7)

Ruskin's understanding of the term 'modernist' here is primarily political rather than literary, suggesting someone favouring progress over tradition. Nevertheless, in spite of such points of disagreement, Ruskin's appreciation of Dickens's writing never waned, and as Charles Swann puts it, 'Ruskin speaks so perceptively of Dickens because he writes from the deep recognition that comes from shared community of concern and vision' (1986: 81). Indeed, to a certain extent it is this very novel, *Hard Times* (1854), which Ruskin praised elsewhere as 'in several respects' Dickens's 'greatest' (*CW* 17: 31), which perhaps best illustrates the sense in which the aesthetics of Dickens's own representations of space were bound up with his 'theoretical' gaze. Notwithstanding his own propensity towards *aesthesis* and *flâneurie* (Hollington 1981), the ways in which he wrote the northern industrial fictional town of Coketown may serve as a point of reference for showing how his earlier works of realism produced a different kind of aesthetic of space from the ones which will primarily concern us in the chapters that follow:

> It contained several large streets all very like one another, and many small streets still more like one another, inhabited by people equally like

> one another, who all went in and out at the same hours, with the same sound upon the same pavements, to do the same work, and to whom every day was the same as yesterday and to-morrow, and every year the counterpart of the last and the next.
>
> [. . .]
>
> You saw nothing in Coketown but what was severely workful. [. . .] All the public inscriptions in the town were painted alike, in severe characters of black and white. The jail might have been the infirmary, the infirmary might have been the jail, the town-hall might have been either, or both, or anything else, for anything that appeared to the contrary in the graces of their construction. Fact, fact, fact, everywhere in the material aspect of the town; fact, fact, fact, everywhere in the immaterial. The M'Choakumchild school was all fact, and the school of design was all fact, and the relations between master and man were all fact, and everything was fact between the lying-in hospital and the cemetery, and what you couldn't state in figures, or show to be purchaseable in the cheapest market and saleable in the dearest, was not, and never should be, world without end, Amen. (2003f: 1.5.27–8)

The various forms of repetition (anaphoras, chiasmuses, epistrophes, epizeuxes, symploches) accentuate the sense in which Coketown was machinic, crafted by mechanical reproduction. In turning man into a machine, modernity eviscerates spiritual life, with Dickens's passage recalling that famous chapter on 'The Nature of the Gothic', published two years earlier, and Ruskin's critique of the ways in which modern industrial society devalued the individual soul, in passages that also critique utilitarianism and 'the modern English fact-hunter' (*CW* 10: 221). Indeed, insofar as 'the jail might have been the infirmary' and 'the infirmary might have been the jail', Dickens's chiasmus is Foucauldian, linking two of those spaces that served to discipline those who were unable or unwilling to work. Moreover, in linking both to the 'town-hall' he suggests that the political superstructure was not simply criminal or sick, but sought to situate itself outside of the circuits of labour while simultaneously feeding off them, vampirically – like capitalism for Marx (1990: 342) or the Law in *Bleak House* (*BH* 60.924).[16] In reading the city as a visible record of both the conditions and relations of production in Marx's terms, as Engels would also do in his reading of the conditions of the English working classes, Dickens's gaze is 'theoretical', and finds no beauty in such a space.

To see beauty in such spaces requires a different mode of vision, the sort which Ruskin marvelled at in Turner. More specifically, it requires a mode of seeing which is aesthetic rather than theoretical.

It is this way of reading spaces, and the tension between the theoretical and aesthetic impulses, that link the different writers discussed in this book. My selection of writers is, I hope, somewhat logical, although as always, the grounds for any selection requires some justification. The figures chosen trace the ways in which Ruskin's distinction between *theoria* and *aesthesis* is developed, first in the late Dickens, and then by Pater, Wilde and James, who are all, to greater or lesser degrees, associated with aestheticism. The conclusion briefly considers the ways in which the tradition of the aesthetics of space came to be developed in modernism, focusing on Virginia Woolf, James Joyce (1882–1941) and Marcel Proust (1871–1922). This kind of modernism, in drawing on the 'impressionism' of the tradition of the aesthetics of space which preceded it, is characterised by an awareness that 'all that is solid melt into air', the title of Marshall Berman's affirmative take on the modern city (1988). Berman is quoting Marx and Engels's *Communist Manifesto* (2002: 223), referring to the ways in which modernity is defined by a series of revolutions in the means of production which reconstructed both social relations and the spaces which they produced. But my conclusion also looks forward to the role played by representative spaces in such a process, which register aesthetic dream spaces, and the tension this implies between the unproductive consumption of space (in pleasure or *jouissance*) (*PS* 353), and what Lefebvre calls the 'productive consumption of space' (*PS* 359), which produces surplus value, here also implying new ways of consuming representative spaces, shorn of the 'realist' impulse.

Nevertheless, my selection of authors begs two questions: firstly, the question of nationality. As I have argued, while a French tradition of an aesthetics of space grounded in a response to Baudelaire has been previously studied, the British version of this tradition has yet to be fully traced. Of course, Baudelaire is important to the British tradition under consideration (Clements 1985), although this differentiates itself by the ways in which it also responds to Ruskin and Dickens. If my prologue dealt with Huysmans, it did so less as part of the French tradition than as a writer who was positioning himself 'after Dickens' and in focusing on a text which was widely read by the British aesthetes; the same is true for my reading, in the conclusion, of Proust, who features in his capacity as a respondent to the British tradition of the aesthetics of space. Likewise, this book reads James as a part of this tradition, both in the sense in which he is clearly responding to Ruskin, Dickens and aestheticism, and insofar as he was, in practice, a European writer, if one whose American heritage led him to write particularly insightfully about transatlantic relationships. With the exception of a year spent living on Paris's *rive gauche*, and two trips back to America, one of which concerns us in this book, James lived in London for close to half a century from 1869 until his death in 1916. As he wrote to Norton, 17 November 1878, if not wholly Anglicanised, 'I am thoroughly Londonized' (*LHJ* 2: 197). It is in the capacity of a British-based author writing back about America that I read him as part of this tradition of the aesthetics of space.

The second question that the selection begs is that of gender. In focusing on a tradition that links Ruskin with the late Dickens and with Pater, Wilde and James, and with the notable exception of Woolf, are the aesthetics of space and the aesthetic consumption of space to be taken to be intrinsically patriarchal? On the one hand, space was gendered in the nineteenth century: public space was the male preserve, private domestic space the female, something that Ruskin and James were particularly attuned to and an idea we have already seen Huysmans play on in his critique of Dickens. Of course, such binaries of active/passive, consumer of space/object of the gaze, *flâneur* walking the crowd/domestic angel of the house are eminently deconstructable, and important work on the forgotten female aesthetes has shown such dichotomies represent an oversimplification of the actual contours of nineteenth-century literary history.[17] In view of this important body of criticism, this book might equally well have focused a chapter on the figure of Octavia Hill (1838–1912), one of Ruskin's friends, whose ideas of creating 'aesthetic' spaces for the poor were important factors in broadening the doctrine of aestheticism socially. Likewise, the book could have included a chapter on the writings of Vernon Lee (1856–1935), whose responses to Venice are clearly deeply informed by both Ruskin's own reading of the city and the distinctions between *aesthesis* and *theoria*.[18] Better yet, a chapter might have focused on Lee's lover, Clementina 'Kit' Anstruther-Thomson (1857–1921), who was not only attuned to, but actively theorised, the ways in which the body was affected by the sensuous experiences of different kinds of spaces. Pioneering the idea of an 'experimental aesthetics', informed by psychological theories of Gustav Theodor Fechner (1801–87), Anstruther-Thomson, who 'had always been a great reader of Ruskin' (1924: 27), wrote a series of notes in which she discussed the power of architecture to affect the body of the spectator (1924: 185–206). This having been said, I have not chosen to focus on figures such as Lee or Anstruther-Thomson, both on the grounds of length, and because the writers that I do discuss are all intentionally canonical. In linking these figures in a new fashion, what this book seeks to establish is the existence of this relatively understudied dimension to their works, all informed to a greater or lesser extent by Ruskin's distinctions between *theoria* and *aesthesis*, and by a reaction against the project of 'realism'.

The starting point is Ruskin, both chronologically and thematically. The first chapter reads carefully both his discussions of the idea of the 'truth of space' and his distinction between *theoria* and *aesthesis* as developed in the first and second volumes of *Modern Painters*. The argument is that this distinction fundamentally underwrites Ruskin's attempts to write Venetian space in *The Stones of Venice*, published a few years later. The second volume of *The Stones*, entitled *The Sea Stories*, which focuses on the moment of Venice's historical pomp and on the Ducal Palace as the visible symbol of this power, is read as an exercise in a 'theoretical' reading of space. But throughout *The Stones*, and especially in the concluding paragraphs of *The Sea Stories* and the final volume, *The Fall*, it becomes clear that Ruskin is unable to maintain this 'theoretical' gaze: it is consistently undercut by a more 'aesthetic' appreciation, revelling in a sensuousness which inflects his appreciation of these spaces.

Chapter 2 deals with the late Dickens, focusing on his final novel, *The Mystery of Edwin Drood*. The chapter argues both that this novel is engaged with Ruskin's writings on the Gothic, and that it represents the occasion for a 'late' meditation on the part of Dickens with respect to both his own prior works and realism (the 'late Dickens' writing 'after Dickens', as it were). If realism, in seeking to see through the housetops, is allied to Ruskin's idea of *theoria*, then *Edwin Drood* instead develops an aesthetics of space. It does so, first and foremost, through opposing the Ruskinian spaces of the fictional cathedral city of Cloisterham to the 'dream space' of London's East End. But it does so only insofar as it shows that Cloisterham itself is resistant to the 'theoretical' gaze of a Ruskin, and shows the sense in which this ancient cathedral city and the capital of modern London are locked in a dialectical, chiasmic structure, doppelgängers of one another.

Chapter 3 considers Pater's response to Ruskin on the Gothic in his imaginary portraits, and his attack on his concept of *theoria* and its distinction from *aesthesis* developed in *Marius the Epicurean*. Showing Pater's subtle attempts to pull these concepts out of Ruskin's Christological interpretation and resituate them within their classical context, the chapter then turns to consider various aesthetic spaces in Pater's works. It focuses on Pater's sensitive descriptions of the ways in which the spaces of the childhood home, the morgue and the cemetery are particularly hospitable to the aesthetic gaze, before reading Pater's reply to realism and Ruskin in the course of his appreciation of the spaces of the Rome of the Antonines in *Marius*.

Chapters 4 and 5 turn to Wilde and James respectively. Replying to those readings of his work that suggest that Wilde is a 'stock' imagist, who uses space as a psychological code or an 'aesthetic' backdrop, empty of historical context, this chapter shows in detail the ways in which his aesthetics of space, while offering another reply to Dickens, can only be properly understood as a politically 'engaged' one. In this chapter, in particular, my method of closely situated analysis draws inspiration from the 'geocriticism' of Bertrand Westphal (2011). Chapter 5 considers James's reply to Ruskin on the 'picturesque' in *The American Scene* (1907). Developing an 'impressionistic' aesthetics of space which is clearly rooted in a response to Pater, this travelogue sees James struggling with how best to read his homeland, and particularly New York. Throughout, the desire to pass moral judgement and gain a vantage point that might allow a 'theoretical' comprehension of the whole of the American scene – one which proves impossible precisely owing to the nature of modern American space, which is both too vast and traumatic – conflicts with an aesthetic pleasure which James cannot help but enjoy.

In discussing these less widely discussed points of comparison between these five canonical writers, this book hopes to illuminate an important tradition of nineteenth-century British writing that has received less critical attention. While this book is obviously limited in terms of what it can do, it seeks to work towards establishing this idea of a tradition of the aesthetics of space, both in the hope that others may find fruitful its readings of individual works, spaces, or the idea of a tradition of the aesthetics of space more generally, or insofar as they may assist in reading other writers or spaces which I have not had the time to address in the pages that follow.

Notes

1. My treatment of realism here and throughout this book is strategic, and I am aware that it is partial, tending to conflate formal and genetic realism, and adopting a view of realism as allied with panopticism. But then again, as Villanueva points out, misquoting George Moore's (1852–1933) *Confessions of a Young Man* (1886/8), it is difficult to speak of realism in general terms and not risk hyperbole (1997: 1). But

I say my treatment of realism is strategic, insofar as it was this partial image of realism against which aesthetes such as Wilde reacted. For a useful selection of nineteenth-century documents representing some of the definitional battle-lines of realism, see Becker 1963. More broadly, beyond Villanueva's excellent work, see the essays collected in Beaumont 2007 for a far more thorough overview of literary realism than it is possible to provide here.

2. For other critical approaches to *fin-de-siècle* London which read space psycho-textually, see Beckson 1992 and Mighall 2003.
3. Lefebvre's own response to psychoanalysis has been criticised: see Pile 1996: 145–72.
4. On Defoe's London, see Lindsay 1976.
5. I am thinking here in particular of Pater's idea of a 'poetic', decadent prose, developed in the chapter 'Euphuism' in *Marius the Epicurean*, and a few years afterwards in his essay on 'Style'. On this, see Dowling 1986: 104–74, and for an initial consideration of the significance of the idea to Wilde, see Whiteley 2017b.
6. The Kantian philosophical underpinnings of the so-called 'project of enlightenment', linked to the broader European cultural movement of the eighteenth and nineteenth centuries, have been influentially discussed, from diverse political perspectives, by figures such as Adorno, Max Horkheimer and Jürgen Habermas.
7. I quote *The Picture of Dorian Gray* from the 1891 edition, unless otherwise indicated.
8. On Foucault's contribution to spatial theory, see Soja 2010: 16–21.
9. On Marx and the uncanny, see Vidler 1992: 3–5.
10. See Hollington 1989. On Benjamin and Dickens, see Piggott 2012.
11. Lefebvre too considers war the catalyst for the production of space in Western Europe: 'the space of history, of accumulation, of investment' (*PS* 277).
12. On Deleuze and urban space, see the essays collected by Frichot, Gabrielsson and Metzger 2016. For a brilliant synthetic reading of Baudelaire through Deleuze, see Holland 1993.
13. See the essays collected by Ford, Keates and Pulham 2015, although barring a few passing discussions in the course of pursuing other topics, these essays do not focus on the question of space.
14. With respect to studies of specific authors under consideration: on Dickens, see particularly Schwartzbach 1979; Tambling 1995, 2009, 2015; Wolfreys 1998, 2012; on Ruskin see Tanner 1992; Hewison 2009; on Wilde see von Eckardt, Gilman and Chamberlin 1987; Cook 2013; Stokes 2013; on James see Kimmey 1991; Tambling 2001; Brooks 2007; Levenson 2010. With respect to specific cities: on Paris, see Clark 1984; Ferguson 1997; Harvey 2006; Kerr 2013; on London see Briggs 1963; Robinson 2004; Freeman 2007; Agathocleous 2011; McKee 2014; Beaumont 2016; on Venice see Norwich 2003.

15. I discuss the idea of Dickens being 'late' in more detail in Chapter 2, as well as the 'lateness' of Ruskin, Pater and James in Chapters 1, 3 and 5 respectively.
16. In am thinking here of Foucault's idea that the 'enlightened' gaze figured madness as the 'absence of work' in *Folie et Déraison* [*Madness and Civilization*, later translated as *History of Madness*] (2009 [1961]: 541–9), and his readings of the disciplinary gazes of both the clinic and prison in *Naissance de la clinique* [*The Birth of the Clinic*] (2003 [1963]) and *Surveiller et punir* [*Discipline and Punish*] (1991 [1975]).
17. On female aestheticism, see Schaffer 2000. More broadly on gender and space, see Rose 1993, and on the *flâneuse*, see Wolff 1985, Feldman 1993 and Parsons 2000.
18. On Lee's Venice, see Maxwell 2010.

Chapter 1

John Ruskin: Towards a Theoretics of Space

In letter 79 of *Fors Clavigera*, June 1877, Ruskin reviewed the inaugural exhibition at the Grosvenor Gallery, Bond Street. The Grosvenor positioned itself as a more radical venue than the conservative, established Royal Academy, based at Burlington House, Piccadilly, a point which Wilde plays upon in having Lord Henry recommend Basil exhibit his portrait of Dorian at the new gallery (*DG* 1.170). As a younger man, Wilde had reviewed the exhibition for the *Dublin University Magazine* in July 1877, praising Whistler's 'colour symphonies' and particularly *Nocturne in Black and Gold: The Falling Rocket*, one of 'the most abused pictures in the whole exhibition' (2013a: 8). This alluded to Ruskin's complaint that he had 'never expected to hear a coxcomb ask two hundred guineas for flinging a pot of paint in the public's face' (*CW* 29: 160). Whistler sued Ruskin, and on 25 and 26 November 1878, the Court of Exchequer heard the case, deciding in the painter's favour.[1] Although he was awarded only a farthing in damages, the publicity made Whistler's name, the trial becoming a European event that pitted the new 'aesthetic' movement against an older order.

Defining Ruskin's relationship with the so-called 'aesthetic' movement is a notoriously difficult exercise, and not simply because precisely what constitutes this movement is a fraught historical question.[2] Ruskin's spat with Whistler must be weighed against the critic's support for a number of earlier exemplars of aesthetic theory. Famously, while Wilde was an undergraduate at Oxford, Ruskin pressed the young aesthete-in-the-making into building roads in the summer of 1874, but this was a younger Wilde. More significant was Ruskin's close friendship with, and financial support of, Daniel Gabriele Rossetti and the other pre-Raphaelites Millais and Holman Hunt (1827–91). This early enthusiasm turned sour around 1865, with Ruskin critical of the later, more sensuous developments in Rossetti's art (*CW* 36: 489), but the critic would still praise his former friend in *The Three Colours of Pre-Raphaelitism* (1878). Ruskin was also friends with Algernon Charles Swinburne (1837–1909), who had first tried to introduce him to Whistler (*CW* 36: xlviii–xlix) many years before *Fors*. Ruskin loved Swinburne's poetry, calling *Atalanta in Calydon* (1865) 'the grandest thing ever yet done by a youth' in a letter to Norton, and while reticent on the amorality of the 'Demoniac youth', he nevertheless considered his 'foam at the mouth' 'fine' (*CW* 36: 501). This moral problem gets to the heart of Ruskin's quarrel with the aesthetic movement, one that was apparent, if only in germ, as early as the first volume of *Modern Painters* (1843), clarified and systematised in the second (1846). Crucially for our purposes, these critical interventions were ones that were informed by a certain question of the 'truth' of aesthetic attempts to represent or capture an image of spaces. Moreover, the key distinctions Ruskin developed between *theoria* and *aesthesis* were ones which we can see informing his own attempts at writing Venetian space in *The Stones of Venice* (1851–3).

My interest in this chapter is primarily in the early Ruskin, from *Modern Painters* to *The Stones*, and in how the ways in which he approaches Venice tell us how he suggested his readers read space. For Philip Mallett, what marks Ruskin's greatness is 'his extraordinary desire, and ability, to see' (1995: 49), and it is this desire which I trace, inspired in particular by Tony Tanner's reading of *The Stones* (1992: 67–147), but differing from him in the ways in which I read the latter text through the prism of *Modern Painters*. In what follows, I focus on Ruskin's key distinction between *aesthesis* and *theoria*, and a series of interconnected ideas that come to circumscribe the tradition of writing the aesthetics of space that develops in Ruskin's shadow, including those of mimesis and imitation, 'realism' and 'naturalism' in art, sensuousness, materiality and the body, ornamentalism, decadence, and the 'truth of space'. Beginning by reading Ruskin's *Modern Painters* slowly and patiently, in order to establish the theoretical ground for his discussions of the aesthetics of space of *The Stones*, this chapter lays the foundations for the analyses that occupy the rest of the book.

Modern Painters I: From the 'Truth' of Painting to the 'Truth of Space'

Modern Painters is primarily interested in the development of a modern 'picturesque', defending Turner's 'superiority' to 'classical' artists

(*CW* 3: 83). The first volume begins with a statement of aims, ones that would later be clearly echoed, but also subtly called into question, in the language of Pater's preface to his *Renaissance* thirty years later. Criticism, Ruskin contends, seeks to 'distinguish what is really excellent', differentiating its informed appreciation from 'transitory' 'opinion' (*CW* 3: 79; compare *SHR* xx–xxi). It aims to identify 'greatness' in art, what Ruskin will later call, citing Sir Joshua Reynolds (1723–92), the 'grand style' (*CW* 5: 17–34),[3] and in evaluating this greatness, a critic must aim to determine general rules (*CW* 3: 79). It is an operation partly – although only partly – of 'taste' (*CW* 3: 84), a quality possessed by the well-educated 'few' who operate as arbiters of public opinion, 'deciding [. . .] for them' (*CW* 3: 80). Notwithstanding the socialism of his later years, these kinds of earlier claims tie Ruskin to an elitism that puts him close to the aestheticism of a Wilde or a James, whose distaste for modern America is driven by the ways in which its spaces are produced by a certain kind of 'democracy'. But it is only partly an operation of taste, precipitated 'by the cultivation of sensibility and judgment', since this faculty can only determine what is beautiful, not distinguish what is 'excellent' (*CW* 3: 96).

For his definition of 'greatness' in art in the second chapter of *Modern Painters*, Ruskin's basic argument is idealist: landscape painting imitates the natural world in order to give us a better sense of its 'truth'. Ruskin considers painting a kind of language, its aim mimetic, 'the art of representing any natural object faithfully' (*CW* 3: 87). Moreover, throughout the five volumes of *Modern Painters*, Ruskin is at pains to draw the parallel between painting and writing, often resorting to quoting Romantic poetry and Dickens to better prove his points.[4] Such a clear parallelism invited his readers to extrapolate conclusions from one art form to the other, so that those writers who followed Ruskin could be justified in applying some of his suggestions regarding the best ways to represent the 'truth of space' to their own attempts to write aesthetic spaces.

For Ruskin, technique is a mode of expression, but great painting, like great poetry, is not determined by 'the mode of representing and saying, but by what is represented and said' (*CW* 3: 88), another idea Pater would echo (1910a: 38). The difficulty in both painting and literature lies in determining 'where the influence of language stops, and where that of thought begins' (*CW* 3: 89), which is to say, in determining where style is an intrinsic or extrinsic element of the expression. As early as this, the second chapter of the first part of *Modern Painters I*, Ruskin is at pains to make the 'distinction [. . .] between what is ornamental in language and what is expressive', 'that part of it which is necessary to the embodying [. . .] of the thought' and that which is not (*CW* 3: 89–90; compare Pater 1910a: 18–20). This question of the ornamental will haunt Ruskin's later writing on architecture, as we shall see. Ruskin is interested in trying to identify what Immanuel Kant (1724–1804), in his *Kritik der Urteilskraft* [*Critique of the Power of Judgment*] (1790), calls the 'parergon' (2000: 110–11; Derrida 1987: 37–118), and like Kant before him, Ruskin gives the example of the frame as a kind of limit point for the picture (*CW* 3: 90).[5] For Ruskin, the status of the ornamental is determined by its formal quality as a certain kind of surface effect, insubstantial as such, included only to give pleasure. For this reason, 'language is [. . .] to be distinguished from, and held subordinate to, that which it conveys' (*CW* 3: 91).

Ruskin's general theory of mimesis builds upon classical rather than Romantic foundations. Considering the '*false use of the term*', Ruskin cites Edmund Burke (1729–97) on the sublime and Samuel Taylor Coleridge's (1772–1834) distinction between imitation and copying, the former representing 'the legitimate function of art – the latter as its corruption' (*CW* 3: 99). For the Romantic tradition, mimesis was one of the highest expressions of art, but for Ruskin, the '*real meaning of the term*' instead lies in the 'pleasurable surprise' produced by a 'resemblance being so great as *nearly* to deceive' (*CW* 3: 100). In this sense, Ruskin distinguishes imitation from simulacrum: the differences between reality and the aesthetic image remain intact, and pleasure comes not from deception, but from almost being deceived. Imitation is 'the evidence that a thing is not what it appears to be' (*CW* 3: 100), Ruskin continues, citing Aristotle in his footnotes, and 'the degree of pleasure depends on the degree of difference and the perfection of the resemblance' (*CW* 3: 101). But while Ruskin recognises the pleasures of imitation, such pleasures are '*the most contemptible that can be derived from art*' (*CW* 3: 101), both because imitation is 'a strictly sensual pleasure' (*CW* 3: 102), a trick of the eye, and because its subjects are 'mean and paltry': 'it is impossible to imitate anything really great'. Imitation addresses either 'contemptible subjects' or 'contemptible parts of them, bits of dress, jewels, furniture, etc.', aesthetic effects, the parergonal or the extrinsic (*CW* 3: 102).

Ruskin warns his readers to be wary of 'the mere sensual pleasure of the eye' (*CW* 3: 91), and this emphasis on the sensual, and guarded comments on mimesis, anticipate *Modern Painters II*, and his key distinction between *theoria* and *aesthesis*. His argument rests upon empiricist and utilitarian foundations, citing John Locke's

(1632–1704) theory of sensation (*CW* 3: 91–2) and, notwithstanding his distate for utilitarianism, reworking Jeremy Bentham (1746–1832) in arguing that 'the greatest picture is that which conveys the greatest number of the greatest ideas' (*CW* 3: 92). But it is also idealist, since 'great' art expresses 'great' ideas, 'and I call an idea great in proportion as it is received by a higher faculty of mind' (*CW* 3: 92). More specifically, art must give an idea of 'Truth', rather than simply an image of material things. Ruskin understands truth to be 'the faithful statement, either to the mind or to the sense, of any fact of nature' (*CW* 3: 104). 'There is a moral as well as a material truth', Ruskin clarifies: imitation 'speak[s] to the perceptive faculties only; truth to the conceptive' (*CW* 3: 105), and 'nothing can be beautiful which is not true' (*CW* 3: 108). To be sure, in one sense, 'any material object which can give pleasure in the simple contemplation of its outward qualities' may be called 'beautiful' (*CW* 3: 109), and such contemplation of beautiful things is divinely ordained, indicative of 'a healthy and cultivated state of mind' (*CW* 3: 109). The appreciation of beauty is a kind of 'sanity' in its etymological sense, implying at once corporeal cleanliness and mental health and carrying '*effets hygiéniques*' (*AR* 11.201; 132), which may be compared with the decadence of the 'foaming' Swinburne.[6] In these pages of *Modern Painters*, Ruskin makes clear that art should not appeal to 'animal feelings', but constitute an 'awakening' of a personal appreciation of 'truth' (*CW* 3: 135).

Part two of the first volume deals 'Of Truth', addressing the 'realism' of the landscape painter, whose aim must be 'the faithful conception' of natural objects (*CW* 3: 133).[7] But Ruskin's 'realism' is compromised by idealism. He argues that nature is only faithfully represented if read from a specific vantage point, the painter guiding 'the spectator's mind to those objects most worthy of its contemplation' (*CW* 3: 133), taking up the position of a kind of ideal subject, enabling the viewer to see the 'Truth of Space'. The first truth of space is that it is 'dependent on the focus of the eye' (*CW* 3: 319), so that 'if in a painting our foreground is anything, our distance must be nothing' (*CW* 3: 321). The second truth of space is that 'its appearance is dependent on the power of the eye' (*CW* 3: 327). The texture of the stuff which makes up space contains more than can be clearly discriminated, but the eye still registers an impression of this excess. 'Every space [. . .] in which we can see everything, or in which we can see nothing, is false', 'every touch is false which does not suggest more than it represents, and every space is false which represents nothing' (*CW* 3: 330), Ruskin argues. It is a point he also takes up in *The Stones*, noting that 'the eye is continually influenced by what it cannot detect' (*CW* 10: 154). For Ruskin, only Turner captures the truth of space; Ruskin compares Turner's vision of London with the Venice of Giovanni Antonio Canaletto (1697–1768), whose *Piazza San Marco* (1723) is the 'drawing of a model, not of a building' (*CW* 3: 337).

In the conclusion to the first volume of *Modern Painters*, the force of Ruskin's title begins to become apparent: the book is not simply about modern painters, but what it means to be a painter of modern life. Ruskin, of course, is not Baudelairean in his understanding of the subject, but the pressing concern of precisely how to represent modernity is common to them,[8] as it will be to all those who follow him and who help to forge the tradition of the aesthetics of space. For Ruskin, it is precisely insofar as Turner is able to represent the truth of modern space that he has been rebuked by critics for breaking with the 'classical' tradition (*CW* 3: 619). Unimpressed with those young artists who philosophised with 'their unformed conceptions of the Beautiful' (*CW* 3: 623), Ruskin argues artists have a duty to be 'humble and earnest' and trace 'the finger of God' (*CW* 3: 623). At this key moment, Ruskin emphasises the moral import of painting, anticipating the central argument of *The Stones* by announcing that art 'should be full of failures; for these are the signs of efforts' (*CW* 3: 623). Ruskin juxtaposes the classically inspired moderns with the new 'aesthetic' school, the cult of 'perfection' with that of artificiality, and in a footnote approvingly quotes from the Bristol School painter Edward Villiers Rippingille (1798–1859): 'Talk of improving nature when it *is* Nature – Nonsense' (*CW* 3: 627). The idea anticipates critically the aestheticism of Huysmans's des Esseintes, announcing that 'Nature has had her day' (*AR* 2.89; 36). For Ruskin, aestheticism would understand nothing of the truth of painting or the truth of space, unable or unwilling 'to distinguish between the real work of nature and the diseased results of man's interference with her' (*CW* 3: 627). It is this distinction between healthy and diseased art that will underwrite Ruskin's later distinction between *theoria* and *aesthesis* in *Modern Painters II*, and his own attempt to represent the 'truth' of Venetian space in *The Stones*.

Modern Painters II: Aesthetic Theory

The second volume of *Modern Painters*, 'Of the Imaginative and Theoretic Faculties', highly influential on the development of the pre-Raphaelites, aims to make broad methodological claims about art in general, from not only an aesthetic but a moral perspective. Ruskin rereads the first volume as an inquiry which dealt 'not of things outward, and sensibly demonstrable, but of the value and meaning of mental impressions' (*CW* 4: 25). Art demands 'heedful and serious examination', offering 'no relief of the ennui of boudoirs' (*CW* 4: 26), with the French terms tellingly implicating these superficial fopperies with a certain proto-aestheticism. The criticism of art 'must be understood and undertaken seriously, or not at all', Ruskin opines, and in footnotes added in the 1883 edition comments: 'I wish the "must" were indeed imperative. The violently increasing number of extremely foolish persons, who now concern themselves with pictures, may be counted among the meanest calamities of modern society' (*CW* 4: 26). Such 'persons' no doubt included Pater, whose star had risen so far by the 1880s that he came to be spoken of alongside Ruskin as one of the greatest art critics of their generation.

Ruskin differs from the aesthetes in his aim of summoning 'the moral energies of the nation to a forgotten duty' (*CW* 4: 28). Reacting against contemporary utilitarianism, he claimed that art is 'useful' whenever it enables the artist 'to be the witness of the glory of God' (*CW* 4: 28). And if Ruskin, writing after his '*un*-conversion' of 1858 (*CW* 29: 89), came to react against these passages for their 'aggressive' 'pietism' when he later revised *Modern Painters*, he did not cut or amend them. This is Ruskin at his most Sage-like, weaving biblical allusions to create a kind of prophetic text, damning utilitarianism as a 'Nebuchadnezzar curse' (*CW* 4: 30). Moreover, what is at stake in art is not simply humanity's moral energy, but specifically that of the British nation itself, which has fallen into 'decay'. It is a task which Ruskin feels urgently, and one which is explicitly linked to the state of contemporary life which 'modern painters must seek to capture' (*CW* 4: 31).

For Ruskin, such a task is intricately intertwined with the question of modern space in mid-nineteenth-century Europe:

> At this time, when the iron roads are tearing up the surface of Europe, as grapeshot do the sea; when their great net is drawing and twitching the ancient frame and strength together, contracting all its various life, its rocky arms and rural heart, into a narrow, finite, calculating metropolis of manufactures; when there is not a moment throughout the cities of Europe that speaks of old years and mighty people, but is being swept away to build cafés and gaming-houses; when [. . .] exchequers are exhausted in luxury of boudoirs and pride of reception-rooms; when we ravage without a pause all the loveliness of creation which God in giving pronounced Good, and destroy without a thought

> all those labours which men have given their lives and their sons' sons' lives to compete, and have left for a legacy to all their kind, a legacy more of their hearts' blood, for it is of their souls' travail; – there is need, bitter need, to bring back into men's minds, that to live is nothing, unless to live be to know Him by whom we live; and that He is not to be known by marring His fair works, and blotting out the evidence of His influences upon His creatures; nor amidst the hurry of crowds and crash of innovations, but in solitary places, and out of the glowing intelligences which He gave to men of old. (*CW* 4: 31–2)

This remarkable passage, written after Dickens, is Dickensian in its use of repetition, in the cumulative power of its adjectives and in its syntactic parallelism. The image is one of trauma, the earth torn up by the progress of modernity, symbolised by the communications routes of the iron roads. This progress is driven by industrialism, turning the city into a 'calculating metropolis of manufactures', the adjective double, emphasising both economic utilitarianism and a callous disregard for the value of its subjects. It is fuelled by a consumerism which, by extension (the use of 'boudoir' again), seems to be emanating from Paris, the capital of the nineteenth century. Space itself has been reterritorialised in modernity. If all of human history may be understood through the production of space, as Lefebvre's Marxist historiography suggests, then what is new here is the speed of modernity, which is itself traumatic, and which compares with the slow, cumulative 'legacy' of ages. It is worth recalling that in *Modern Painters I*, Ruskin 'scorned' the 'velocity' of young, 'aesthetic' artists (*CW* 3: 623). To see such a space means missing what has been effaced, the trace of God, that moral insight which gives meaning to life. Like Wordsworth, his 'most persistent poetical voice' (Austin 1990: 583), and as a late Romantic, Ruskin eschews the 'hurry of crowds' of the city, seeking out 'solitary places' in nature.

It is directly following these remarkable passages dealing with the 'modernity' of contemporary European space that Ruskin introduces his key terms:

> the Theoretic faculty, is concerned with the moral perception and appreciation of beauty. And the error respecting it is, the considering and calling it Æsthetic, degrading it to a mere operation of sense, [. . .] so that the arts which appeal to it sink into mere amusement, ministers to the morbid sensibilities, ticklers and fanners of the soul's sleep. (*CW* 4: 35–6)

Theoria is interested in the intrinsic quality of the 'truth' of the artwork, appealing to the 'moral' sense, while *aesthesis* is interested in the sensory effects of the beautiful. *Theoria* is higher and more worthy than *aesthesis*, since the latter's operation is diminished by the repeated adjectival 'mere'. *Aesthesis* is 'morbid', indicative of a mind diseased (Latin: *morbus*), and the aesthetes are those who encourage forgetfulness and slumber. *Theoria*, on the other hand, is 'the intellectual lens and moral retina' of true artists (*CW* 4: 34).

Ruskin's choice of terms needs to be carefully contextualised, for he was well aware that his 'substitution of the term "Theoretic" for "Æsthetic"' was idiosyncratic (*CW* 4: 42). The move is significant rhetorically, first and foremost, because it allowed Ruskin as a Protestant to read and value Catholic art, as Michael Wheeler argues (1999: 53–4). But the concept itself was drawn from fourth-century Greece, when the newly termed 'philosophers' developed the idea that 'the supreme form of wisdom is *theoria*, the rational "vision" of metaphysical truths' (Nightingale 2004: 3). In book five of the *Republic*, Plato had defined the true philosopher as one 'for whom the truth is the spectacle of which they are enamored' (5.475e), and as Andrea Nightingale has demonstrated, the concept of *theoria* was appropriated and reworked from a specific cultural practice, a religious pilgrimage of the same Greek name (2004: 40–71). Ruskin's use of the word, however, is inconsistent, seeming to switch back and forth from Plato to Aristotle. In his initial definitions in *Modern Painters II*, he approvingly quotes Aristotle's *Nichomachean Ethics* (3.10.1118a), where the philosopher argues that some men are prone to 'indulge in excess' (*CW* 4: 43), particularly when it comes to the 'inordinate pleasures of touch and taste'. But 'men are held intemperate, only when their desires *overcome or prevent the action of their reason*' (*CW* 4: 44; emphasis Ruskin's in the 1883 edition), Ruskin comments, associating *theoria* with *sophrosyne*.[9] As such, *aesthesis* without *theoria* risks a kind of madness (*CW* 4: 45).

However, as his argument continues, we swiftly see that the distinction Ruskin seeks to draw between *theoria* and *aesthesis* is precarious at best. He tells us that 'the mere animal consciousness of the pleasantness I call Æsthesis; but the exulting, reverent, and grateful perception of it I call Theoria' (*CW* 4: 47), a difference of degree rather than a distinction of faculties. It makes an aesthetic appreciation preliminary to a theoretical one, in which animal pleasure is sublimated into 'the full comprehension and contemplation of the Beautiful as a gift of God' (*CW* 4: 47). This 'aspirational', upward-striving quality is something which Ruskin will also praise in Gothic architecture in *The Stones* (*CW* 10: 247), and which marks his 'ascentual' style (Tanner 1992: 95). Topographically, Ruskin's argument is closer to

Plato than Aristotle, and he would later speak of his 'Spiritual Platonism' (*CW* 36: 592). Indeed, by the time of writing the second volume of *The Stones*, Ruskin seems to recognise that his version of *theoria* owes more to Plato than to Aristotle. He praises Platonism as being 'profoundly spiritual', coherent with 'the great Christian virtue of Holiness' (*CW* 10: 368), and criticises Aristotle's system for being 'so false, so forced, and so confused' (*CW* 10: 374).

This shift from Aristotle to Plato, however, necessarily introduces the problem of the body. In his 1873 lectures at Oxford, 'Love's Meine', delivered the same year that Pater scandalised the city with the publication of his *Renaissance*, Ruskin writes that by *theoria*, he means 'Plato's word, which is the proper word in Greek, and the only possible *single* word that can be used in any other language by any man who understands the subject', explicitly meaning it to '*include* bodily sensation' (*CW* 25: 123). So Ruskin actively associates *theoria* with Plato's bodily idealism; indeed, accentuates its bodily nature 'somewhat more than Plato's' (*CW* 25: 124). At the same time, however, Ruskin's original formulation – designed to deny 'that the impressions of beauty are in any way sensual' (*CW* 4: 42) – makes clear that it is precisely the bodily nature of *aesthesis* that is the issue, its lack of deeper or higher 'moral insight'. His image of the critic ascending through the process of appreciating beauty – one of the quintessentially 'philosophical' images, as Deleuze reminds us (2004: 145) – focuses not on beauty itself, but on 'ideas of beauty', which are 'the subject of moral, and not of intellectual, nor altogether of sensual pleasure' (*CW* 4: 48). Not 'altogether' sensual pleasure, but only partly so, so that such pleasures may be redeemed in a higher synthesis, 'accompanied first with joy, then with love of the object, then with the perception of kindness in a superior intelligence, finally, with thankfulness and veneration towards that intelligence itself' (*CW* 4: 48). Read after psychoanalysis, Ruskin's distaste for the 'sensual' suggests the operation of sublimation, spiritualising desire. It would be reductive to suggest that his own unfulfilled sexual desire found a kind of redemption in these pages, particularly since the second volume of *Modern Painters* predates his wedding to Effie Gray (1828–97) of 1848, which famously went unconsummated (Hilton 1985: 117–20).[10] Nevertheless, it remains true that it is precisely the 'sexual instinct' that Ruskin sought to attack, those 'feelings of the beautiful, which we share with the flies and spiders' (*CW* 4: 63). But as in Plato's *Symposium*, this ladder towards the *eidos* is prone to collapse, as in the famous Alcibiades moment, where the object of divine theoretic contemplation is revealed in a moment of bathos to be far less ideal than the philosopher-king may let on.[11] We will need to consider again the ways in which the tradition of aesthetics of space that builds on Ruskin responds to this question of the place of the body in aesthetic appreciation.

Another important context for understanding Ruskin's choice of terms is German. Although he dismissed German philosophy on the grounds of his 'steady pursuit of Naturalism as opposed to Idealism' (*CW* 5: 424), and famously critiqued 'German dullness, and English affectation' in discussing the 'pathetic fallacy' (*CW* 5: 201),[12] he himself makes a comparison between *theoria* and an *Anschauung* in these same pages of *Modern Painters II* (*CW* 4: 57). An *Anschauung* is an intuition, an idea associated less with Kant (with whom Ruskin's treatment of aesthetic judgement, the ethical and the 'will' has far more in common than he may have realised)[13] than with the attempts of Johann Gottlieb Fichte (1762–1814) and Friedrich Wilhelm Joseph Schelling (1775–1854) to respond to the seemingly impregnable barrier between the phenomenal and noumenal, the sensible and rational.[14] Ruskin understands *theoria*, as an *Anschauung*, to be the 'dwelling upon and fond contemplation' of the object (*CW* 4: 57), foreshadowing Heidegger, who writes perceptively on the Greek word *theoria* (1977b: 163–6), as well as elsewhere on the significance of the idea of *Wohnen* (dwelling) (1977a: 141–60). But the distinction between *aesthesis* and *theoria* also had a prehistory, whether or not Ruskin was aware of it, in Alexander Gottlieb Baumgarten (1714–62). It was as a 21-year-old that he had introduced the word 'aesthetics' into modern European thought in his doctoral dissertation, *Meditationes philosophicae* (1735). In his *Aesthetica* (1750), Baumgarten famously defined *aesthesis* as the 'lower theory of knowledge', constituting a 'science of sensuous cognition' (1750: 1; § 1).[15] *Aesthesis* is 'sensation', what Ruskin calls the appreciation of differences in the sensible (*CW* 25: 123), linking to the etymology of the word, derived from the Greek for perception. Like Baumgarten, Ruskin considered the aim of aesthetics to be the 'perfection' of the faculty of sensible cognition, which is to say, the realisation of the beautiful (1750: 6; § 14), and both argue that we must exclude the common beauty ascribed to objects or matter (1750: 8; § 18). Ruskin's introduction of this distinction into English in *Modern Painters II* marked a turning point in the burgeoning discipline of nineteenth-century British aesthetics.

But if the distinction was useful when Ruskin wrote *Modern Painters*, then by the time of coming to revise it in the 1870s, he had come to associate *aesthesis* with a 'general tendency of modern art, under the guidance of Paris'. In 'Love's Meine', announcing that he would reprint the volume, Ruskin bemoaned the fact that 'the "general student" has plunged himself into such abysses, not of analytic, but of dissolytic, – dialytic – or even diarrhœic – lies, belonging to the sooty and sensual elements of his London and Paris life' (*CW* 25: 122). This returns us to the question of space: the aesthete, identified with decadent metropolitan space, is attacked for his moral depravity and intellectual arrogance, for not imagining 'that there were people before *he* lived, who knew what "æsthesis" meant, though they did not think that pigs' flavouring of pigs'-wash was ennobled by giving it a Greek name' (*CW* 25: 122), and for seeking beauty only 'in the model-room, or the Parc aux Cerfs' (*CW* 25: 123), where Louis XV (1710–74) notoriously housed his young mistresses. The aesthetes are accused of 'wallowing with swine', recalling Horace's famous quip on Epicureanism (*Epistle* 1.4.16). Ruskin's phrasing recalls his attack on the traumatic speed and spaces of modernity in *Modern Painters*:

> the entirely infernal atmosphere of the common cafés and gambling houses of European festivity, infecting every condition of what they call 'æsthesis', left in the bodies of men, until they cannot be happy with the pines and pansies of the Alps, until they have mixed tobacco smoke with the scent of them; and the whole concluding in the [. . .] enjoyment – of the most squalid conditions of filth in our capital cities, that have ever been yet recorded, among the disgraces of mankind. (*CW* 25: 127–8)

The hedonistic tendencies of aestheticism, fanned by metropolitan flames, serve to blunt rather than sharpen the appreciation of beauty, the aesthete's palate pampered 'until the appetite is lost in its sickened satiety, incapable of pleasure' (*CW* 4: 61). Any beauty found in their works is 'merely *æsthetic*' (*CW* 4: 211). By contrast, it is only a theoretical gaze that produces that special kind of 'realism' which Ruskin calls 'Imaginative Verity', 'the power of every picture depend[ing] on the penetration of the imagination into the TRUE nature of the thing represented' (*CW* 4: 278). Reading the conclusions of the second volume of *Modern Painters* back into the first, it becomes clear that representing the 'truth of space' is less an aesthetic operation than a theoretical one. Turner's ability to stay true to both the focus and the power of the eye, while also capturing the sensuous realities of space, was not simply attentive to *aesthesis* but captured a 'theoretical' truth of space. Such a theoretical gaze was precisely what Ruskin sought to prioritise and elevate. It was a kind of way of reading spaces that he himself would put into practice a few years later in *The Stones*.

Venice and *Theoria*: *The Sea Stories* and the Gothic

Ruskin visited Venice in 1849 in preparation for writing *The Stones of Venice*. This trip was bound up with his attempts to defend Turner in *Modern Painters* (*CW* 9: 85), and he considered the final volume of *The Stones* to be a kind of 'introduction' to *Modern Painters II*, in which, as we have seen, he had differentiated *theoria* and *aesthesis*. This 'very interesting connection' between the two works was outlined in a letter to his father, 22 February 1852. For Ruskin, the 'peculiar love of landscape' that is 'characteristic' of the nineteenth century, and of Turner as the pride of 'modern' painters, was a result of the artistic 'decline' following the Renaissance (*CW* 10: 208), and symptomatic of the 'desire to escape out of our modern cities' (*CW* 10: 207). The point will be important as we continue to trace the tradition of the aesthetics of space, which is marked by a complex relationship with the tradition of the 'picturesque'.

As Lefebvre argues, Venice is 'a space which is fashioned, shaped and invested by social activities' and, at its peak, may be considered less a 'product' than a 'work' of art (*PS* 73). In *The Stones*, Ruskin's deals with this relationship between the social and Venice as a work of art. The work is divided into three volumes, the first dealing with *The Foundations* of the Byzantine city, which witnessed 'a people struggling out of anarchy into order and power' (*CW* 9: 20); the second devoted to *The Sea Stories* told by Venice's Gothic, the period of her rise, pomp and power; the final volume to *The Fall* and Venice's 'decline'. It images Venice in her decadence, 'a ghost upon the sands of the sea', the city a phantasm, so that 'we might well doubt, as we watched her faint reflection in the mirage of the lagoon, which was the City, and which was the Shadow' (*CW* 9: 17). Ruskin considers this decline a symptom of her mode of government, one which can be read theoretically through her stones. To this end, Ruskin aims to read Venice 'stone by stone' (*CW* 9: 4), to make both the stones of Venice and *The Stones of Venice* 'touch-stones' (*CW* 9: 57). It takes architecture as text, looking for an 'architectural rhetoric' (*CW* 9: 62). As in *Modern Painters*, the aim is didactic, so that the reader of *The Stones*, whether they be in Venice or back in London, may be able to 'distinguish the noble from the ignoble work' 'by a glance of the eye' (*CW* 9: 62). Moreover, Ruskin's book was explicitly aimed at British readers, seeking to warn them to see clearly the signs of their own decadence, and to compare Venice and her fall with modern London (*CW* 9:10). The title of the final volume and such a comparison would have recalled for his readers Edward Gibbon's (1737–94) popular *The History of the Decline and Fall of the Roman Empire* (1776–89), one of the first histories to consider the reasons behind the fall of a great empire. Ruskin differs from Gibbon, however, who saw Christianity behind Rome's decline, whereas for Ruskin, Venice's fall comes precisely in turning away from Christianity during the Renaissance. But Venice was always precarious, geographically and culturally, poised somewhere in between the Occidental and Oriental:

> Opposite in their character and mission, alike in their magnificence of energy, they came from the North and from the South, the glacier torrent and the lava stream: they met and contended over the wreck of the Roman empire; and the very centre of the struggle, the point of pause of both, the dead water of the opposite eddies, charged with embayed fragments of the Roman wreck, is VENICE. (*CW* 9: 38)

The juxtapositions, the isocola, the use of balanced subordinated clauses, the chiaroscuro, techniques which we see repeated in the pages that follow, here seek to hold things in place, to name that which is held in place, inscribed in capital letters to mark and secure its presence, as Venice.

As the story of 'the causes and consequences of the rise and fall of Art in Europe' (*CW* 10: 327), Ruskin's reading of Venice turns on the Ducal Palace, which is figured as 'the central building of the world' (*CW* 9: 38) in the final chapter of *The Sea Stories*. The title of this volume puns on both the architectural feature (*CW* 10: 146) and the ways in which these features narrate the past, 'writ[ing] her history on the white scrolls of the sea-surges' (*CW* 10: 15). Ruskin's linking of the architecture to the sea is important, since it shows the ways in which, in Lefebvre's terms, 'the representation of space (the sea at once dominated and exalted) and representational space (exquisite lines, refined pleasures, the sumptuous and cruel dissipation of wealth accumulated by any and every means) are mutually reinforcing' (*PS* 74). Ruskin begins with a description of a modern approach to the city, seeing Venice's palaces as 'desecrated ruins', the city 'defaced' (*CW* 10: 7), and the whole of *The Stones* is an exercise in reading ruins, both architectural and those Benjaminian 'spoils' of civilisation (*SW* 4: 391). Beginning in the suburbs of Torcello and Murano, already displaying Venice's 'decay' (*CW* 10: 36–7), Ruskin gradually moves the reader closer to the centre of the city and the

Ducal Palace. He pauses at St Mark's, historicising its construction, use of stone, and the costs and effort required to import it (*CW* 10: 95–6), as well as the ways in which its builders reused stones from earlier constructions, so that the edifice became a historical palimpsest (*CW* 10: 96–7). Venice was a text which had been endlessly rewritten in an 'architecture of incrustation' (*CW* 9: 323). Most significantly, its power was 'dependent for its charm' on its lack of completeness (*CW* 10: 104), and St Mark's is read as a kind of religious text, in an idea which became influential on Proust. Ruskin advocates 'reading a building as we would read Milton or Dante, and getting the same delight out of the stones as out of the stanzas' (*CW* 10: 206). For Ruskin, St Mark's must be considered 'a Book of Common Prayer, a vast illuminated missal' (*CW* 10: 112), and the widespread destruction of Gothic style in cities like London is one of the great errors of modern metropolitan spaces, resulting in its subjects losing the ability to truly appreciate beauty (*CW* 10: 122).

The glory of St Mark's lies in its 'realism', both its theoretic insight into the truth of things, and its connection to the reality of the life of the city around it (*CW* 10: 120–2). It is in this context that we should read the 'decadence' of Renaissance Venice:

> When in her last hours she [Venice] threw off all shame and restraint, and the great square of the city became filled with the madness of the whole earth, be it remembered how much her sin was greater, because it was done in the face of the House of God, burning with the letters of the Law. Mountebank and masquer laughed their laugh, and went their way; and a silence has followed them, not unforetold. (*CW* 10: 141–2)

The style recalls Thomas Carlyle, *The Stones* written shortly after *Latter-Day Pamphlets* (1850), showing its influence not only in its attack on laissez-faire economics but also in Ruskin's prose.[16] The Renaissance brings a Dionysian excess, with Venice gradually becoming 'drunk with the wine of her fornication' (*CW* 10: 177, alluding to Revelation 17: 2). Ruskin's version of the decadent city figures 'Venice as festival', to quote Lefebvre (*PS* 73). And the masque, confusing identities, a theme that fascinates Bakhtin (1984: 122–32), recalls the ways in which Ruskin viewed Renaissance Venice as the 'masque of Italy' (*CW* 10: 177), quoting Byron (*Childe Harold's Pilgrimage* 4.3.27). The allusion to Byron's Venice, to which we will return, shows already the extent to which even Ruskin's explicitly 'theoretical' reading of space ends up being conditioned by prior aesthetic traces.

The central pillar of Ruskin's 'theoretical' reading of Venetian space is the famous chapter on 'The Nature of the Gothic'. Defining the Gothic is difficult, 'like defining a language' (*CW* 10: 180), so that Ruskin instead speaks of 'a greater or lesser degree of *Gothicness*' (*CW* 10: 181). But just as the aesthetic approach is differentiated from the theoretical one, so too a similar operation can help define the 'Gothic':

> Gothic architecture has external forms and internal elements. Its elements are certain mental tendencies of the builders, legibly expressed in it [. . .] Its external forms are pointed arches, vaulted roofs, etc. And unless both the elements and the forms are there, we have no right to call the style Gothic. (*CW* 10: 183)

That the 'Savageness' of Gothic had been treated as 'a term of unmitigated contempt' reflects the classical ideal, but Ruskin holds the existence of such an ideal symptomatic of decadence: 'the fallen Roman, in the utmost impotence of his luxury, and insolence of his guilt, became the model for the imitation of civilized Europe' (*CW* 10: 185). Moreover, Ruskin puts some of this historical distaste for the Gothic aesthetic down to questions of space. He imagines:

> the Mediterranean lying beneath us like an irregular lake [. . .] for the most part a great peacefulness of light, Syria and Greece, Italy and Spain, laid like pieces of a golden pavement in to the sea-blue, chased [. . .] with bossy beaten work of mountain chains, and glowing softly with terraced gardens, and flowers heavy with frankincense, mixed among masses of laurel, and orange, and plumy palm, that abate with their grey-green shadows the burning of the marble rocks, and of the ledges of porphyry sloping under lucent sand. (*CW* 10: 184)

The important point is that climate implies a certain kind of production of space (*PS* 77). Commenting on the 'picturesque' style of passages such as these, Mallett suggests that Ruskin attempts 'to recreate Turner's effects of colour and light' in his prose through 'verbal accumulation, participial adjectives, above all the control of rhythm' (1995: 41).[17] These are stylistic effects present here, and are ones which Ruskin will later redeploy when attacking the 'monotony' of city life. But regardless of its Turneresque qualities, what is certain is that Ruskin's operation in the passage is 'eco-mimetic', to use Timothy Morton's terms (2007: 32–3). Connoting at the level of vocabulary and style the sunny pleasure of the Mediterranean he describes, Ruskin accentuates the warm colours and sensuous imagery of incense and perfume, while the alliterating bilabials ('bossy beaten', 'plumy palm'), subtle assonance and sibilance ('lucent sand') give a sense of substantial luxuriousness. As the passage continues, Ruskin moves northwards up Europe, through the 'vast belt of rainy green' of Switzerland and Germany, to a more primordial landscape, where 'the earth heave[s] into mighty masses of leaden rock and healthy moor' (*CW* 10: 184), eventually arriving at a 'wall of ice', 'deathlike' in its grip (*CW* 10: 187). These spaces produce a different way of living, a 'wildness of thought, and roughness of work' (*CW* 10: 188). For Ruskin, Gothic architecture is produced by this kind of Northern space, considered as an index not simply 'of climate, but of religious principle' (*CW* 10: 188).

It is in this context that Ruskin returns to the subject of ornamentation that had concerned him in *Modern Painters*. Explicitly referring to this earlier work (*CW* 9: 267–8, 304, 306), he had argued in *The Foundations* that 'noble ornamentation' is 'the expression of man's delight in God's work' and '*ig*noble ornamentation' is 'the expression of man's delight in his *own*' (*CW* 9: 253). In the following chapter, Ruskin distinguishes between servile, constitutional and revolutionary ornamentation (*CW* 9: 291), and argues that ornaments should be adapted to the power of the eye (*CW* 9: 292–4), best viewed at 'a *given* distance' (*CW* 9: 296), linking the glory of the Gothic to the 'truth of space'. In *The Sea Stories*, Ruskin develops the point: servile ornamentation is associated with the architecture of the Greeks, Nenevites and Egyptians, where 'the workman was [. . .] a slave' (*CW* 10: 189), comparing with the medieval system of ornament in which 'this slavery is done away with altogether; Christianity having recognised, in small things as well as great, the individual value of every soul' (*CW* 10: 189–90). Gothic architecture openly 'confesses its imperfection' and considers it a spiritual strength (*CW* 10: 190).[18] The 'modern English mind', by contrast, is closer to the Greek in 'that it intensely desires, in all things, the utmost completion or perfection compatible with their nature' (*CW* 10: 190), with Ruskin suspicious of the classical ideal that many of his aesthete heirs would put on a pedestal.[19] The 'modern' subject, as much as the classical one, is no more than a 'machine', producing imitations 'with admirable speed and perfect precision', but without thought, investment or soul, becoming little more than an 'animated tool' (*CW* 10: 192). Famously, Ruskin now addresses his reader directly and asks them to consider the space in which they currently sat:

> Look around this English room of yours, about which you have been proud so often [. . .] Examine again all those accurate mouldings, and perfect polishings, and unerring adjustments of the seasoned wood and tempered steel. [. . .] Alas! if read rightly, these perfectnesses are signs of a slavery in our England. (*CW* 10: 193)

'If read rightly', Ruskin admonishes his readers – which is to say, if read 'theoretically'. The middle-class home is considered spiritually devoid, indicative of a pernicious class structure which sends British subjects 'like fuel to feed the factory smoke' (*CW* 10: 193). Ruskin hears a 'great cry that rises from all our manufacturing cities' (*CW* 10: 195), so that the conditions of nineteenth-century metropolitan space are linked to the spatial environments of the rooms of his readers, and both spaces require a theoretical rather than aesthetic reading.

On these grounds, Ruskin pre-emptively argues against the foundations of aestheticism. He recommends that only articles that are 'absolutely necessary' should be manufactured (*CW* 10: 195), so that his proto-socialism, which so influenced William Morris (1834–96), may be compared with that of Wilde, influenced by both, in 'The Soul of Man under Socialism' (1891).[20] Ruskin also argues that one should never 'demand an exact finish' (*CW* 10: 198), that the aim should not be for perfection but for spiritual invention. There is a 'fatal error' in 'despising the manual' (*CW* 10: 201), and instead, true Christianity for Ruskin is characterised by this quality of 'touch', an idea which Derrida will also pursue (2005: 99–103). '*The demand for perfection is always a misunderstanding of the ends of art*' (*CW* 10: 202), Ruskin argues, since art should not exist simply for its own sake, but in order to communicate its deeper 'truth'. When read through Ruskin's theoretical gaze, the Renaissance, that period which Pater would idealise twenty years later, is revealed to be precisely the moment of European decadence, its aesthetic expression, characterised by a 'relentless requirement of perfection', 'the first cause of the fall of the arts' (*CW* 10: 204).

For Ruskin, the pride of Venice is the Ducal Palace, 'which at once consummates and embodies the entire system of the Gothic architecture' (*CW* 10: 327), testifying to the fact that '*the root of all that is greatest in Christian art is struck in the thirteenth century*' (*CW* 10: 306). Ruskin reads the Ducal Palace theoretically, as a text that reveals the history of the rise and fall of Venice. Its first stone dates to the city's 'birth' in 813, the Gothic Palace to 1297, when the Venetian government was overhauled under Doge Pietro Gradenigo (1251–1311), so that 'the Gothic Palace was, in its foundation, coeval with that of the aristocratic power' (*CW* 10: 340). Venetian space is produced as political space, and the Gothic Palace was built over the next hundred and twenty-five years, so that the project of its construction was coeval with 'the central struggle of [Venice's] life' (*CW* 9: 20), the commencement of the Renaissance Palace coeval with the moment of her decline (*CW* 10: 346). The Renaissance rang Venice's death knell: when 'the central epoch of her life was past; the decay had already begun' (*CW* 10: 352). Ruskin reads the stones in detail, throughout guided by a theoretical understanding of the relationship between space and the 'moral vigour' of the builders and the city that they built. Reading Venice with Ruskin is an exercise in *theoria*, through which he called his readers to see the 'truth of space', to engage in a 'theoretics' of space.

Venice and *Aesthesis*: Reading and Rereading the Fall

The Sea Stories ends with Ruskin imagining future defacement of the Ducal Palace 'that made [its] walls as precious as so many kingdoms'. The phrase is followed by a semi-colon, linking seemingly unconnected passages, breaking into a piece of dramatic descriptive prose with which the volume concludes:

> so precious, indeed, and so full of majesty, that sometimes when walking at evening on the Lido, whence the great chain of the Alps, crested with silver clouds, might be seen rising above the front of the Ducal Palace, I used to feel as much awe in gazing on the building as on the hills, and could believe that God had done a greater work in breathing into the narrowness of dust the mighty spirits by whom its haughty walls had been raised, and its burning legends written, than in lifting the rocks of granite higher than the clouds of heaven, and veiling them with their various mantle of purple flower and shadowy pine. (*CW* 10: 438–9)

The contingency of this image, one which occurs only 'sometimes', suggests that the sublime moment, or rather, the moment of Ruskinian sublime (Thomas 1986), is a question of temperament, and that only certain kinds of metropolitan spaces may be sublime, linking sublimity to *theoria*. The image again positions Ruskin as a Victorian Sage, showing how his own appreciation of the 'picturesque' was not only aesthetic but theoretical, guided by an unseen moral read into space.

These concluding moments of *The Sea Stories* may be compared with their counterparts in *The Foundations*. There, Ruskin had returned to the problem of imitation, quoting from a recent book by Edward Lacy Garbett (1824–1900) on the theme of the aesthetic 'correcting' nature: 'I say correction, for though it is the highest aim of every art to imitate nature, this is not to be done by imitating any natural form, but by *criticising* and *correcting* it' (*CW* 9: 407; quoting Garbett 1850: 74). For Ruskin, by comparison, the aim is 'not to improve, but explain' (*CW* 9: 409), a hermeneutic operation; he is closer to Arnold in his definition of the function of criticism than to Pater. Indeed, what is at stake is exactly a question of 'realism' in representation (although meaning here something different from the word's connotations in the nineteenth-century literary tradition), so that we can read Ruskin's discussion of Gothic Naturalism, 'the love of natural objects for their own sake, and the effort to represent them frankly' (*CW* 10: 215), as offering an anticipatory reply to aestheticism. Throughout *The Stones*, Ruskin differentiates Western from Oriental art, 'the mindless luxury of the East' with its love of 'arabesques' (*CW* 9: 15), an aesthetic which Wilde, influenced by Poe, would deploy as a cypher for decadence.[21] But in considering the 'representationalism' of Western art, Ruskin has cause to differentiate three kinds of 'realism': Purism, Naturalism and Sensualism. Purists represent only what is good in nature, whereas Naturalists proper 'render all that they see in nature unhesitatingly, [. . .] sympathising with all the good, and yet confessing, permitting good out of the evil also', in a 'chiaroscuro equally balanced between light and dark' (*CW* 10: 222). It is a kind of comic realism, mixing styles, to use Auerbach's terms. In art it is represented by Turner and Hunt (*CW* 10: 222, 228), and in literature, although Ruskin does not name him here, perhaps best by Dickens, whose humour Ruskin praised (*CW* 36: 431). Sensualists, on the other hand, 'perceive and imitate evil only', Ruskin remarks, pursuing 'evil for its own sake' (*CW* 10: 224), anticipating almost verbatim Jean-Paul Sartre's (1905–80) famous estimation of Baudelaire (1967: 71).[22] Whereas the Naturalists show the 'Divinely guided glance' of *theoria* (*CW* 10: 223), Sensualists gorge in an *aesthesis* unredeemed. They 'delight in the beggary and brutality of the human race, their colour is for the most part subdued or lurid, and the greater spaces of their pictures are occupied by darkness' (*CW* 10: 222). Their landscapes are scenes of 'decay, disorder, and disease' (*CW* 10: 229), visions of excess, as in Laureamont's Paris or Wilde's East End. Ruskin links this Sensualism with the 'morbid condition' he had previously diagnosed in *Modern Painters* (*CW* 10: 229). Aestheticism is opposed to a theoretical engagement with space.

Still, Ruskin was not wholly averse to writing (of) dark spaces. In the chapter on 'The Two Boyhoods' of the fifth volume of *Modern Painters* (1860), written after *The Stones*, Ruskin compares the childhood homes of Turner and Giorgione (1477–1510) and considers the effects of spaces on their art. Giorgione's Venice is a space of 'brightness' and 'balm', with 'no foulness, nor tumult, in those tremulous streets' (*CW* 5: 375). Turner, on the other hand, born in 1775, grew up 'near the south-west corner of Covent Garden, [where] a square brick pit or well is formed by a close-set block of houses, to the back windows of which it admits a few rays of light' (*CW* 5: 375). Turner was remarkable insofar as he learnt to 'endure ugliness' and find beauty in such spaces: 'Dead brick walls, blank square windows, old clothes, market-womanly types of humanity – anything fishy and muddy, like Billingsgate or Hungerford Market, had great attraction for him; black barges, patched sails, and every possible condition of fog' (*CW* 5: 377). If Ruskin himself was Turneresque in his ability to capture an aesthetics of such spaces in his prose, his ability to write the city, as much as his ability to read it, draws comparison with Dickens. It does so not only in terms of substance, with Swann noting similarities between their 'brilliantly detailed (and creative) readings of the details of buildings as the indices of a society's moral vigour' (1986: 75), but also in terms of style. Like Dickens before and after him, Ruskin recognised that metropolitan space challenged the visual, and that the conditions of modern life led to 'a radical shift in the way the eye functioned' (Mallett 1995: 51), an insight that anticipates Benjamin. For Simmel, who makes Ruskin and Friedrich Nietzsche (1844–1900) strange bedfellows, linked through their 'passionate hatred' of the city (1950: 413), modern spaces made hitherto unimaginable mental demands on their inhabitants. This is a point that Ruskin develops in 'Fiction, Fair and Foul': 'the resulting modes of mental ruin and distress' (*CW* 34: 268) are not simply overwhelming, but are overwhelmingly 'new', returning eternally as a mass of sensory impressions which threatened the fabric of the subject.

We see the influence of the novelist on the critic markedly in the famous description of Croxted Lane in 'Fiction, Fair and Foul', and the detritus strewn either side of the road:

> ashes and rags, beer-bottles and old shoes, battered pans, smashed crockery, shreds of nameless clothes, door-sweepings, floor-sweepings, kitchen garbage, back-garden sewage, old iron, rotten timber jagged with out-torn nails, cigar-ends, pipe bowls, cinders, bones and ordure, indescribable;

> and variously kneaded into, sticking to, or fluttering foully here and there over all these, remnants, broadcast, of every manner of newspaper, advertisement or big-lettered bill, festering and flaunting out their last publicity in pits of stinking dust and mortal slime. (*CW* 34: 267)

The effects are quintessentially Dickensian. Mallett comments: 'indefinitely extensible, non-hierarchical, the list allows the suggestion that the disorder of modern city life defeats the rationality of syntax' (1995: 48). In both topic and style, the passage recalls Esther's first arrival at Krook's, describing the rag-shop window (*BH* 6.67–8), and *Bleak House* is a novel which turns upon the idea of London as a vast dump, an economy of rubbish (Chappell 2013). Indeed, in 'Fiction, Fair and Foul' Ruskin explicitly considers Dickens's novels, comparing his 'fimetic art' to the nightmarish aesthetics of Gustave Doré (1832–83), thinking in part of *London: A Pilgrimage* (1872), which drew inspiration from *Edwin Drood*. Indeed, what is at stake with such a 'fimetic art' is precisely a question of 'truth' and its representation for Ruskin. As he admitted in a letter to Norton, 8 July 1870, Dickens was Ruskin's superior 'in every mental quality but one – the desire of truth without exaggeration' (*CW* 37: 10). For all his ardent social commentary, Dickens's 'delight in grotesque and rich exaggeration' was fascinated by, luxuriating in, the decadence it sought to illuminate. This critique of a theoretical gaze compromised by a tendency towards *aesthesis* is one that equally may be levelled at Ruskin, occluded to his own aesthetic pleasures, anticipating Proust's attack on his work, discussed in Chapter 3. But it was for this very reason that Ruskin considers Dickens the quintessential writer of Victorian London, and *Bleak House* the text which defined for the metropolitan subject 'the horrors [. . .] of Death' (*CW* 34: 271), with Dickens playing a similar role for Ruskin to that which Nietzsche will for Simmel in his analysis of the metropolis and mental life (1950: 413).

Ruskin understood that on both the grounds of capitalist economics and the principles of the division of labour, 'we are forced, for the sake of accumulating our power and knowledge, to live in cities' (*CW* 9: 411). But in congregating in cities, any advantages gained are 'counterbalanced by our loss of fellowship with Nature' (*CW* 9: 411). It is this that explains the impulse towards the picturesque in modern art, a form of nostalgia for a simpler, rural life. As Robert Hewison argues, Ruskin disliked the picturesque because 'it was a false vision of nature, the product of an approach which made only a superficial study of the outward forms of natural scenery', composing 'an idealized picture which bore no resemblance to the "facts"' (1976: 46). As a 'superficial study', the picturesque was always on the side of *aesthesis* rather than *theoria*, prioritising both momentary pleasure and aesthetic form over true insight. It makes the fact that Williams omitted Ruskin from his treatment of *The Country and the City* all the more remarkable. And it also explains the fact that Ruskin defines 'the modern feeling of the picturesque', which is to say, 'surface' rather than 'noble' picturesque, by its 'delight in ruin' (*CW* 6: 9), which, in Benjaminian terms, marks its melancholia. As Ruskin put it in *The Seven Lamps of Architecture* (1849), this kind of picturesque constitutes a '*Parasitical Sublimity*' (*CW* 8: 236), a delight in an aesthetics of 'universal decay' (8: 235), a point he drew from his reading of 'a recent critic on Art', the physiologist Alexander Walker (1779–1852).[23]

For Ruskin, the space of modern London is itself decadent, characterised by 'grim railings and dark casements, and wasteful finery of shops, and feeble coxcombry of club-houses' (*CW* 9: 411). It is the subject of letter 44 of *Fors* (August 1874), on 'The Squirrel Cage. English Servitude', where London, the 'vicious centre', enslaves the country, the capital exacting 'tribute' (*PS* 234), forced to furnish the trappings of an 'accursed life': 'over the whole country the sky is blackened and the air made pestilent, to supply London [. . .] with [. . .] vulgar upholstery, jewels, toys, liveries, lace, and other means of dissipation and dishonour of life' (*CW* 28: 136). Aesthetic effects here are visible signs of social alienation. It turns the people into a 'fermenting mass of unhappy human beings, – news-mongers, novel-mongers, picture-mongers, poison-drink-mongers, lust and death-mongers' (*CW* 28: 137). Everyone is a 'monger', selling something, and the slide of predicates shows the ways in which capitalism is ultimately an economics of death.

In *The Stones*, it is precisely at this moment of reckoning against 'that great foul city', as he puts it in *The Crown of Wild Olive* (1866), 'rattling, growling, smoking, stinking, – a ghastly heap of fermenting brickwork, pouring out poison at every pore' (*CW* 18: 406), that Ruskin turns back from London to Venice. In the final pages of *The Foundations* he invites his readers to 'come with me, for I have kept you too long from your gondola: come with me, on an autumnal morning, through the dark gates of Padua, and let us take the broad road leading towards the East' (*CW* 9: 412). The vocative is deployed here, as it will be in the corresponding passage concluding *The Sea Stories*: it asks the reader to follow Ruskin's writing as he moves through space, but it also masks rhetorically an attempt to interpellate the subject (Althusser 2008: 48–9). Yet if Ruskin aims to force his readers to read space theoretically, to see its truth from the position of his own attuned eye, then there is something else also at work here, an aesthetics of space that he could hardly have countenanced given his expressly 'theoretical' aims. Style once again intervenes, with its ornamental flourishes, and an aesthetic quality that brings the body into play. In this sense, Ruskin's own writing is revealed as implicated in precisely the kind of decadence that he had sought to attack in *The Stones*. For him, Venice was 'in her fall the most corrupt, of European states' (*CW* 9: 46), but his own prose shows this decadence in its 'jewelled style'.[24]

We sense this early in *The Foundations* when Ruskin invites his readers to follow him into 'the streets of the Sea city' and 'to submit ourselves to their undistinguished enchantment' (*CW* 9: 59). One 'submits' oneself to the domineering power of such a space, its aesthetic fascination, so that to write such a space means to become lost in this 'enchantment'. Stephen Kite has usefully shadowed Ruskin through Venice, reading *The Stones* as the product of the gaze of a *flâneur*, exposing 'a tension between ethics and aesthetics' (2012: 110). For all his millenarian and apocalyptic imagery, and for all his searing indictments of the 'signs of the times' (*CW* 34: 41), phrasing implying Carlyle, Ruskin's prose is nevertheless also aesthetic in the most visceral of ways. Indeed, the moral can easily get lost in the pleasures of style, in its 'unfettered soaring of half-free association, the self-renewing, self-amplifying, proliferating embellishment' (Tanner 1992: 72). Such a style is both a kind of aestheticism, in the sense in which these associations become self-sufficient, and anticipates modernism, in its syntactic approximation of stream of consciousness.[25] Indeed, Ruskin's earlier appreciations of Turner's Venice in *Modern Painters I*, written before he had firmed up his distinction between *theoria* and *aesthesis*, see him describing the Venetian sky as 'a visible infinity – liquid, measureless, unfathomable, panting and melting through the chasms', 'dreamlike' (*CW* 3: 257). This Venice is apolitical, characterised by a complete lack of 'theoretical' interest, and a stylistic 'self-excitation' that is 'little short of orgasmic' (Tanner 1992: 75).

In the final paragraphs of *The Foundations*, Ruskin takes his readers on a journey through the countryside of Veneto, moving eastwards towards the city, following the Brenta:

> a muddy volume of yellowish-grey water, that neither hastens nor slackens, but glides heavily between its monotonous banks, with here and there a short, babbling eddy twisted for an instant into its opaque surface, and vanishing, as if something had been dragged into it and gone down. (*CW* 9: 412)

Another 'ecomimetic' passage in the onomatopoeia of the 'babbling eddy', Ruskin's prose expresses the sensuous pleasure of language experienced in its own materiality. It also connotes a sense of loss and *jouissance*, in an image of drowning, a topic we will return to in the next chapter. Ruskin tells us that as we travel, the eye is caught by things that it would be better not dwelling on, such as 'the much vaunted "villas on the Brenta"' (*CW* 9: 412), which stand for the decadence of Renaissance imitation. More than a theoretic reaction, these villas carry unwanted aesthetic traces, 'much vaunted' owing to their connotations with Byron, who rented one, La Mira, immortalising it in *Don Juan* (1819–24) (1.212.1693). In *Praeterita* (1885), Ruskin admitted Venice had been 'chiefly created' for him through Byron (*CW* 35: 295), but the problem was that the poet's city was precisely the kind of aesthetic construct that ended up intervening in any attempt to read the city theoretically. In a lengthy passage early in *The Sea Stories*, Ruskin had considered Byron's power to read proleptically the stones of Venice:

> The Venice of modern fiction and drama is a thing of yesterday, a mere efflorescence of decay, a stage dream which the first ray of daylight must dissipate into dust. No prisoner, whose name is worth remembering, or whose sorrow deserved sympathy, ever crossed that 'Bridge of Sighs', which is the centre of the Byronic ideal of Venice; no great merchant of Venice ever saw that Rialto under which the traveller now passes with breathless interest: the statue which Byron makes Faliero address as of one of his great ancestors was erected to a soldier of fortune a hundred and fifty years after Faliero's death; and the most conspicuous parts of the city have been so entirely altered in the course of the last three centuries, that if Henry Dandolo or Francis Foscari could be summoned from their tombs, and stood [. . .] at the entrance of the Grand Canal, [. . .] the painter's favourite subject, the novelist's favourite scene, [they] would literally not recognise one stone of the great city. (*CW* 10: 8–9)

Venice itself is an aesthetic construct, Ruskin points out, not simply 'there', but one which is read, consciously or unconsciously, through its prior aesthetic representations. The allusion is to *Childe Harold's Pilgrimage* (1812–18), where the Byronic hero stands 'in Venice, on the Bridge of Sighs' (4.1.1), marking the site as the 'centre' of future aesthetic representations of the city. The allusion to Verocchio's statue of Bartolommeo Colleoni is to Byron's *Marino Faliero* (1821) (3.1.89–92), which has Faliero, who died in 1355, apostrophise a statue not erected until 1496. Byron's Venice is not '*the real thing*' (*CW* 10: 436), yet its power over the imagination means that it anticipatively rereads

Venetian space. This tension between 'aesthetic' space and 'real' space is one which the writers in the tradition of the aesthetics of space all have to deal with in different ways. If Venice admonishes a theoretical inquiry into 'the true nature' of the city and the space where she was founded, 'built by iron hands and patient hearts, contending against the adversity of nature and the fury of man' (*CW* 10: 9), then Ruskin was unable to cast off the traces of the Byronic city that had first caught his attention.

These prior aesthetic traces of 'much vaunted' spatial features which consistently haunt Ruskin's Venice tend towards the deconstruction of the lofty pretensions of his theoretical visions. His gaze ends up wallowing in the sensuous, obsessed with ruins, and with reading them 'romantically'. At the piazza in Dolo, for instance, Ruskin gazes at a villa of 'the old Venetian type', one that is 'sinking fast into utter ruin, black, and rent, and lonely'. In a 'Puritan' gesture, Ruskin admonishes his readers, 'Do not look that way' (*CW* 9: 413), but this advice only comes after his having dwelt on these ruins for a paragraph, luxuriating in their wreckage. Indeed, in passages such as these, we anticipate the Venice of *The Fall*, and the 'attraction of repulsion', to use the Dickensian phrase (*UT* 263), that Ruskin clearly felt towards the decadent city. Take the moment in the penultimate paragraph of *The Foundations*, when Ruskin changes horse for gondola at Mestre, and makes his final approach to Venice:

> Stroke by stroke, we count the plunges of the oar, each heaving up the side of the boat slightly as her silver beak shoots forward. [. . .] In front, nothing to be seen but long canal and level bank; to the west, the tower of Mestre is lowering fast, and behind it there have risen purple shades, of the colour of dead rose-leaves, all round the horizon, feebly defined against the afternoon sky, – the Alps of Bassano! Forward still: the endless canal bends at last, and then breaks into intricate angles about some low bastions, now torn to pieces and staggering in ugly rents towards the water, – the bastions of the fort of Malghera. Another turn, and another perspective of canal; but not interminable. The silver beak cleaves it fast, – it widens. (*CW* 9: 414–15)

Two things should be taken from this passage: most obviously, the ways in which it seeks to write space topographically, using punctuation and syntax to image both the winding of the river and the suspense that precedes each new image that meets the eyes. But moreover, the eroticism. The imagery recalls Enobarbus on the 'purple' sails of Cleopatra's barge (*Anthony and Cleopatra*, 2.2.203), whose vaginal connotations are impressed onto the Vicentine Alps. As in

Shakespeare, the 'strokes' of the oars imply a double meaning,[26] as if the boat itself were 'heaving' and 'plunging' with its 'silver beak' shooting forward, in an image which Ezra Pound (1885–72) certainly read as erotic (*Canto* 17.75; Aji 2003: 139). It is a moment of *jouissance*, with Ruskin entering Venice, finally, here in the penultimate paragraph of the book.

'Tis a consummation devoutly to be wished, no doubt, but one that Ruskin finds frustrated by the interruption of 'a low and monotonous dockyard wall' (*CW* 9: 415), the railway bridge. In a letter of 10 September 1845, Ruskin remarked upon the first time he saw that bridge: 'We turned the corner of the bastion where Venice once appeared, and behold the Greenwich railway, only with less arches and more dead walls, entirely cutting off the whole open sea and half the city' (*CW* 4: 41). Ruskin associates the bridge, completed in 1846, with London, so that London here seems to be invading Venice, the train figuring for speed and modernity. Indeed, the Venice that he arrives at recalls not only London, but the industrial north, 'a straggling line of low and confused brick buildings, which [. . .] might be the suburbs of an English manufacturing town' (*CW* 9: 415). This is neither the 'gorgeous' Venice that Dickens had encountered in 1846, nor the Romantic one of Byron: Ruskin arrives at a ruined city. In *Praeterita*, Ruskin reflected on these passages as a product of 'the melancholy experience of 1852', rather than his earlier trips, 'when there was not even beginning of railway bridge' (*CW* 35: 294). The bridge becomes a fixation, that which ruins Venice and interrupts thought, just as 'the accursed whistling of the dirty steam-engine of the omnibus of the Lido' (*CW* 27: 328), signifying tourism, prevents him from writing in letter 19 of *Fors* (July 1872). On an earlier trip, 'everything, muddy Brenta, vulgar villa, dusty causeway, sandy beach, was equally rich in rapture, on the morning that brought us in sight of Venice' (*CW* 35: 294); now, by contrast, 'the object which first catches the eye is a sullen cloud of black smoke brooding over' the city (*CW* 9: 415). Ruskin just about resists the pathetic fallacy, a tightrope act he also attempts in later work, as when reading Manchester in *The Storm-Cloud of the Nineteenth Century* (1884) (Swann 1986), as though in a momentous effort of self-restraint. But with the smoke 'brooding' over the city, the image anticipates Conrad's *Heart of Darkness*, another decadent city (2008a: 103), suggesting latter-day Venice as an apocalyptic space.

Breaking the paragraph, Ruskin announces simply 'It is Venice', a rhetorical move perhaps borrowed from Dickens's announcement of London in *Nicholas Nickleby* (2003g: 32.390). The story of the decadence of this 'melancholy' Venice is the subject of the final volume, *The Fall*. To be sure, this subject is one that Ruskin had proleptically anticipated throughout *The Stones*, expressing a compulsion to repeat, but it is only in *The Fall* that we see its precise causes. In the opening paragraphs, Ruskin compares an image of Venice at 'its period of greatest energy and prosperity' with London, asking 'what have been the causes which have induced so vast a change in the European mind' (*CW* 11: 4). For Ruskin, Venice's decadence follows a historical pattern oft repeated: 'luxuriance of ornament, refinement of execution, and idle subtleties of fancy, taking the place of true thought and firm handling' (*CW* 11: 5). Imitation confuses categories, makes buildings lie, so that they seem to be something other than they are, speaking in someone else's tongue. It recalls the fact that in *The Foundations*, Ruskin associates Renaissance ornamentalism with forgery (*CW* 9: 52), so that in *The Fall*, we find that its decline was precisely one from representation to imitation (*CW* 11: 5). Mimesis makes space hard to read, and the theoretical gaze wont to get lost in the fopperies of aesthetic façades. Ruskin's desire to return to '*the real thing*', 'however ruinous, however obscured and defiled' (*CW* 10: 436), is a vital crusade against 'the increase of the ersatz, the encroachment of the pseudo, the proliferation of the fake' (Tanner 1992: 112). The Renaissance fell into *aesthesis*; hence its obsession with 'the luxury of the body' (*CW* 11: 76). Venice forgot God in her pride, her 'unscrupulous and insatiable pursuit of pleasure', which led to her 'irremediable degradation' (*CW* 11: 133–4). 'In the ingenuity of indulgence, in the varieties of vanity', Ruskin writes, with his alliteration giving him partly away, Venice 'drank with deeper thirst from the fountains of forbidden pleasure, and dug for springs, hitherto unknown, in the dark places of the earth' (*CW* 11: 195). The allusion is to Psalm 74: 20, in another striking anticipation of Conrad's London (2008a: 105). Both Venice and London are untimely, hearts of darkness, cities teetering precipitously on the brink.

For Ruskin, the subject of Renaissance art was no longer the glory of God, but art itself. 'The images summoned by art began gradually to assume one average value in the spectator's mind' (*CW* 11: 130), regardless of its subject: 'the hearts of men hardened as their handling softened, until they reached a point when sacred, profane, or sensual subjects were employed, with absolute indifference, for the display of colour and execution' (*CW* 11: 131). Precisely, *aesthesis*. Gradually the European mind 'congealed into that state of utter apathy' (*CW* 11: 131), Ruskin concludes: that constituted its fall, its decadence. It was an ennui beginning in the Renaissance and would reach a crowning glory in the figure of the aesthete, with his disinterested doctrine of *l'art pour l'art* and fascination with ornamental excesses, the luxury of the body that privileged the pleasures of the senses and the gratifications of the flesh.

The Stones of Venice is the story of the rise and fall of a city, but also of the production of a series of different kinds of spaces. It was a chance for Ruskin to put into practice ideas developed in *Modern Painters* a few years beforehand: to read space and read it 'right'. But as we have seen, Ruskin's theoretical gaze is never fully untainted, always laced with the traces of an aesthetic pleasure which threatened to overwhelm his moral rectitude. It is the conflict between a theoretical and aesthetic approach to space, inherited from Ruskin and contested by those who succeeded him, which will concern us in the chapters that follow.

Notes

1. On the trial, see Merrill 1992.
2. On Ruskin and the aesthetes, see Shrimpton 1999.
3. Although *Modern Painters* as a whole offers a rebuke of many of Reynolds's other ideas: see Alexander 1973: 140–3.
4. See for instance Ruskin's discussion (*CW* 3: 347) of Dickens's description of 'looking through, rather than at, the deep blue sky' in *American Notes* (2003a: 2.2.170).
5. On Pater's treatment of parerga, see Whiteley 2013.
6. Ruskin himself would later suffer a number of mental breakdowns, in 1871, 1878, 1880, 1885 and 1888 (Hilton 2000: 205–9, 343–51, 374–94, 419–25, 512–19, 566–8), but this is the later figure who only peripherally concerns us in this chapter.
7. Not that an artist's aim must always be 'realist', since Ruskin also acknowledges the beauty of non-representational art (*CW* 3: 92).
8. For one attempt at reading Baudelaire and Ruskin comparatively, see Wettlaufer 2003.
9. Whether Ruskin himself would have seen it this way is debatable: in *The Stones*, he criticises Aristotle for supposedly mistaking the operation of temperance for the essence of the virtues (*CW* 10: 374). On *sophrosyne*, see in particular Foucault 1992.
10. For a similar point, noting that *The Stones* was written while Ruskin was with Effie in Venice, reading the city rather than his wife as the object of his 'unresting desire', see Tanner 1992: 68–9.
11. Compare Plato's *Symposium* 212d–e, where Socrates' lover, Alcibiades, returns home drunk and disorderly, immediately following a speech

on how the love of beautiful young men may offer a preliminary step towards a higher 'theoretical' insight. On *theoria* in the *Symposium*, see Nightingale 2004: 83–6.

12. By 'English affectation', Ruskin is referring to Coleridge, as he made clear in a footnote.
13. Ruskin considers sensory impressions to be 'a subject of *will*, and therefore of moral duty' (*CW* 4: 52), and that man has a duty to prefer certain sensory impressions to others, assuming he is not suffering from 'diseased conditions of the organs' (4: 53). 'Good' taste can be cultivated (4: 58) through the right operation of 'habit' (4: 58), claiming for itself a kind of subjective 'universality' (4: 60). One cannot decide what sensations one will receive (4: 54–5), but one can decide which ones to cultivate, an argument that has a number of points of similarity with Kant, although less with the third than the second *Kritik*.
14. Ruskin apparently regretted the analogy, adding in a footnote of 1883 that 'I have not the least idea, now, what the "anschauung" of the Germans is, and whatever it may be, beg my pupils have nothing to do with it' (*CW* 4: 57), an odd qualification, since if he was unaware of its significance, why warn his readers away from it? For a discussion of Schelling's attempts to overcome both Kant's and Fichte's concepts of the *Anschauung*, his role in popularising the term, and the ways in which the term came to prominence in British literary circles, see Whiteley 2018b.
15. Translations are my own.
16. See for instance where Ruskin alludes to Carlyle's *Latter-Day Pamphlets* on the idea of the 'human-beaver' (*CW* 9: 67; compare Carlyle 1897: 20: 185).
17. In a different, but not unrelated sense, Tony Tanner speaks of Ruskin's '*erotics* of colour' (1992: 110).
18. This is true not only of Gothic architecture, but of Gothic style: 'It is that strange *disquietude* of the Gothic spirit that is its greatness; that restlessness of the dreaming mind, that wanders hither and thither among the niches, and flickers feverishly around the pinnacles, and frets and fades in labyrinthine knots and shadows along wall and roof, and yet is not satisfied, nor shall be satisfied' (*CW* 10: 214). As Tanner comments, 'whatever else it is describing, this is writing describing itself' (1992: 103).
19. On the Victorian reception of classical Greece, see Jenkyns 1980 and Turner 1981. For work specifically on the aestheticism of Pater and Wilde respectively, see Martindale, Evangelista and Prettlejohn 2017 and Ross 2013.
20. The classic study of Ruskin and social theory is Anthony 1983.
21. See, for instance, 'The Harlot's House': 'Like strange mechanical grotesques, / Making fantastic arabesques, The shadows raced across the blind' (ll. 7–9). Wilde's rhyme suggests Poe's *Tales of the Grotesque and Arabesque* (1840).

22. Indeed, Ruskin is blind to the pleasures of sadism, at least in *The Stones*: 'Everybody likes to do good; but not one in a hundred finds this out. Multitudes think they like to do evil; yet no man ever really enjoyed doing evil since God made the world' (*CW* 9: 71).
23. With reference to this passage, George Landow quotes from Ruskin's diaries: '"Walker on the Picturesque" Universal decay is the essence of the picturesque. In landscape, therefore, the picturesque stands in the same relation to the beautiful and sublime that the pathetic does to them in poetry' (1971: 233). The verbatim quotation, which Landow could not locate, was drawn from Walker's *Beauty; Illustrated by an Analysis and Classification of Beauty in Woman* (1836: 123). The timing of this citation of Walker's misogynistic theory of aesthetics in *The Seven Lamps of Architecture* in 1849, while Ruskin's marriage to Effie remained unconsummated, is suggestive.
24. I appropriate the phrase from Boyiopoulos's reading of Wilde (2015: 63).
25. On Ruskin and modernism, see Feldman 2002: 17–55, and the essays collected in Cianci and Nicholls 2001.
26. Compare Enobarbus: 'amorous of their strokes' (*Anthony and Cleopatra*, 2.2.206).

Chapter 2

Charles Dickens: After Realism

Travelling to Venice in 1844, Dickens wrote effusively to John Forster (1812–78), recording his first impressions of the city:

> Nothing in the world that ever you heard of Venice, is equal to the magnificent and stupendous reality. The wildest visions of the Arabian Nights are nothing to the Piazza of Saint Mark [. . .] The gorgeous and wonderful reality of Venice is beyond the fancy of the wildest dreamer. Opium couldn't build such a place, and enchantment couldn't shadow it forth in a vision. (*LCD* 4: 217)

Although Ruskin had noted in *The Stones of Venice* the ways in which Venice invited a reading through the *Arabian Nights* (*CW* 10: 76), Dickens wrote this letter before Ruskin's version of the city came to dominate the Victorian imaginary and its aesthetics of space. Dickens's Venice is instead closer to Byron's, but transcends both his poetry and Turner's 'noble' painting, operating 'beyond all pen or pencil' (*LCD* 4: 217). As Dickens recalls in *Pictures from Italy* (1846), sitting in an Italian church in the evening 'is like a mild dose of opium' (2003i: 5.46), recalling Marx on religion as the '*opium* of the masses' (1992: 244). In this first encounter with Venice, the city emerges as a space of dream, inverting reality. 'Plashing through the silent and deserted streets', Dickens 'felt as if the houses were reality – the water, fever-madness' (*LCD* 4: 217). Both city and 'reality' are precarious. Dickens remarks on the pleasure of moving between these two worlds, 'diving down [. . .] into its wickedness and gloom – its awful prisons, deep below the water; its judgment chambers, secret doors, deadly nooks', against which Venice's surface-level charms amounted to 'insubstantial Magic' (*LCD* 4: 217). This imagery is repeated in *Pictures from Italy*, there displaced onto St Peter's in Rome, 'so silent and so close, and tomb-like', its hidden dungeon 'so black, and stealthy, and stagnant, and naked' (2003i: 11.137). In

Lefebvrean terms, Dickens sees the ways in which Christian Rome, as opposed to the ancient city, came to identify absolute space with subterranean space (*PS* 254). For Dickens, 'this little dark spot becomes a dream within a dream' (2003i: 11.137), a phrase which echoes from *Martin Chuzzlewit* (1999: 17.287), with the vision of the palatial surface vaulted over an unconscious violence in the depths that threatens to 'undermine the city' (2003i: 11.137).

'Venice is a bit of my brain from this time', he remarked to Forster (*LCD* 4: 217), and Dickens's version of the city foreshadows the ways in which an aesthetics of opium dreaming comes to circumscribe the spaces of *The Mystery of Edwin Drood*. Unfinished at Dickens's death, this novel opens in the dens of Bluegate Fields in Shadwell, on the docks of the Thames, a kind of dark mirror of Venice, as in 'Down with the Tide' (*Household Words*, 5 February 1853), where Dickens writes that, viewed from the river at night, the East End might be mistaken for 'the narrower bye-ways of Venice' (1998: 121). This chapter focuses on Dickens's final novel and on what I want to call the 'late Dickens', an idea based in part on Adorno's idea of 'late style'.[1] In Dickens's case, it is marked by a dark, obsessive meditation on death and on motifs of decadence and decay, as well as by repetitions that rework his earlier work thematically and lexically. I would argue that Dickens becomes 'late' at that moment when his realism, a quality which had been hitherto linked to a desire to see the city, to understand it as a product of society, and as a way of intervening in social questions, gives way to a less optimistic form of fiction. In Dickens, in other words, *Spätstil* is a response to *Spätzeit*, the 'lateness' of modernity.[2]

The very idea of late Dickens implies the idea that Dickens is himself writing 'after Dickens', and a certain Dickensian image of London, had come to dominate the popular imagination. Certainly, we see the characteristics of late Dickens in *Edwin Drood*, a murder mystery where the eponymous Edwin is the presumed victim, and his uncle, John Jasper, the presumed murderer, his possible motive being his love for Rosa Bud, Edwin's fiancée. Jasper himself is a doppelgänger figure, who works as a socially respectable choirmaster at the cathedral in the fictional city of Cloisterham, based on Rochester, but who hides a dark side. He is addicted to opium, which he takes both in the dens of East London and in the privacy of his home in Cloisterham, so that the traces of an Oriental decadence journey from the Empire and the capital's docklands back into the Home Counties, here figuring for Britain's domestic ideal, in an *unheimlich* movement. While London itself is a peripheral presence in the novel, or at least, in what remains of it, with most of the action focused on Cloisterham, the cathedral city and the capital form a kind of doppelgänger pair, linked through Jasper, so that any discussion of the one space ends up implicating the other. Moreover, the representation of the aesthetics of London space in *Edwin Drood* is key insofar as it complicates both Dickens's pretensions to write urban realism and the terms of any post-Ruskinian 'theoretical' approach to the modern metropolis.

Writing in *Unto this Last* (1860), Ruskin admitted that, in spite of their differences, Dickens was 'entirely right in his main drift and purpose in every book he has written', and if his treatment was occasionally 'partial', then 'his view was finally the right one, grossly and sharply told' (*CW* 17: 31). In the previous chapter, we have already discussed some of the ways in which Ruskin wrote 'after Dickens', and as Nicholas Shrimpton has argued, Dickens betrays the influence of Ruskin in his descriptions of 'the moralized landscapes of his later work' (1981: 62). The idea is interesting, but is not the one pursued here: instead, this chapter focuses less on Dickens's debt to Ruskin on *theoria* than on how *Edwin Drood*, written 'after Ruskin', favours *aesthesis*, in something of a reply to Dickens's earlier realism, producing an aesthetics of space. For while we can be sure that Dickens had been influenced by Ruskin's thinking about Gothic architecture,[3] and that *Edwin Drood* was written in the context of the Gothic Revival and a post-Ruskinian debate regarding the value of architecture and the significance of reading space 'theoretically', what is at stake here is not simply a question of direct influence.[4] If Dickens's realism is allied with *theoria*, then the late Dickens, and particularly *Edwin Drood*, problematises this kind of moral insight precisely insofar as it represents space not only as unreadable, so that it cannot be squared with the realist project of removing the housetops, but also as being 'unreal' (*ED* 23.261). It is not simply that metropolitan space is visionary in this text, or that such vision is linked to opium, for these are ideas with a long prehistory: as early as 1846, Dickens was calling London his 'magic lantern' (Forster 1966: 1: 420), a phrase Benjamin quotes (*PW* 426; M4a,4), and the idea of the modern city as an aesthetic 'dream space' appears famously in works such as de Quincey's *Confessions*, which no doubt influenced *Edwin Drood*. Instead, what marks the late Dickens and this final novel is that it addresses the ways in which visionary space always already precedes our engagement with reality. My analysis is informed by that of Tambling on the 'poetry' of *Edwin Drood* (2015: 204–19), but differs in its focus, emphasising Dickens's engagement with the Gothic and the presence of Ruskin haunting the text, as well as the ways in which such a 'poetry' creates an aesthetics of space. It is not that Dickens simply chooses to write an aesthetics of space; rather, the text registers the sense in which, 'after Dickens' and 'after Ruskin', it is no longer possible to read space theoretically. As such, the novel is not a record of an aesthetic choice but an aesthetic compulsion, a recognition that space must be approached aesthetically.

Dickensian Dream Spaces I: Bluegate Fields

The unconscious, Freud reminds us, knows no time (*SE* 14: 187). The same is true of the intoxicated subject, a point that Benjamin develops in 'Hashish in Marseilles' (1932). He gives Baudelaire's *Les paradis artificiels* (1860) as exemplary, and quotes Ernst Joël (1893–1929) and Fritz Fränkel (1892–1944), for whom narcotics unleash 'images and chains of images, long submerged memories' (*SW* 2: 673). The idea rests upon Freud, who, in the *Interpretation of Dreams* (1900), suggested that dreams allow us limited access to our unconscious memories, which are played out in a displaced form (*SE* 4: 305–9) metonymically in 'chains' of images or signifiers (Lacan 2007a: 676). Benjamin links metonymy with the allegorical mode of writing, and with the idea of trauma. In dreams, 'space can expand', Joël and Fränkel remind us (*SW* 2: 673), since time can also expand, creating a kind of 'chronotope', to use Bakhtin's term. This is an idea that has been used to think about Dickens's London previously (Gomel 2011: 297–309), but here, the chronotope ruptures the stability of the singular subject, so that 'connections become difficult to perceive, owing to the frequent sudden rupture of all memory of past events' (*SW* 2: 673). Without these kinds of connections to offer a stable ground, the subject becomes divided from themselves and reality.

Benjamin develops the point in *Das Passagen-Werk*, where he meditates on the idea of the 'dream city', linking the allegorical mode of writing about nineteenth-century space with alienation, consumer culture, dreaming and intoxication:

> The nineteenth century a spacetime < *Zeitraum* > (a dreamtime < *Zeit-traum* >) in which the individual consciousness more and more secures itself in reflecting, while the collective consciousness sinks into ever deeper sleep. But just as the sleeper – in this respect like the madman – sets out on the macrocosmic journey through his own body, and the

> noises and feelings of his insides, such as blood pressure, intestinal churn, heartbeat, and muscle sensation [. . .] generate, in the extravagantly heightened inner awareness of the sleeper, illusion or dream imagery which translates and accounts for them, so likewise for the dreaming collective, which, through the arcades, communes with its own insides. (*PW* 389; K1,4)

In this complex set of considerations, Benjamin associates the dreamer and the madman. It recalls Dickens on one of his 'Night Walks' (*All The Year Round*, 21 July 1860), who, passing Bethlem, muses whether 'the sane and insane' are 'equal at night', for our dreams 'nightly jumble events and personages, and times and places' as the mad do daily (*UT* 153). For his part, Benjamin associates the dreamer and madman with the intoxicated, so that sleep, insanity and intoxication alike are all states of ecstasy, an *ekstasis* which is a being-out-of-place. Such ecstatic states are proper to the experience of nineteenth-century metropolitan space. Benjamin suggests that city space implicates the body, the visions of the dreamer translating bodily stimuli as somatic products. Through an 'extravagantly heightened inner awareness', the city communes 'with its own insides', a scene staged in the arcades, where desire plays out. According to Benjamin, the 'spacetime' (*Zeitraum*) of the nineteenth-century city is also a kind of 'dreamtime' (*Zeit-traum*), punning on the German. The city mobilises desire while simultaneously 'de-realising' this space. In the nineteenth-century city, 'reality' is deterritorialised through and as dream, with the past a relic or a ruin, untimely in the sense of Dickens's Old Curiosity Shop, which finds itself always already displaced and out-of-time.[5] Benjamin quotes Baudelaire in 'L'art philosophique' (1859), where 'everything is allegory, allusion, hieroglyph, rebus' (*PW* 238; J5a,6; quoting Baudelaire 1961: 1101; 1964: 207), linking dreamtime and the dream city with the allegorical. As in de Quincey's *Confessions*, noting the ways in which the intoxicated subject finds that time is lost in space in 'labyrinthine' London, modern space is characterised by 'knotty problems of alleys', 'enigmatical entries', 'sphynx's riddles of streets without thoroughfares' (de Quincey 2008: 48). For Benjamin, such spaces can only be read allegorically, a power that the dreamer harnesses in order to mobilise desire, as in Baudelaire's 'Le Cygne' (*SW* 3: 39). As ruin, modern metropolitan space must be represented through an aesthetics of space. It is this kind of deterritorialisation of dreamer and madman alike that Dickens registers in the idea of Jasper's 'scattered consciousness' (*ED* 1.7).

As Benjamin argues, the city 'is only apparently homogenous' (*PW* 88; C3,3), with those perceived boundaries that supposedly divide it and orientate 'the magnetic field of trajectories just as they haunt dreams' (Certeau 2002: 104), in a constant state of flux and transgression. 'Nowhere, unless perhaps in dreams, can the phenomenon of the boundary be experienced in a more originary way than in cities' (*PW* 88; C3,3), Benjamin remarks, so that in a city, boundaries are both actual, mapped by street names and district divisions, and virtual, since things rarely remain in their proper place. This kind of osmosis is registered visually in Charles Booth's (1840–1916) famous poverty map (1889), where more affluent areas front less salubrious ones.[6] One such boundary is that between West and East in London, or the line of Cable Street that marks the boundary of the area known as Bluegate Fields. This location houses the den where Jasper wakes in the first paragraph of *Edwin Drood*. Dickens knew the area first hand, noting the 'exact' realism of his descriptions in a letter to John Bowring (1792–1872) (*LCD* 12: 520). Under police escort, he had travelled to Shadwell with the American journalist Thomas James Fields (1817–81) to visit the 'horrid opium dens', finding 'in a miserable court [. . .] the haggard old woman blowing at a kind of pipe made of an old penny ink-bottle' (Fields 1876: 105–6). This 'haggard' woman was Opium Sal, the model for *Edwin Drood*'s Princess Puffer, and Fields recalled the 'deep sympathy' Dickens had for 'these outcasts of London' (1876: 106), aware as he was of the socio-economic systems that propped up the opium trade, linking London to the Empire.[7]

Populated by what Booth terms the 'lowest class, vicious, [and] semi-criminal', Bluegate Fields was associated with Asian immigrants. The Chinese had settled Limehouse, just under a kilometre east, in the early years of the century (R. Porter 1998: 302). Bluegate Fields joined London Docks to its south, with the East End stretching from here to St Katharine at the edge of the City. Investment would rebuild the entire area during the 1800s, with then prime minister, William Pitt the Younger (1759–1806), laying the foundation for the West India Docks in 1800. Opening in 1802 on the Isle of Dogs, the Docks were twenty-four acres in size and at capacity could accommodate 600 ships. The West India Docks stimulated competition: the London Docks were opened in 1805, the East India Company opened docks at Blackwall in 1806, St Katharine Dock opened in 1828, the Royal Victoria Dock in 1855, the Millwall Dock in 1868, the Albert Dock in 1880 and the East and West India Company (merged in 1838) at Tillbury in 1886 (Tambling 2009: 282–3). The East End stretched

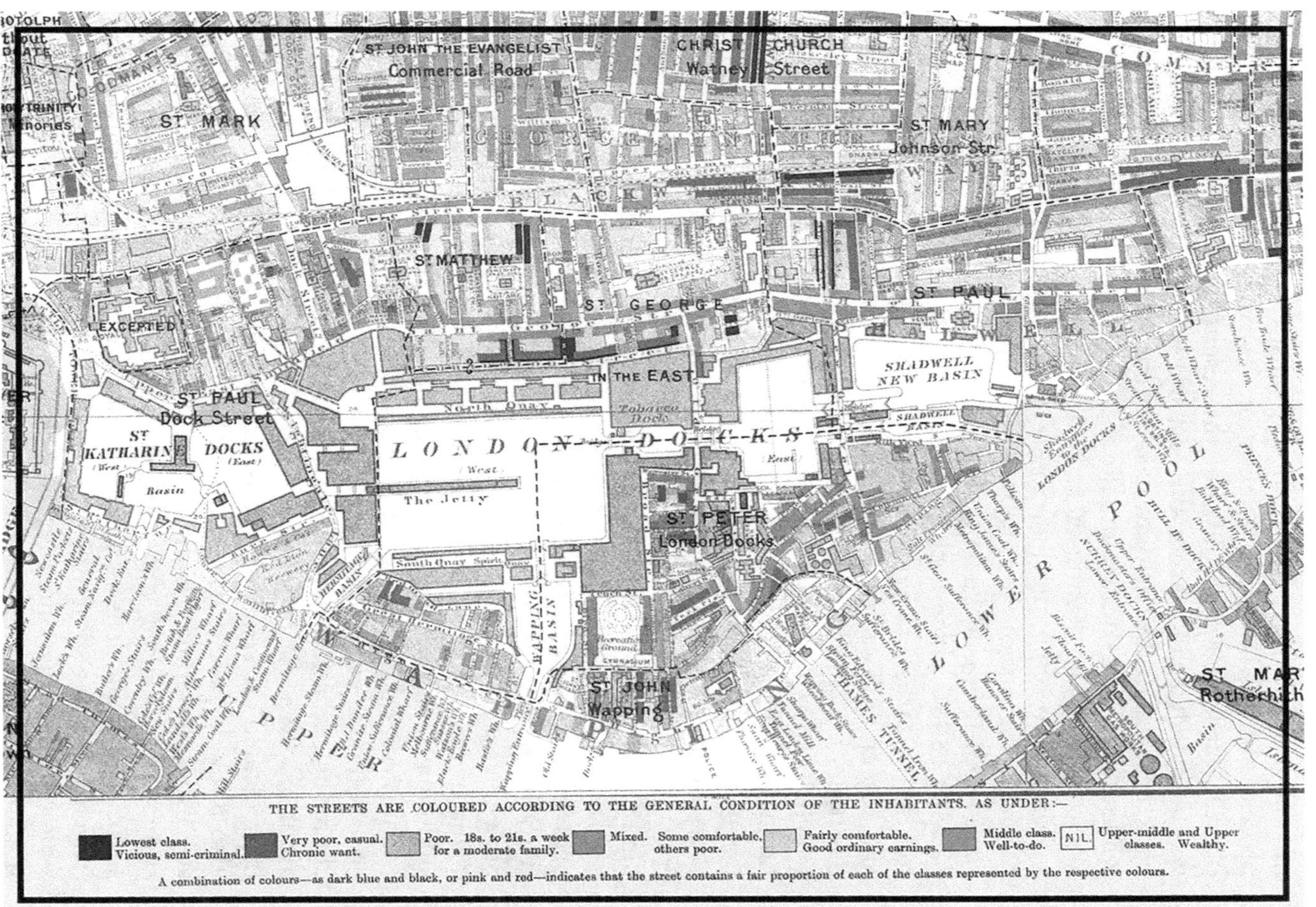

Figure 2.1 Bluegate Fields

ever-eastwards, in that famous image opening Conrad's *Heart of Darkness*, where the Thames is seen reaching outwards as an 'interminable waterway'. It figures for capitalist expansion, that endless process of imperial reterritorialisation rewriting the 'blank spaces o[f] the earth' (2008a: 108). But the result of this over-expansion was ultimately financial ruin: the East and West India Company went bankrupt, and by the end of the century many of the docks lay empty, while the labourers drawn into the area by the prospect of work were left to poverty and destitution.

This socio-economic palimpsest, and particularly that of the Asian immigrants of the area, was drawn by Joseph Charles Parkinson (1833–1908) in 'Lazarus, Lotus-Eating' (*All The Year Round*, 12 May 1866), which Dickens clearly read closely. In it, Parkinson follows 'Lazarus', 'one of the poor wretched Chinamen who shiver and cower and whine at our street corners' (1866: 421), as he meanders through East London. The opium den in Bluegate Fields which Lazarus frequents offers an image of both the Empire and London in microcosm, with 'no limit to the variety of nationalities patronising this wretched hovel', and customers harking 'from every quarter of the globe, and more immediately from every district in London' (422). It is this social seepage which will allow figures like Wilde's Dorian to encounter both Adrian Singleton, a nobleman, and James Vane, a sailor, in the same establishment, figures of vastly different circumstances meeting 'on perfect equality' (Parkinson 1866: 423). More importantly, London itself is seen to be a microcosm of the globe, with the opium den revealing the thanatic underside of its cosmopolitanism.[8] It is another world, subhuman in a racist motif, with the Bengalee 'incoherent' and the Manileño speaking in a 'semi-idiotic jabber' (423). Similar incoherence will be registered by Dickens's Jasper, the 'wild chattering and clattering', where 'when any distinct word has been flung into the air, it has no sense or sequence' (*ED* 1.10), suggesting that 'sense' is predicated on 'sequence', causality or chronology. But Parkinson also finds that the den is 'alive with [. . .] humanity' (1866: 423), suggesting an affinity is dimly discernible between those who are supposedly 'civilised' and those whom they look down upon. As such, the opium dens of Bluegate Fields do not simply stand for 'psychic context', but offer us a view of a reality not only possible but, in Benjaminian terms, precisely 'proper' to such a space. If such spaces are invested psychoanalytically, they are present in Dickens's novel not simply as literary effects, but registering a complex social reality.

When Jasper wakes in the den to be confronted by 'a Chinaman, a Lascar, and a haggard woman' (*ED* 1.7; compare Parkinson 1866: 424), these figures are both 'real', based on Dickens's own experiences, and simultaneously allegorical, death's heads. The passage recalls another in 'A Small Star in the East' (*All The Year Round*, 19 December 1868), prompted by the uncommercial traveller's recollection of his recent perusal of Hans Holbein's (1497–1543) *Danse Macabre* (1523–5) (Dickens bought a copy in 1841), foreshadowing an apparition of a 'weird skeleton rattl[ing] along the streets' of East London (*UT* 354). For his part, Parkinson describes a customer of the opium dens as having a 'livid, cadaverous, corpse-like visage' (1866: 423), and Lazarus as having 'sunken eyes, fallen cheeks, cadaverous parchment-like skin, and deathly whiteness', resembling 'a hideous and long-forgotten mummy' (424), the opium addict a gothic monster.[9] This idea of the mummy may be partly recalled in Dickens's novel by Edwin 'going to wake up Egypt' (*ED* 8.72), at once a motif of imperial domination (Park 2002) and an expression of the death-drive, with Rosa fearful of being buried alive in the Pyramids, her life smothered under Edwin's ambition (*ED* 3.32). As allegorical figures of the Empire, the customers of the opium den also signify the rotten core of the imperial project, and the ways in which the nineteenth-century city, built upon such dreams, confuses categories. Princess Puffer has 'opium-smoked herself into a strange likeness of the Chinaman' (*ED* 1.8), we are told, phrasing again implying Parkinson, who speaks of the customers 'smok[ing] themselves into dreamy pleasant stupefaction' (1866: 423). Strange likenesses and uncanny repetitions, these are ruined figures and figures of ruin. It shows the political unconscious of the nineteenth-century city, less its wish-image than return of the repressed.

Fields recalled that they had heard Sal uttering the same lines Dickens put into Puffer's mouth: 'There was something hideous in the way this woman kept repeating, "Ye'll pay up according, deary, won't ye?"' (1876: 106; *ED* 1.8) It suggests that some of the opium den scene is 'real'. But whether real or not, the scene is also inscribed with aesthetic traces. Parkinson tells us that Lazarus's den seemed charged by dreams, hinting at secrets of 'strange unholy pleasures' and offering glimpses of 'barbaric life' (1866: 425). He speculates on the 'visions' that the space had witnessed, expanding to house 'the mighty feasts; the terrible dramas; the weird romances; the fierce love; the strange fantastic worship; the mad dreams; the gorgeous processions; the brilliant crowds; the mystic shadows' (Parkinson 1866: 425). Similar

IN THE COURT.

Figure 2.2 Luke Fildes, 'In the Court' (1869)

'gorgeous processions' concern Dickens in the opening paragraph of 'The Dawn', the first chapter of his novel:

> An ancient English Cathedral town? How can the ancient English Cathedral tower be here! The well-known massive grey square tower of its old Cathedral? How can that be here! There is no spike of rusty iron in the air, between the eye and it, from any point of the real prospect. What IS the spike that intervenes, and who has set it up? Maybe, it is set up by the Sultan's orders for the impaling of a horde of Turkish robbers, one by one. It is so, for cymbals clash, and the Sultan goes by to his palace in long procession. Ten thousand scimitars flash in the sunlight, and thrice ten thousand dancing-girls strew flowers. Then, follow white elephants caparisoned in countless gorgeous colours, and infinite in number and attendants. Still, the Cathedral tower rises in the background, where it cannot be, and still no writhing figure is on the grim spike. Stay! Is the spike so low a thing as the rusty spike on the top of a post of an old bedstead that has tumbled all awry? Some vague period [MS: centuries] of drowsy laughter must be devoted to the consideration of this possibility. (*ED* 1.7)

The passage immediately situates the reader in space, only to then question the reality in which Jasper finds himself. Lying in the den, Jasper sees Cloisterham Cathedral in front of him, 'well-known', but here displaced to 'where it cannot be', anatopic. Time and space are confused in the dream, as Freud reminds us (*SE* 5: 308). In the accompanying plate, Luke Fildes's (1843–1927) 'In the Court' seems to show

ST. GEORGE'S IN THE EAST FROM LONDON DOCKS

Figure 2.3 Phil W. Smith, 'St. George's in the East from the London Docks' (1923)

the prospect of something dimly visible through the window.[10] The outline may suggest a church steeple, and depending on the orientation of the den, Jasper would almost certainly have been able to see the 'real prospect' of St George in the East through such a window: the church towered above the neighbourhood, as contemporary illustrations demonstrate. Designed by Nicholas Hawksmoor (1661–1736), it was one of six London churches built after the 1711 Act of Parliament for the building of fifty new churches, prompted by London's rapid growth. St George in the East was suburban, dating from the period when the location was more prosperous, housing rich merchants, but by Jasper's time, the social topography had altered dramatically. As such, St George in the East registers the speed of modernity, just as Cloisterham Cathedral stands for a parochial attempt to resist this change: church and cathedral are both out of time.

Cloisterham maps onto the real place of Rochester, its name 'a fictitious mask' (*ED* 3.22). Dickens lived at nearby Gad's Hill Place in Higham, purchased in 1856 and becoming his sole residence from 1860, a property he had had designs upon since he was a boy, an idea which he dramatised in 'Travelling Abroad' (*All The Year Round*, 7 April 1860). There, the uncommercial traveller meets 'a very queer small boy' 'midway between Gravesend and Rochester', the two travelling together towards Gad's Hill, with the boy recollecting his father telling him that if he worked hard, he 'might some day come to live in it' (*UT* 86). The incident is uncanny, since the 'queer' boy here figures for the younger Dickens, who had been told the same by his own father (*LCD* 11: 265–6). Later in his life, Dickens had expressed a desire to be buried in Rochester, amongst the 'old 'uns' as Durdles puts it (*ED* 12.135), making such passages indicative of a death-drive which we find throughout the late Dickens and particularly this novel. The cathedral in Jasper's dream is 'ancient': Rochester Cathedral dates to the Norman period, an example of Romanesque architecture.[11] In the opening passage of the novel, the age connotes the idea of the building as a social and political fulcrum for the surrounding countryside, a point which is re-emphasised by the description of the cathedral with the three descriptives 'well-known massive grey', words suggesting the substantiality of the structure, its monumental function as an expression of the will to power and the desire to 'transcend death' (*PS* 221). Here, the imagery of home, at least for Jasper, functions as a wish-image: it speaks to his desire for certainty, and for an identity that does not slip, a consciousness which is not 'scattered'.

The narrator continues from Jasper's point of view: 'There is no spike of rusty iron in the air, between the eye and it, from any point of the real prospect.' Jasper finds something out-of-place, an *ekstasis* which is proper to the idea of his opium-induced ecstasy. 'What IS the spike that intervenes, and who has set it up?', Jasper asks himself. It registers that moment of 'impediment, failure, split' in the dream, through which we may gain a partial glimpse into the unconscious, and which speaks of 'a strange temporality' (Lacan 1998b: 25). The spike 'intervenes' into the vision, as an object which cannot be there 'in reality', and so one which disrupts the fantasy. It 'inter-venes', comes in between reality and the vision, the spike being, we soon realise, the 'top of a post of an old bedstead that has tumbled all awry'. 'Maybe' it has been erected on the 'Sultan's orders', Dickens continues, with the transitional adverb contingent, so that Dickens's phrasing imitates the metonymic slide of dream language. The next sentence – 'It is so, for cymbals clash, and the Sultan goes by to his palace in long procession' – moves from possibility to certainty, the sibilance carrying the reader through the fantasy. In fact, the whole passage is sibilant, making the reader slip and slide, speeding the text up, while the dental alveolars and the voiceless velars arrest the text, fragmenting it, so that the reader gets no sense of control or mastery over either space or time. Through the 'poetry' of his prose, Dickens implicates the reader's bodies in his text, his language giving a precise sense in which *Zeitraum* becomes *Zeit-traum*.

It is at this point that the trace of a prior text invades Dickens's writing. The allusions have been assumed generic, suggesting the *Arabian Nights*, one of his favourite texts, but Dickens silently quotes the Romantic poet Robert Southey's (1774–1843) epic, *The Curse of Kehama* (1810).[12] Such textual effects create an aesthetic space, so that Dickens's Oriental fantasy of 'ten thousand scimitars flash[ing] in the sunlight' picks up on Southey's description of Kehama's massacre of a thousand archers, 'ten thousand scymitars [. . .] / Flash[ing] up, like waters sparkling to the sun' (8.169–70).[13] While Dickens may have recorded the line automatically, transcribing the image unconsciously,[14] there could have been other reasons why he might have mobilised a subtle allusion to Southey's poem. *The Curse of Kehama* follows the figure of Ladurlad, cursed by Kehama, who becomes a kind of undead figure, living a life suspended 'in a delirious state between sleeping and waking' (*ED* 10.109), just as Jasper does when he is under the influence of opium.[15] Regardless, what is certain is that either consciously or unconsciously, Southey's text 'intervenes' into Dickens's text. Its sadism at once inflects and infects the image of the cathedral, so that the symbol of Christianity and imperialism is envisaged as under siege from the Orient and the Other. The East

End here is also the East, with the docks the gateway to the Empire, and from there the infection is seen to be spreading out into the Home Counties. Indeed, the idea of infection is proper to intoxication in *Edwin Drood*, as we see when Jasper catches the 'unclean spirit of imitation' from Puffer: 'As he watches the spasmodic shoots and darts that break out of her face and limbs, like fitful lightning out of a dark sky, some contagion in them seizes upon him' (*ED* 1.2). The image of Cloisterham Cathedral under siege by Kehama is one of decadence, so that the novel feels like a later, *fin-de-siècle* one: its spaces are millenarian, apocalyptic, anticipating the 'invasion literature' which Moretti discusses (1998: 137–40) as a response to an Empire in crisis. It is as though Dickens's novel comes too early, if we think here of Nietzsche and another idea of the untimely (Nietzsche 2005: 3, 100).

The decadence of *Edwin Drood* is both political and personal, given that this text is Dickens's last novel, tinged with a repetition compulsion and with the death-drive. Its sadism openly invokes a certain *jouissance*, since Kehama's 'ten thousand scimitars' immediately give way to 'ten thousand dancing-girls', where the parallelism links sex and death. This kind of erotic tumult recalls the orgiastic Venice that the 'puritan' in Ruskin desperately seeks to subsume in his 'theoretical' gaze, an unbridled 'sensualism' that revels in the pleasures of *aesthesis*. What is at stake is a question of desire, a libidinal investment in space. Dickens's allusion to the white elephants, animals which are ornamental as much as ceremonial, also suggests the figurative use of the phrase. As a burdensome or costly enterprise, undertaken mainly for the conspicuousness of the consumption, 'white elephant' is a term associated with capitalism (*OED* n.2, dating the first use to 1721). The associations turn Jasper into an aesthete who fetishises the commodity.

But Jasper is not wholly lost in the dream. 'Still, the Cathedral tower rises in the background', we are told, with the adverb stubborn, the building impressing itself upon Jasper's vision. 'Verticality and great height have ever been the spatial expression of potentially violent power', Lefebvre writes (*PS* 98), with the visionary cathedral here suggesting the Law of the Father, and as such implying a very different kind of sadism from that of Kehama. It figures the cathedral as panopticon (Tambling 1995). Hence Jasper's incredulity, not at the violence of the scene but at its absence, its *sanity*, the fact that there is 'still no writhing figure [. . .] on the grim spike'. 'Writhing' here semi-rhymes both with the tower 'rising' and with the bedstead tumbled 'awry' (Tambling 2015: 204), a kind of lexical echo we find

Figure 2.4 Gustave Doré, 'Opium Smoking – The Lascar's Room in "Edwin Drood"' (1872)

throughout this novel and the late Dickens, speaking towards his own compulsion to repeat. This bedstead is a ruin or a 'wreck', as in Blanchard Jerrold's (1826–84) description of a similar scene in *London: A Pilgrimage* (1872: 147). This book was illustrated by Doré, and the accompanying plate, 'Opium Smoking – The Lascar's Room in "Edwin Drood"', makes clear the sense in which Doré's aesthetic envisions London through the late Dickens. For Ruskin, Doré's decadent aesthetics is characterised as the 'slimy efflux of the waters of Styx' (*CW* 25: 170), but Dickens appreciated his art (Jerrold 1870: 240), and the feeling was mutual.[16] In the vision in *Edwin Drood*, this ruinous bedstead is rusty red, connoting blood, and its spike is 'grim', suggesting an agency in place and space and in the thing. The adjective recalls the church of Saint Ghastly Grim of 'The City of the Absent' (*All The Year Round*, 18 July 1863), based on St Olave's, Hart Street. Fronted by 'a ferocious, strong, spiked iron gate, like a jail', 'ornamented with [stone] skulls', 'it [. . .] came into the mind of Saint Ghastly Grim, that to stick iron spikes a-top of the stone skulls, as though they were impaled, would be a pleasant device' (*UT* 263).

In this echo, Cloisterham Cathedral passes a kind of subtle comment on the role of the church in the modern city. The uncommercial traveller notes his 'attraction of repulsion' to the scene, with 'the skulls most effective, having the air of a public execution, and seeming, as the lightning flashed, to wink and grin with the pain of the spikes' (*UT* 263). 'Attraction of repulsion' is a phrase that Forster also uses to discuss Dickens's London (1966: 1: 14), and which Philip Collins takes as emblematic of his divided approach to the city (1973: 537). It makes Dickens, as much as Jasper, a split subject.

When the vision is finally arrested by 'reality', with the spike revealed to be the 'top of a post of an old bedstead', it prompts 'some vague period of drowsy laughter', or 'centuries of laughter' in the manuscript, compressing time in the instant (*SE* 5: 63), and expanding endlessly in another spacetime-cum-dreamtime. The next paragraph begins with Jasper 'shaking from head to foot', piecing together his 'scattered consciousness' (*ED* 1.7), discovering himself neither in Cloisterham nor Kehama's Orient, but in Bluegate Fields. Jasper 'gropes his way down the broken stairs' and leaves, with the chapter ending as follows:

> That same afternoon, the massive grey square tower of an old Cathedral rises before the sight of a jaded traveller. The bells are going for daily vesper service, and he must needs attend it, one would say, from his haste to reach the open Cathedral door. The choir are getting on their sullied white robes, in a hurry, when he arrives among them, gets on his own robe, and falls into the procession filing in to service. Then, the Sacristan locks the iron-barred gates that divide the sanctuary from the chancel, and all of the procession having scuttled into their places, hide their faces; and then the intoned words, 'WHEN THE WICKED MAN –' rise among groins of arches and beams of roof, awakening muttered thunder. (*ED* 1.11)

A jasper is a type of precious stone, valued for its green colour. Ruskin notes its presence throughout Venice, associating it with ornamentalism (*CW* 10: 83). Another green stone is jade, which is associated with East Asian culture during the period, linking to the Chinese immigrants of Bluegate Fields. Jasper is the 'jaded traveller', the colour suggesting his envy of his nephew's fiancée, or perhaps intended to connote a sense of 'decadence', as Wilde might say (*CR* 108). But is it actually Jasper whom we see? It is '*a* jaded traveller' (my emphasis) who returns, and not necessarily the one from beforehand, the same jaded traveller. Is this then the dream or the 'reality'? If Jasper maintains the trace of another's 'scattered consciousness' with him, then which Jasper is it that journeys back to the Home Counties?

This final paragraph of this first chapter of the novel makes clear that space as it is written and encountered in *Edwin Drood* will be removed from the 'realism' characterising Dickens's earlier novels. The image here, concluding a chapter that opens with a vision of a cathedral, ends with the 'jaded traveller' arriving home at this same cathedral, having journeyed there in his dreams earlier that day, for this is 'that same afternoon'. It is the same 'well-known' 'massive grey square tower' that rises here, as it rose before Jasper's eye, but this time seen from a point of 'the real prospect'. The cathedral which begins the novel is this same cathedral, but otherwise, seen in a vision, so that when we arrive at the cathedral for the first time in reality, it is uncanny. As such, an aesthetics of space has preceded our encounter with 'reality', rereading it, haunting it, as a simulacrum that precedes the original experience. Indeed, there is no original here, but simply an echo of an echo, 'a dream within a dream' (2003i: 11.137). In *Edwin Drood*, this final scene of 'The Dawn' performs in reality the vision of Jasper's dreams.

Indeed, the whole scene repeats the prior dream, but in a manner displaced, carried metonymically away from the vision, a repetition with a difference. The 'bells' are ringing, echoing in a more homely, domesticated manner, the 'cymbals' that 'clash' in the vision. The 'white robes' recall the 'white elephant', the choir the host, the choral 'procession' the 'long procession' of soldiers and dancing-girls. The 'iron-barred gates that divide the sanctuary from the chancel' recall the spike-cum-rusty bedstead top that intervenes in Jasper's initial vision. If Jasper himself is the 'Wicked Man', he is asked to consider the lines from Ezekiel – 'When the wicked man turneth away from his wickedness that he hath committed, and doeth that which is lawful and right, he shall save his soul alive' (18: 27), which, at the Anglican Evensong, is followed by Psalms 51: 3: 'I acknowledge my transgressions: and my sin is ever before me.' But Jasper's sin is both before and behind him, precisely insofar as his visions collapse chronological relations between space and time, and precisely since a 'scattered' consciousness, lacking identity, cannot acknowledge its transgressions as its own. The whole scene is a performance of the ritual, one that is eminently familiar and domestic, but through repetition becomes uncanny. Moreover, this ritual is explicitly aesthetic, so that the long 'procession' becomes a rehearsal voided of reference, a pantomime miming an opium dream, yet one more simulacrum. In this, the first chapter of Dickens's final novel, we find ourselves far removed from Ruskinian *theoria*. The Gothic space of Cloisterham Cathedral cannot be *read* as such, but can only ever be approached as *aesthesis*. From 'The Dawn' onwards, *Edwin Drood* becomes an exercise in an aesthetics of space.

English Gothic: Cloisterham

If Jasper is 'the man whose scattered consciousness has [. . .] fantastically pieced itself together' (*ED* 1.7), Dickens's language skirts that of Parkinson, whose Lazarus sees 'shadows which fantastically combine together' (1866: 421). The adverb registers the fact that such a consciousness is only held together through the operation of fantasy, losing that stable ground that would allow a more thorough self-relation. As Benjamin reminds us, the narcotic dream is 'typified by a continual oscillation of dreaming and waking states, a constant and finally exhausting oscillation between totally different worlds of consciousness' (*SW* 2: 673). Jasper is clearly a doppelgänger, whose subject is oscillating, passing from one to the other 'without the smallest stage of transition between the two extreme states' (*ED* 2.21). He is prone to losing consciousness, when 'a strange film' comes over his eyes (*ED* 2.18), as a 'curious film passes over' Puffer (*ED* 14.160). The echo in the text registers the sense in which Puffer is a double of Jasper, both with 'spasmodic' faces (*ED* 1.10, 23.260), but *Edwin Drood* is a novel in which doubles proliferate at a dramatic rate. As well as doubling for the 'haggard and red-eyed' Jasper (*ED* 16.186), the 'haggard' Puffer is echoed in Neville after he has escaped to London (*ED* 17.193): haggardness is a property of the city space, the price of its transgressions, as Dorian Gray's portrait will later make clear (*DG* 8.256). Neville is the twin of Helena (*ED* 7.64), the two looking 'much alike' (*ED* 6.58), with Helena dressing up as a boy, troubling gender; as doppelgängers, they seem to have a telepathic connection (*ED* 7.64), accentuating the uncanny (*SE* 17: 234). Helena also substitutes for Rosa, in a chiastic relationship (*ED* 8.73; Tambling 2015: 208), where Edwin becomes a suitor to Helena and Neville holds designs upon Rosa, who is herself her mother's double (*ED* 11.125, 20.223). Edwin, for his part, is a kind of self-reflexive non-person, allowing him to also double himself, implied at that moment when he is first introduced to Neville and Mr Crisparkle spells out his name 'D-r-double o-d' (7.65), inserting the double into the name. Mr Grewgious tells Edwin that the true lover lives 'at once a doubled life and a halved live' (*ED* 11.121), living and dying through the other, a fate which Rosa, who admits that 'I don't understand myself' (*ED* 7.70), clearly fears as much as Edwin does. And if Drood is a double, he mirrors not only Neville, but also Jasper, both of whom are described as 'brooding' (*ED* 14.156; 12.141), almost a homonym for his surname, with a draft title for the novel having been *The Loss of Edwyn Brood*.

The idea of brooding is important in Dickens's novel. In *The Stones*, Ruskin associates brooding with the modernity of the city and its decadence (*CW* 9: 415). For Freud, 'brooding' [*grübeln*] is a defence mechanism in which 'the thought process itself becomes sexualized', attracting excess libidinal energy and 'divert[ing] it into the sphere of thought' (*SE* 10: 245).[17] To brood implies repetition, reworking desire in an obsessive or neurotic thinking about thinking. Both Drood's and Jasper's brooding displaces erotic energy: Drood, insofar as he does not seem to desire Rosa sexually,[18] and Jasper, insofar as his brooding foreshadows his plans to murder his nephew. But the figure of the brooder may also be linked to that of the aesthete. Considering Baudelaire, Benjamin argues that the *Grübler* is another kind of allegorist:

> What fundamentally distinguishes the brooder from the thinker is that the former not only meditates a thing but also meditates his meditation of the thing. The case of the brooder is that of the man who has arrived at the solution of a problem but has then forgotten it. And now he broods – not so much over the matter itself as over his past reflections on it. [. . .] Brooder and allegorist are cut from the same cloth. (*PW* 367; J79a,1)

Like the melancholic, the brooder has lost the object of desire. It is in this sense that we can unpack Jasper's dreams in the opium den. There, much to Puffer's frustration, Jasper seems unable to recall the 'matter itself', the murder, but instead only the 'journey'. His repetition of this journey, undertaken 'many times' over (*ED* 23.261), marks him as a *Grübler*.

Regardless, what is clear is that all of these uncanny repetitions suggest something at work in the unconscious, a repetition complex that permeates the late Dickens. If the characterisation of Miss Twinkleton as one who has 'two distinct and separate phases of being' (*ED* 3.24) also seems to describe Jasper, then her state is that of hypocrisy (Tambling 2015: 208), as that which seems to be proper to Cloisterham and to the type of parochialism it represents. Jasper's condition is apparently more severe: having a 'scattered consciousness' implies a kind of dissociative personality disorder. According to Forster, the unwritten ending of *Edwin Drood* would have seen the murderer

> review his career by himself at the close, when its temptations were to be dwelt upon as if, not he the culprit, but some other man, were the tempted. The last chapters were to be written in the condemned cell, to which his wickedness, all elaborately elicited from him as if told of another, had brought him. (1966: 2: 366)

Tambling reads Jasper as a psychotic (2015: 216–17), but it is not only Jasper who suffers from a 'scattered consciousness': nearly all of the characters in the novel suffer from various degrees of splitting. Perhaps Dickens presents Jasper as exemplary or different precisely in order to fool the reader into thinking that he is the exception; it allows the reader to pass over the deeper recognition, namely that we all suffer from 'scattered consciousness', that we are all Jasper. Deleuze and Guattari (2004a) argue that capitalism and schizophrenia are locked in a chiastic structure: capitalism, precisely through the process of deterritorialisation, produces schizophrenic subjects, ones whose desire has been deterritorialised. While schizophrenia does not itself imply a dissociative personality disorder, the schizophrenic, like Jasper, is prone to substance abuse and becomes unable to differentiate different states of 'reality'. Watching himself 'as if' he were another, and speaking in another's tongue, Jasper seems to suffer from a form of schizophrenia. And if Jasper's 'scattered consciousness' is associated with Bluegate Fields, then it is also associated with the deterritorialisation of capitalism: less the consumerism of the arcades that fascinated Benjamin than the compulsion to enjoy (Lacan 2015: 18) that drives him towards the transgression of both the law and the boundaries of his subjectivity. In this sense, if *aesthesis* is about the mobilisation of desires, then *theoria* seeks its repression.[19] Little wonder in this context that Ruskin's theoretics of space railed against modern capitalism.

If London is a site of enjoyment in *Edwin Drood*, the city is another one of the novel's doppelgängers. Cloisterham doubles for London and for an older version of the city and of what it means to be 'English', a master-signifier in Lacanian terms, an empty signifier without a signified, the façade of which not even Cloisterham can manage to maintain. Jasper's division is a tale of two cities: the modern capital, which mobilises desire, and the old cathedral city, which attempts to repress it. Cloisterham itself is localised by three spaces, the cathedral, the castle and the High Street, which speak to three localising points that ground a certain sense of what it meant to be English in the mid-Victorian period: religion, politics and commerce. The age of Cloisterham signifies a conservatism that is rooted in the stones out of which it is built:

> An ancient city, Cloisterham, and no meet dwelling-place for any one with hankerings after the noisy world. A monotonous, silent city, deriving an earthy flavor throughout, from its Cathedral crypt, and so abounding in vestiges of monastic graves, that the Cloisterham children grow small salad in the dust of abbots and abbesses, and make dirt-pies of nuns and friars. (*ED* 3.22–3)

This age is often noted – the city has 'ancient streets' (*ED* 6.59) – as is the sense of a past and of the violence Cloisterham had once seen: 'swaggering fighting men had had their centuries of ramping and raving about Minor Canon Corner, and beaten serfs had had their centuries of drudging and dying there' (*ED* 6.53). Literally built out of the bones of the dead, the 'earthy' flavour of the city, a point repeated in the text (*ED* 3.23, 4.43, 5.48, 23.270), anticipates Pater's 'Duke Carl of Rosenmold' (1887), where 'time [. . .] seem[ed] to have been standing still almost since the Middle Age' (*IP* 116), and the 'sleepy' ceremonialism of Rosenmold reflects the ways in which its ancestors are 'buried' beneath its stones (*IP* 117, 123). For Pater, culture is ultimately a culture of death, a 'turning over of the earth', an idea which he takes etymologically from German philology and Andrew Lang (1844–1912) (Dowling 1988: 220; Whiteley 2010: 50–2). 'Earthy' implies decay and mould – as in Pater's 'Rosenmold' (*IP* 116) – and links Cloisterham and its cathedral with a church like St James Garlickhythe, discussed in 'City of London Churches' (*All The Year Round*, 5 May 1860). Rebuilt by Wren after the Great Fire, St James Garlickhythe seems to be fashioned out of the dead:

> The snuff seems to be made of the decay of matting, wood, cloth, stone, iron, earth, and [. . .] the decay of dead citizens in the vaults below [. . .] Dead citizens have got into the very bellows of the organ [. . .] We stamp our feet, to warm them, and dead citizens arise in heavy clouds. Dead citizens stick upon the walls, and lie pulverised on the sounding-board. (*UT* 110)

The phrasing recalls J. Hillis Miller on 'the general pulverization' of the London of *Our Mutual Friend* (1958: 195), and in 'The Study of Architecture in Schools' (1865), Ruskin figures the city subject as simply 'one atom in a drift of dust' (*CW* 19: 24). Such echoes between Cloisterham and St James Garlickhythe make its version of London another expression of the death-drive, if differing from that of Bluegate Fields, binding both like Jasper as two different phases of being.

Cloisterham is bisected by 'the cheerfully frequented High Street' (*ED* 12.134). At one end lies the river, standing for the Medway, which is 'confused' by the tide (10.102), 'heaving with restless knowledge' (12.137) as it flows east to the sea. The river seems to signify death, with Edwin's watch found at the weir, so that he may be presumed drowned, a threat that is marked and repeated in the novel: Rosa's mother had drowned (11.124) and Tartar once saved Crisparkle from drowning (21.232). Near the cathedral, to its east, the High Street houses Jasper's Gate House, as well as Mr Tope and, later, Dick Datchery; to the south lie Mr Sapsea's House and Eastgate House. On the other side of the cathedral lies Minor Canon Corner, with the castle to its north on the banks of the river, and to the south the Monk's Vineyard, remnants of the 'monastery ruin' (*ED* 2.11). The whole city is architecturally defined by its cathedral. It recalls Ruskin's point that the Gothic is not an especially ecclesiastical style, but originally defined entire cities. Tope's house 'partook of the character of a cool dungeon', its rooms seemingly excavated out of its 'massive' ancient walls (*ED* 18.205), and when Datchery arrives in Cloisterham, he seeks 'something venerable, architectural, and inconvenient': something 'Cathedraly' (*ED* 18.274).

As for the rest of the city, we are told that it offers 'no thoroughfare' (*ED* 3.23), a phrase which is an autocitation of earlier work,[20] and implies repression, an inability to pass through. Cloisterham is 'a city of another and bygone time', anachronistic or untimely, out of place in the modern world. Considering anachronism, Tambling quotes *Bleak House* on the aristocracy wanting to put back 'the hands upon the Clock of Time, and cancel [. . .] a few hundred years of history' (*BH* 12.189), noting the novel's contemporaneity with the Gothic Revival (Tambling 2010: 1). In Cloisterham too, 'all things in it are of the past' (*ED* 3.23), as marked by the fact that it has no railway station and 'never would' according to Mr Sapsea, the mayor: 'Express Trains don't think Cloisterham worth stopping at, but yell and whirl through it on their larger errands, casting their dust off their wheels as a testimony to its insignificance' (*ED*. 6.57). This suggests that the action takes place in the past, before Staples Inn had been overshadowed by 'neighbouring architecture of lofty proportions' (*ED* 11.113), seemingly between 1846 and 1861, when Rochester was connected to London on the Chatham Line.[21] Sapsea, for his part, is a fitting mayor, Cloisterham's 'purest jackass' and pre-eminent hypocrite. He represents the Law of the Father, both in his official role and since his premises on the High Street sport 'a wooden effigy' of his own father over his door. But this also suggests the Law's impotence (Lacan 1998b: 103), since this effigy is only 'about half life-size' (*ED* 4.36). Sapsea lacks the astuteness to see his own hypocrisy, or what his effigy signifies. Of those who live in Cloisterham, only Durdles, 'the chartered libertine of the place' (*ED* 4.41), is permitted to speak the truth, playing the role of Fool and refusing to respect Sapsea's façades (*ED* 18.209). Perhaps this privilege relates to the fact that he is another divided subject, 'as seldom drunk as sober' (*ED* 4.42), who recognises that character is always a kind of fantastic imposition (Tambling 2015: 210), hence 'often speak[ing] of himself in the third person; being perhaps a little misty as to his own identity when he narrates' (*ED* 4.41). His nickname, Stony, is of uncertain origin, a point which Jasper presses, asking whether it stands for Tony (*ED* 4.44), but it also stands for being 'stoned' (*ED* 5.46). In this, he becomes another of Jasper's doubles.

Durdles is Cloisterham's stonemason, seen 'sitting on all manner of tombstones' (*ED* 4.41), and is associated with the cathedral. He is found amongst its many 'secluded nooks' (*ED* 12.134), recalling the uncommercial traveller, who 'haunts' the 'deserted nooks' of London's old churchyards (*UT* 262). In *Edwin Drood*, Durdles and the cathedral are bound in an uncanny 'connexion' (*ED* 5.48), and as Elizabeth Bridgham rightly notes, he figures as the cathedral's gargoyle (2008: 127–9), and is 'always prowling among old graves and ruins, like a Ghoule' (*ED* 12.132). But Bridgham does not point out that Dickens's understanding of the significance of gargoyles and the Gothic grotesque would have been informed by that of Ruskin (Hollington 1984: 192–215; Thomas 1986: 87). Perhaps Durdles represents the Ruskinian 'noble grotesque' in comparison to the 'terrible grotesque' (*CW* 11: 166–7) of Puffer, who is 'as ugly and withered' as one of the cathedral's 'fantastic carvings' (*ED* 23.271). Durdles lives in the ruins of the old Norman city, and discussing St Mark's, Ruskin notes that the Venetians 'had been accustomed to build with their ruins' (*CW* 10: 96): traces of Byzantine structures are written into its stones, with the Gothic literally built out of the material of the Venetian past. So too Durdles, who 'lives in a little antiquated hole of a house that was never finished', built 'of stones stolen from the city wall' (*ED* 4.42). This quality of unfinishedness, which Ruskin considers the quintessential characteristic of the Gothic, and which he reads 'theoretically' as revealing the 'truth of space', extends to the approach to Durdles's house, 'ankle-deep in stone chips, resembling a petrified abode of tomb-stones, urns, draperies, and broken columns, in all stages of sculpture' (*ED* 4.42). Intimate connection with the past can have the sense of petrifying life, turning it to stone. More broadly, the wider city takes its character from this recycling of older stones: 'Fragments of old wall, saint's chapel, chapter-house, convent, and monastery, have got incongruously or obstructively built into many of its houses and gardens' (*ED* 3.23). In this, Cloisterham is figured as a 'ruin', a 'picturesque' image of the city most obviously traced during Jasper's 'moonlight expedition' with Durdles (*ED* 12.128). But this tendency to read space picturesquely was a motif of which Ruskin was always wary in Dickens. Writing in a letter of 6 June 1841, reflecting on his recent reading of *Old Curiosity Shop*, Ruskin remarked that Dickens should try to hold himself 'to a far higher standard, giving up that turn for the picturesque which leads him into perpetual mannerism' (*CW* 36: 26). Ruskin's suspicion towards the picturesque, as we have seen, was rooted in his belief that it represented a repressive gesture, turning away from the social reality of city space. But in this case, it is not Dickens who reads Cloisterham as picturesque, but Jasper, in a way that is symptomatic of his modernity in Ruskinian terms.

The cathedral stands for tradition and the Law. There is an ancient hierarchy that structures Cloisterham life, old titles which demand respect – Reverend, Dean, Mayor – a social fabric which the imposing presence of the building maintains. The theme recalls Ruskin, reflecting on the Gothic in *The Sea Stories*. Before coming to discuss St Mark's, Ruskin makes a comparison to 'a quiet English cathedral town', inviting his readers to 'walk with me to the west front of its cathedral' (*CW* 10: 78). The 'generic' description may suitably describe Cloisterham, the 'retired' main street, the 'old-fashioned groups of somewhat diminutive and excessively trim houses' (*CW* 10: 78), the gardens 'which show here and there [. . .] the vestiges of an old cloister arch or shaft' (*CW* 10: 79). Ruskin stands at the cathedral's west front 'looking up at its deep-pointed porches and the dark places between their pillars where there were statues once' (*CW* 10: 79), asking his readers to consider both the scene's 'sublimity' and 'its small formalisms', which in turn mark the town's subjects:

> Estimate its secluded, continuous, drowsy felicities, and its evidence of the sense and steady performance of such kind of duties as can be regulated by the cathedral clock; and weigh the influence of those dark towers on all who have passed through the lonely square at their feet for centuries. (*CW* 10: 80)

In medieval times, the northern Gothic cathedral gathered space around it (*PS* 220), producing space and distributing it around this privileged focal point so that it 'appears to come under the thrall of a divine order' (*PS* 235). For Ruskin, the 'generic' cathedral impresses itself on all who saw those 'dark towers [. . .] rising far away over the wooded plain' (*CW* 10: 80), so that the architecture has an 'influence' on the subjects approaching it, a disciplinary power. In *Edwin Drood*, this panoptic gaze is carried by Cloisterham Cathedral's 'hoarse rooks', which are always present, overlooking the action from their perch, and are paired with 'its hoarser and less distinct rooks in the stalls far beneath' (*ED* 3.23). Ruskin compares the doves of St Mark's with the birds of the English cathedral, 'the restless crowd, hoarse-voiced and sable-winged' (*CW* 10: 84). In *Edwin Drood*, Rosa is a dove (*ED* 21.230) whereas Jasper is associated with the 'hoarse' rooks. In context, Ruskin's allusion to 'sable-wings' cites Marlowe – 'Doth shake contagion from her sable wings' (*Jew of Malta*, 2.1.4) – marking the birds as ravens, another member of the corvidae family: it suggests that the English cathedral brings neither light nor peace but darkness and 'contagion', that quality associated with decadence and opium in Dickens's novel (*ED* 1.10). But the rooks' panoptic gaze is revealed to be limited, for they are notably absent at the moment of the murder itself, unable to see the crime. They are signified only synecdochally by their nests, torn into 'great ragged fragments' by the storm that night, when 'chimneys topple' (*ED* 14.165), echoing the millenarian darkness of *Macbeth* (2.3.61). The next morning, Cloisterham awakes to find that 'the hands of the Cathedral clock are torn off' (*ED* 14.166), erasing that symbolic structure that Ruskin credits with the ability to 'regulate' time and local life (*CW* 10: 80).[22] It suggests that a 'scattered consciousness' misplaces and displaces time, recalling John Elliotson's (1791–1868) *Human Physiology* (1835), where a drunken porter forgets where he has left a parcel, and is unable to find it when sober, only discovering it when drunk again. Dickens had alluded to the story earlier in the novel (*ED* 3.24), as his friend Wilkie Collins (1824–89) had in *The Moonstone* (1868) (2008: 2.3.10.386). Later, Crisparkle finds Edwin's gold watch (*ED* 16.182), taken synecdochally for his dead body. Both the watch and the clock mark Cloisterham as a space and time out of joint.

The 'drowsy' felicities of Ruskin's English cathedral (*CW* 10: 80) are recalled in Dickens's 'drowsy' Cloisterham (*ED* 3.23, 23.255). But the city's drowsiness also seems to reflect somehow that of the 'scattered consciousness' manifested in Jasper's 'drowsy laughter' (*ED* 1.7), in Durdles's drunkenness (*ED* 12.137), and in Puffer, whose 'drowsy repetition' of Edwin's name as 'Eddy' (*ED* 14.161) connotes a link between drowsiness and drowning (Tambling 2015: 206). Drowsiness suggests the death-drive, as does Cloisterham's 'monotony', differing from London's 'ghastly monotony' (*UT* 354) in its untimely status as a 'never-changing place' (*ED* 5.48). Through the figure of Sapsea, this monotony is associated with Cloisterham's parochialism and hypocrisy (*ED* 12.126), that 'cloistered', suffocating environment that leads Jasper to speak of 'the cramped monotony of my existence' (*ED* 2.19). Jasper associates this with 'grinding', and previously we have been told that Cloisterham has been ground out of the bones of the dead (*ED* 3.23). Jasper's 'existence grinds me away by the grain' (*ED* 2.19); he calls himself 'a poor monotonous chorister and grinder of music' (*ED* 2.20). He is not alone in being a 'grinder', with Grewgious (*ED* 9.86), Neville's stepfather (*ED* 7.62) and Billickin (*ED* 22.252) all either grinders or ground up. The allusion recalls Dickens's earlier 'grinders', notably Thomas Gradgrind, whose name suggests the punishing brutality of modern life. In *Hard Times*, being ground down is a product of Coketown, whose steam-engines 'worked monotonously up and down, like the head of an elephant in a state of melancholy madness' (2003f: 1.5.27). The simile associates industrialism and monotony, not only suggesting that the city turns one mad, but also making the point, as Ruskinian as Benjaminian, that monotony automates. The original object or cause has been lost, and the action comes to be performed for its own sake, producing melancholia as that which is proper to the age of mechanical reproduction.

While Ruskin had his issues with *Hard Times*, he would have agreed with Dickens's attack on the 'monotony' of London (*CW* 34: 270), but would differentiate this from the 'monotone grey' of the English cathedral, which he praises as a product of time and nature (*CW* 10: 109). Ruskin would consider Jasper's hatred of his 'quiet life' (*ED* 2.19) his decadence, seeking to differentiate Gothic 'changefulness' from the 'diseased love of change' (*CW* 10: 209), a 'morbid' idea indicative of *aesthesis*. After Edwin's disappearance, Jasper suggests that 'a man leading a monotonous life [. . .] dwells upon an idea until it loses its proportions' (*ED* 14.164), fixation being another kind of madness. Psychoanalytically, fixation (*Fixierung*) relates to fetishism: it represents a cathexis in a partial object, one which stands in metonymically for some other cause, and is associated with neurosis. Capitalism produces fixations through consumerism, but more broadly, is invested ideologically in grinding its subjects down, seeking to produce neurotics, as Deleuze and Guattari have argued (2004a: 133–41), developing an argument first made by Freud (*SE* 21: 87). Taken in this context, Jasper's brooding Cloisterham monotony suggests monologism, a single state rather than one of difference. Monotony leads to a reterritorialisation of the subject as fixated and neurotic, and stands opposed to the other kind of subject which capitalism produces in spite of itself, that of the 'scattered consciousness', the schizophrenia of a deterritorialised *aesthesis* which knows no lost object but which liberates desires.

Ruskin remarks that although the English cathedral is 'no longer dedicated to the kind of services for which it was intended by its builders and finds itself 'at variance [. . .] with the temper of the people by whom it is now surrounded', it still retains a trace of its religious influence through its architectural power (*CW* 10: 91). The cathedral stands in for God, for the lawful life, warning man against the decadence of modernity. But with its broken clock hands (*ED* 14.166), Cloisterham Cathedral no longer stands for God, and implies synecdocally God's absence, during a period when the relevance of religion appears to be waning. It marks space monumentally as an untimely reminder of lost time. But if Cloisterham Cathedral stands for an absent God, then it also functions as a memento mori. Notably, Ruskin's comparison between St Mark's and his generic English cathedral asks his readers to walk with him in approach to the western façade. In *Edwin Drood*, Grewgious, looking for Jasper, makes a similar journey, passing from the Gate House across the Close before standing at the western door of the cathedral. From this vantage point, he remarks that 'it's like looking down the throat of Old Time' (*ED* 9.94). Allegorically, Father Time, a perversion of the figure of Saturn-Cronus (mistaking Cronus for Chronos), is typically portrayed as a winged figure carrying a scythe in one hand, in a corrupted image of the grim reaper, and an hourglass in the other, signifying the passing of time, reminding us that we all end up in the crypt. On the western façade of Rochester Cathedral, the tympanum

Figure 2.5 Rochester Cathedral: tympanum

Figure 2.6 Rochester Cathedral: Great West Door

above the door features a central figure, which is defaced, missing both his face and his right hand, with a book in his left hand. Perhaps Grewgious mistakes this image of Christ for Old Time, a Christian image for a pagan one.

There may be an echo of this later in the novel when Edwin, having met Puffer and hearing from her an uncanny version of his name, finds himself alone and fearful, 'surrounded by vestiges of old time and decay' (*ED* 14.162). Earlier, Dickens's narrator takes up Grewgious's allusion, personifying the Cathedral:

> Old Time heaved a mouldy sigh from tomb and arch and vault; and gloomy shadows began to deepen in corners [. . .] Within the grill-gate of the chancel, up the steps surmounted loomingly by the fast darkening organ, white robes could be dimly seen, and one feeble voice rising and falling in a cracked monotonous mutter, could at intervals be faintly heard. [. . .] In the Cathedral, all became grey, murky, and sepulchral, and the cracked monotonous mutter went on like a dying voice, until the organ and the choir burst forth, and drowned it in a sea of music. (*ED* 9.94–5)

The scene is another refrain on repeated motifs, and of the uncanny compulsion to repeat which marks this novel and the late Dickens. 'Gloomy shadows' picks up on Cloisterham as a 'gloomy place' (*ED* 2.19), the 'gloomy smile' of one of the customers at Bluegate Fields (1.10), Jasper's gloomily neurotic state of mind (*ED* 14.164), and his gloominess on the day following Edwin's disappearance (*ED* 19.212). The word connotes the presence of danger within it, containing the idea of 'looming', and gloominess also suggests melancholia, brooding and the name of Drood. The 'fast darkening organ' recalls the first night at the cathedral, when Jasper, Tope and Crisparkle look upon 'the fast darkening scene' in which the building seems as though it is being reclaimed by the earth, suffocated under 'pendant masses of ivy and creeper' (*ED* 2.13). The phrase also foreshadows the night of the murder, when 'the rooks hovered above [. . .], darker splashes in the darkening air' (*ED* 13.152). But most significantly, it replays the processional evensong of the final paragraph of 'The Dawn', which itself reworks Jasper's dream vision of the opening paragraph: the 'grill-gates' recall the 'iron-barred gates', both picking up the iron spike that impales Kehama's foes and the iron spike of the bedstead in Bluegate Fields, the 'white robes' in both passages ghost the 'white elephants', and so forth. If things are hard to make out, discriminate clearly, only 'dimly seen' and 'faintly heard', this is in part because they have already been seen and heard before, losing their distinctness through the repetition. The 'monotonous' voice is presumably Jasper's, his 'cracked monotonous mutter' picking up on the 'muttered thunder' of the final words of 'The Dawn' (*ED* 1.11). Here, as there, it signifies the coming violence, anticipating the stormy night of Edwin's disappearance, with Jasper's voice eventually 'drowned', as Edwin is presumed to be. Cloisterham Cathedral gives an image of Old Time, but less of the Christian version of the figure than its original persona, in a kind of Heinean-Paterean motif of malevolent deities returning to wreak havoc in a later time. Everything becomes crypt-like, 'sepulchral', so that God's house is vacated by Christian spirit, its 'theoretical' depth excavated: all that remains is aesthetic play. It is uncanny: the 'generic' Ruskinian space of the English Gothic, so familiar to so many of his readers, becomes defamiliarised. A repetition of a repetition of a repetition, a 'dream within a dream', the scene is another simulacrum, voided of reference.

Simulacral Space: Ghosting London

Cloisterham is 'quiet' for the most part, its streets 'silent', although we are told that they are 'prone to echo on the smallest provocation' (*ED* 3.23). Echoes are repeated in the novel. Cloisterham Cathedral's bell seems to toll a 'solemn echo' of Edwin's disquiet (*ED* 14.162), and we hear echoes in the Cathedral Close (*ED* 2.11) and the 'footsteps of rare passers' (*ED* 6.53). People begin to echo one another's speech, Edwin echoing Bazzard (*ED* 11.119), the Dean echoing Tope (*ED* 12.128). But speech is also 'shattered' and 'fragmented' by all these echoes, so that even if meaning is 'still capable of being pieced together' (*ED* 12.133), nuances may be missed and messages lost. These persistent echoes register the uncanny, troubling the order of things, as in the ghosting in the novel. Mrs Tisher rustles about 'like the legendary ghost of a dowager in silken skirts' (*ED* 3.29), and the girls at the Nun's House are eager for some ghostly adventures (*ED* 13.142); Cloisterham's citizens avoid the 'eerie' Precincts, with rumours abroad of 'a mysterious lady, with a child in her arms and a rope dangling from her neck' (*ED* 12.134); Neville is haunted by his past in London (*ED* 17.198), and Tartar is a 'ghost' from Crisparkle's past (*ED* 21.232). Durdles for his part speaks of 'ghosts of other things', of 'sounds' and 'cries' (*ED* 12.135). But it is Jasper who is the most significant ghostly presence in the novel, a revenant, a 'ghastly figure' whom Grewgious sees 'ris[ing], open-mouthed, [. . .] and lift[ing] its outspread hands' (*ED* 15.176). This ghostly presence is associated with opium, through which Jasper 'delivers himself to the Spectres' (*ED* 5.51). He 'terrifies' Rosa, 'haunting' her thoughts (*ED* 7.53), his gaze mesmeric, making Rosa 'a slave [. . .] with his looks' (*ED* 7.70). 'The fascination of repulsion had been on her so long, and now culminated so darkly, that she felt as if he had the power to bind her by a spell' (*ED* 20.221). 'Fascination of repulsion' recalls the 'attraction of repulsion' that London produces in Dickens (*UT* 263), suggesting Jasper's mesmerism to be a 'dark' quality of the modern city, which 'fascinates'.

The murder, as has been already noted, does not take place as such in the novel, but is foreshadowed and echoed everywhere. When Crisparkle goes walking, he finds himself drawn, almost automatically, to Cloisterham Weir. The location has a 'haunted air' (*ED* 16.182), making the space difficult to read, where 'signals of strange shapes showed like spectres' (*ED* 15.173), the sibilance adding to the ghostly effect. Realising where he has found himself, Crisparkle has the uncanny sense that there must have been some unconscious purpose behind his journey:

> 'How did I come here!' was his first thought, as he stopped.
> 'Why did I come here!' was his second. (*ED* 16.181)

Neither question is asked, the punctuation marking both as exclamations, as though the answer is already known. 'Listening intently to the water', he found that 'a familiar passage in his reading, about airy tongues that syllable men's names, rose [. . .] unbidden to his ear' (*ED* 16.181). John Milton's (1608–74) line (*Comus* l. 208) impresses itself onto his mind without his bidding, obeying his unconscious, speaking to the ways in which our engagement with space is always mediated through prior aesthetic traces. He cannot shake 'the strange idea that something unusual hung about the place' (*ED* 16.181). That night, 'the Weir ran through his broken sleep' (*ED* 16.145), reminding him of the presence of what he had not seen. What is the syllabled name that he cannot quite hear? Listening to the water, perhaps Crisparkle catches an onomatopoeic 'eddy' of the weir, or rather the echo of 'Eddy', since when he returns, he catches sight of, is 'fascinated' by, Edwin's gold watch (*ED* 16.182). 'Eddy' is a 'threatened' and 'dangerous' name, Puffer remarks (*ED* 14.127), and moreover, implies the whirlpool (*OED* 'eddy' n.1), and thus a loss of identity. The *OED* gives no original etymology for the word, but speculates a connection with the prefix *ed-*, to return or go back: as Eddy, Drood is an echo, a signifier of death and a function of the drive to repeat.

These echoes allow the city to speak otherwise, so that Cloisterham is haunted both by its past and by the city of London. The capital is always there in the background, the humming presence of 'external mankind' (*ED* 6.57). The cathedral city represents an older way of life, one closer to the theoretical space that Ruskin finds so lacking in London. But to react against London means in part to admit its overwhelming power, against which the subject is powerless. For the most part, London's power in the novel lies in the 'attraction of repulsion' that drives Jasper to Bluegate Fields. Moretti contends that Dickens's city differs from Balzac's, for while Paris is 'oriented by desire, and held together by *reverie*', a quality which makes it 'legible', London 'can never become an object of desire' and so cannot be read (1998: 100). But London is precisely a question of desire for Jasper, and if it is made 'legible' in this novel, it is as 'dream space', disorienting the city, reversing the operation, since this desire is always laced with the death-drive. Jasper is unable to resist this compulsion, almost admitting as much when he dwells melancholically on the fact that Cloisterham offers 'no whirl and uproar', 'no distracting commerce or calculation, no risk' (*ED* 2.19). The phrasing suggests the unconscious linkage which binds pleasure, intoxication (opium) and capitalism. Assuming Jasper is a stable single subject, the line would make Jasper a hypocrite, like Miss Twinkleton, where hypocrisy marks *ressentiment*, a powerlessness to alter the 'monotony' of life, 'the tedious unchanging round of this dull place' (*ED* 8.76). But Jasper is not single; escaping to London, hoping to get 'relief' (*ED* 23.261), his power lies in 'scattering' his consciousness.

In this, Jasper compares with Neville, another of his doubles (*ED* 15.172). After having been accused of Edwin's murder, Neville moves to London, hoping to find 'anonymity' away from the prying eyes of the residents of Cloisterham. But he is unable to 'persuade myself that the eyes of even the stream of strangers I pass in this vast city look at me without suspicion'. He feels 'marked and tainted' (*ED* 17.194), scapegoated in another image of infection. For his part, Neville's 'weakness' is born of having been 'tyrannically held down by the strong hand' (*ED* 6.64), marking his anger as another kind of *ressentiment*. This 'strong hand' is associated with his stepfather, but also with British colonial power, since he hails from Ceylon. Allusions to his 'tigerish' blood (*ED* 7.64, 8.80, 8.81) are racist in their connotations, suggesting an animal violence linked to his 'dark' skin (*ED* 6.79), and they are connotations which Jasper will mobilise to his advantage – although he too is 'dark' (*ED* 2.14, 21.231) – when attempting to pin the murder of Edwin on one whose 'complexion is "Un-English"' (*ED* 14.162). But these same allusions also mark an anxiety over the Father's impotence: *Edwin Drood* was written and published (if not set) after the 'Mutiny' of 1857, by which time the tiger had become a symbol of a colonial resistance that Britain could neither wholly subdue nor contain (Miller 2012).

That London is space which is overdetermined (*SE* 4: 283–84; Althusser 2005: 82–128) is implied by Grewgious's chambers at Staples Inn in Holborn. It is one of the few definite locations given in the novel, alongside Billickin's apartments in Southampton Street, Bloomsbury Square. Holborn gives a different, more 'homely' image of London than Bluegate Fields. Staples Inn is 'a little nook composed of two irregular quadrangles' (*ED* 11.112), the 'nook' drawing attention to similarities with Cloisterham Cathedral (*ED* 5.35, 12.105). Holborn is a place 'where certain gabled houses some centuries of age still stand looking on the public way, as if disconsolately looking for the Old Bourne that has long run dry' (*ED* 11.112), asserting what James calls London's 'value of *names* even when all the rest is gone' (*CNJ* 278). Like London's old churches, 'monuments of another age', Holborn's houses seem to 'echo, not unharmoniously, to the time when [. . .] London really was London' (*UT* 116). Holborn is a place out of place, harking back to a past that has been culverted, banished underground like the Old Bourne. In chapter 20, 'A Flight', Rosa arrives in front of Grewgious's chambers, standing 'on P.J.T.'s doorsteps, wondering what P.J.T had done with his street door' (*ED* 20.223). The allusion is to a 'mysterious inscription' over the door:

P
J T
1747.

The narrator speculates that 'it might mean Perhaps John Thomas, or Perhaps Joe Tyler' (*ED* 11.113), 'Pretty Jolly Too' (*ED* 11.119) or 'Possibly Jabbered Thus' (*ED* 11.126). Overdetermined, such signs give themselves to be reread endlessly by the urban subject who, like Wordsworth in *The Prelude*, hopes to fix meaning once and for all, to produce a cognitive map of modern space. Grewgious himself is a man of somewhat limited 'conversational powers'. 'I cannot express what I mean', he remarks, adding the alternative that 'having no meaning, I do not mean what I fail to express' (*ED* 11.121). Language fails to capture his meaning, as when he remarks that 'Life is pounds, shillings, and pence. Death is —' (*ED* 9.88), where the aposiopesis registers something that resists symbolisation, or rather, the lack grounding the symbolic order itself.

Rosa has recently escaped from Jasper's mesmeric power, taking a train into London. 'As the evening grew darker and darker, [. . .] the great city impended nearer and nearer' (*ED* 20.222), the verb connoting a sense of violence hanging over (*OED* 'impend' *v.*[2] 1), brooding over the city. She fears 'what might become of her, alone, in a place so strange and crowded' (*ED* 20.222), and her anxiety picks up on economic language, with 'a multitude of such uneasy speculations' disturbing her 'more and more as they accumulated' (*ED* 20.222), so that the 'strangeness' of London is linked to capitalism. Her approach to London riffs on familiarly Dickensian themes: 'At length the train came into London over the housetops; and down below lay the gritty streets with their yet un-needed lamps a-glow, on a hot, light, summer night' (*ED* 20.222). The image of the train passing over the rooftops recalls the 'theoretical' motive of Dickens's

Figure 2.7 Gustave Doré, 'Over London by Rail' (1872)

realism to 'take the house-tops off' (2002a: 47.685), and the passage perhaps provided partial inspiration for Doré's 'Over London by Rail', which looks down on rows of houses from a viaduct. But unlike in *Dombey and Son*, where Dombey rides the train from the city to Leamington, seeing 'close at hand' 'through the battered roofs and broken windows, wretched rooms' (2002a: 20.299), there is no possibility of *theoria* in *Edwin Drood*. The lives beneath the house-tops remain invisible.

Arriving in London, Rosa finds herself:

> rattling away again in a cab, through deserts of gritty streets, where many people crowded at the corner of courts and byways to get some air, and where many other people walked with a miserably monotonous noise of shuffling of feet on hot paving-stones, and where all the people and all their surroundings were so gritty and so shabby! (*ED* 20.222)

Repetition defines London, but somewhat differently from the way in which it defines Cloisterham. The cab 'rattles', an onomatopoeic word (*OED* 'rattle' *v.*[1]), registering a kind of aural shock, with noise 'the principal medium of urban perception' (Wolfreys 2012: 6). 'Rattle' is also an echo, both of Puffer's 'querulous, rattling whisper' (*ED* 1.8) and of the violent wind of the night of Edwin's disappearance (14.165), as well as connoting money, with Datchery 'rattling his loose' change, making Puffer's ears 'greedy' (23.266). The 'shuffling of feet on hot paving-stones' gives Dickens's London 'something like an image of classical hell' (Welsh 1971: 65), while their 'monotonous noise' means that London echoes Cloisterham, its monotony reversed but related, recalling Jasper's version of the cathedral city as 'devilish', not 'celestial' (*ED* 2.19).

In London, both the space and its people are 'gritty', and it is unclear which gives character to the other: the space or the people. The choice of this adjective, used twice in the passage (*ED* 20.222), and so soon after the 'gritty streets' of the previous paragraph, suggests a lack of imagination on Rosa's part, an inability to see differences in the city: it anticipates chapter 22, 'A Gritty State of Things Comes On'. There, Rosa and Grewgious take a trip with Tartar in his boat, moored at Temple Stairs, up the river, dining 'in some everlastingly-green garden', impossibly Edenic, a space which the narrator does not locate, it 'needing no matter-of-fact identification here' (*ED* 22.247). The trip is 'idle' and 'restful', the river 'obliging', sensuously indulgent, the boat making a 'sweet return among delicious odours of limes in bloom, and musical ripplings' (*ED* 22.247). But 'the rare glimpses of another city are glimpses only' (Welsh 1971: 136), and the return to London brings a different prospect: 'all too soon, the great black city cast its shadow on the waters, and its dark bridges spanned them as death spans life, and the everlastingly-green garden seemed to be left for everlasting, unregainable and far away' (*ED* 22.247). 'Dark' and 'impending', London seems to Rosa 'very gritty again, and everything had a strange and an uncomfortable appearance of seeming to wait for something that wouldn't come' (*ED* 22.247), an uncanny 'air' that she cannot shake off (22.253). It associates London's grittiness, itself a product of aesthetic repetition, with deferral, a quality that defines modern American space for James. In Lacanian terms, it also figures the city's neurosis: waiting defers an engagement with the repressed (Lacan 1991: 286–7).

In 'Night Walks', Dickens quotes Macbeth, himself 'scattered', speaking of himself in the third person, on sleep as 'the death of each day's life' (2.2.39), adding that dreams are 'the insanity of each day's sanity' (*UT* 154). Dreams are the subject of the final chapter of the novel, 'The Dawn Again', which, in both topic and title, echoes the first, 'The Dawn'. This repetition is a question both of plot and of inscription, forcing the reader to approach the chapter and its narrative through the title, which insists here and forewarns us in advance that what is at stake will be precisely a question of repetition. Indeed, the final chapter is driven by the compulsion to repeat and by the death-drive. Jasper leaves for London, taking a hotel 'in a little square behind Aldergate Street, near the General Post Office'. From there he travels 'eastward and still eastward through the stale streets' (*ED* 23.256). This clause, not even a whole sentence, is important, because it is the only time we see Jasper walk London. He differs in this crucial manner from de Quincey's opium-influenced *flâneur* in the *Confessions*, who 'makes the streets a phantasmagoria' (Hollington 1981: 76).

Jasper finally 'reaches his destination: a miserable court, specially miserable among many such' (*ED* 23.256) – scant descriptive prose – and when he enters, Puffer recognises his condition as a case of 'the all-overs' (23.206). Smoking opium, Jasper converses in a dream state, recalling 'a journey, a difficult and dangerous journey [. . .] over abysses where a slip would be destruction'. This is a journey that has been made 'hundreds of thousands of times', 'so often, and through such vast expanses of time, that when it was really done, it seemed not worth the doing, it was done so soon' (23.260). Simultaneously a contraction and expansion of space and time, a 'period' which inflates impossibly (as in the manuscript version of 'The Dawn'), this 'journey' which cannot take place may refer to the moment of the murder, with the event 'foreclosed' to Jasper (Tambling 2015: 216–17). But it is also a question of space, as he makes clear in the previous sentence, saying 'I did it [the journey] here hundreds of thousands of times' (*ED* 23.260), situating it as something that takes place in the den. This is confirmed by the clarification Puffer immediately suggests, 'That's the journey you have been away upon', or rather 'remarks' upon, since it is not phrased as a question, and which Jasper affirms. More specifically, this journey is defined by repetition, 'always in one way' (*ED* 23.260). Puffer reads the journey as the narcotic trip, saying 'you come o' purpose to take the journey' (*ED* 23.261), but remains aware that Jasper does not take it alone. He agrees:

> 'To think,' he cries, 'how often fellow-traveller, and yet not know it! [. . .]'
> [. . .]
> 'Yes! I always made the journey first, before the changes of colours and the great landscapes and glittering processions began. They couldn't begin till it was off my mind. I had no room till then for anything else.' (*ED* 23.261)

'Glittering processions' recalls the 'glorious processions' of Lazarus (Parkinson 1866: 425), so that the journey figures the entrance to the dream state, with its vibrant 'colours' and 'great landscapes'. But these 'glittering processions' also recall those of Cloisterham Cathedral, so that 'The Dawn Again' repeats 'The Dawn', first Jasper's dream and then its simulacrum, which is to say, the 'real' events of that evening when Jasper takes up his place in the procession at Cloisterham Cathedral.

When the vision begins to subside, Jasper considers it 'too short and easy', with 'no struggle, no consciousness of peril, no entreaty' (*ED* 23.263). But 'The Dawn Again' is not a repetition without a difference, for Jasper starts, marking something that he had never seen before. The object that has caught his attention is never made clear in the novel, but Jasper's description is telling: 'Look at it! Look what a poor, mean, miserable thing it is! *That* must be real' (*ED* 23.263). Reality is 'poor, mean, miserable' when compared to the dream. Eventually, Jasper leaves the den, returning to Cloisterham, although this time followed by Puffer. There we see the dawn again, 'a brilliant morning [that] shines on the old city', which seems to suggest an idea of renaissance, a 'glorious light' 'penetrat[ing] into the Cathedral, subdu[ing] its earthy odour, and preach[ing] the Resurrection and the Life' (*ED* 23.270). But 'earthy' in this novel connotes death, not life, and cannot be 'subdued', so that we cannot shake the feeling that this 'real' event of the dawn is not the one that the chapter title had referred to. The 'theoretical' gesture is bathetic, undercutting any implied Christian idea of spiritual rebirth.

Indeed, it is precisely the sense in which the spaces of this novel speak to aesthetic repetition, rather than theoretical insight, that is the lasting impression of *Edwin Drood*. In the throws of his opium ecstasy, Jasper exclaims 'When it comes to be real at last, it is so short that it seems unreal for the first time' (*ED* 23.261). This is a phrase which may describe the foreclosed moment of murdering his nephew, but which equally well sums up the novel's aesthetics of space. Indeed, Jasper's comment also describes the experience of reading not only 'The Dawn Again' but also, necessarily, 'The Dawn', which from its very first images offers only *aesthesis*. In this sense, when we encounter the 'unreal' vision in 'The Dawn Again', we recognise it as a repeated experience, and we remember that in 'The Dawn', Cloisterham Cathedral is itself 'unreal', first seen in the vision, so that, when it is encountered in 'reality' at the end of the chapter, what is real is 'unreal'. Moreover, since the cathedral stands for history, 'Englishness' and a stable sense of the past, it is precisely this kind of 'reality' which has become 'unreal'. Dickens's last novel is fascinated less by the 'realism' of seeing what lies beneath the housetops than by the ways in which late nineteenth-century metropolitan space mobilises desire to deterritorialise itself as 'dream space'. It is for this reason that we find that when Cloisterham Cathedral appears in the final paragraph of 'The Dawn', finally encountered as 'real at last', 'it seems unreal for the first time'.

Notes

1. For Adorno on late style, see 2002: 564–8. See Hutchinson 2016: 257–73 and Spencer 2016: 220–34, and more broadly on Adorno and 'lateness', see Jameson 2007.
2. For one reading of *Edwin Drood* that emphasises the sense in which it constitutes a response to his earlier work and riposte to realism, see Meckier 1987: 153–200. The 'late Dickens' becomes particularly marked after his survival of the Staplehurst rail crash, 9 June 1865: in this sense, lateness is partly biographical, as Edward Said has argued (2017). For one interesting attempt to link the early and late Dickens, see Cockshut 1962, although I would dispute his suggestion that *Edwin Drood* sees Dickens's styles 'reconciled'. Rather, following Adorno, I would argue that Dickens's lateness is characterised by a style which 'embod[ies] the contradictions [. . .] in its innermost structure' (1967: 32).

3. When he arrived in Genoa in 1844, he bemoaned the fact that his copy of the *Seven Lamps* had been delayed at customs, suggesting that this work was a significant presence for the younger Dickens (Johnson 1952: 514). My thanks to Wendy Nakanishi for helping me locate this reference.
4. Ruskin did not even own a copy of the novel (Dearden 2012: 93–4), although his allusion to the novelist's 'jackdaw sentiment for cathedral towers' (*CW* 37: 7), possibly suggesting *David Copperfield* (2004: 16.235, 39.570), may also suggest he was reading *Edwin Drood* at the time of Dickens's death, reacting partly against it.
5. On the significance of the inability to locate the shop, see Tambling 2009: 86–94.
6. On the differences between reading such a map on the 'macroscopic' and 'microscopic' levels, see Moretti 1998: 76–9.
7. Dickens had published George Dodds's (1808–81) articles on the Opium Wars in *Household Words* (1 August 1857, 104–8; 22 August 1857, 181–5), and years earlier, he would have encountered Henry Morley's (1822–94) romanticised portrait of opium smoking drawn in 'Our Phantom Ship' (*Household Words*, 28 June 1851, 325–31). On opium consumption during the period, see Berridge and Edwards 1981.
8. A 'contrapunctal' reading would find the traces of the opium trade throughout Dickens: beyond *Bleak House*'s Nemo, see for instance Xu 1997, reading *Little Dorrit*. In *Our Mutual Friend*, John Harmon is drugged with opium and when Bella and her father leave London for Greenwich, they sit in a tavern watching the ships bound for China 'to bring back opium' (1997: 2.8.315). As Hollington notes, Dickens's allusions to opiates operate as a 'persistent theme whose dimensions are primarily sociological rather than psychological' (1984: 232).
9. Perhaps also a biblical allusion: Lazarus's name implies the figure whom Jesus brings back to life, and who walks out of his burial cave with 'hands and feet wrapped with strips of linen, and a cloth around his face' (John 11: 44).
10. In this, Fildes's illustration follows from the original sketches by Charles Collins (1828–73), reproduced in Raven 2000: 119. On Collins and Fildes, see Cohen 1980: 210–28.
11. In this sense, Rochester Cathedral contrasts aesthetically with the mismatch of St George in the East, Gothic in outline, but with classical ornamentation. Nevertheless, if Hawksmoor's church lies behind the vision, Jasper's confusion is not wholly inexplicable: the cathedral's current spire was erected in 1904, with its nineteenth-century tower crenellated, as was the tower of St George in the East. Given this fact, the skylines might have been more easily mistaken during the Victorian period, particularly given the context of Jasper's state of mind.
12. For more on this allusion, previously unnoted, see Whiteley 2018a.

13. Southey has 'scymitar' with the 'y', an exotic spelling the *OED* shows dying out at the end of the Romantic period, around 1832. But perhaps a trace of Southey's 'y' was retained somewhere in Dickens's mind when he wrote the plans for *Edwin Drood*. The manuscript of projected names and titles has a number of jarring 'ys' jumping out from his list of the projected draft names of his eponymous hero: 'Edwyn' (four times) and 'Selwyn'. Perhaps this 'y', which marks Southey's scimitar as Oriental, and which typographically gives a cutting, a violence in the text, was insisting somewhere in Dickens's mind even at the planning stage.
14. Dickens owned the 1818 two-volume edition of Southey's poem (Stonehouse 1935: 103), and he read the epic in 1839 (*LCD* 1: 640), but we cannot be sure if or when he reread it. However, we can be sure that Dickens was rereading Southey while writing *Edwin Drood*, with the name of Dickens's murderer seemingly based on his reading of the ballad 'Jaspar' (1798): see Shatto 1985.
15. Indeed, while Southey's epic fell from critical view for many years, it had been highly thought of, at least by his fellow poets. Coleridge obviously borrows from the *Curse of Kehama* in 'Kubla Khan' (1816), and the young Percy Bysshe Shelley (1792–1822) considered it exemplary, taking imagery from this very same incident of the massacre of the thousand archers in his 'A Retrospect of Times of Old' (c. 1812) (ll. 37–8). In other words, Dickens may well have reasonably expected readers of *Edwin Drood* to have got the allusion.
16. Jerrold's retrospective (1870) recalls meeting Dickens in May, a month before he passed away, when he asked after Doré.
17. Freud sees this kind of brooding at work in Leonardo da Vinci (*SE* 11: 78–9), in an analysis which may recall Pater (*SHR* 97). Freud was aware of Pater's essay, citing it in his work (*SE* 11: 68, 110, 111).
18. For more on sex in the novel, see McKnight 2013.
19. As Lacan argues with reference to Aristotle (2007b: 23), the 'master's discourse' of *theoria* simultaneously produces the *objet a* as surplus *jouissance* in spite of itself (what he calls elsewhere *Mehrlust*, and associates with capitalism, comparing with Marx's *Mehrwert*, surplus value).
20. Before *No Thoroughfare* (1867), co-written with Collins, Dickens had considered the title for what became *Our Mutual Friend*.
21. On the dates suggested by Dickens's various modes of transport, see Paroissien in his edition of *ED*, 307–8.
22. It was only with the introduction of railway time that time was standardised across Britain: the Great Western Railway adopted GMT in November 1840 and the rest of the country gradually followed suit. But if *Edwin Drood* is set in 1846, Cloisterham would not yet have standardised with London, meaning that the loss of the cathedral clock marks a loss of temporal reference.

Chapter 3

Walter Pater: Towards an Aesthetics of Space

In a piece published in the *Speaker*, 26 August 1899, an undergraduate recollected a meeting 'In Pater's Rooms', Old Lodge 4 and 5, Brasenose College, Oxford, dating to sometime between 1892 and Pater's death in 1894. 'F' recalls the interior being decked out in the trappings of an aesthete, with stencilled walls, cushions, table covers and curtains all shades of blue, accented by white books, natural woods and polished brass.[1] This interior space compared with the view from Pater's window:

> The room was small, but the Gothic window with its bow enlarged it, and seemed to bring something of the outside Oxford into the chamber [. . .] The Radcliffe just a few hand-breadths from the pane, the towers and crockets of All Souls beyond, and to the right the fair dream of St. Mary's spire, filling up the prospect with great suggestions – [. . .] and they seemed for the moment to become almost the furniture of the student's chamber. (1899: 207)

Figure 3.1 Walter Pater's rooms, Brasenose College: Gothic window

Figure 3.2 Walter Pater's rooms, Brasenose College: view of the Radcliffe Camera

Figure 3.3 Walter Pater's rooms, Brasenose College: view of All Souls

Whereas Ruskin argues in *Modern Painters* that window frames are extrinsic to aesthetic contemplation, 'a vague, flitting, obscure interruption to whatever is perceived beyond it' (*CW* 3: 320), for 'F', the focus of Pater's room was the window, which 'frames' Oxford outside. Pater's fictional writings are replete with examples of windows that allow communion between spaces, so that the relations of inside and outside become permeable, as well as examples of how architecture can frame the world as art. His own rooms thus played out the architectonics so memorably sketched in the infamous 'Conclusion' to his *Renaissance*, in which the exterior and interior worlds reflect one another as two modes of flux (*SHR* 186–8). But what is perhaps most striking for our purposes is the immediate presence of Oxford: framed by a Gothic window, the first view is of the Radcliffe Camera, designed by James Gibbs (1682–1754) and built in 1737–49 in English Palladian style; east across Radcliffe Square, All Souls College and the crockets of the Codrington Library, designed by Hawksmoor and built in 1716–51 in his idiosyncratic Gothic style; south of Radcliffe Square, St Mary's, with its famous Gothic spire, dating to the 1320s, a 'fair dream' to the undergraduate spectator, recalling Arnold's description of Oxford's 'dreaming spires' (l. 21) in 'Thyrsis' (1865). Pater's rooms were located in the architectural centre of Oxford: it contextualised his workspace and informed his writing.

There was perhaps no writer who was more attuned to the aesthetic power of space in the later nineteenth century than Pater. In his fiction, as well as in his essays, place and space shape the characters he portrays, particularly in his imaginary portraits. But as the leading figure of British aestheticism during the period, Pater is a significant figure for thinking through the tradition of the aesthetics of space, not simply given his marked interest in both space and questions of the aesthetic, but insofar as he engages with Ruskin's distinction between *theoria* and *aesthesis*. As Harold Bloom puts it, Ruskin had been Pater's 'prophet of the eye' (1974: 168), but his own mode of vision developed into something which placed an emphasis on the sensuous and the body in a manner that Ruskin would not have admitted, at least consciously. This chapter begins by analysing Pater's debt to Ruskin, Pater's reply to Ruskin's ideas on the Gothic and qualifications regarding *theoria*, before discussing various different ways in which Pater's own aesthetics of space operates. The chapter examines the ways in which space determines the aesthetic sensibility, concluding with an analysis of Pater's treatment of metropolitan space in *Marius the Epicurean*.

After Ruskin

Pater's relationship with Ruskin is difficult to reckon.[2] For Bloom, it was marked by an anxiety of influence, explaining the lack of open acknowledgement of debt in Pater's published and unpublished work (1974: 181–2). Certainly, there was something of a professional rivalry there. In a letter to H. J. Nichols, 28 November 1881, Pater refers to his essay on Sandro Botticelli (1445–1510), tersely remarking that it was 'the first notice in English of that old painter. It preceded Mr. Ruskin's lectures on the same subject by I believe two years' (*LWP* 41). Ruskin, for his part, had been reading Pater's essay in 1872, but seemingly did not know the author's name, calling him simply 'an Oxford man'.[3] This relative anonymity was perhaps unsurprising. Pater had gained a classical fellowship at Brasenose in 1864, but Ruskin would return to Oxford as the first Slade Professor of Fine Art in 1869. Without question, it was Ruskin who was the pre-eminent force in Oxford during this period, although things would soon shift: a year after this dismissive reference, Pater's name would have been impossible to forget, when his signature appeared on the *Renaissance*. When Wilde entered Oxford in 1874, he felt the pull of Ruskin and Pater equally strongly (Ellmann 1988: 46), and Pater's reputation was so great by the mid-1880s that, when Ruskin announced his resignation of the Slade Professorship in 1884, Pater put his name forward as arguably the outstanding candidate, although hostility from above meant he withdrew from consideration. Still, as a young man in the 1860s, Pater had been deeply inspired by Ruskin (Wright 1907: 1: 232), as we can see in one of his unpublished imaginary portraits, 'An English Poet' (c. 1878). Following the artistic development of its protagonist, one of Pater's many autobiographical projections, this particular poet discovers inspiration in a series of nineteenth-century English writers, including the 'master of imaginative prose who might seem to bear on his single shoulders the whole Alpine world with no detail missing from root to crest' (*IP* 151), an allusion to the fourth volume of *Modern Painters* (1856).[4] And while Pater would move away from Ruskin in the later 1860s and 1870s as he forged his new aesthetic doctrine, his appreciation for Ruskin's achievements remained (Wright 1907: 2: 23).

Indeed, the debt that Pater owed Ruskin is clearest in his treatment of the Gothic, perhaps unsurprisingly given the situation of his rooms at Brasenose.[5] Broadly speaking, Pater agrees with Ruskin in recognising the historical, political and spiritual significance of Gothic architecture, although he would also subtly and consistently problematise Ruskin's idealism. Pater's final published essays before his death were a pair dealing with 'Some Great Churches in France' on 'Notre-Dames d'Amiens' and 'Vézelay', appearing in the *Nineteenth Century* in March and June 1894 respectively, intended to form the beginnings of a series, with a further study of 'Notre-Dames de Troyes' left among his unpublished manuscripts.[6] The topic takes up what Erwin

Panofsky (1892–1968) calls the 'visual logic' that informed medieval social practice and produced new forms of space (1951: 58). As Lefebvre comments, this logic went 'far beyond Gothic architecture and involves the towns, political action, poetry and music, and thought in general' (*PS* 260).

Dealing with 'the greatest and purest of Gothic churches' (*MS* 109), 'Notre-Dames d'Amiens' never mentions Ruskin by name but finds itself in dialogue with *The Bible of Amiens* (1884). For Ruskin, the cathedral's Gothic is 'clear of Roman tradition, and of Arabian taint; Gothic pure, authoritative, unsurpassable, and unaccusable' (*CW* 33: 121–2), but while Ruskin considers this a spiritual question, Pater links its 'purity' to the city's 'civic pride', allowing Amiens to promote 'the new, revolutionary Gothic manner, at the expense of the derivative and traditional, Roman or Romanesque, style' (*MS* 110). Little wonder that in his translation of Ruskin's work Proust complained with some impatience as to 'why Ruskin's name is never once mentioned' in Pater's essay (Ruskin 1926: 250; Proust 1987: 83). For Pater, Notre-Dames d'Amiens ranks as one of the first examples of pointed style, 'monuments for the most part of the artistic genius of laymen' (*MS* 110), and he emphasises the sense in which the cathedral was designed both structurally and aesthetically to be a communal space: 'Light and space – floods of light, space for a vast congregation, for all the people of Amiens, [. . .]; – you see at a glance that this is what the ingenuity of the Pointed method of building has here secured' (*MS* 111; compare *CW* 33: 122–3). This 'enlightening' of the space precisely corresponds to Panofsky's 'visual logic' (*PS* 259). Like Ruskin in *The Stones of Venice* and Mr Grewgious in *The Mystery of Edwin Drood*, so too Pater invites us to the western door of the cathedral to take in the spectacle, from where

> at one view the whole is visible, intelligible; – the integrity of the first design; how later additions affixed themselves thereto; how the rich ornament gathered upon it; the increasing richness of the choir; its glazed triforium; the realms of light which expand in the chapels beyond; the astonishing boldness of the vault, the astonishing lightness of what keeps it above one; the unity, yet the variety of perspective. (*MS* 113)

Pater's style here itself constitutes an aesthetics of space, imitative of its subject, a form of architectural writing in which the semi-colons literally build up an image of the structure that lies before the reader's eyes. It recalls the sense in which Pater considers all writing a form of 'literary architecture' (1910a: 20), and style a question of 'stately and regular word-building' (*ME* 1: 1.6.97), a motif which, as Frank has noted, was inherited from Ruskin and became influential on Proust (1979: 17–49). Indeed, this essay sees Pater arguably at his most Ruskinian. Like Ruskin, he holds that 'in architecture, close as it is to men's lives and their history, the visible result of time is a large factor in the realised aesthetic value' (*MS* 118), accentuating the mnemonic dimension of the Gothic that Ruskin had championed in *The Seven Lamps of Architecture* (*CW* 8: 221–47). Likewise, Pater holds that 'a false restoration only frustrates the proper ripening of his work' (*MS* 118; compare *CW* 10: 434–7). Moreover, Pater considers the pointed style an appreciation of 'the freshness as of nature itself, seen and felt for the first time', compared to which 'those older cloistral workmen had but fed their imagination in an embarrassed, imprisoned, and really decadent manner' (*MS* 119). So while Ruskin is never named in the text, his presence is consistently guiding Pater's eye as the prior aesthetic trace which makes the cathedral legible. But if Notre-Dames d'Amiens offers itself to be read as a Bible, for Pater, unlike Ruskin, it is 'an open Bible', 'a book about men and women, and other persons equally real' (*MS* 199). In other words, Amiens is a work of what Ruskin would call 'Naturalism' proper (*CW* 10: 215). Pater, like Ruskin, recognises that in the person of the Gothic workman, 'art has at last become personal', and claims that 'the artist, as such, appears [. . .] in the thirteenth century' (*MS* 120). But unlike Ruskin, Pater links this freedom to the classical spirit, considering the workman at Amiens 'no longer a Byzantine, but a Greek – an unconscious Greek' (*MS* 120).[7]

In his unfinished novel, *Gaston de Latour* (1888), Pater again takes up a dialogue with Ruskin on the Gothic. Something of a sequel to *Marius*, 'dealing with the same problems under altered historical conditions' (*LWP* 65), the novel follows its protagonist's intellectual journey during the period of the Wars of Religion in sixteenth-century France. The narrative is situated in the context of the topography of France, spreading from the north to 'that south-west country of peach-blossom and wine' (*GL* 2.56), where the architecture as well as the contours of the land itself changes (*GL* 4.77), recalling Ruskin's mapping of European space, climate and temper in *The Stones* (*CW* 10: 184).[8] *Gaston* begins in the country of La Beauce, 'the great corn-land of central France' (*GL* 1.37), located between the Seine and Loire rivers, and the 'abode' of the Latour family, 'the work, in large measure, of Gaston [. . .] left unfinished at his death, some time about the year 1594' (*GL* 1.37). In what may be read as an autobiographical comment on Pater himself and on his relationship with Ruskin, we are told that Gaston was 'an enemy of all Gothic darkness or heaviness', and that upon his return many years later, 'full of a later taste' (*GL* 1.39), he sought to modify the Gothic of his home town and particularly his local church of Saint Hubert (Pater's invention):

> A thicket of airy spires rose above the sanctuary; the blind *triforium* broke into one continuous window; the heavy masses of stone were pared down with wonderful dexterity of hand, till not a hand's-breadth remained uncovered by delicate tracery, [. . .] not a space was left unsearched by cheerful daylight, refined, but hardly dimmed at all, by painted glass mimicking the clearness of the open sky. (*GL* 1.39)

This later taste would have been defined in some measure by the Renaissance, with French society then 'somewhat distraught by an artificial aesthetic culture', 'filled with wild passions, and wildly dramatic personalities', and offering 'a scene already singularly attractive for aesthetic beauty' (*GL* 1.44).

Aged about twelve, Gaston travels to Notre-Dame de Chartres, that cathedral which Huysmans would write so memorably about in *La Cathédrale* (1898). Entering through its 'great western portal', Gaston discovers that 'it was a world to explore, as if one explored the entire Middle Age; it was also one unending, elaborate, religious function – a life, or a continuous drama, to take one's part in' (*GL* 2.50). As Lefebvre notes, entering a Gothic cathedral means 'plung[ing] into a particular world, that of sin and redemption', which also implies an 'ideology' (*PS* 221). But most notable is Gaston's particular mode of appreciating the Gothic, less a question of 'scale' or of spiritual 'impression', than something else:

> The somewhat Gothic soul of Gaston relished there something strange, or even bizarre, in the very manner in which the building set itself, so broadly couchant, upon the earth; in the natural richness of tone on the masonry within; in its vast echoing roof of timber, the 'forest', as it was called; in the mysterious maze traced upon its pavement; its maze-like crypt, centering in the shrine of the sibylline Notre-Dame, itself a natural or very primitive grotto or cave. (*GL* 2.50)

Perhaps in this emphasis on the Gothic 'bizarre', Gaston already recognises the sense in which humanity itself is 'gothic', the human mind 'like the grotesques which some artists of that day loved to joint together' (*GL* 5.86). And while Pater was working on the novel as late as 1893, the year before he died, he did not live to finish *Gaston*, and so we can only speculate as to how this love of the Gothic 'bizarre' might have played out. Still, from the clues in the first chapter regarding Gaston's belated return home and modification of Saint Hubert, we may assume that he would gradually find the influence of what Ruskin calls the 'Grotesque Renaissance' (*CW* 11: 133–95) making greater and greater claims on him.[9]

Gothic architecture also plays a prominent spatial role in Pater's imaginary portraits, a number of which are set in the Middle Ages, or in cities defined by their Gothic heritage. In 'Denys l'Auxerrois' (1886), Pater's narrative is set in thirteenth-century Auxerre, the narrator beginning by surveying the French countryside, discussing Auxerre's architecture alongside that of Troyes and Sens, as 'each gathered, as if with deliberate aim at such effect, about the central mass of a huge grey cathedral' (*IP* 4.81). Troyes's Cathédrale Saint Pierre et Saint Paul is 'visible far and wide over the fields' (*IP* 4.82), 'gathering' space in Lefebvrean terms, its Gothic marked as '*Flamboyant*' or late, with its streets carrying 'a peculiar air of the grotesque, as if in some quaint nightmare of the middle age' (*IP* 4.82). Pater's italicisation of 'flamboyant' implies the French, and elsewhere Pater would translate the term as 'gothic "flamings"' (*GL* 3.67), but it had been incorporated into English by Edward Augustus Freeman (1823–92), Regius Professor of History, in *An Essay on the Origin and Development of Window Tracery in England*, published in 1851.[10] In its late style, the Gothic of Troyes compares with that of Sens's Cathédrale Saint Étienne, which is marked instead with 'an almost English austerity' (*IP* 82). The narrator notes the similarity to Canterbury Cathedral, a space Pater knew well, having been schooled in the city in 1853–8; both churches were partly designed by William of Sens (?–1180). The 'severity' of its style associates the cathedral with a disciplinarity which seems to be proper not simply to the Gothic in general, but more specifically to the English Gothic, and which may also pass something of a subtle comment on Ruskin. It recalls Pater's later imaginary portrait, 'Emerald Uthwart' (1892), the first half of which, following Emerald's education, was based on Pater's experiences at King's School, Canterbury. Its Gothic has 'something of the discipline, of monasticism' about it, 'gravely magnificent' (*IP* 179), where Pater's use of the adjective also suggests a sense of death.[11] Like the stones of Dickens's Cloisterham, the school's walls are 'a composite of minute dead bodies' (*IP* 259). In this imaginary portrait, Emerald's eye is drawn to another 'dreaming spire', the 'Angel's steeple' of

Canterbury Cathedral, dating to the sixteenth century, through which 'everything seems challenged to follow the upward lead of its long, bold, "perpendicular" lines' (*IP* 179–80). This sense of the vision being challenged is key: 'The very place one is in, its stonework, its empty spaces, invade you; [. . .] – challenge you, so to speak, [. . .] to systematise your vagrant self; which however will in any case be here systematised for you' (*IP* 180). The subject recognises themselves as being 'hailed' in the disciplinary gaze, and in answering the challenge is interpellated, becoming precisely a 'subject' (Althusser 2008: 47). The Gothic is ideological, 'mould[ing] all who enter [. . .] to a perfect, uninquiring, willing or unwilling, conformity to itself' (*IP* 180). Such are its panoptic dreams. And for Pater, there is a beauty in all this discipline, 'the beauty of the *ascêsis* (we need that Greek word) to which he not merely finds himself subject, but as under a fascination submissively yields himself' (*IP* 181).[12] This kind of 'submissive' 'fascination' with power, experienced as a kind of pleasure, suggests Pater's masochism.

In 'Denys l'Auxerrois', Auxerre too is defined by the Gothic, 'the three great purple tiled masses of Saint Germain, Saint Pierre, and the cathedral of Saint Étienne, rising out of the crowded houses'. 'Here, that rare artist, the susceptible painter of architecture, if he understands the value alike of line and mass of broad masses and delicate lines, has "a subject made to his hand"' (*IP* 83), Pater remarks, quoting Robert Browning's (1812–89) 'A Light Woman'(1855) (l. 56).[13] Pater's narrative focuses on the influence of the character of Denys upon the community, which is then invested in the completion of the cathedral's great tower.[14] This building project has an explicitly communal and political connotation:

> Auxerre had its turn in that political movement which broke out sympathetically [. . . in] the towns of France, turning their narrow, feudal institutions into a free, communistic life – a movement of which those great centres of popular devotion, the French cathedrals, are in many instances the monument. (*IP* 85)

The passage compares with one in his essay on 'Notre-Dames d'Amiens' in which Pater points out that this cathedral likewise was the product of the towns rising 'against the feudal establishment', developing 'the local and municipal life of the commune' (*MS* 109). It is an idea that Pater derives, at least in part, from Eugène Viollet-le-Duc (1814–79), who maintained a 'rationalistic' interpretation of the French Gothic. He is cited twice in the essay on 'Vézelay' (*MS* 135, 138), and quoted silently in 'Notre-Dames d'Amiens' when Pater comments that, 'strange as it may seem, in this "queen" of Gothic churches, *l'eglise ogivale par excellence*, there is nothing of mystery in the vision' (*MS* 112).[15] Ruskin had also read Viollet-le-Duc, quoting 'deservedly' his appreciation of Notre-Dames d'Amiens as 'The Parthenon of Gothic Architecture' (*CW* 33: 121), and referring to his work appreciatively in *Praeterita* (*CW* 35: 384).[16] But Ruskin appears to have been less impressed with Viollet-le-Duc's secular emphasis, which reads the Gothic as the style which produces social rather than spiritual space. In this, Pater differs from Ruskin, for while the 'nature of the Gothic' is a question of politics for both of them, for Ruskin this politics is explicitly Christological, whereas for Pater it is a question of another form of community.

In the figure of Denys, working on the construction of Saint Étienne, Pater gives us something of a version of Ruskin's ideal workman. He carved 'unconsciously', expressing his own individuality 'with the chisel', but Pater's portrait also suggests the limitations of Ruskin's idealised view of the medieval artist. Denys begins in 'wild gaiety, exuberant in a wreathing of life-like imageries', his work indicative of Ruskinian 'Naturalism', that kind of realist aesthetic 'from which nothing really present in nature was excluded' (*IP* 92). But 'as the soul of Denys darkened', his work 'passed into obscure regions of the satiric, grotesque and coarse' (*IP* 92). Pater's phrasing suggests Ruskin's distinctions between the 'noble grotesque' and its 'ignoble' forms, already discussed with reference to Dickens. More specifically, it recalls the ways in which Ruskin sees the Renaissance develop an interest in what he calls the 'satirical grotesque', which results 'from the malice of men given to pleasure, and in which the grossness and foulness are in the workman as much as in his subject' (*CW* 11: 176). In context, we can see that Denys undermines Ruskin's idealistic understanding of the ways in which the medieval workman's soul may be impressed into the Gothic. Like Gaston's preference for the Gothic 'bizarre', Denys's soul is not simply 'noble', but inflected with the Dionysian.[17]

A similar critique of Ruskin's idealism is also discernible in 'Apollo in Picardy' (1893), the last imaginary portrait Pater published before his death. This narrative turns on the story of Prior Saint-Jean, who, leaving his monastery in medieval France, travels to the Carthusian monastery of Chartreuse Notre-Dame des Prés in Neuville-sous-Montreuil (now Pas-de-Calais), taking with him a younger companion, Hyacinthus; there they meet Apollyon, a version of the god Apollo in exile, a motif borrowed from Heinrich Heine (1797–1856) (Harrison 1924). It is an encounter which sends the Prior insane, and the narrative has been read as a complex meditation by Pater on the legacy of the 'monkish' (Jean) Ruskin, who had himself gone insane five years beforehand (Keefe 1986). If this is indeed somewhere in Pater's mind, it suggests that the power of the Gothic lies in its sanity, the way in which its disciplinarity stabilises the subject and its desires. But this sanity is also a form of imprisonment, and Pater puns on the Prior's 'inner cell' (*IP* 201), as he does in 'Emerald Uthwart' (*IP* 178), with both allusions recalling the image of the solipsistic dreaming 'prisoner' of the 'Conclusion' (*SHR* 188). In this sense, if the Prior is a partial portrait of Ruskin, he is also something of a partial portrait of Pater himself (Shuter 2001),[18] and the monastery in which the Prior first begins the narrative figures as an image of Oxford:

> He [. . .] was grown almost as necessary a part of the community as the stones of its material abode [. . .] The structure of a fortified medieval town barred in those who belonged to it very effectively. High monastic walls intrenched the monk still further. From the summit of the tower you looked straight down into the deep narrow streets, upon the houses [. . .] climbing as high as they dared for breathing space within that narrow compass. But you saw also the green breadth of Normandy and Picardy, this way and that; felt on your face the free air of a still wider realm beyond what was seen. (*IP* 200)

Far from providing the kind of spiritual release that Ruskin identified in the Gothic, the architecture limits the free expression of the subject's desire, just as Oxford's conservative culture sought to regulate Pater's own desire. The city is fortified from outside and encloses those within, its streets claustrophobic. Indeed, in the 'freedom' of the countryside, having come under the influence of Apollyon, the Prior begins to experiment architecturally on the construction of a barn for the community. This project marks precisely the sense in which Lefebvre argues that modern forms of space 'emerged' in Western Europe during the Middle Ages, that moment when 'abstract' gave way to 'secular' space (*PS* 256). The countryside, hitherto populated by spaces of 'unnatural magic' (*IP* 203), what Lefebvre calls 'demonic' and '"heterotopical" places' of 'sorcery and madness' (*PS* 263), gains a new sense of spatiality through its Gothic cathedrals, which become focal monuments to Christianity, ones which also serve a politicising function. But this particular barn possesses 'a sort of classical harmony in its broad, very simple proportions, with a certain suppression of Gothic emphasis' (*IP* 204), most notably of the buttress. Ruskin considers the buttress a key compositional strength of the Gothic (*CW* 9: 202–10), noting that the feature is less favoured in the architecture of the Venetian 'fall' (*CW* 9: 248). In context, Pater's description suggests the ways in which the Prior begins to anticipate the Renaissance, if only 'unconsciously', just as Denys had in Auxerre. For the Prior, the structure marks 'a welcome contrast [. . .] to the sort of architectural nightmare he came from' (*IP* 279–80), a development 'not so much of style as of temper' (*IP* 204).

In this sense, while we say that Pater broadly follows Ruskin in his writings on the Gothic by situating it historically and politically, and by recognising it as an aesthetic expression of the individual workman's soul, we also see in these portraits enough of a critique to suspect something significant at issue between the two. Indeed, in *Marius*, Pater had made clear a crucial distinction between their positions. Pater's novel was conceived as offering a reply to misunderstandings of his earlier aesthetic philosophy and particularly that 'Conclusion' to the *Renaissance* which he had suppressed in the second edition (1877) for fear 'it might possibly mislead some of those young men into whose hands it might fall', only to reinstate it in the third edition (1888) by stating that he had 'dealt more fully in *Marius the Epicurean* with the thoughts suggested by it' (*SHR* 186). Following the intellectual development of its eponymous protagonist living in the Rome of the Antonines, the novel sees Marius continually testing new philosophical theories in an effort to find one which does justice to his own aesthetic appreciation of life. In one of the central chapters, with the events dating to when he is around nineteen years old, Marius evaluates the old Cyrenaic philosophy in a prelude to developing his 'New Cyrenaicism':

> How earnest and enthusiastic, how true to itself, under how many varieties of character, had been the effort of the Greeks after Theory – *Theôria* – that vision of a wholly reasonable world, which, according to the greatest of them, literally makes man like God. (*ME* 1: 2.8.140)

Marius's speculations here are clearly rooted in Greek intellectual history, and in *Plato and Platonism* (1893), his late series of lectures on the subject, Pater makes clear the ways in which, for 'the greatest of them', namely Plato, 'all gifts of sense and intelligence converge in one supreme faculty of theoretic vision, *θεωρία*, the imaginative reason' (1910f: 140). Nevertheless, even given this explicitly classical context, there is little doubt that Pater's Victorian readers would have immediately recognised another figure underwriting this discussion: Ruskin. But Pater's version of *theoria* differs subtly from that of Ruskin, for what Pater was seeking was a very special kind of 'vision':

> To be absolutely virgin towards [. . .] experience, by ridding ourselves of such abstractions as are but the ghosts of bygone impressions – to be rid of the notions [. . .] that so often only misrepresent the experience of which they profess to be the representation – *idola*, idols, false appearances, [. . .] to neutralise the distorting influence of metaphysical system by an all-accomplished metaphysic skill. (*ME* 1: 2.8.141)

Pater alludes here to the problem that, misunderstood, Epicureanism 'may perhaps open a wide doorway to human weakness' (*ME* 1: 2.8.141), that unscholarly version of 'hedonism' which he was at pains to try to dissociate from his own aestheticism.[19] It was this distinction which underwrote Pater's dissatisfaction with Wilde's Dorian, whom he deemed 'a quite unsuccessful experiment in Epicureanism' (Beckson 1998: 85). But while acknowledging this point, Pater also suggests a limitation in Ruskin's version of *theoria*. For Pater, Ruskin's idea is too closely associated with his Christianity, the Greek concept morphed out of recognition. Such a rebuke of Ruskin is of added significance given the fact that in *Modern Painters*, nearly thirty years beforehand, he had made absolutely clear the relative merits of Christian and Epicurean *theoria* as he understood them: 'the Christian *Theoria* seeks not, though it accepts and touches with its own purity, what the Epicurean sought; but finds its food and the objects of its love everywhere, in what is harsh and fearful as well as in what is kind' (*CW* 4: 50). Pater would consider this treatment of Epicureanism far too one-sided, but he would also dispute this reading of *theoria* more broadly. For Pater, Ruskin's uncritical assumption of Christianity as the model of 'theoretical' truth made his *theoria* the organ of precisely the sort of dominating moral system or 'unverified hypothesis' which would make too much of a claim upon the aesthete (*ME* 1: 2.9.149).

In this sense, Pater's allusion to Ruskinian 'idols' in this passage foreshadows Proust. For Ruskin, 'idolatry [. . .] is no encourager of the fine arts' (*CW* 10: 131), constituting 'not the mere bowing down before sculptures, but the serving or becoming the slave' of them (*CW* 10: 451). But for Proust, Ruskin was guilty of precisely this kind aestheticist idolatry (Karlin 2005: 30–1). Proust makes the arresting comparison between Ruskin and the symbolist painter Gustave Moreau, so influential on Huysmans's des Esseintes (*AR* 5.123–5; 63–4) and the 1890 incarnation of Wilde's Dorian (*DG* 9.124). For Proust, both Ruskin and Moreau are susceptible to 'a certain fetishism in the worship of the symbols themselves' (Ruskin 1926: 64; Proust 1987: 39):

> Ruskin never ceased to commit the sin of idolatry. At the very moment that he was preaching sincerity, he was himself lacking in it, not by what he said, but the way in which he said it. The doctrines he professed were moral doctrines and not aesthetic doctrines, and yet he chose them for their beauty. And since he did not wish to present them as beautiful but as true, he was forced to deceive himself about the nature of the reasons that made him adopt them. (Ruskin 1926: 79–80: Proust 1987: 50–1)

In this percipient analysis, Proust shows the ways in which *theoria* was always liable to slip into *aesthesis*, a 'fall' which we have discussed in reading Ruskin's aesthetics of Venetian space. For Proust, the beauty of Ruskin's style – that which first attracted the young Pater to read him so appreciatively – not only ended up overwhelming the matter at hand, but speaks to unconscious desires to which Ruskin was unable to admit.[20]

For Pater, Epicureanism is primarily a visual doctrine, which provides

> insight [. . .] into all that the present moment holds in trust for us, as we stand so briefly in its presence. From that maxim of *Life as the end of life,* followed, as a practical consequence, the desirableness of refining all the instruments of inward and outward intuition, of developing all their capacities, of testing and exercising one's self in them, till one's whole nature became one complex medium of reception, towards the vision [. . .] of our actual experience in the world. (*ME* 1: 2.8.142–3)

Most significantly, *theoria* does not stand in opposition to *aesthesis* for Pater, as it had for Ruskin, but must be particularised through aesthetic appreciation. It is precisely on the question of the body that the two diverged. Marius ranks the body as 'the highest potency of all the beauty of material objects' (*ME* 1: 1.6.92), and later in the novel, he considers the stoicism of Marcus Aurelius (AD 121–80) to be 'theoretically' compromised by 'some flaw of vision' with respect to his 'contempt' for the body, 'some diseased point of thought' (*ME* 2: 3.18.54). In this sense, it is ironic that Ruskin explicitly appeals to Plato when justifying his use of the Greek word (*CW* 25: 123–4), for in Pater's reading, Plato's *theoria* is not simply 'bodily', but a question of erotic desire. In Plato, 'the sensuous lover becomes a lover of the invisible, but still a lover, after his earlier pattern, carrying into the world of intellectual vision, of *θεωρία*, all the associations of the actual world of sight' (Pater 1910f: 146). Moreover, in this Platonic association of *theoria* with the 'sensuous lover', one must bear in mind the Greek context: this vision eroticises first and foremost the athletic male body, as Pater would do in his late essay on 'The Age of Athletic Prizemen' (1894). This homoeroticism is something which Pater intends to mobilise, so that his eroticisation of Ruskin's *theoria* is also a 'queering' of it.[21] Ruskin, on the other hand, seeks to efface the body, extricating *theoria* from its Greek context, part of his war on the 'decadence' of *aesthesis*. So whereas Ruskin sought to distinguish sharply between two supposedly distinct 'faculties', Pater showed the ways in which *theoria*, when placed in a classical rather than Christian context, itself constituted *aesthesis*, grounded in aesthetic appreciation and the body.

Spaces of Beginning and Ending: Homes, Morgues, Crypts

For Pater, the home has a special place in the narrative of the aesthetic education of the subject. Writing before Freud and Gaston Bachelard (1884–1962), he anticipates them both in understanding home as the space which roots the subject: for Pater, the aesthetic sensibility is first formed through an aesthetics of space. Three Paterean homes in particular deserve consideration: that of his first imaginary portrait, 'The Child in the House' (1878); Marius's ancestral home, *White-nights*; and Cecilia's house in *Marius*.

'The Child in the House' is one of Pater's most autobiographical works, describing the house in which he lived as a young boy in Enfield, Middlesex. In *Modern Painters*, Ruskin argues that a child, shorn of 'all conventional and authoritative thoughts', is best placed to experience *theoria* (*CW* 4: 77–8), but for Pater, it is the faculty of *aesthesis* that is peculiarly keen in the child. In this, he anticipates Lefebvre, who argues that only young children can truly live in representational spaces (*PS* 50). The portrait begins with the protagonist, Florian Deleal, meeting an old man who 'chanced' to name 'a little place in the neighbourhood of a great city', where Florian 'had passed his earliest years' (*IP* 133). Later, Florian dreams of the place 'with a great clearness, yet, as sometimes happens in dreams, raised a little above itself, and above ordinary retrospect' (*IP* 133). The dream gives reality a heightened aesthetic touch, 'with tints more musically blent on wall and floor, and some finer light and shadow running in and out of its curves and angles, and with all its carvings daintier' (*IP* 133). The portrait becomes a recollection both of the house and of the 'story' of Florian's 'spirit' (*IP* 133). Documenting the 'aesthetic education' of the child and the objects which make up the texture of their reality, Pater shows how space and subject become intertwined, 'inward and outward being woven through and through each other into one inextricable texture' (*IP* 133).

The 'aspirational' motif so intrinsic to Ruskin's writing, discussed in Chapter 1, is recalled in the ways in which Florian initially traverses his dream house, moving from the ground floor up the staircase until he arrives at the roof:

> The old-fashioned, low wainscoting went round the rooms, and up the staircase with carved balusters and shadowy angles, landing half-way up at a broad window, with a swallow's nest below the sill, and the blossom of an old pear-tree showing across it in late April, against the blue, below which the perfumed juice of the find of fallen fruit in autumn was so fresh. At the next turning came the closet which held on its deep shelves the best china. Little angel faces and reedy flutings stood out round the fireplace of the children's room. And on the top of the house, above the large attic, where the white mice ran in the twilight – an infinite, unexplored wonderland of childish treasures, glass beads, empty scent-bottles still sweet, thrum of coloured silks, among its lumber – a flat space of roof, railed round, gave a view of the neighbouring steeples. (*IP* 134)

The topography recalls the ways in which Bachelard, in the first chapter of *La poétique de l'espace* [*The Poetics of Space*] (1958), moves from cellar to garret. Pater's focus is on the sensuous, and 'The Child in the House' becomes a document of 'the rapid growth' of his 'capacity of fascination by bright colour and choice form', 'the lust of the eye' (*IP* 137; quoting 1 John 2: 16), *aesthesis* rather than *theoria*. In the passage where Florian first maps the house, the chiaroscuro, the strong colours, the focus on scent and perfume, give a kind of aesthetic phenomenology of space.[22] The house is full of curiosities, the china, the beads and bottles, rich and sensual objects: they are aesthetic effects, objects in which the wishes and desires of the child are invested. These curiosities 'reverberate' in the subject's memory, as Bachelard writes, so that they precipitate 'resonances, sentimental repercussions, reminders of the past' (1994: xxiii). Such a phenomenology reminds us of the *mémoire involontaire* of *À la recherche du temps perdu* [*In Search of Lost Time*]

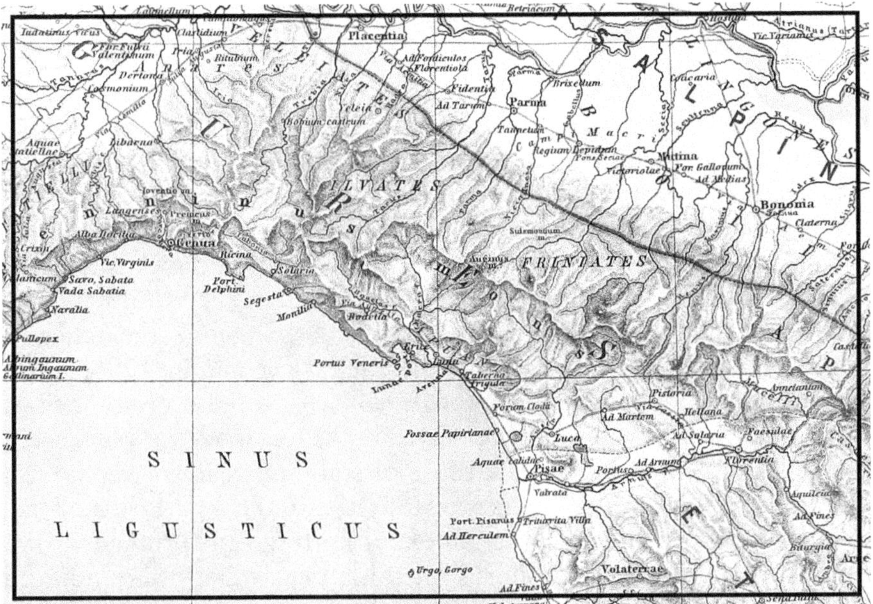

Figure 3.4 Liguria

(1913–27), and the unacknowledged debt that Proust owes to Pater, the former having read a number of Pater's works, including the posthumous *Miscellaneous Studies* (1895) which featured 'The Child in the House'.[23] Thinking topographically and recalling the sense in which Pater considers the human body a work of architecture (*IP* 205), the 'infinite, unexplored wonderland' of the attic suggests the space of the imagination, so that Pater's image anticipates Carl Jung's (1875–1961) famous dream house (1989: 158–9). By extension, the spaces that lie below the surface (cellars, crypts) connote the unconscious and death.[24] Certainly, such spaces are 'psychic' (*PS* 186), but, grounded in the subject's memories, they are nevertheless also 'real' and 'lived'.

The home of 'The Child in the House' can be compared to *White-nights*, Marius's ancestral villa, another dream space (*ME* 1: 1.2.14).[25] As Lefebvre has shown, the Roman villa represents 'the concretization, within agro-pastoral space, of a codified, law-bound spatial practice, namely private ownership of the land', and 'emerges' precisely in the period of Rome's 'decadence' as a 'generator' of a new kind of spatiality built around the abstract principle of property (*PS* 252). Located on the slopes south of Luna in today's Liguria, *White-nights* has a view east towards 'the pallid crags of Carrara' in northern Tuscany, and west across the Riviera towards Portus Veneris (today Portovenere), with 'the lighthouse temple of *Venus Speciosa* on its dark headland, amid the longdrawn curves of white breakers' (*ME* 1: 1.2.20). There, Marius can see the 'freight of white marble going to sea', marking the port as a mercantile centre and implying subtly the space of imperialism. It foreshadows already the ways in which *Marius*, a historical novel which maps in detail the space of second-century Italy, also maps nineteenth-century Britain.[26] Pater's narrator remarks that travellers would pause 'to read the face, as it were, of so beautiful a dwelling place' (*ME* 1: 1.2.19). The motif implies prosopopoeia (Greek: *πρόσωπον*, 'face'), and suggests the sense in which the home may be read as allegorical (Benjamin 1998: 166), so that *White-nights* stands metonymically for a sense of security or 'homeliness', a 'dwelling place'. 'Dwelling' foreshadows Heidegger, for whom *Wohnen* connotes a sense of stability, peace or repose, an emotional 'attachment' to a place (1977a: 146–7). By Marius's time, *White-nights* presents itself as 'an exquisite fragment', ruined with a 'graceful wildness', possessing 'something pensive, spell-bound, and but half real' (*ME* 1: 1.2.20).

Both the '*White-nights*' chapter of *Marius* and 'The Child in the House' chart the ways in which the aesthetic sensibility is formed not only through childhood cathexes, but also insofar as the sanctity of these 'homes' becomes violated. In Pater's historical novel, it is Marius's ophidiophobia that produces this change:

> One fierce day in early summer, as he walked along a narrow road, he had seen the snakes breeding, and ever afterwards avoided that place and its ugly associations, for there was something in the incident which made food distasteful and his sleep uneasy for many days afterwards. (*ME* 1: 1.2.23)

Psychoanalytically, the snake figures the threat of castration, as in Freud's reading of 'Das Medusenhaupt' (1922), and we have already been told that *White-nights* is famous for its 'head of Medusa' (*ME* 1: 1.2.19).[27] In Lacanian terms, castration is the price paid for entry into the symbolic order, contrasting with the image of a home that offers the prelapsarian fantasy of wholeness, of a subject not inscribed by lack. Later in his life, we are told that in Pisa, Marius 'came upon an African showman exhibiting a great serpent' (*ME* 1: 1.2.23), and again, 'that at Rome he saw, a second time, a showman with his serpents' (*ME* 1: 1.2.24). In both, the associations simultaneously connote the sense of the city's cosmopolitanism and the space of the Empire as producing an anxiety of that which lies without or beyond. Similarly, in 'The Child in the House', it is the presence of the metropolitan which initially produces this sense of violation in Florian. The house neighbours a 'great city', with distant steeples visible from the roof, and 'high walls' partitioning the space inside from 'the gloom and rumours of the town' (*IP* 135). Always present in the background, the city haunts the 'homely' space, as London ghosts Cloisterham in *Edwin Drood*. Through an open window enter 'two streams of impressions, the sentiments of beauty and pain' (*IP* 137), that bring with them the consciousness of death, as when Florian walks in a neighbouring churchyard:

> In a bright dress he rambled among the graves, [. . .] and so came, in one corner, upon an open grave for a child – a dark space on the brilliant grass – the black mould lying heaped up round it, weighing down the little jewelled branches of the dwarf rose-bushes in flower. And therewith came, full-grown, never wholly to leave him, [. . .] the physical horror of death, with its wholly selfish recoil from the association of lower forms of life, and the suffocating weight above. (*IP* 142)

The strong imagery of the 'dark space' contrasted with the 'brilliant grass' and the 'jewelled branches' marks the experience as an aesthetic one. It links Pater's aestheticism with the death-drive, so that death adds intensity to aesthetic experience. For Florian, the 'desire of physical beauty mingled itself early [with] the fear of death – the fear of death intensified by the desire of beauty' (*IP* 141). This is a realisation that leads him to recall later experiences at the morgues of Paris and Munich.

Before discussing these passages in more detail, we must consider the extent to which Pater, writing after Ruskin, is also writing after Dickens. Pater owes more to Dickens than one might initially suspect, particularly given the dismissive and elitist tone of his (reported) complaint to his friend Richard Charles Jackson (1851–1923) that Dickens was 'a monument to wasted energy, but then he wrote for the unlettered' (Wright 1907: 2: 116).[28] Still, while a schoolboy at King's, Pater was apparently 'forcibly attracted' by Dickens's 'story-telling power' and 'humour' (Wright 1907: 1: 123), and he would later write appreciatively of Dickensian humour in his 1878 essay on Charles Lamb (1775–1834) (1910a: 106). Pater also revelled in the fact that King's was the model for Dr Strong's school in *David Copperfield*. With his friends John McQueen and Henry Dombrain, Pater eagerly read *Little Dorritt*, just then being serialised, the three of them 'often making merry, as they walked together in the Precincts, over Flora Finching and Mr. F.'s Aunt' (Wright 1907: 1: 124). Moreover, Pater's style obviously owes something to Dickens as well as to Ruskin. In an 1886 review article for the *Guardian*, Pater meditates on one of his persistent concerns, the possibility of writing a 'poetic' prose which might best represent the contemporary age, 'the wild mixture of poetry and prose, in our wild nineteenth century, under the influence of such writers as Dickens and Carlyle' (1910b: 6). So while Pater may have come to have issues with Dickens's 'realism', his own contributions towards crafting an English 'decadent' style must be contextualised as being, in part, a response to the novelist.

Without question, Pater's discussion of the spaces of the Paris and Munich morgues should be read in the context of Dickens and Zola:

> Hitherto he had never gazed upon dead faces, as sometimes, afterwards, at the *Morgue* in Paris, or in that fair cemetery at Munich, where all the dead must go and lie in state before burial, behind glass windows, among the flowers and incense and holy candles – the aged clergy with their sacred ornaments, the young men in their dancing-shoes and spotless white linen – after which visits, those waxen, resistless faces would always live with him for many days, making the broadest sunshine sickly. (*IP* 141)

To a Victorianist, what is perhaps most arresting in this passage is the way it treats the Paris Morgue as incidental. Built in 1867 and located on Île de la Cité, the Morgue replaced the 1804 one, a casualty of Haussmannisation (located on Quai du Marche Neuf). As Vanessa Schwartz has argued, the Morgue was conceived from the outset as a 'mass' and 'spectacular' space (1999: 45–88), and crowds of people came to visit, whether to identify the bodies or simply for the sake of 'curiosity'. Most famously, the Morgue features in *Thérèse Raquin* (1867), where Zola remarks that it was 'a sight within reach of everybody, and one to which passers-by, rich and poor alike, treat[ed] themselves' (1984: 13.105; 2008: 76). Dissolving class distinctions, the Morgue became part of the wider experience of the nineteenth-century city, implying the 'anonymity' of the crowd, linking voyeur to *flâneur*. It consisted of rows of metal benches on which the bodies lay, with water dripping onto them to preserve the corpses, their clothes hung on hooks behind. Viewers were separated from the bodies by a plate-glass window, which in the later Morgue was accented by curtains. In this sense, the bodies were literally staged for the gaze of the spectators. Unsurprisingly, the Morgue became a well-known tourist destination during the period, not only popular with Parisians, but noted by the French for the huge numbers of British visitors

(Vita 2003: 241). Every guidebook from *Baedeker's* to *Murray's* featured a paragraph on the Morgue, and by the time that Pater published 'The Child in the House' in 1878, the Morgue had featured in a great deal of British literature, most notably in Browning's 'Apparent Failure' (1864) and in Dickens's journalism. Forster remarks that Dickens 'went at first rather frequently to the Morgue, until shocked by something so repulsive that he had not courage for a long time to go back' (1966: 1: 445), but eventually he did return, drawn there irresistibly, the space marked by the compulsion to repeat. As the uncommercial traveller puts it, 'whenever I am at Paris, I am dragged by invisible force into the Morgue. I never want to go there, but am always pulled there' (*UT* 88). The experience is uncanny, as was the theatrical spectacle of the corpses. Dickens remarks in 'Some Recollections of Mortality' (*All The Year Round*, 16 May 1863) that the Morgue's bodies look like 'waxworks' (*UT* 223), as Pater also remarks in 'The Child in the House' (*IP* 141), and Freud notes the waxwork's uncanniness, imitating life at a distance (*SE* 17: 225).[29]

In chapter 13 of *Thérèse Raquin*, Laurent watches some young boys gratify their lust while looking at dead female flesh (1984: 13.107; 2008: 77), and the eroticism of the Morgue is something that Benjamin discusses (*PW* 410–11; L3,3). 'Overcome by revulsion and horror' (1984: 13.104; 2008: 75), Laurent nevertheless admits to 'strange pleasure' in the sights, fascinated in particular by a woman who was 'provocatively offering her bosom to his gaze' (1984: 13.105; 2008: 75), giving the corpse agency. 'Strange pleasure' again implies the death-drive, as does Laurent's 'strange attraction' to the space (1984: 13.107; 2008: 77). This emphasis on the erotic is marked aesthetically by the luxurious sensualism of Zola's language, that excessive quality which, as we have seen, Auerbach considers proto-aestheticist and a quintessential element of naturalism, marking it off from earlier nineteenth-century realism (2003: 497–9). But for his part, there appears to have been something about the Morgue which could not quite satisfy Pater's 'curiosity', perhaps owing to the fact that it was a 'mass' space of consumerism and commodification. Zola notes how 'the glass screen which separated the onlookers from the corpses' (1984: 13.103; 2008: 74) recalls the arcades, the visitors inspecting the bodies 'as if they were staring in the window of a fashion store' (1984: 13.106; 2008: 76). Consumerism is linked to Laurent's necrophilic gaze: sexual and commodity fetishism alike empty the object of life, an eroticisation of that which is dead. In 'Railway Dreaming' (*Household Words*, 10 May 1856), Dickens also makes the analogy: 'the bodies lie on inclined planes within a great glass window, as though Holbein should represent Death, in his grim

Dance, keeping a shop, and displaying his goods like a Regent Street or Boulevard linen-draper' (1998: 375). As Tambling argues (2009: 55), Dickens's allusion to Holbein makes the corpse allegorical, and links allegory to the commodity and fashion to death in a move that is precisely Benjaminian. In 'Travelling Abroad', the uncommercial traveller strolls in the Palais Royal, 'lazily enjoying the shop windows' (*UT* 91), when images of a corpse he had earlier viewed at the Morgue overwhelm him: the fetish is not simply the dead object in which the subject has invested, but the presence of death has become something which insists in the commodity. Interestingly, Dickens associates this sense of being 'haunted' by the Paris Morgue with 'the intensity and accuracy of an intelligent child's observation', both of which produce 'fixations' (*UT* 91). Pater, for his part, also registers the 'haunting' quality of the faces which lived with him 'for many days, making the broadest sunshine sickly' (*IP* 141), and links it to a moment of fixation in the development of the child.

The Morgue, then, was a loaded space, but what is arresting in Pater's portrait is that, regardless of whether he is thinking of the old or new Morgue,[30] he alights in Paris only briefly, instead immediately displacing the scene to 'that fair cemetery at Munich', the Alter Südfriedhof. This relocation is important: it moves the events from a 'mass' space, associated with tourism and consumerism, to one which was far less well known during the period. There seems to have been only one allusion to the Munich cemetery in the travel literature of the period predating Pater's portrait, in Murray's *Handbook for Travellers in Southern Germany* (1871), where it receives only one, parenthetical line.[31] Likewise, Munich was not yet a site for Anglophone literature: Pater's imaginary portrait predates Mark Twain's (1865–1910) visit to the cemetery in 1879 by a year, and Twain's short story, 'A Dying Man's Confession' (1883), in which it featured, by five years. In its relative anonymity, the space it figures is a more exclusive destination for an aesthete, offering the possibility of a more personal appreciation: solitude, time, contemplation. And this kind of experience is captured by Pater's famously measured and elongated prose style, his syntax marked by those rich subordinate clauses, those pauses for additions and amendments which 'arrest' time and death in a moment of 'insight' in the instant of aesthetic appreciation.[32]

In *Marius*, it is Cecilia's house which offers a moment of aesthetic 'arrest'. The location is introduced in the final part of the book, opening with two chapters on 'Two Curious Houses'. The first is Cicero's villa at Tusculum, where he had penned the *Tusculanae Disputationes* (c. 45 BC), and where Marius travels to meet Apuleius:

> he mounted to the little town on the hillside, [. . .] under shadow of the 'haunted' ruins of Cicero's villa on the wooded heights. He found a touch of weirdness in the circumstance that in so romantic a place he had been bidden to meet the writer who was come to seem almost like one of the personages in his own fiction. (*ME* 2: 4.20.76)

The scene suggests Pater's late Romanticism (Hutchinson 2016: 178–85), as does his comment that the 'wild country figures' of the Latium countryside 'inclined him to poetry' (*ME* 2: 4.20.77). It recalls an earlier allusion, comparing the Ligurian peasantry to Wordsworth's 'common man' (*ME* 1: 1.1.5). As Stefano Evangelista reminds us, Pater's Rome was 'consciously modelled on the city of the Romantic imagination', with Marius himself resembling a sentimental traveller (2012: 321; Vance 1997: 213–16). But this scene in particular is 'weird' for two other reasons. Firstly, there is the uncanny sense of repetition in meeting Apuleius, a figure whom he feels as though he already knows, having read the so-called 'golden book' *Asinus Aureus* earlier in the novel. There, Apuleius stands for 'modernity', comparing with Gaston's discovery of Pierre de Ronsard's (1524–85) *Odes* (1550), and both standing in relation to Baudelaire's *Les fleurs du mal*, published when Pater was eighteen, about the age when his two protagonists discover their respective texts.[33] Secondly, meeting Apuleius in such a space is weird because he is a foreigner, a Numidian living under Roman rule. Marius notes in Apuleius 'a piquancy in his *rococo*, very African', which gives him a kind of 'perfumed personality' (*ME* 2: 4.20.85). It is partly this status as an outsider that marks his decadence and produces 'modernity' as the conjunction of the cosmopolitan and the Empire.

If Cicero's villa is 'weird', marked both by a Romanticism which is resistant to the city and by a visitor who makes this a foreign space at home, the second 'curious house', Cecilia's, offers a 'strange contrast' (*ME* 2: 4.21.92). Marius is returning towards Rome accompanied by his friend, Cornelius, a soldier of the Twelfth Legion and a Christian. As a soldier, he represents Rome's imperial power, as well as an 'ordered' understanding of the space of the city (*PS* 244); as a Christian, he represents the sense in which the representational space of Rome 'founds' that of Christianity (*PS* 245). The two are travelling along the Via Latina:

> The seemingly endless line of tombs and cypresses had been visible for hours against the sky towards the west; and it was just where a cross-road from the Latin Way fell into the Appian, that Cornelius halted at a doorway in a long, low wall – the outer wall of some villa courtyard. (*ME* 2: 4.21.94)

'The Queen of Ways', as the narrator notes later, was 'in reality the favourite cemetery of Rome' 'closely crowded, in every imaginable form of sepulchre' (*ME* 2: 4.24.142). Many of Pater's readers may have thought of Giovanni Battista Piranesi's (1720–78) 'Appian Way', the frontispiece for the second volume of his *Le antichità romane* [*Antiquities of Rome*] (1756), which images the road in a baroque fantasy, teeming with towering structures, teetering and toppling, accented by cypresses and smoking perfume, the Pyramid of Cestius in the background, the whole scene one of decadence and ruin. But Pater's interest is less in funereal absolute space (*PS* 235) than in what lies behind it: coming to a doorway, Marius and Cornelius slip 'into the court or garden of a villa [. . .] the spaciousness of which surprised Marius [. . .], being thus wholly concealed from passengers along the road' (*ME* 2: 4.21.95). Cecilia herself is the widow of a Christian martyr, marking Marius's first encounter with this new religion. Her house, built out of 'the fragments of older architecture', which, when 'juxtaposed', became 'aesthetically, very seductive' (*ME* 2: 4.21.96), stands as an image of Christianity itself – predicated on the idea of rebirth and composed out of earlier religious practices. Being in the house awakens Marius's 'old native susceptibility to the spirit, the special sympathies, of places' (*ME* 2: 4.21.96), and memories of *White-nights*.

Wandering through the house, Marius comes to a flower garden at the rear, bound by a 'low, grass-grown hill':

> A narrow opening cut in its steep side, like a solid blackness there, admitted Marius [. . .] into a hollow cavern or crypt, neither more nor less in fact than the family burial-place of the Cecilii, to whom this residence belonged, brought thus, after an arrangement then becoming not unusual, into immediate connexion with the abode of the living. (*ME* 2: 4.21.98)

This crypt reworks the representational spaces of ancient Roman culture: 'the realm of the dead, chthonian and telluric forces, the depths and the heights' (*PS* 231). But if the immediate comparison is with the funeral monuments on the Via Appia, Marius finds this space unlike any cemetery he had previously seen, with its 'long, apparently endless, yet elaborately designed galleries, [. . .] increasing so rapidly': 'Originally a family sepulchre, it was growing to a vast necropolis, a whole township of the deceased, by means of some free expansion of the family interest beyond its amplest natural limits' (*ME* 2: 4.21.99). It rests on the idea of 'immediate connexion' between life and death, like the Heideggerean *mundus* (*PS* 242), and anticipates the ways in which the nineteenth century saw cemeteries as 'the "other city" where each family possessed its dark dwelling' (Foucault 2000a: 181). This space has an 'air of venerable beauty' (*ME* 2: 4.21.99), which differs from that of the Morgue. Pater associates that experience, whether at Paris or Munich, at least partly with 'what French writers call the *macabre* – that species of almost insane pre-occupation with the materialities of our mouldering flesh, that luxury of disgust in gazing on corruption', as he puts it earlier in *Marius* (*ME* 1: 1.5.60). And if the image of the necropolis, a space which lies beneath the structures of the surface, may recall Dickens's vision of the 'labyrinths' beneath Rome (2003i: 11.137), they serve a very different purpose in Pater's historical novel. For Dickens, these substructures 'undermine' the visions of the surface, speaking of the unconscious that cannot be brought to light.[34] Cecilia's crypt, by contrast, is defined by 'visibility' (*ME* 2: 4.21.103). Of course, Marius is not simply converted, for as he notes 'it was still [. . .] to the eye, to the visual faculty of mind, that those experiences appealed' (*ME* 2: 4.21.106); in other words, he is not a Christian, still fascinated first and foremost by the aesthetic qualities of experience. But this is precisely what Pater means by *theoria*. He gives us an aesthetics of space that is not doctrinal, but curious, sympathetic and, above all, bodily, attuned to beauty wherever the eye may alight.

The Aesthetics of Metropolitan Space in *Marius the Epicurean*

In 1869, Pater moved from his college rooms north to 2 Bradmore Road, Oxford. He became neighbours with another Fellow of Brasenose, Thomas Humphry Ward (1845–1926), and his more illustrious wife, the novelist Mary Augusta Ward (1851–1920), author of *Robert Elsmere* (1888), and niece of Matthew Arnold. She remembered the house as being

> 'Paterian' in every line and ornament. There was Morris paper; spindle-legged tables and chairs; a sparing allowance of blue plates and pots, bought, I think, in Holland [. . .]; framed embroidery of the most delicate design and colour, the work of Mr. Pater's elder sister; engravings, [. . .] from Botticelli, or Luini, or Mantegna; a few mirrors, and a very few flowers, chosen and arranged with a simple yet conscious art. I see that room always with the sun in it, touching the polished surfaces of wood and brass and china, and bringing out its pure bright colour. (1918: 1: 165)

This was a period of turmoil in Oxford, turmoil which would soon embroil Pater. The bishop preached against his 'Conclusion' from the pulpit at Christ Church Cathedral; a year earlier, Pater had been caught in a compromising relationship with a young male undergraduate, William Money Hardinge (1854–1916), and Benjamin Jowett (1817–93), Regius Professor of Greek and Master of Balliol, blackmailed Pater out of running for promotion (Inman 1991). Oxford was suffocating him; he found it 'impossible [. . .] to escape the ruts of convention' (Wright 1907: 2: 41).

Born a cockney in Stepney, Pater returned to London in August 1885, renting a house with his sisters at 12 Earls Terrace, Kensington. Sir Charles John Holmes (1868–1936), a student of Pater's at Brasenose and later Slade Professor, recalled two different men, the spaces reflected in their respective appearances: at Oxford, Pater's 'hair was left to grow rather long, his moustaches to droop, his walk was a paddle', whereas in Kensington, 'he tripped along in a smart top-hat and black jacket, with stiff clipped moustache, neatly rolled umbrella and dog-skin gloves' (1936: 102). In the West End, Pater socialised with literary figures including Henry James, Vernon Lee, Arthur Symons, and Frank Harris (1855–1931), but he also travelled around the churches of the East End on Sundays, in search of aesthetic effects (Wright 1907: 2: 34). Jackson recalls Pater's interest in the interior spaces of these churches:

> He delighted in high altars banked with flowers – the arum, the narcissus, the jonquil – innumerable candles forming a pyramid of points of fire, priests in transplendent copes stiff with gold, incense rising in swelling clouds, bells ringing, genuflections. (Wright 1907: 28–31)

In his reminiscences, 'F.' recalls that Pater discussed modern architecture as well as his love of the Gothic, and 'instanced as nearest to perfection St. Philip's Church, which lies behind the London Hospital. What led Water Pater to ill-odoured Whitechapel I cannot guess' (1899: 208). No doubt it was one of these Sunday pilgrimages that first took him to that site, built by Arthur Cawston (1857–94), completed in 1892.[35] Given that F.'s audience with Pater must have occurred after the publication of Wilde's *Dorian Gray*, which had made very clear the decadent attractions that East London might provide, his question speaks of either wilful or strategic ignorance, but his suggestion was that the East End was no fit place for the aesthete.

Still, the '*urbanity*' (*IP* 135) of metropolitan space is an insistent presence in Pater's work, with the city associated with decadence.

The young Gaston speaks of 'the presence and perfume' of the capital (*GL* 2.57), with readers perhaps thinking more of modern Paris than the city preparing to celebrate St Bartholomew's Day 1572, when the narrator describes it as 'adorned' 'if with something of artifice [. . .], almost to illusion' (*GL* 6.101–2). Pater was also aware of the different claims that city and natural spaces respectively might make upon aesthetic judgement. Reviewing Ward's translation of Henri-Frédéric Amiel's (1821–81) *Fragments d'un journal intime* (1884), Pater sounds like Ruskin discussing Turner in 'The Two Boyhoods' when remarking that aesthetic pleasure derived from an appreciation of space becomes more remarkable 'when [. . .] we feel that there has been, and with success, an intellectual effort to get at the secret, the precise motive, of the pleasure' (1910b: 25–6), before he quotes Amiel's description of 'an effect of fog, which we commend to foreigners resident in London'. Fog has 'a poetry of its own – a grace, a dreamy charm', an 'elegiac' quality that marks it off from an experience of reality (1910b: 26; quoting Amiel 1885: 215), and marks the writing of such spaces as 'poetical' in its distance from 'realism'.

Read as a nineteenth-century novel, *Marius* certainly seems to be a riposte to the realism that was dominant during the period. If the nineteenth century was the great age of historical novels, and a period when an awareness of historicity defined a new sense of what it meant to be a subject during the period, as both Auerbach (2003: 458–9) and Georg Lukács (1885–1971) (1983) have argued, then the spatiality of Pater's historical novel differs markedly from that which was typical. In comparison to works such as Edward Bulwer-Lytton's (1803–73) *The Last Days of Pompeii* (1834) or Charles Kingsley's (1819–75) *Hypatia* (1853), *Marius*'s strong centripetal pull makes the novel more realist, at least in terms of structure (Moretti 1998: 33); more contemporary in its plotting, as with Dickens's young men who are dragged towards the capital as Marius is drawn to Rome. The protagonist's first taste of metropolitan life, however, is in Pisa, fifty kilometres north from Luna along the shore:

> The partly decayed pensive town [. . .] had lent, at one time the vivid memory of its fair streets of marble, at another the solemn outline of the dark hills of Luna on its background, at another the living glances of its men and women, to the thickly gathering crowd of impressions, out of which his notion of the world was then forming. (*ME* 1: 1.4.44–5)

Enrolled in an Academy in the suburbs, Marius finds the 'decayed' town awakening his sense of decadence: he had 'yielded himself [. . .]

to the seductions of that luxurious town', marking his 'early corruption' (*ME* 1: 1.4.52–3). Most significantly, Marius finds amongst 'the urbanities, the graceful follies' of Pisa that 'it was the reality, the tyrannous reality, of things visible that was borne in upon him' (*ME* 1: 1.4.47). Decadence is linked precisely with *aesthesis*, with metropolitan space awakening a new mode of vision.

Following the death of his school friend Flavian from the Antonine plague, an event that prompts Marius's first major reconsideration (his 'New Cyrenaicism', which involved Pater's rereading of Ruskin on *theoria* and *aesthesis*), he determines to move to Rome to act as amanuensis to the Emperor Marcus Aurelius. He travels 'by the byways among the lower slopes of the Apennines of Luna, to the town of Luca' (*ME* 1: 2.10.159), before 'surrender[ing] himself, a willing subject, as he walked, to the impressions of the road' (*ME* 1: 2.10.160). Marius takes the Via Cassia, 'where the figures and incidents of the great high-road seemed already to tell of the capital, the one centre to which all were hastening' (*ME* 1: 2.10.161), a marker of imperial power, the Roman road linking 'the *urbs* to the countryside over which it exercises dominion' (*PS* 245). The route takes him through 'the heart of the old, mysterious and visionary country of Etruria' (*ME* 1: 2.10.161), whose earlier civilisation had been subsumed by the rise of Rome, and Marius muses on 'its strange religion of the dead, reinforced by the actual sight of the funeral houses scattered so plentifully among the dwelling-places of the living' (*ME* 1: 2.10.161).

The ruins of this older civilisation contrast with more modern ones Marius sees as he draws closer to Rome. Earlier in the novel, we have been told that the Antonine plague had been brought in the 'train' of Lucius Verus (AD 130–69) returning 'from the East' and the Marcomannic Wars (AD 166–80) (*ME* 1: 1.7.111), an Oriental motif that adds to the sense of decadence. The narrator notes that 'in Rome itself many thousands perished', with 'whole towns, and even entire neighbourhoods' lapsing 'into wildness or ruin' (*ME* 1: 1.7.112). With farms 'less carefully tended than of old' and villas also 'partly fallen into ruin', the narrator notes that 'the picturesque, romantic Italy of a later time – the Italy of Claude and Salvator Rosa – was already forming, for the delight of the modern romantic traveller' (*ME* 1: 2.10.163). The allusion is to Claude Lorrain (1600–82) and Salvator Rosa (1615–73), the latter of whom painted *Marius meditating among the ruins of Carthage* (c. 1650), both of whom were famous for their romanticised images of the Italian landscape, populated by peasantry and scattered ruins. The Italian 'picturesque', something that fascinates James in the essays collected in *Italian Hours* (1909), and a quality that he writes against in *The American Scene*, is here imaged through the baroque, and both are seen to be the result of a historical trauma leaving its traces on both the space and its aesthetics. Pater's point is that an aesthetics of space, when read carefully, is found to be always already historical and political, linking *aesthesis* and *theoria*, recalling the ways in which ruins are associated elsewhere in Pater's fiction with war.[36]

In *Marius*, this image of the ruined landscape is precisely a sign of 'decadence'. After he has arrived in Rome and met Aurelius, Marius considers the city's 'melancholy grandeur' and associates it with a sense of death, 'all that was monumental in that city of tombs' (*ME* 1: 2.12.200). Aurelius himself is a baroque thinker, able to 'discern a death's-head everywhere' (*ME* 1: 2.12.201), recalling Benjamin, who notes that 'everything about history [. . .] that has been untimely, sorrowful, unsuccessful' is expressed in 'a death's head' (1998: 166). These thoughts which associate Aurelius and Rome's decadence lead Marius to 'forsee [*sic*]' a vision of 'the ruins of Rome', 'a grass-grown Forum, the broken ways of the Capitol, and the Palatine hill itself in humble occupation' (*ME* 1: 2.12.200). It is an image that Pater himself would have seen when he visited Rome in 1882 to research the novel, but in context, it turns Marius into an Antonine version of Balzac, a man whom Benjamin credits with being able to see 'the monuments of the bourgeoisie as ruins before they have crumbled' (*SW* 3: 44). For Marius, this 'impression connected itself with what he had already noted of an actual change even then coming over Italian scenery' (*ME* 1: 2.12.200).

At Urbs Vetus, today's Orvieto in Umbria, Marius first meets Cornelius, who is returning from campaign to take up his quarters on the Palatine. The two travel together for a few days until 'Rome was seen at last'. 'It was dark, before they reached the *Flaminian* Gate' (*ME* 1: 2.10.170), north of the city on the east bank of the Tiber, so that Marius's first impressions of the metropolis must wait. Awaking the next morning, he considers himself 'fortunate in the time of his coming to Rome', which had just 'reached its perfection in the things of poetry and art – a perfection which indicated only too surely the eve of decline' (*ME* 1: 2.11.172). The point recalls Gibbon, and by extension, given the intended ways in which Pater's Rome is placed into dialogue with modern London, Ruskin on the fall of Venice. Marius has arrived precisely at the tipping point, the present moment auguring the Sack, 'the enemy on the Danube [. . .] but the vanguard of the mighty invading hosts of the fifth century' (*ME* 2: 3.17.29). Marius likens Rome to 'some vast intellectual museum', with the majority of its great buildings still intact (*ME* 1: 2.11.173).[37] The idea once again combines a classical and a Victorian perspective. In *Middlemarch* (1871–2), George Eliot had called Rome 'the city of visible history, where the past of a whole hemisphere seems moving in funeral procession with strange ancestral images and trophies gathered from afar' (2003: 2.20.192). Freud plays on a similar idea in *Civilization and Its Discontents* (1930), comparing the past of the mind with the past of the city (*SE* 21: 69–71). In Antonine Rome, the past survived as 'antique, quaint, immeasurably venerable, like the relics of the medieval city in the Paris of Lewis the Fourteenth', preserved as the 'picturesque' (*ME* 1: 2.11.173). Marius likens the older Rome, predating Emperor Nero's (AD 37–68) rebuilding efforts following the Great Fire of AD 64, to the Gothic, which the Sun King, Louis XIV (1638–1715), promoted in France. The connotations suggest Rome as a space of curiosity, but also of death, as in Adorno, for whom museums are 'the family sepulchres of works of art' (1967: 175). And reading Rome as a museum anticipates the figure of Marcus Aurelius himself, who is a collector (*ME* 1: 2.12.204), and who later determines 'to sell by auction the accumulated treasures of the imperial household' (*ME* 2: 3.17.35) to fund his expedition against the Iazyges, AD 169.

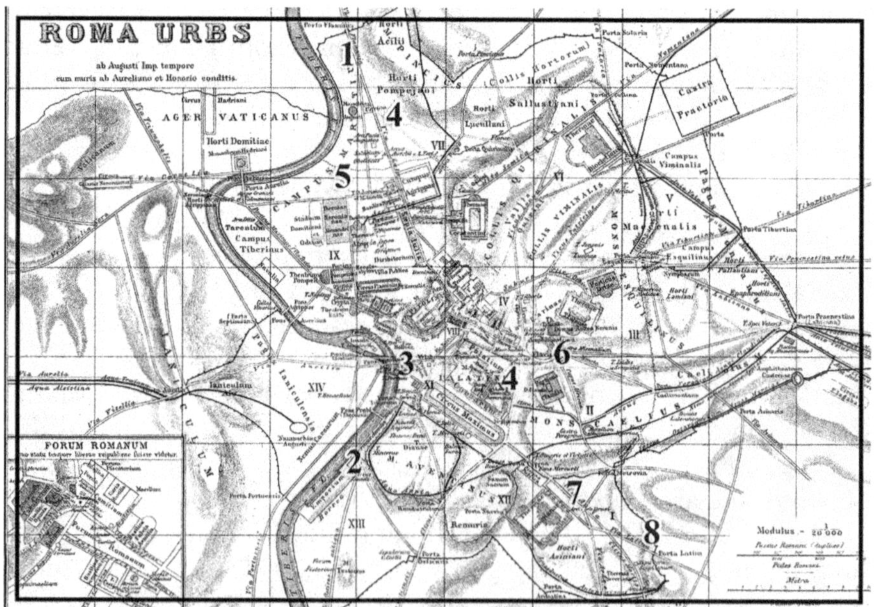

Figure 3.5 Ancient Rome

1. Porta Flaminia; 2. Marmorata; 3. Temple of Portunus; 4.Via Flamina; 5. Campus Martius; 6. Colosseum; 7. Via Appia; 8. Via Latina

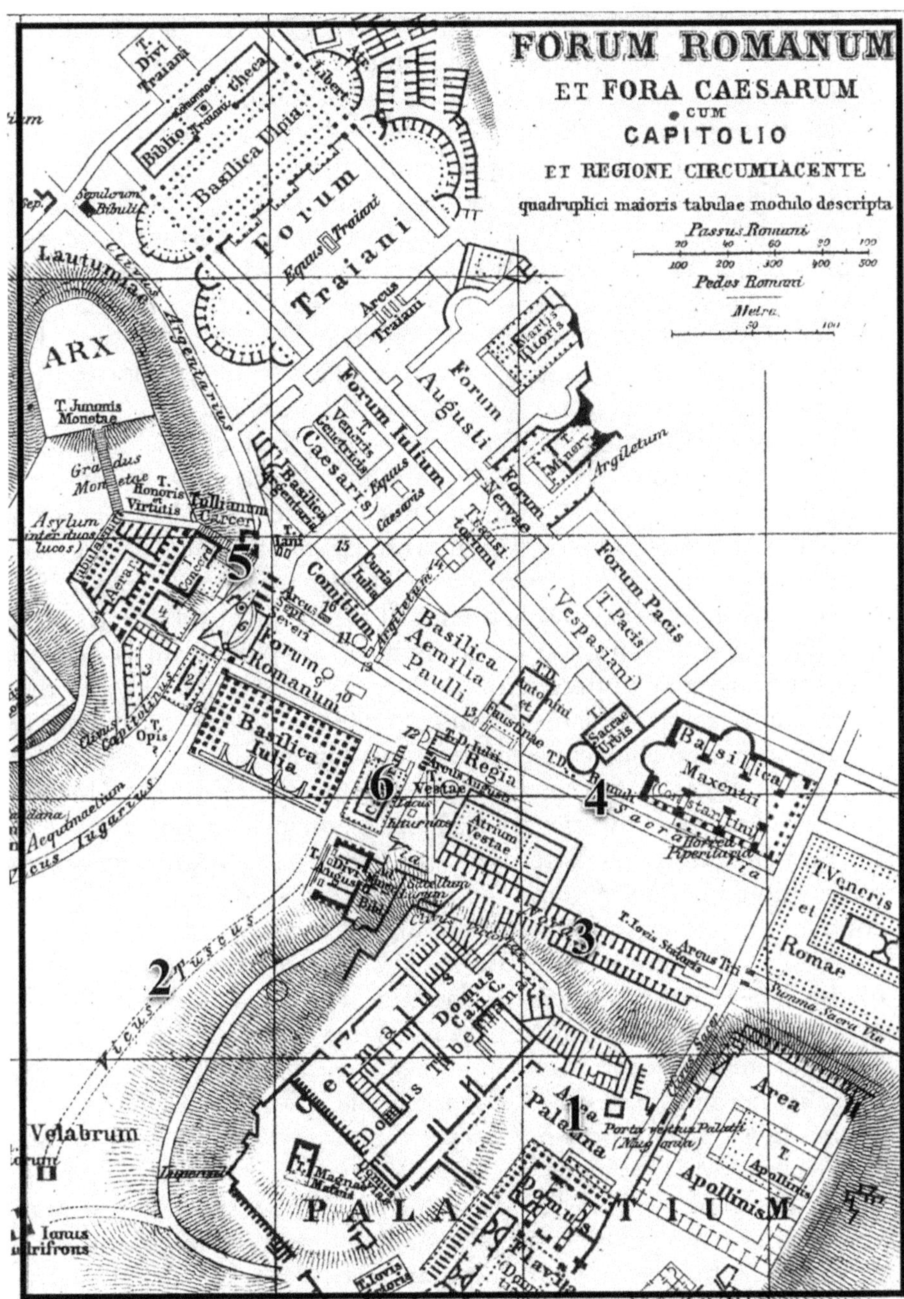

Figure 3.6 The Roman Forum

1. Palatine Hill; 2. Vicus Tuscus; 3. Via Nova; 4. Via Sacra; 5. Templum Pacis; 6. Templum Castorum (Temple of the Dioscuri)

Chapter 11 of the novel sees Marius walk Rome as a metropolitan *flâneur*. Here, ancient Rome also becomes unmistakably a portrait of contemporary metropolitan space. As the narrator notes later in the novel, 'that age and our own have much in common – many difficulties and hopes. Let the reader pardon me if here and there I seem to be passing from Marius to his modern representatives – from Rome, to Paris or London' (*ME* 2: 3.16.14).[38] Certainly, Marius's *flâneurie* implies Baudelaire, and elsewhere, Pater quotes from the essay on 'Le peintre de la vie moderne', with the famous encomium on the *flâneur*, when Gaston defines modernity as 'the transitory, the fugitive, the contingent' (*GL* 3.65; quoting Baudelaire 1961: 1163; 2006: 403).[39] On his 'free wandering through Rome', Marius descends from his apartment, overlooking the Palatine, strolling through 'the dun coolness of the narrow streets' (*ME* 1: 2.11.174) to meet Cornelius, though 'certainly not by the most direct course' (*ME* 1: 2.11.175). Together, they descend to the Vicus Tuscus, running on the west side of the Forum, noting its 'rows of incense-stalls' (*ME* 1: 2.11.175), imported from Arabia, another mark of the Empire and Rome's cosmopolitanism. Walking south, they join the Via Nova, which met the Vicus Tuscus at the intersection with the Ara Maxima. There, 'the fashionable people were busy shopping' (*ME* 1: 2.11.175), showcasing the importance of conspicuous consumption, linking the Rome of the Antonines to the capitals of the nineteenth century. Likewise, Marius is amazed by 'the frizzled heads, then *à la mode*', where the French term immediately draws attention to parallels between the fashionable hairstyles of the period, described by Juvenal, and contemporary Parisian 'style'. Looking past the Altar to the south, Marius has 'a glimpse of the *Marmorata*', the docks on the east side of the Tiber at the foot of the Aventine Hill, 'where specimens of all the precious marbles of the world were lying amid great white blocks from the quarries of Luna', again a reminder of the Empire. They also remind him of 'his distant home' (*ME* 1: 2.11.175), with *White-nights* distant now not simply geographically, but also culturally. Marius and Cornelius then 'visited the flower-market, lingering where the coronarii pressed on them the newest species, and purchased zinias, now in blossom (like painted flowers, thought Marius), to decorate the folds of their togas' (*ME* 1: 2.11.175). Located next to the Temple of Portunus in the Forum Boarium, the Smithfield of Rome, this market sold exotic flowers extolled by Marcus Fronto (AD 100–66?), one of Marius's contemporaries (Fronto 1919: 164–5).[40] But the incident is jarring, anachronistic, with zinnias, native to the Americas, unavailable in ancient Rome.[41] Likened to 'painted flowers', they remind the reader of the artificiality of the scene, perhaps recalling *À rebours*, where des Esseintes collects fake flowers, 'almost miraculously executed in rubber and wire, calico and taffera, paper and velvet', until, 'tired of artificial flowers aping real ones', he turns to 'natural flowers that would look like fakes' (*AR* 8.160; 97).

Leaving the flower market, Marius and Cornelius 'loiter' 'at the other side of the Forum', near to 'great Galen's drug-shop' (*ME* 1: 2.11.175), located on the Via Sacra, running north along the Forum to the Colosseum at the east. The Via Sacra itself housed goldsmiths and jewellers, and was a prestigious shopping location (Holleran 2012: 55). After glancing 'at the announcements of new poems on sale attached to the doorpost of a famous bookseller', the two friends then enter

> the curious library of the Temple of Peace, then a favourite resort of literary men, and read, fixed there for all to see, the *Diurnal* or Gazette of the day, which announced, together with births and deaths, prodigies and accidents, and much mere matter of business. (*ME* 1: 2.11.175–6)

Built in AD 71 by Emperor Vespasian (AD 9–79), the Templum Pacis was located at the Forum Vespasiani at the western end of the Via Sacra, facing towards the Colosseum, but here is unmistakably a Gentleman's Club like those populated by Wilde's London dandies. Later in the novel, Marius will hear Fronto speak there, and the narrator again makes the parallel between his time and the reader's, describing the site as having 'grown into an institution like something between a college and a literary club' (*ME* 2: 3.15.3). Reading the *Diurnal*, the Roman version of the *Pall Mall Gazette*, Marius is struck by a story of 'a *chronique scandaleuse*' concerning a 'great lady' (*ME* 1: 2.11.176), Empress Faustina (AD 120–75), reminding the reader of the various scandals that preoccupied contemporary readers in the nineteenth century. Leaving the Forum, the two friends walked north to the Via Flaminia, a space 'already bordered with handsome villas', 'turning presently to the left, into the *Field-of-Mars*, still the playground of Rome' (*ME* 1: 2.11.177). By Marius's time, 'vast public edifices were grown to be almost continuous over the grassy expanse' of the Campus Martius (*ME* 1: 2.11.177), and later in the novel, the site will host the ceremonial burning of the body of Verus (*ME* 2: 3.17.31). It recalls the original purpose of the Campus Martius as a civic space, comparable to a nineteenth-century city park, foreshadowing Wilde's Hyde Park and James's Central Park.

On the occasion of an earlier stroll, Cornelius and Marius stop to stand with a 'crowd [. . .] to watch a party of athletes stripped for exercise' (*ME* 1: 2.11.177), mobilising a homoerotic gaze.[42]

In Pater's descriptions of Rome, emphasis is placed upon the city as a site of ceremony and ritual. These rituals are polytheistic, for Rome is a city that worships a vast array of gods, some of which come from the East, another decadent motif. As 'a spectator in the streets of Rome', Marius watches the spread of a 'delirious sort of religion [. . .] during the seven days of the *Lectisternium*', noting that 'some jaded women of fashion [. . .] found in certain oriental devotions, [. . .] an opportunity for personal display' (*ME* 2: 3.17.38), so that for them, at least, *theoria* is simply a matter of *aesthesis*. On such occasions, fashion means being seen, but at other times, it also means retiring from the city to the country, as when Marius finds himself remaining in Rome 'long after the very latest roses were faded, when "the town" had departed to country villas, or the baths, or the war' (*ME* 2: 3.16.14).[43] It recalls Dickens's 'Arcadian London' (*All The Year Round*, 29 September 1860), recounting walking the 'fashionable' areas around Burlington Arcade when 'the baneful influences of ultra civilisation' are on holiday (*UT* 185). Consisting of a single straight arcade of shops specialising in luxury goods, Burlington Arcade opened in 1819, and was built for Lord George Cavendish (1754–1834) by Samuel Ware (1781–1860), in imitation of Paris's Passage des Panoramas. By contrasting the arcades with the 'Arcadian' ideal, Dickens's irony registers the difference between the utopia supposedly promised by consumer capitalism and the pastoral paradise of ancient myth. It anticipates James, who will later compare the fantasy image projected by New York to a 'New England Arcadia' that supposedly grounds it in *The American Scene*. For Dickens, however, 'Arcadian London' is short lived, for 'the iron age will return', and the 'fashionable' people 'will grind Arcadia away, and give it to the elements in granite powder' (*UT* 189).

Marius's most notable experience of being part of the crowd, while being simultaneously distanced from it, occurs at the Colosseum. His senses are overwhelmed by the detail of the vision:

> the sunshine, filtered into soft gold by the vela, with their serpentine patterning, spread over the more select part of the company; the Vestal virgins, taking their privilege of seats near the empress Faustina, who sat there in a maze of double-coloured gems, changing, as she moved, like the waves of the sea; the cool circle of shadow, in which the wonderful toilets of the fashionable told so effectively around the blazing arena, covered again and again during the many hours' show, with clean sand

> for the absorption of certain great red patches there, by troops of white-shirted boys, for whom the good-natured audience provided a scramble of nuts and small coin, flung to them over a trellis-work of silver-gilt and amber, precious gift of Nero, while a rain of flowers and perfume fell over themselves, as they paused between the parts of their long feast upon the spectacle of animal suffering. (*ME* 1: 2.14.235)

Pater's narrator makes the striking comparison between the Colosseum's theatrical scenes of bloodletting and the realist novel as forms of entertainment: Rome's shows were 'the novel-reading of that age', a 'mass' form of entertainment providing 'help [. . .] for sluggish imaginations'. Indeed, just as in the realist novel which, in its theoretical gaze, portrays the ugly side of life only to impart its moral lessons, so too the 'macabre' aspects of reality, those 'grisly accidents, such as might happen to one's self', are played out in the Colosseum at a distance, 'with every facility for comfortable inspection' (*ME* 1: 2.14.239). In this sense, Pater's critique of the moral vacuity of the Colosseum recalls Huysmans's image of the 'cosy ark' of Dickens's realism (*AR* 11.209; 138). Moreover, Pater warns his readers against complacency, comparing the amphitheatrical spectacle to the slave trade, implying the comparison once again between the Roman Empire and the British one, 'each age in turn, perhaps, having its own peculiar point of blindness, with its consequent peculiar sin' (*ME* 1: 2.14.242).

Marius notes that 'the spectacle of the amphitheatre was, after all, a religious occasion', lending 'to its grim acts of blood-shedding a kind of sacrificial character' (*ME* 1: 2.14.236–7). It stands symbolically for imperial Rome more broadly, a civic space attesting to its power. As always, power is bound to ritual in Pater's Rome, with Marius watching Aurelius, 'clad in the civic dress of the chief Roman magistrate, and with a crown of myrtle upon his head', solemnly process along the Via Sacra 'to offer sacrifice to the national gods'. The attendant priests are 'clad in rich white vestments', followed by 'a company of flute-players, led by the great choir-master, or conductor, of the day' (*ME* 1: 2.12.188). In the context of our discussion of the aesthetics of space, the reference recalls Dickens's Cloisterham processions – certainly, the ritualistic aesthetic of Christianity that Pater sought out on his trips to the East End. Standing among the 'vast crowd', Marius saw 'the world's masters pass by' (*ME* 1: 2.12.188), marking his gaze as Hegelian.[44] In Rome, processions link religious ritual with the ceremonies of war, as when, later in the novel, Marius finds himself carried along with 'the younger element' to watch 'the famous procession, or *transvectio*, of the military knights [. . .] passing over the Forum, from their trysting-place at the temple of Mars, to the temple of the Dioscuri' (*ME* 2: 3.15.12):

> Through that light trellis-work, Marius watched the riders, arrayed in all their gleaming ornaments, and wearing wreaths of olive around their helmets, the faces below which, what with battle and the plague, were almost all youthful. It was a flowery scene enough, but had to-day its fulness of war-like meaning; the return of the army to the North, where the enemy was again upon the move, being now imminent. (*ME* 2: 3.15.13)

The aesthetic pomp, the 'gleaming ornaments' and ceremonial wreaths, as well as the eroticism of the 'youthful' male faces, belie the traces of imminent violence, so that the Forum, a public space now become a ceremonial one, is penetrated unnervingly by a sense of what lies outside the city walls. If the public space of Rome is inscribed militarily as a space of power, then the 'youthful' faces also suggest a certain impotence of the Empire at its crisis point, registered when Aurelius returns in 'triumph', his ceremonial re-entry into the city, AD 176. Then, Marius watches from 'almost at the exact spot' (*ME* 2: 4.27.197), but finds it a 'vulgar spectacle', as well as uncanny, with the 'repetition' 'prophetic, so to speak, and evocative of ghosts' (*ME* 2: 4.27.199), the déjà vu presenting a sense of loss and death.

Pater was interested in melancholia, famously reading the 'brooding' portrait of Leonardo da Vinci's (1452–1519) *La Gioconda* (c. 1505) through Albrecht Dürer's (1471–1528) *Melancholia* (1514) (*SHR* 97). For his part, Marius's melancholic sense of belatedness, to use Bloom's term, of coming late and of a loss which he cannot quite explain or locate, sees him read Rome in a 'melancholy aspect' which comes to triumph over its 'superficial gaudiness' (*ME* 2: 4.24.170). It links to Aurelius himself, who strikes Marius as 'the most melancholy' figure 'in the entire history of Rome' (*ME* 2: 3.17.33). This melancholia is expressed in part by his status as a collector, a figure more emblematic of the later nineteenth century than of ancient Rome. For Benjamin, the collector seeks to 'divest [. . .] things of their commodity character by taking possession of them', but in so doing 'bestows on them only connoisseur value' (*SW* 3: 39). The collector becomes conceivable as an allegorist (*PW* 206; H2,1), and as such, melancholic, for 'as far as the collector is concerned, his collection is never complete' (*PW* 211; H4a,1), always in need of the lost object. The dream of the collector is to construct 'a whole magic encyclopaedia, a world order' (*PW* 207; H2,7), and so too Aurelius's collection speaks of a similar impulse towards a 'theoretical' vision of the world and universe as a totality. It is this desire for precisely the lost object which both underwrites his vision of 'cosmopolitanism' and divides Pater's *aesthesis* from Ruskin's *theoria*.

'Cosmopolitanism' is, of course, a key term during the period, significant to Wilde, and one which carried important connotations for late nineteenth-century readers, associating the metropolitan with the transnational, but was also coded, implying both a critical stance towards homoerotic desire and the possibility of a 'reverse discourse'. In this sense, the utopianism of Aurelius's meditations on the cosmopolitan ideal would be one further example of how Pater invites his readers to see *Marius* through a double lens, both as a historical novel and as one commenting on contemporary concerns. Aurelius's cosmopolitanism, 'the great Stoic idea, that we are all fellow-citizens of one city' (*ME* 1: 2.13.219), offers an idealised projection, extrapolating from the reality of the city in which he lived. It is Rome at once *orbis* and *urbs*, the city as an *imago mundi* (*PS* 243–4). In the *Discourses*, the narrator notes, 'Aurelius speaks often of that *City on high*, of which all other cities are but single habitations', 'incorporate somehow with the actual city whose goodly stones were lying beneath his gaze', but meaning by it 'more than the whole commonwealth of Rome, in any idealisation of it, however sublime' (*ME* 2: 3.17.37). In an earlier chapter, when Aurelius had lectured on a similar theme, Marius finds himself frustrated precisely by the 'theoretical' nature of the emperor's vision, 'in search of its visible locality and abiding-place, the walls and towers of which, so to speak, he might really trace and tell, according to his own old, natural habit of mind' (*ME* 2: 3.15.11). But Aurelius's *theoria* is less interested in the 'reality' of his vision (*ME* 2: 3.17.39), aware on some level that, like Prior Saint-Jean, he is unable to 'arrest [. . .] this beam of insight, or of inspiration (*IP* 209). 'However distinct the mental image', the narrator notes, 'with the descent of but one flight of steps into the market-place below, it must have retreated again, as if at touch of some malign magic wand, beyond the utmost verge of the horizon' (*ME* 2: 3.17.40). The presence of the reality of the market space – replete with its sensory affects, its urgency, its visual and olfactory impact – undercuts Aurelius's ideal. Indeed, he soon recognises this vision to have been 'a confused place, [. . .] and haunted by strange faces, whose novel expression he, the great physiognomist, could by no means read' (*ME* 2: 3.17.40), so that all is allegory once again. Noting Plato's articulations on the subject, Aurelius muses that his Greek forebear 'had but divined, by a kind of generosity of spirit, the void place, which another experience than his must fill' (*ME* 2: 3.18.41). Aurelius's attempted *theoria* is symptomatic of melancholia, and, like Christianity in this novel, cosmopolitanism offers nothing other than 'a pledge of something further to come' (*ME* 2: 4.28.220). Written over a 'void place', the cosmopolitan ideal attempts to name and fix that lost object that forever eludes us.

In this sense, the metropolitan space of Rome in *Marius* is placed in contrast with *White-nights*, and by extension, the home of 'The Child in the House'. The latter are homely yet uncanny spaces, where the subject and their aesthetic sense are formed. By contrast, Rome, decadent, perfumed and spectacular, puts this subject into question. The experience of the city is overwhelming and cannot be rationalised through *theoria*. It is intoxicating, and navigating such a space necessarily implicates the body. Faced with the reality of Rome, at the height of its pomp and the precise moment of its decline and fall, Aurelius's 'theoretical' vision of a cosmopolitan ideal is frustrated. Rather, the cosmopolitan reality of such a space can only ever be experienced through *aesthesis*, as is demonstrated in Pater's extraordinary recreation of Marius's *flâneurie* through ancient Rome.

Notes

1. For more on Pater's rooms, see Crook 2008: 271–84.
2. See Daley 2001 for the most comprehensive treatment of the topic currently available, although he makes little mention of Pater's fiction or *Marius the Epicurean*, where Pater's most significant rebuke of Ruskin appears.
3. On Pater and Ruskin on Botticelli, see Tucker 2002.
4. See Østermark-Johansen's note in her edition: *IP* 291.
5. Although Ruskin himself was less enamoured of the location. In one of his Slade Lectures on 'The Relation to Art of the Science of Light' (1872), Ruskin remarked that 'at the very foot of the dome of the Radclyffe, between two principal colleges, [. . .] – Brasen-nose Lane – is left in a state as loathsome as a back alley in the East end of London' (*CW* 22: 205).
6. For his part, Ruskin remarked that he was 'more disappointed' with Vélazay 'than ever with anything' (*CW* 33: xxxv).
7. Under the influence of German aesthetic theory, Pater considered Greek art the ideal (*SHR* 168–79). For Ruskin, however, Greek art compares unfavourably with Christianity, making it 'full of danger to the student in proportion to his admiration of it': 'The Greek could not conceive a

spirit: he could do nothing without his limbs; his God is a finite God' (*CW* 4: 329). In other words, it is precisely the material, the bodily, *aesthesis*, that is so dangerously seductive in Greek art.

8. A similar distinction between the 'severe northern air' of Cumberland and the 'feverish southern land' (*IP* 149) of Normandy features in 'An English Poet'; likewise, in 'Denys l'Auxerrois', Pater's narrator remarks on Auxerre's 'happy mean between northern earnestness and the luxury of the south' (*IP* 83).
9. In the unpublished eighth chapter of the novel, Gaston travels through the 'quiet monastic neighbourhood of Saint-Germain-des-Prés' in Paris to the house of his friend Jasmin de Villebon, a Gothic structure of the late fifteenth century which speaks of 'certain inward tendencies towards relaxation of the *moral* fibre' and which Gaston's eyes find 'delightful' (*GL* 8.123).
10. We can be sure Pater knew of his work, for 'F' recalls him lauding 'the "stirring, interesting writing of Professor Freeman, which I love to read"' (1899: 208).
11. For a comparable point, dealing with Pater's punning on 'grave' words in the essay on 'Style' (1888) (1910a: 15), see Dowling 1986: 129.
12. Pater's phrasing here recalls his essay on another type of schooling and the 'military monasticism' (1910f: 220) of 'Lacadæmon' (1892), composed during the same period as 'Emerald Uthwart'. There, *ascêsis* is also associated with homoeroticism as proper to a specifically 'male beauty' (1910f: 222).
13. The phrase anticipates Wilde's Dorian, who is a 'subject made to [Lord Henry's] hand' (*DG* 4. 219). Wilde reviewed Pater's *Imaginary Portraits* for the *Pall Mall Gazette*, 11 June 1887: see Wilde 2013a: 178–80.
14. Østermark-Johansen points out that this is an error on Pater's part: the tower was not completed until nearly a century later than the action takes place: *IP* 261 n.
15. On Pater's reading of Viollet-le-Duc, see Inman 1990: 482.
16. In 'Val d'Arno' (1874), Ruskin also recommends Viollet-le-Duc to the audience of his 1873 lectures at Oxford (*CW* 23: 94).
17. In Pater's portrait, this incident occurs when Denys has returned to Auxerre after having gone on 'a long journey' (*IP* 179). In the context of Heine's motif of the gods in exile which underwrites Pater's portrait, this suggests a trip to the East, Dionysus returning as Dionysus Zagreus. His 'satirical grotesque' can therefore be read not simply in the terms of the Renaissance, but also in relation to an Oriental influence. It recalls Pater's discussion of 'Vézelay' which, in its 'eccentricity' when compared to other Romanesque Gothic, has 'at least for English eyes, something of a Saracenic or other Oriental character', as though the architects who worked on it 'had seen things undreamt of by other Romanesque builders, the builders in England and Normandy'. These Oriental dreams give an 'almost savage character' to the work, 'full of

wild promise in their coarse execution, cruel, [. . .] in the realisation of human form and features', recalling the associations of sadism and violence mapped in the aesthetic spaces of Dickens's *Edwin Drood*. 'Irresistibly they rivet attention' (*MS* 134), Pater notes, 'fascinating' the Christian gaze.

18. Shuter 2001 reads 'Apollo in Picardy' as a narrative in which a narcissistic younger man destroys the life of an older one, linking the portrait to Wilde's introduction of Lord Alfred Douglas (1870–1945) to Pater in 1892, the year before its publication.
19. As he writes in *Marius*, 'Words like "hedonism" – terms of large and vague comprehension – above all when used for a purpose avowedly controversial, have ever been the worst examples of what are called "question-begging terms"' (*ME* 1: 2.9.150–1). In private, Pater famously remarked: 'I wish they would not call me a hedonist. It gives such a wrong impression to those who do not know Greek' (Gosse 1896: 258).
20. For a critique of Proust's attack on Ruskin, read as too heavily influenced by his own sympathy with French 'decadence', see Hewison 1976: 193–5. On Ruskin and idolatry, see Tanner 1992: 99–101.
21. On the ways in which Pater and others during the period sought to recodify Greek homeoerotic culture, see Dowling 1994.
22. On Pater and perfume, see Maxwell 2017; on Pater and phenomenology, see Whiteley 2010: 23–4.
23. Proust's friend Robert de Billy appears to have first introduced him to Pater's works, recommending *Greek Studies* and *Marius*, and Proust's writings also show the influence of the *Renaissance*. Working from manuscript evidence, Emily Eells has traced the ways in which the character of Bergotte in the draft of *À la recherche du temps perdu* cites Pater's works, allusions which were then suppressed when it eventually came to print (Eells 2002: 151–4, 175–6).
24. On 'The Child in the House' and the uncanny, see Vidler 1992: 57–62 and Whiteley 2010: 81–4.
25. On the ways in which Pater mixes classical and Victorian in his representation of Roman houses in *Marius*, see Hales 2017.
26. One of the most striking of these moments of anticipation occurs when Marius recalls in his diary a tragic incident which might have been set in Gaskell's industrial north: 'At the baths, a party of labourers are at work upon one of the great brick furnaces, in a cloud of black dust. [. . .] A man comes along carrying a boy whose rough work has already begun – the only child – whose presence beside him sweetened the father's toil a little. The boy has been badly injured by a fall of brick-work, yet, with an effort, he rides boldly on his father's shoulders. It will be the way of natural affection to keep him alive as long as possible, though with that miserably shattered body [. . .] and yet surely not without a heartbreaking sigh of relief, alike from him and them, when the end comes' (*ME* 2: 4.25.176).

27. For a reading of Pater's discussion of the Medusa alongside Freud's fragment, see Hillis Miller 1976: 98–103.
28. Jackson was one of Thomas Wright's primary sources for his 1907 biography of Pater, but is an unreliable witness, and quotations reported by him must be treated with caution. While Jackson seems to have known Pater to some degree while in London, there appears to be a good deal of exaggeration in what he claims about their relationship.
29. For his part, Adorno links waxworks with the commodity in his reading of *The Old Curiosity Shop* (1992: 171–7).
30. The date of the portrait implies the new Morgue, by then nearly a decade old, but considering the events autobiographically, the experience may date to 1864, when Pater and his sisters visited Paris for the long vacation.
31. 'On the S. side of it [the Southern Cemetery], after passing a semicircular vaulted building containing the Leichenhaues (i.e. dead-house, where the bodies of all the persons who die are exposed to public view – a painful sight), lies the New Friedhof' (Anon 1871: 81).
32. On Pater's 'arresting' syntax, see Dowling 1986: 129–30. My idea of the aesthetic moment 'arresting' time in the instant is informed by Blanchot 2000.
33. Baudelaire is clearly evoked when Gaston speaks of the *Odes* as offering '"flowers of evil", among the rest' (*GL* 3.72). On Baudelaire as a model for Apuleius and Ronsard, see Monsman 1980: 137–8.
34. In 'Night Walks', Dickens writes of London and of the overwhelming and suffocating demand of the dead in a phantasmagoric vision of the return of the repressed: 'the vast armies of dead [. . .] overflow[ing] the hills and valleys beyond the city, and [. . .] stretch[ing] away [. . .] seemingly to the confines of the earth' (*UT* 154).
35. The year after work on St Philip's Church ended, Cawston published *A Comprehensive Scheme for Street Improvements in London* (1893), which argued for a drastic demolition and reconstruction of London under the influence of Haussmann's Paris, widening the streets, creating more public spaces and increasing 'visibility'. It was not well received.
36. In *Gaston de Latour*, Gaston travels the French countryside 'with a delightful sense of peril': 'they passed from time to time half-ruined or deserted farm-buildings where the remnants of the armies might yet be lingering' (*GL* 3.62). Indeed, capturing the image of the ruin at a later date is precisely an 'aesthetic' question which drives to the heart of the problem of realism, as Pater makes clear in 'Emerald Uthwart': 'Had a draughtsman equally truthful or equally "realistic", as we say, accompanied them and made a like use of his pencil, he might have been mistaken at home for an artist aiming at "effect", by skilful "arrangements" to tickle people's interest in the spectacle of war – [. . .] ignoble ruin everywhere' (*IP* 191). The final adjective engages Ruskin once again.

37. For a fascinating discussion of the ways in which Roman habits of collecting turned the capital into a kind of museum, see Rutledge 2012.
38. Paris had featured in *Gaston de Latour* and Pater's third projected volume of the trilogy was to be set at 'the end of the last century – and the scene, England' (*LWP* 65). A few manuscript fragments titled 'Thistle' may represent working notes for this final novel, to have been set partly in Oxford, but also to involve a stay in the capital. In one of the fragments, Pater gives us an aesthetics of London space, presumably intended for this work: 'the women outside the Guildhall. how he goes about London' (bMS Eng 1150 (31), held at the Houghton Library, Harvard University).
39. Likewise, Marius's view of the modernity of Antonine Rome is mediated via Baudelaire, as when Marius considers the world 'as a hospital of sick persons' (*ME* 2: 4.25.174), quoting the first line of Baudelaire's 'Any Where Out of the World' (1867) (1961: 303; 2010: 92).
40. While there were other stalls selling flowers in the city, it seems highly likely that Pater is thinking of the Portunia, given the presence of Fronto as a character in the novel and the fact that Pater drew on Fronto's letters as sources for other aspects of the novel. Pater owned a copy of Fronto's letters in Samuel Adrianus Naber's (1828–1913) edition (1867): see Inman 1981: 337. On the curiously ahistorical portrait Pater draws of Fronto as a stoic, see Rutherford 2017: 122–3.
41. On the significance of anachronism in *Marius*, although without reference to this specific point, see Porter 2017.
42. On the question of gender and social space in Pater's Rome, see Eastlake 2019: 190–203.
43. At other times, however, Marius does leave the city, retreating 'to one of his favourite spots on the Sabine or Alban hills' (*ME* 2: 3.19.62). Such occasions show Pater's post-Darwinian late Romanticism, awareness of geological deep time, and appreciation of the natural sublime: 'An air of immense age possessed [. . .] the vegetation around – a world of evergreen trees – the olives especially, older than how many generations of men's lives! fretted and twisted by the combining forces of life and death, into every conceivable caprice of form' (*ME* 2: 3.19.65–6).
44. Pater had read Hegel closely (Shuter 1997: 61–77; Ward 1966: 53–77; Whiteley 2010). In a famous letter to Friedrich Niethammer (1766–1848), 13 October 1806, Hegel discussed Napoleon seen riding through Jena as the 'spirit of the world' (1984: 114).

Chapter 4

Oscar Wilde: Cosmopolitan Space

In 1874, the young Oscar Wilde had been one of the undergraduates who had taken part in John Ruskin's road-building scheme in North Hinksey, a project which was an important element of his political and social activism following his appointment to Oxford (Eagles 2011: 103–14). But if Wilde was interested in Ruskin the social thinker, he was also interested in Ruskin the aesthetician. In 'The Critic as Artist', Gilbert exclaims, 'Who cares whether Mr. Ruskin's views on Turner are sound or not?' His 'mighty and majestic prose [. . .], so fervid and so fiery-coloured in its noble eloquence, so rich in its elaborate symphonic music' is itself a 'work of art', speaking to the reader's 'soul [. . .] with lofty passion and with loftier thought' (*CR* 156). This exaltation of *Modern Painters* is immediately followed by a similar passage extolling Pater's *Renaissance*, the proximity of the two thinkers' names speaking of their respective influence upon Wilde.

Reading Wilde through Ruskin's distinction between *theoria* and *aesthesis* allows us to gain another kind of appreciation of the former's writing of space. As we have seen, the significance of Wilde's literary treatment of metropolitan space can be easily underestimated as 'psychic' context or 'stock' imagery. Certainly, Wilde was not a fan of realism, and while he read Dickens, he had no appetite for the novelist's romanticism, famously quipping that one needed 'a heart of stone to read the death of Little Nell without laughing' (Ellmann 1988: 441). Likewise, Wilde was less than enamoured of the grubbiness and 'bourgeois' mentality – the 'dreary vices' and 'drearier virtues' (*CR* 79) – of the naturalism of Zola and Eliot: for Wilde, art should not be judged by 'any external standard of resemblance' (*CR* 89). But this distaste notwithstanding, is it really true to claim that Wilde gives us nothing more than 'stock' images of London? Offering close readings of *The Picture of Dorian Gray* and 'Lord Arthur Savile's Crime' (1887), this chapter reads Wilde's aesthetics of space as engaged, socially and politically. Like Pater in *Marius the*

Epicurean, Wilde holds that the aesthetic effects of space are always already rooted in the real social and political histories of these spaces. Defined as much by that which is foreign as that which is 'proper' to it, by a strange alterity that calls into question the panoptic dreams of *theoria*, Wilde's cosmopolitan aesthetics reveals London as a space of otherness that precipitates 'curious effects'. Situating Wilde's writing within the spatial practice of late nineteenth-century London in a methodology informed by Westphal (2011), this chapter argues that Wilde's city is at once 'real', politically charged, and an aesthetic 'cosmopolitan' space.

London's 'Curious Effects'

Revising his novel for publication as a book in 1891, Wilde expanded what became chapter 19 of *Dorian Gray*, adding a striking passage in which London is described as a city 'rich in curious effects':

> I was going through the Park last Sunday, and close by the Marble Arch there stood a little crowd of shabby-looking people listening to some vulgar street-preacher. As I passed by, I heard the man yelling out [a] question to his audience. It struck me as being rather dramatic. London is very rich in curious effects of that kind. A wet Sunday, an uncouth Christian in a mackintosh, a ring of sickly white faces under a broken roof of umbrellas, and a wonderful phrase flung into the air by shrill, hysterical lips – it was really very good in its way, quite a suggestion. I thought of telling the prophet that Art had a soul, but man had not. (*DG* 19.350)

The fact that he added this passage, having first serialised the narrative in *Lippincott's Monthly Magazine* in 1890, prompts the question as to how Wilde's readers are being invited to approach this 'curious' moment: how should we read the *fin-de-siècle* city in Wilde?

This Sunday jaunt might be dismissed as offering little more than a snapshot of the city, another 'stock' image of London. Wilde's interest in adding the passage seemingly lies in the idea of the aesthetic 'effect', one which is 'curious', and thereby seemingly desired, in part, for the sake of 'curiosity'. Lord Henry appears to be privileging this 'effect' over the political reality of the late nineteenth-century city, not only treating life in the spirit of art, but reducing this *Lebenswelt* (Husserl 1970: 48–53) to nothing but a series of aesthetic 'effects'. And yet, there may be more to this 'effect' than is initially apparent. Lord Henry narrates a specific event, grounded in real-life social practice, capturing the 'rhythm' of 'everyday life' (de Certeau 2002: 91–110). As Lefebvre puts it, 'what we *live* are rhythms – rhythms experienced subjectively', which 'invest' space (*PS* 206). The vignette refers to a clearly identifiable social space, Speakers' Corner, lying at the north-eastern corner of Hyde Park next to Marble Arch, a politicised space, where public speaking was permitted. The image of a 'vulgar street-preacher' initially suggests religion, particularly since the day in question was Sunday, so that London seems to be figured as a godless city, the preacher's millenarianism paying a kind of 'hysterical' lip service. It suggests sermons are cant, repetition for repetition's sake, the orator's 'rather dramatic' words (the qualifier here already bathetic) evacuated of any referential significance in late nineteenth-century London. Read thus, the curious aesthetic effects of Wilde's London seem allied to *fin-de-siècle* nihilism.

But alongside the religious connotations present in the scene, there is also a political undercurrent: the preacher is 'vulgar', common; his audience 'shabby-looking', poorly dressed. The adjectives imply class, recalling, subtly but necessarily for Wilde's late nineteenth-century audience, the revolutionary history of Speakers' Corner. In 1855, Hyde Park had witnessed riots over the Sunday Trading Bill, with Marx, living in exile, speaking at the rally and writing about the disturbances of the consecutive Sundays of 24 June and 1 July for the *Neue Oder-Zeitung*.[1] Hyde Park was invaded by protestors, angry at the proposals, with picketers blocking the gentry riding on Rotten Row – this was the space, running on the south side and linking Hyde Park Corner with the Serpentine Road, where it was most fashionable to be 'seen' in nineteenth-century London, a consumption of public space integral to contemporary upper-class life.[2] Commenting on the riots, Marx, impassioned, but ultimately getting ahead of himself, announced that it was no 'exaggeration to say that the *English Revolution began in Hyde Park*' (1973: 290). But its revolutionary spirit would be rekindled nearly thirty years later when William Morris attended a demonstration at Speakers' Corner on 21 July 1884 in support of what would become the Representation of the People Act. Things turned violent, and 'Morris fought like a man with the rest of us', according to Sam Mainwaring (1841–1907) (MacCarthy 1994: 489). Mainwaring would go on to found the Socialist League in late December that year, with Morris editing the League's journal, *Commonweal*. Morris returned to Speakers' Corner two years later, on Saturday 12 June 1886, and Wilde met him two years after that.[3] Both Wilde and his audience would have been aware of Speakers' Corner's history as a space for revolutionary agitation.

A few years after meeting Morris, Wilde published his essay on 'The Soul of Man', engaging with *News from Nowhere* (1890) (*CR* 236, 560 n.). The essay was written during the period when he was revising this very same passage of *Dorian Gray*, and it is precisely this question of the 'soul of man' that is posed obliquely by the street-preacher. It suggests that Wilde may have been inviting his readers to approach the moment politically. The context for Lord Henry's story has him musing on the biblical motif (Mark 8: 36) of how it profits a man to 'gain the whole world and lose [. . .] his own soul'. The question jars Dorian, the connotation here double, linking to the Faust myth, with Wilde's eponymous protagonist figuring for Faust and Lord Henry for Mephistopheles, so that the 'effects' of the city are demonic.[4] But the question is also one which had socialist connotations, as in *Die heilige Familie* [*The Holy Family*] (1845), considering 'the Critical *salvation*' of the soul. As Marx writes there against Bruno Bauer (1809–82), 'what profit is it to me if I gain the whole world, including the lower classes of the people, and suffer the loss of my own soul?' (Marx and Engels 1975: 135). While Wilde would not have known this passage (untranslated until 1956), the biblical phrase would nevertheless have maintained political connotations for him through Morris's *The Earthly Paradise* (1868–70).[5] In this manner, the 'vulgarity' of Lord Henry's street-preacher and his audience has political connotations which would have been carried to Wilde's late nineteenth-century audience implicitly. The vignette here gives a stock image of *fin-de-siècle* London, but one that is also precisely located in real social praxis. In this sense, Speakers' Corner speaks to Wilde's readers, connoting a politics that cannot be wholly isolated from the space.

It is not that Lord Henry's aestheticisation of Speakers' Corner means that he has dispensed with social reality (Murray 2016b: 221–2). Rather, Wilde's aesthetics of space builds on a political reality that his writing incorporates as an indispensable 'effect' of its textual surface. The scene strikes Lord Henry as 'being rather dramatic', as though the event, and the space itself, is being staged. The 'curious effects' which it produces are given in a single sentence, or rather sentence fragment, a chain of dependent noun phrases: 'A wet Sunday, an uncouth Christian in a mackintosh, a ring of sickly white faces under a broken roof of umbrellas, and a wonderful phrase flung into the air by shrill, hysterical lips' (*DG* 19.350). Borrowing a poetic technique from French symbolism, Lord Henry's sentence builds a series of grammatically disconnected clauses to construct a picture that is causally incoherent, while simultaneously focalised, grounded

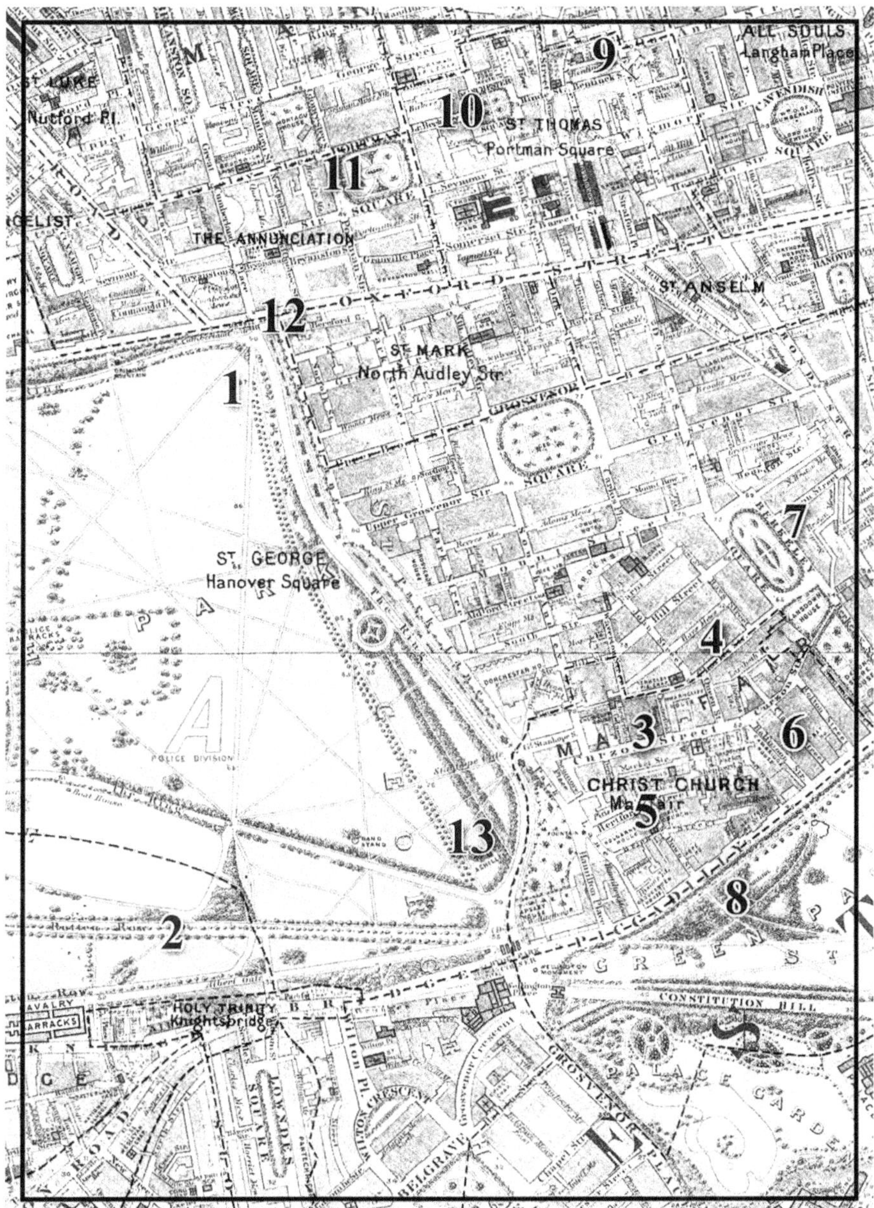

Figure 4.1 Hyde Park and Piccadilly

1. Speakers' Corner; 2. Rotten Row; 3. Curzon Street, home of Lord Henry in *Dorian Gray*; 4. 9 Charles Street, Wilde's home 1883–5; 5. 152 Hertford Street, home of Alan Campbell in *Dorian Gray*; 6. 7 Half Moon Street, James's home 1868; 7. Berkeley Square, home of Lady Agatha in *Dorian Gray*; 8. Piccadilly; 9. Bentinck Street, home of Lady Windermere in 'Lord Arthur Savile's Crime'; 10. Manchester Square; 11. Portman Square; 12. Marble Arch; 13. Wellington Monument (statue of Achilles)

and 'real'. The 'wet Sunday' perhaps carries the echo of de Quincey's *Confessions*, where the opium eater describes the moment when he stepped into a druggist near the Pantheon, just over a mile east down Oxford Street from Speakers' Corner: 'It was a Sunday afternoon, wet and cheerless: and a duller spectacle this earth has not to show than a rainy Sunday in London' (2008: 42). But while de Quincey's Romantic finds that only opium can illuminate the 'spectacle' that is London, Wilde's aesthete considers the drug simply one of many different aesthetic approaches towards seeing the city. For Benjamin, to recall our discussion of Dickens in Chapter 2, the dream is proper to nineteenth-century city space: there, 'spacetime' (*Zeitraum*) becomes 'dreamtime' (*Zeit-traum*), and the dream city is approached as allegorical (*PW* 389; K1,4). Wilde's image is allegorical in Benjamin's sense, with Lord Henry's fragmentary series of noun phrases relating metonymically, but lacking a stable signified to ground them. They also depend on an absent verb to direct them, so that they become detached from 'reality', outside of the order of things. At the same time, and by the same token, this allegorical composite simultaneously comments on the scene, not only through the implied politics of the social practice, but in the syntactic form itself. The impressionistic image is of the city as itself fragmented; it images London as ruin, but also gives a vibrant aesthetic vision of the *fin-de-siècle* city, focused on its 'curious effects'.

Social Space: Hyde Park and Piccadilly

Lord Henry resides in Curzon Street in Mayfair, the heart of society London, running east from Park Lane, curving north to Berkeley Square, where it meets Charles Street, where Wilde moved (no. 9) in 1883. Curzon Street is where Lady Clentina Beauchamp lives in 'Lord Arthur Savile's Crime' (*SF* 67), and where Mrs Erylnne takes a house in *Lady Windermere's Fan* (1892), shockingly since the street is purportedly so 'respectable' (1.241–73). It was associated historically with the peerage (hence the space of Lord Henry) and politicians, home to Benjamin Disraeli (no. 19) from 1880 until his death in 1881. During the period, Piccadilly, alongside St James's, was the heart of fashionable London.

Leaving Curzon Street in chapter 3, Lord Henry 'strolls' (suggesting *flâneurie*) over to Albany to visit his uncle, Lord Fermor (*DG* 3.194). The walk would take only a few minutes, passing Hertford Street to his right, where Dorian's former lover Alan Campbell lives (no. 152)

(*DG* 14.304). A set of bachelor's apartments, built in 1802–3, the Albany was located on Half Moon Street, connecting Curzon Street to Piccadilly. James had been resident at 7 Half Moon Street in the late 1860s, and in *The Importance of Being Earnest* (1895), Algernon has a flat there, with Jack his neighbour at B.4 The Albany (1.162–3). Peter Raby notes (Wilde 2008: 358–9 n.) that Wilde had originally written the apartment number as E.4, but later changed it to B.4: E.4 had been occupied by George Ives, and was where Wilde met Jack Bloxam in 1894. This rewriting suggests that Wilde mapped his London onto reality, but then subtly 'de-realised' space. It sees E.4 become B.4, so that Jack Worthing (a name connoting worthiness, although here a false identity; his 'real' name is Ernest, connoting earnestness) masks two real-life figures: firstly Ives, then Bloxam, so that Jack in fiction masks Jack in reality. The 'reality' of this kind of textual space within Wilde's writing cannot be easily untangled from its aesthetic representations.

Leaving his uncle, Lord Henry 'passed up the low arcade into Burlington Street, and turned his steps in the direction of Berkeley Square' (*DG* 3.198), implying Burlington Arcade.[6] Passing from Piccadilly to Bond Street, Burlington Arcade reaches Burlington Street, before then turning west towards Berkeley Square, where Lady Agatha resides; it runs parallel to Old Bond Street, where Agnew's was, and still is, located (no. 43), whose owner is said to have attempted to buy one of Basil's landscapes to no avail (*DG* 1.177).[7] Benjamin links these arcades to consumerism, alienation and dream space, with Wilde's reference reinforcing the motif of *flâneurie*. Characterising Piccadilly as 'arcadian' recalls Dorian discussing the area and the way in which all of nineteenth-century London can be read as a kind of arcade:

> As I lounged in the Park, or strolled down Piccadilly, I used to look at every one who passed me, and wonder, with a mad curiosity, what sort of lives they led. Some of them fascinated me. Others filled me with terror. There was an exquisite poison in the air. I had a passion for sensations. (*DG* 4.211)

'Strolling' (that term again) down Piccadilly, Dorian gazes at the crowd. His 'passion for sensations' is synaesthetic: gazing here activates his sense of smell, the scent of 'an exquisite poison in the air', with both phrases also richly sibilant. It is an aesthetic dream state, where sensory impressions merge and boundaries between them blur. Regardless, Wilde's aesthetics of space produces an interpenetration of sense and substance which is 'curious', a term associated here with madness.

From the Latin *curiosus*, Dorian's 'curiosity' in the gaze, through which space is treated in the spirit of art, recalls the cognate term 'curio'. Describing an *objet d'art* or piece of bric-à-brac valued as a curiosity or rarity, 'curio' entered into English in the mid-nineteenth century (the *OED* gives 1851 as the first use). In this context, Dorian's 'mad curiosity' can be seen as a kind of 'curiomania', a condition symptomatic of the decadent. It was attacked in an article under that name in the *Pall Mall Gazette*, 13 January 1886, which Wilde would have read as a regular contributor to the periodical. The anonymous writer describes curiomania as 'a morbid craving after the acquisition of curios' (Anon. 1886: 4), tingeing it with the death-drive. The curiomaniac can be compared to the figure of the collector, like Pater's Marcus Aurelius, but if the latter figure is proper to the nineteenth century more generally, as Benjamin argues, then the curiomaniac is emblematic of the *fin de siécle* in particular. Curiomania is a recent 'disease', the subject suffering 'from pure lust of possession, and because the acquisition of them [the curios] in itself seems a sufficient ground for acquiring them' (1886: 4). After psychoanalysis, this idea of 'sufficient ground' may be read as phantastic, as is the entire curiomaniacal operation: it is 'pure lust', less art for art's sake than desire for desire's sake. Indeed, in a striking anticipation, the anonymous author considers the curiomaniac as stuck in the oral phase, stating that 'as a baby is moved to put everything it sees into its mouth, so the curiomaniac seeks to make everything within the limits of the craze his own' (1886: 4). Freud links the oral phase to the loss of the primary object – the (m)other – as sufficient ground and considers it a form of auto-eroticism (*SE* 7: 179–85): it reveals the essential lack which grounds being as such. The phenomenon of curiomania is thus a metonymy of desire, the subject revealing through his mania what Lacan would call his 'lack of being [*manque à être*]' (2007a: 524). Using the example of the curiomaniac who collects nothing but teapots, the writer in the *Pall Mall Gazette* continues: 'Teapot after teapot will be annexed, until the habit of teapot getting for its own sake becomes fixed, and a mania is established' (1886: 4). The associations would have been with George du Maurier's (1834–96) pastiche of the Æsthetic Bridegroom living up to his blue china in 'Six-Mark Tea-pot' (*Punch*, 30 October 1880), and James Hadley's (1837–1903) Aesthetic Teapot for Royal Worcester (1882). Moreover, the clause 'for its own sake' diagnoses the curiomaniac as decadent, here referring to a form of mania, a falling away (Latin: *decadere*) from excellence, a healthy state (Latin: *sanus*). To separate the healthy from the diseased, the collector from the curiomaniac, the aesthete from the decadent, is apparently an urgent biopolitical project for the author, but is beset by problems, for 'the border-line between sanity and mania' is 'so indefinite that it is not easy to state with accuracy where one leaves off and the other begins' (1886: 4; compare *SHR* 188). Curiomania precipitates and produces 'a pronounced egotism', characterised by a 'want of sympathy' with others (1886: 4).

Describing his own 'mad curiosity', Dorian speaks of it as a 'fascination' (*DG* 4.211), a word derived from the Latin *fascinare* ('to bewitch, enchant'), so that his mania is an 'enchantment' with the spectacle of the city.[8] The term is important: as Maurice Blanchot (1907–2003) argues, the phenomenon of fascination destabilises precisely the 'real' in constructing an aesthetic relation of space (1982: 32–3), linking once more to the states of dreaming and intoxication. Another of Wilde's dandies 'fascinated' with space is the protagonist in 'Lord Arthur Savile's Crime'. The short story opens with a reception held by Lady Windermere at Bentinck House, on Bentinck Street in Marylebone, at which Lord Arthur is told by the cheiromantist Septimus Podgers that he will one day commit murder. Unable to process this, Lord Arthur leaves the party, walking west-south-west just over half a mile to Hyde Park, somewhere near Marble Arch. 'The night was bitter cold, and the gas-lamps round the square flared and flickered in the keen wind' (*SF* 59), Wilde writes, in 'stock' phrasing recalling Huysmans reading Dickens (*AR* 11.203; 134), referring seemingly to either Manchester Square or Portman Square. As Lord Arthur proceeds 'with the gait of a drunken man', another form of intoxication, we see the social topography materialised by the figure of law, a policeman, juxtaposed with a beggar who grows frightened of Lord Arthur, 'seeing' in him 'misery greater than his own' (*SF* 59).[9]

Hyde Park also features in chapter 5 of *Dorian Gray*, but there seen from the perspective of the lower classes. Sybil Vane lives somewhere on 'the dreary Euston Road' (*DG* 5.225), running from King's Cross Station in the east (opened in 1852 as the hub for the Great Northern Railway) to Regent's Park, where it joins Marylebone Road. Her 'lodging-house' is 'shabby' (*DG* 5.229), the same adjective that Lord Henry will use to describe the preacher's audience. Sybil and her brother James take a walk west from the family home and arrive at Hyde Park, where she briefly catches sight of Dorian riding in an open carriage with two ladies on the Row. The siblings then walk north to Marble Arch, passing the statue of Achilles (*DG* 5.228) on the south-east at Hyde Park Corner. It is there, 'in front of that dreadful statue', the monument to the Duke of Wellington (1769–1852), cast by Richard Westmacott (1775–1856) and erected in 1822, that Tommy proposes to Mabel Chiltern in *An Ideal Husband* (1895) (2.466). The site is erotically charged, and the statue's nakedness was criticised upon its first erection. But there is another political connotation here, implied when Mabel exclaims 'really, the things that go on in front of that work of art are quite appalling. The police should interfere' (2.467–8). On 21 February 1886, the police interfered with a Social Democratic Federation rally, led by Henry Hyndman (1842–1921), in front of the statue, precipitating violent scenes.

When Lord Arthur arrives at the Park, however, there is a different set of political connotations implied. With its 'sombre woodland' 'fascinating' him, Lord Arthur 'leaned wearily up against the railings' (*SF* 59). These railings were erected during the 1820s along Park Lane, replacing the wall and opening up the park to public consumption. To 'lean' on these railings would have recalled for some of Wilde's readers the so-called 'Hyde Park Railing Affair', when the police blocked off the park from a rally of the Reform League led by the Chartist John Bedford Leno (1826–1894) on 23 July 1866, the protestors breaking down the railings to gain access. More broadly, the railings symbolise the line of duty (the subtitle of the 1891 version of the short story was 'A Study of Duty'): in the context of Hyde Park as social space, Lord Arthur, standing on Park Lane, where his fiancée has her family home (*SF* 66), looks into the public space, but is unable to take her with him until he has fulfilled his 'duty'. '"Murder! murder!" he kept repeating, as though iteration could dim the horror of the word' (*SF* 59), or rather reiteration could empty the signifier of signification. Lord Arthur's epizeuxis recalls less Cassio (*Othello*, 5.1.27) than Iago: 'How silent is this town! Ho, murder, murder!' (5.1.64). The Shakespearean echo makes London complicit with the impending murder, and the social space of the city simultaneously an expression of power.

Labyrinthine Space: St Giles

Leaving the Park, Lord Arthur sets off down Oxford Street, returning northwards, and enters 'narrow shameful alleys':

> Two women with painted faces mocked at him as he went by. From a dark courtyard came a sound of oaths and blows, followed by shrill screams, and, huddled upon a damp door-step, he saw the crook-backed

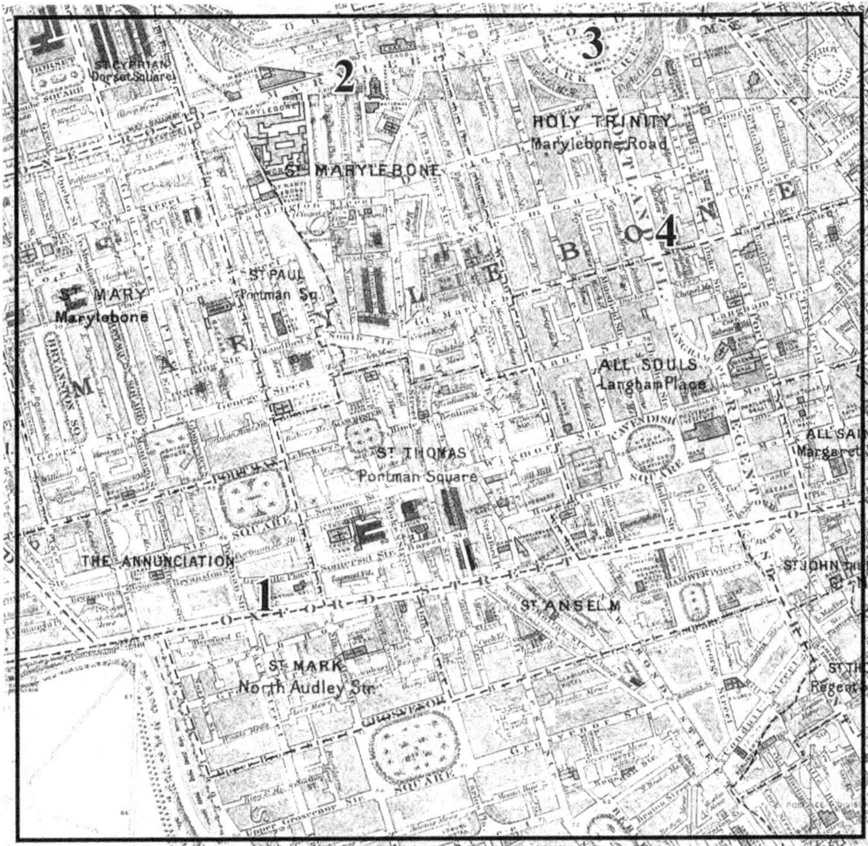

Figure 4.2 Marylebone

1. Oxford Street; 2. Marylebone Church; 3. Park Crescent; 4. Portland Place

> forms of poverty and eld. A strange pity came over him. Were these children of sin and misery predestined to their end, as he to his? Were they, like him, merely puppets of a monstrous show? (*SF* 59)

The passage seems open to the accusation of being 'stock' imagery, but we must be careful not to overlook its intertextual allusions. Wilde's phrasing is an autocitation of 'The Harlot's House' (1885), where prostitutes are figured 'like wire-pulled automatons' (ll. 13–14), and their customer 'a horrible marionette' (l. 22), imagery which will also be recalled in *Dorian Gray* (*DG* 16.325), and later echoed in 'The Ballad of Reading Gaol' (1898) (ll. 295–306). Wilde's image of puppetry also cites the 'Tableaux Parisiens' of Baudelaire's *Les fleurs du mal*, particularly 'Les sept vieillards', suggesting a comparison between the cities. In a reversal of Huysmans's approach to Parisian space through reading Dickens, Wilde's London becomes permeated by Baudelaire's aesthetics of space.

As Wolfreys has argued, the figures of beggars or prostitutes are 'monstrous for the modern subject, in principle and when intimately encountered, living invisibly at the centre of the modern world' (2012: 79). This invisibility is now encountered in the course of Lord Arthur's spatial practice: Marylebone houses not only Bentinck House, but also prostitution, violence and beggars – the striated topographies of the city are ruptured, erupting in a return of London's repressed. Most significantly, what is at stake is not simply the subject's unconscious, but rather a political unconscious, with Lord Arthur 'amazed at the discord between the shallow optimism of the day, and the real facts of existence' (*SF* 59–60). It is another allegorical move, with Lord Arthur reading the 'forms' of poverty and old age, and where what is allegorised is not simply an internal psychological drama, but social relations themselves. London is no utopian cosmopolis in practice.

'After a time', Lord Arthur finds himself, having travelled exactly a mile, 'in front of Marylebone Church' (*SF* 60), where Paul is christened in *Dombey and Son*. With Regent's Park on his left, he looks east along Marylebone Road towards Park Square, seeing 'far into the distance [. . .] the line of flickering gas-lamps' curving, Park Crescent. There, Lord Arthur turns south, walking 'hastily in the direction of Portland Place' (*SF* 60). 'At the corner of Rich Street' (Wilde's invention, suggesting wealth and power)[10] 'stood two men, reading a small bill upon the hoarding'. There, he is overcome by 'an odd feeling of curiosity', that term again, here *unheimlich*. 'The word "Murder", printed in black letters, met his eye' (*SF* 60): the sign (already double) here stands as a phantasm, a figure of reiteration of an event only anticipated, yet to come.

Lord Arthur now 'turned on his heel, and hurried on into the night', a passage which again seems like 'stock' imagery: 'He had a dim memory of wandering through a labyrinth of sordid houses, of being lost in a giant web of somber streets, and it was bright dawn when he found himself at last in Piccadilly Circus' (*SF* 60). Presumably he is heading east, through St Giles's; the passage recalls similar imagery in *Dorian Gray*, where Dorian tires of London's fashionable sights and journeys eastwards: 'I felt that this grey, monstrous London of ours, with its myriads of people, its sordid sinners, and its splendid sins, [. . .] must have something in store for me.' For his part, Dorian describes his journey in only one sentence: 'I don't know what I expected, but I went out and wandered eastward, soon losing my way in a labyrinth of grimy streets and black, grassless squares' (*DG* 4.211). In his edition of the novel, Robert Mighall remarks that the labyrinth was 'a common, if not clichéd, trope for representing the topography of poorer and criminalised districts of the capital at this time' (2000b: 237 n. 6), and we have already noted the way in which Moretti considers the image reductive (1998: 84). But psychoanalytically, the labyrinth is suggestive. Ruskin uses the image in *The Stones* precisely at one of those precarious moments when his theoretical gaze gives way to the pleasures of *aesthesis*, describing the 'whirling, irresistible, labyrinth' of the Rhine or Po rivers contorting into 'twisted eddies' (*CW* 9: 272), a motif linking *jouissance* and death which we have seen already at work in *Edwin Drood*. For his part, Lacan associates the labyrinth with *Zwangsneurose*, obsessional neurosis (2007a: 232, 526), and Freud speaks of getting lost in a very similar labyrinthine city space to the one that Wilde describes, a return which is *unheimlich* (*SE* 17: 237). As such, it is unsurprising to find that the labyrinth is a quintessential representation of space in Lefebvre's terms, primarily conceptual rather than lived (*PS* 233). But we must also situate the image within spatial practice; in Marxist terms, the labyrinth suggests the inability of the lower classes to escape their situation, and the way in which the relations of production were reproduced in and through social space. This 'stock' image speaks powerfully of political realities.

Wilde's description in both texts suggests the infamous Rookery, located between Great Russell Street in the north and the church of St Giles in the Fields to the south. The textual echoes are of de Quincey speaking of losing Ann in 'the mighty labyrinths' around Oxford Street (2008: 36), and Dickens, in particular *Nicholas Nickleby*, where the term is used explicitly in the context of the Rookery, 'that labyrinth of streets which lies between Seven Dials and Soho' (2003g: 64.765). Lost in the 'labyrinth', time is lost in space for Nicholas and Kate Nickleby in the same way as it is for Lord Arthur and Dorian. But something separates the St Giles's of Dickens and Wilde: the construction of New Oxford Street in 1847, bisecting the region. This is a moment of what Lefebvre calls the increased 'visibility' of abstract space, with London's construction of new roads and railways aiming to reconfigure social space. However, New Oxford Street also left many inhabitants homeless, further overcrowding the slums. The very fact that it is the same term, 'labyrinth', that is used is indicative not only of a cliché (a figure of repetition, a cliché already inscribes the trace of difference), but of a precisely Lefebvrean point: such a 'rationalisation' of space was also an 'appropriation' which repeated the relations of production.

St Giles's also features later in *Dorian Gray* after Sybil's disastrous performance at an 'absurd little theatre, with great flaring gas-jets and gaudy play-bills' (*DG* 4.211), identified in the note on the inquest into her death in the *St. James's Gazette* (*DG* 10.273) as the Holborn Royal Theatre (Royal Holborn Empire), 242–5 High Holborn.[11] In these pages, Holborn, one of the alternative theatre districts of London, is associated with its Jewish immigrants, in moments revealing an anti-Semitism that somewhat belies the rhetoric of Wilde's cosmopolitanism.[12] After leaving Sybil, Dorian passes through St Giles's in another passage reliant upon 'stock' imagery:

> He remembered wandering through dimly-lit streets, past gaunt black-shadowed archways and evil-looking houses. Women with hoarse voices and harsh laughter had called after him. Drunkards had reeled by cursing, and chattering to themselves like monstrous apes. He had seen grotesque children huddled upon doorsteps, and heard shrieks and oaths from gloomy courts. (*DG* 7.244)

The lexical echoes here rework 'Lord Arthur Savile's Crime' (*SF* 60), so that the 'dark courtyard' becomes 'gloomy courts', 'oaths and blows' become 'shrieks and oaths', and the 'crook-backed forms of poverty and eld' become 'grotesque children'. The passage seems recycled, and if one description amounts to stock imagery, so too the other. However, this does not preclude the recognition of the way in which it is also very carefully crafted. The first sentence deploys three compound modifiers, with each modifying a noun of location (streets, archways, houses) to describe the space. Each compound modifier, in its turn, is built through noting a certain quality of visibility. Moreover, each compound modifier is progressive, moving from spatial practice to a representation of space in Lefebvrean terms. The first, an empirical observation that the streets were 'dimly-lit', implicitly evokes the fitting of gas street-lighting in London, a point also captured in chapter 16 as Dorian travels towards the East End, where 'the gas-lamps grew fewer, and the streets more narrow and gloomy' (*DG* 16.324). Gas lighting was introduced on Pall Mall in 1807, and was widespread in the West End by the 1830s (R. Porter 1998: 192–3). However, these improvements were distributed disproportionately, so that the city's poorer districts still lacked gas by the time the West End fitted its homes with electricity.[13] Wilde's observation is therefore one grounded in spatial practice. By contrast, his second compound modifier, the 'black-shadowed archways', connotes a representational space, and his final one, the 'evil-looking houses', personifies space, as in allegory, and as in the 'gloomy courts' of the end of the paragraph, the adjective

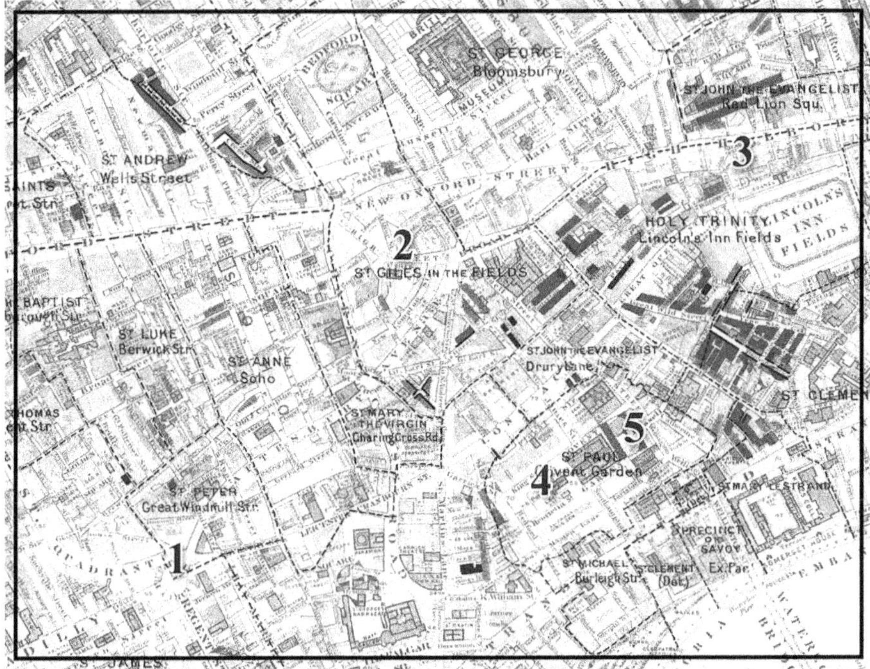

Figure 4.3 St Giles and Covent Garden

1. Piccadilly Circus; 2. St Giles in the Fields; 3. Holborn Royal Theatre, Sybil's theatre in *Dorian Gray*; 4. St Paul's; 5. Royal Opera House

calling into question whether the courts are poorly lit or melancholic. These images give a representation of space in Lefebvre's terms, as does the description of the people, giving a topography of the social space: the prostitutes, 'women with hoarse voices and harsh laughter'; the drunkards, 'chattering to themselves like monstrous apes', figuring a kind of reverse Darwinism, manifesting a fear of what H. G. Wells (1866–1946) calls 'zoological retrogression' (1891); and finally, the children, described as 'grotesque', and thus another figure of allegory, suggesting the perversion or deformation of the future.

Polyrhythmic Space: Covent Garden

In 'Lord Arthur Savile's Crime', the protagonist 'strolls' from the Circus down Piccadilly towards Belgrave Square, recalling the spatial practice associated with Dorian's curiomania. The Circus, built in 1819 under the planning of Nash, was one of the only major monumental spaces constructed in London during the nineteenth century, a significant difference from Haussmann's Paris. En route, Lord Arthur meets 'the great waggons on their way to Covent Garden' (*SF* 60). Covent Garden stretches up to St Giles's at its north end, meeting St James's to the west, linking rich and poor. At the centre lay the market, with St Paul's, designed by Inigo Jones (1573–1652) and completed in 1633, to its south-west, with its famous portico facing the piazza. On the north-eastern side of the market lay the Royal Opera House, then the Theatre Royal (renamed in 1892) and originally constructed in 1732, rebuilt twice following fires in 1808 and 1856, with the new building, designed by Edward Middleton Barry (1830–80), opened in May 1858.[14] Covent Garden was where Dickens's uncommercial traveller was based (*UT* 107), associating the space with *flaneûrie*, and with a certain bustle and excitement. In a famous letter to Wordsworth, Lamb described Covent Garden as a microcosm of London and the city itself as 'a pantomime and a masquerade' that 'impelled' his own noctambulism (1975: 267), a trope that became a staple of mid-Victorian journalism, pioneered by Dickens's protegé George Augustus Sala (1828–95). For his part, Ruskin registers discomfort with the location when commenting that Byron possessed 'a strange taint; and indefinable – evening flavour of Covent Garden' (*CW* 34: 341).

It is there that Dorian arrives after having broken off his engagement with Sybil. Wilde describes the market in another passage rich in 'curious effects':

> He followed [the carts] into the market, and watched the men unloading their wagons. A white-smocked carter offered him some cherries. He thanked him, wondered why he refused to accept any money for them, and began to eat them listlessly. They had been plucked at midnight, and the coldness of the moon had entered into them. A long line of boys carrying crates of striped tulips, and of yellow and red roses, defiled in front of him, threading their way through the huge jade-green piles of vegetables. Under the portico, with its grey sun-bleached pillars, loitered a troop of bedraggled bareheaded girls, waiting for the auction to be over. (*DG* 7.244)

This passage constitutes another reworking from 'Lord Arthur Savile's Crime'. Instead of following the carts into the market, Lord Arthur watches them pass him by on their journey along Piccadilly:

> The white-smocked carters, with their pleasant sunburned faces and coarse curly hair, strode sturdily on, cracking their whips and calling out now and then to each other; on the back of a huge grey horse, the leader of a jangling team, sat a chubby boy [. . .]; and the great piles of vegetables looked

> like masses of jade against the morning sky, like masses of green jade [. . .] Lord Arthur felt curiously affected, he could not tell why. There was something in the dawn's delicate loveliness that seemed to him inexpressibly pathetic [. . .] These rustics, too, with their rough, good-humoured voices, and their nonchalant ways, what a strange London they saw! A London free from the sin of night and the smoke of the day, a pallid ghost-like city, a desolate town of tombs! He wondered what they thought of it, and whether they knew anything of its splendour and its shame, of its fierce, fiery-coloured joys, and its horrible hunger, of all it makes and mars from morn to eve. Probably it was to them merely a mart where they brought their fruits to sell, and where they tarried for a few hours at most, leaving the streets still silent, the houses still asleep. It gave him pleasure to watch them as they went by. (*SF* 60–1)

Three commonalities between the passages should be noted. The first is the eroticism. The market, bordering the poverty of St Giles's and its 'uncared for [. . .] savages' (*UT* 155), was associated with prostitution from the time of Shakespeare until the late nineteenth century. *Harris's List of Covent Garden Ladies* (1757–95) gave an itemised inventory of over one hundred prostitutes working the area: the 'troop of bedraggled bareheaded girls' who 'loiter' under the portico seem to suggest prostitution (to 'loiter with intent' was criminalised by Act of Parliament in 1891, the year of *Dorian Gray*'s publication in book form), as they wait for one auction (the market) to be over before beginning another. But more significant perhaps was the reputation of the area as a homosexual cruising ground (Cook 2003: 10). Covent Garden presents here an image of the erotics of economics and the economics of erotics, of the specific concept of 'desire' developed by Wilde in response to the market society, so fruitfully discussed by Regenia Gagnier (2000: 172) and Jeff Nunokawa (2003: 32–33). Lord Arthur's appreciation marks his scopophilic 'pleasure' in the gaze, that sort of gaze which Proust describes as 'not merely the messenger of the eyes, but a window at which the senses lean out, [. . .] a gaze that would like to touch the body it is looking at, capture it' (*RTP* 1: 139; 1: 142). Likewise, Dorian is also drawn to 'a long line of boys', significant in coming immediately after his break from Sybil.

The second thing to note is the spatial practice. Dorian and Lord Arthur experience London as *flâneurs*. But to the costermongers, it is a space of work. The passage describes their entrance into London, but they are not Londoners, divorced both from its pleasures, the 'sin of night', and from the city itself, the 'smoke of the day'. The city is 'strange' to them, otherworldly. It figures a necropolis, a 'town of tombs', phrasing which recalls James Thompson's (1834–82) 'The City of Dreadful Night' (1880), 'the soundless solitudes immense / Of ranged mansions dark and still as tombs' (ll. 44–5). And yet, while their city is *unheimlich*, the market is theirs as much as it is Lord Arthur's. Two spatial practices, then, and two representational spaces, meet, with Lord Arthur's stroll west encountering the workers' movement east. Lefebvre would term this mobile conjunction 'polyrhythmia' (2013: 77), where diverse rhythms coexist side by side, without producing an 'arrhythmia', a dissonant conflict between the rhythms of those different spatial practices that make up the city. Such a polyrhythmia is characteristic of Wilde's London and offers precisely a theory of 'cosmopolitanism'.

But the third thing to note is the way in which the eroticism and the cosmopolitanism of the social space of Convent Garden come together to construct an aesthetics of this space. The piled vegetables (substantial and dense) are seemingly removed from the realm of the aesthetic, but look 'like masses of green jade', a simile reworked in *Dorian Gray* into the compound adjective 'jade-green' (which Wilde himself may have independently coined).[15] The word 'jade' associates these vegetables with the Oriental, with Wilde's Anglo-Japanesism subtly re-visioning the seemingly mundane street scene, making what is 'natural' (here also implying the domestic) foreign and 'curious'.[16] This 'curiosity' is implied in the moment when the 'white-smocked carter' (specified in both texts) offers Dorian some cherries. The image reveals real spatial practice, with cherries one of the highlights of the market during the season, but while Dorian eats them 'listlessly' (suggesting ennui), the narrator immediately narrativises them: 'they had been plucked at midnight, and the coldness of the moon had entered into them.' They are overdetermined, quasi-mythical yet not quite placed: plucking the fruit at midnight suggests an idea of witchcraft, the coldness of the moon romanticism, the lunar imagery also suggesting eroticism, a motif Wilde mobilises throughout his contemporaneous biblical tragedy, *Salomé* (1891). The associations are sexual, with cherries long having been metaphors for the lips, and more recently having come to be deployed euphemistically for an attractive girl.[17]

But if Wilde's description seeks to activate the eyes and mobilise the reader's desires, then his aesthetics of space also engages their ears. In 'Lord Arthur Savile's Crime', the carters have 'pleasant sunburned faces and coarse curly hair', and are figures who 'strode sturdily on, cracking their whips and calling out', descriptions full of hard consonants, rich in alliteration, so that it is not simply the horses' tack which is 'jangling' but also Wilde's prose. An intrinsically aural quality, one which Wolfreys (2012) considers a marker of Dickens's earlier

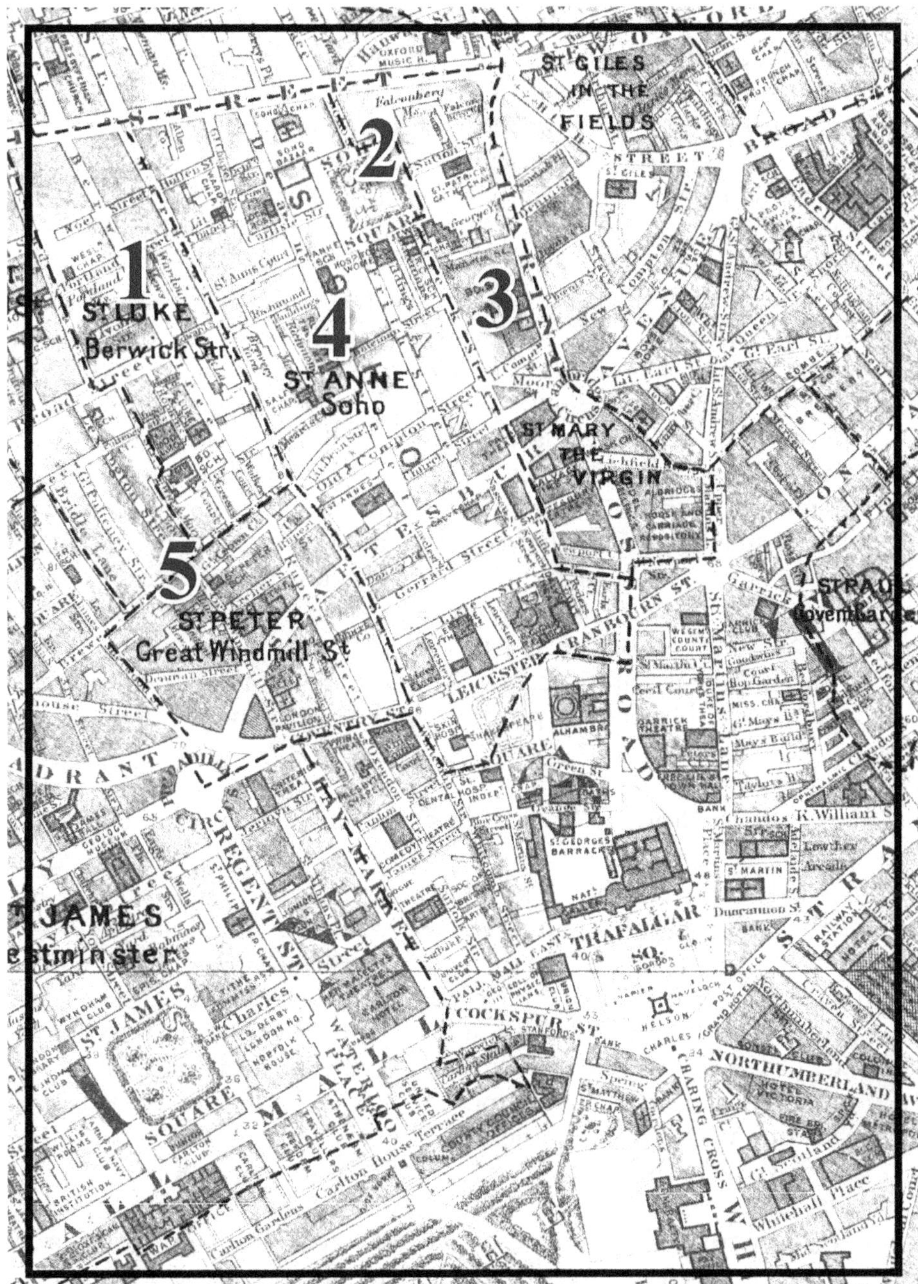

Figure 4.4 Soho

1. Waldour Street; 2. Soho Square; 3. 18 Greek Street, the Universal League for the Material Elevation of the Working Classes; 4. 28 Dean Street, Marx's home 1851–6; 5. Great Windmill Street

phenomenology of the city, also underwrites the description of the 'dawn's delicate loveliness' which follows, one which occasions Lord Arthur's pathetic displacement into the minds of the carters. He wonders 'whether they knew anything of its [London's] splendour and its shame, of its fierce, fiery-coloured joys, and its horrible hunger, of all it makes and mars from morn to eve'. This 'poetic' prose is continued in the final image of London as 'a pallid ghost-like city, a desolate town of tombs', in which the sibilance and the lilting alliterations of the repeated alveolars create a kind of spectral effect. Such effects anticipate Joyce's description of Gabriel Conroy's epiphany in the concluding paragraph of 'The Dead' (1907): 'His soul swooned slowly as he heard the snow falling faintly through the universe and faintly falling, like the descent of their last end, upon all the living and the dead' (2008a: 176). Wilde's city is at once jangling with the hubbub and commotion of the busy scene, those aural shocks proper to this space and the spatial practice that traverses it, and simultaneously a phantom city, its 'streets silent' and, deploying sibilance and prosopopoeia, its 'houses still asleep'. Silently citing Wordsworth's sonnet 'Composed upon Westminster Bridge' (1807), where 'the very houses seem asleep' (l. 13), the final phrase makes Wilde's London a kind of Romantic dream city, 'all bright and glittering in the smokeless air' (l. 8).

Revolutionary Space: Soho

In 'Lord Arthur Savile's Crime', Lord Arthur awaits news of his aunt's death from Venice, smoking cigarettes on the Piazza and dining at Florian's, established in 1720, and Danielli's (*SF* 66), the luxurious hotel overlooking Saint Mark's Basin. It was where Ruskin often stayed (Kite 2012: 111–12), and welcomed Dickens and Georges Sand (1804–76), as James discusses (*IH* 4.67–8). It is another version of the city, implying *The Fall* more than *The Sea Stories*, the decadent space that would be the subject of Thomas Mann's (1875–1955) *Der Tod in Venedig* [*Death in Venice*] (1912). But when the news of Lady Clementina's death arrives in Italy, Lord Arthur returns to London, only to discover she had died of natural causes. Undeterred, his preparations for a second murder attempt take him to Soho.

Lord Arthur's entry into Soho compares with Lord Henry's in *Dorian Gray*, looking for 'a piece of old brocade' in Waldour Street (*DG* 4.209). This runs south from Oxford Street to Pall Mall, and is a haven of antique stores of the type immortalised by Dickens's *Old Curiosity Shop*. But whereas Lord Henry is scouting for bric-à-brac,

Lord Arthur travels to the space for different reasons. He has first visited the lodgings of his friend Count Rouvaloff, 'a young Russian of very revolutionary tendencies' in Bloomsbury, 'generally suspected' of being a 'Nihilist agent' (*SF* 69), and on his directions takes a coach to Soho Square, situated just south of Oxford Street, three streets east of Waldour Street. Lord Arthur 'strolls' (again) south down Greek Street, named after Greek refugees from the Turks made it their home in the 1670s, to Bayle's Court. No Bayle's Court exists off Greek Street, which was cut off by the construction of Shaftesbury Avenue in 1886 (another project designed to make space 'visible'), and it seems likely that the place was deliberately intended by Wilde to be unlocatable.[18] But if Bayle's Court cannot be placed, it is nevertheless located in an explicit space – namely, revolutionary London – precisely insofar as this signifies a social space.[19]

This revolutionary London would later concern Conrad in *The Secret Agent* – published in 1907 but set in 1886, the year before 'Lord Arthur Savile's Crime' was published – where Soho's cosmopolitanism is precisely a question of politics, and where successfully navigating the space becomes a question of knowledge and power. In Wilde's story, Lord Arthur meets Herr Winckelkopf, presumed an exiled revolutionary, at Bayle's Court. In 1862 Mikhail Bakunin (1814–76) had lived on Alfred Street (no. 14), now Huntley Street, located in Bloomsbury, approximately 300 metres north of Soho Square, and he perhaps served as inspiration for Rouvaloff. Winckelkopf, for his part, was probably inspired by the Russian radicals Sergei Stepniak (1851–95), who visited Wilde in Tite Street, and Pyotr Kropotkin (1842–1921), of whom Wilde speaks favourably in *De Profundis* (2005a: 124). The location of Greek Street is in keeping with the political radicalism reconfiguring Soho's social space during the second half of the nineteenth century: running parallel to the west of Greek Street lies Dean Street, where Marx lived (no. 28) between 1851 and 1856, and where he would write *Der 18te Brumaire des Louis Napoleon* [*The Eighteenth Brumaire of Louis Napoleon*] (1852); the German Workers' Education Association, formed in 1840, was based in Great Windmill Street, three streets west of Dean Street, to the other side of Waldour Street; the Universal League for the Material Elevation of the Working Classes (1863) was based at 18 Greek Street; and the International Workingmen's Association (First International) would be founded in 1864 at St Martin's Hall, situated east of Tottenham Court Road and north of Covent Garden. Lord Arthur enters this world deliberately, but Lord Henry would also have found himself in the heart of revolutionary London.

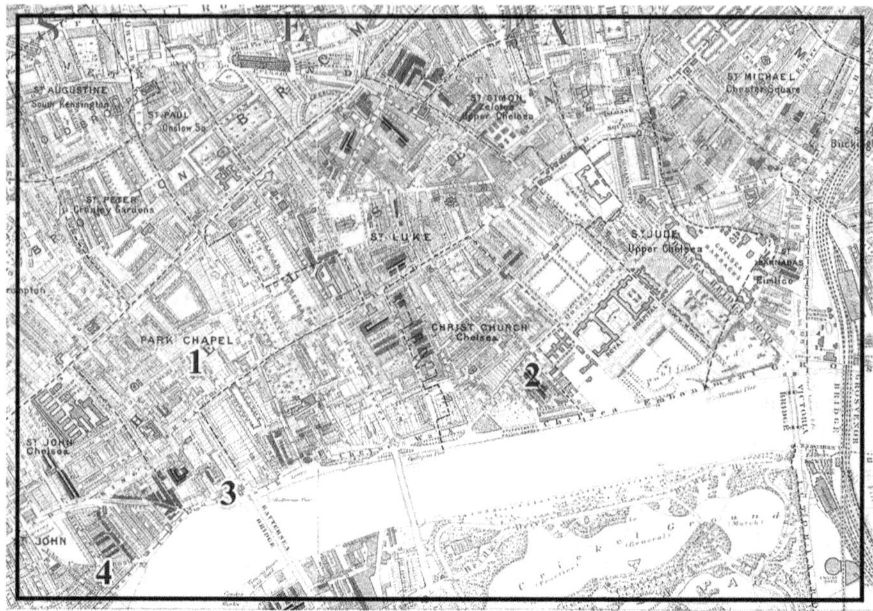

Figure 4.5 Chelsea

1. 1 The Vale, Charles Shannon's home; 2. 34 Tite Street, Wilde's home 1885–92; 3. 96 Cheyne Walk, Whistler's home 1866–78; 4. Cremorne Gardens, closed in 1877

The social space of the Soho of the late 1880s and early 1890s may be usefully compared with Chelsea, where Basil Hallward's studio is located, with the 'dim roar of London' audible (*DG* 1.169). The studio is likely to have been based on 1 The Vale, situated between Fulham Road and King's Road, where the artist Charles Shannon (1863–1937) lived, and Wilde knew the area well, having himself moved from 13 Salisbury Place, off the Strand, to 34 Tite Street in 1885. Located about 600 metres from The Vale, Tite Street was home to Whistler's White House (no. 35), designed by Edward William Godwin (1833–86), with Whistler moving there in 1878 from 96 Cheyne Walk, a short walk away. At the western end of Cheyne Walk lay Cremorne Gardens, opened in 1832, the location of the fireworks display captured in Whistler's *Nocturne in Black and Gold*, that work attacked by Ruskin in *Fors Clavigera* (*CW* 29: 160). The connotations make Chelsea a space of *aesthesis* rather than *theoria*.

The Chelsea of the *fin de siècle* was bohemian and semi-respectable, and, like the Soho of the period, defies any attempts to reduce London to a simple binary. Soho was openly cosmopolitan (Walkowitz 2012: 17–43), incorporating Russians and Germans, and, before them,

Figure 4.6 The Embankment

1. Westminster Bridge; 2. Hungerford Bridge; 3. Big Ben; 4. St Paul's; 5. Cleopatra's Needle

Greeks and Turks, and insofar as this space was associated with the revolutionary. But part of Wilde's aesthetics of space rests on showing how this cosmopolitanism also meant the blurring of discrete striated topographies.[20] It recalls Benjamin, for whom dream space shows the ways in which a city's boundaries function both as limits and as thresholds of transgression, the city being 'only apparently homogenous' (*PW* 88; C3,3), and who links this process of deterritorialisation to dream space. Space in late nineteenth-century London was necessarily interrelated, so that no boundary remained discrete. Lords Henry and Arthur walking through Soho mark a real-life spatial practice that was engaged in this blurring, what Deleuze and Guattari would call a kind of 'nomadism' (2004b: 387–467). It is an idea which Dickens anticipates in 'An Unsettled Neighbourhood' (1854), commenting on the ways in which London was 'unsettled, dissipated, wandering' (1998: 245), and a year later, Baudelaire would expressly link 'cosmopolitanism' with a kind of nomadism in 'L'Exposition Universelle' (1961: 954; 2006: 116). Wilde, building on Baudelaire's cosmopolitanism, understands a blurring of identity, at once personal, sexual and spatial, and linking all three together, as being proper to *fin-de-siècle* Soho.[21] It constitutes a kind of 'cosmopolitan style' (Walkowitz 2006: 4).

Monumental Space: Cleopatra's Needle

Having failed to murder his uncle, Lord Arthur dines at the Buckingham (*SF* 74), suggesting either St James's or Belgravia. From there he 'wanders' south-east towards the Victoria Embankment, perhaps passing Carlton Terrace, where the Windermeres reside in *Lady Windermere's Fan*, a stroll which would have taken approximately half an hour. He sits somewhere between Westminster Bridge, rebuilt in Gothic Revival style in 1862 after a design by Thomas Page (1803–77), and Hungerford Bridge, redesigned by Sir John Hawkshaw (1811–91), which was opened in 1864 and replaced the original suspension bridge designed by Brunel. 'After some time, twelve o'clock boomed from the tall tower at Westminster' (*SF* 75), the chime of Big Ben, with Lord Arthur finding himself at the epicentre of London's political space, the world of Sir Robert Chiltern of *An Ideal Husband*. It is now two o'clock, and Lord Arthur 'strolls' (again) down the Embankment, constructed by the Metropolitan Board of Works between 1865 and 1870. The structure was engineered by Sir Joseph Bazalgette (1819–91), and had a twofold purpose: both to hide the new sewer system running underneath, an essential improvement of public space, and as another moment in the project of making space 'visible', narrowing the Thames, but widening the walkways. Dickens was appreciative, as Ruskin might have expected from his 'modernism' (*CW* 37: 7), and wrote in 1865 that the construction was 'a really fine work' (*LCD* 11: 116). It was lit by gas lamps (reintroduced for reasons of cost in 1884), but Ruskin was less enamoured. For him, said lighting testified to the paucity of British aesthetic 'imagination': 'the utmost, which our modern poetical imagination has been able to invent, is a row of gas-lamps' (*CW* 20: 255).

Irrespective of the artistic merits of the space itself, Wilde's language is certainly aesthetic. It strikes the reader as uncanny, recalling the phrasing used earlier in the text to describe Lord Arthur's walk to Hyde Park. 'The roar of the city' becoming 'fainter', Lord Arthur exclaims: 'How unreal everything looked! How like a strange dream!' (*SF* 75). The anaphoras echo his previous 'discord': 'How incoherent everything seemed! How lacking in harmony!' (*SF* 59). The uncanny registers an untimeliness, in repetitions that augur the approaching murder that is caught in a proleptic pattern of anticipation. With 'the huge dome of St. Paul's' now looming, Lord Arthur comes upon Podgers standing next to Cleopatra's Needle (*SF* 75), and opportunistically murders him. A few days later, a note in the

St James's announces Podgers's suicide: 'the body [. . .] washed on shore at Greenwich, just in front of the Ship Hotel' (*SF* 76). Destroyed in a German air raid in 1941, the Ship Hotel, located south of the river, lay at the present site of the *Cutty Sark*, and was where the wedding banquet of John and Bella takes place in *Our Mutual Friend* (Dickens 1997: 4.4.652–6).

Cleopatra's Needle is one of three Egyptian obelisks removed from Luxor, the others being located in New York and Paris. First presented to Britain in 1819, it would lie in Egypt until 1877, when Sir William Wilson (1809–84) funded its transport in 'a fit of imperial bravura' (D. Porter 1998: 34). The Needle was erected in its present position in September 1878, the location suggesting monumental London. Psychoanalytically, such monumentalism is phallic, an idea which Lefebvre develops (*PS* 262), but Wilde's treatment is more nuanced; in it, we have a 'stock' image which has the potential to transform Wilde's text. The implicit associative traces return us to Soho by way of Paris and the Place de la Concorde.[22] Its Obélisque de Louxor had been presented to France in 1826 and was erected by Louis Philippe (1775–1850) in 1833 on the site where Louis XVI (1754–93) and Marie Antoinette (1755–93) were guillotined. One obelisk implies the other, if only through association. Taken in this context, Wilde's reference to this specific location allows a seemingly incidental ornamentation – both literally and in terms of Wilde's text – to take on renewed significance: the explosive device Winckelkopf makes for Lord Arthur, 'a pretty little French clock, surmounted by an ormolu figure of Liberty trampling the hydra of Despotism' (*SF* 71).

The image of the clock, described as 'pretty' with 'ormulu' decoration, connotes the idea of bourgeois bric-à-brac, a piece of 'kitsch culture' (Jameson 1986: 379) which defines the aesthetic of the nineteenth-century interior. In the realist novel, it is precisely the presence of such objects that gives the 'reality effect', and as such, we may link Wilde's clock to Barthes's analysis of the barometer 'designed to look like a temple of Vesta' in that seemingly incidental description in the first of Flaubert's *Trois Contes* (Flaubert 1952: 1.1.591; 2005: 4).[23] Rereading Barthes politically, Jameson argues that this Flaubertian barometer is not incidental but loaded with meaning, a material expression of 'one of the prime agencies for the rationalization of time and the organization of the modern labour process' during the nineteenth century (1986: 379). But while on the surface Wilde's clock seems like yet another 'aesthetic effect' which risks being reduced in significance, we find that it too is intrinsically political. Given both Winckelkopf and Wilde's own political leanings, the image has socialist significance: it suggests that – like Marx and Engels (1976: 61) – Winckelkopf thinks of the French Revolution as a forerunner of a socialist revolution, and for Wilde the French Revolution constituted 'an admirable result' (*CR* 262). Of 'the cap of Liberty', Jane remarks that 'I didn't think it very becoming myself, but papa says it was historical, so I suppose it is all right' (*SF* 73), so that anything historical may become sartorially acceptable. The joke may be mistaken for a throwaway line, yet almost immediately the question of fashion returns, so that the clock's revolutionary movements, precisely in their bathos (the device does not go off), are supposed by Jane to be 'quite fashionable in London' (*SF* 73), where 'violent Radicals' may be seen at Bentinck House (*SF* 51). In this context, we may recall Benjamin recalling Marx, reminding us that 'the French Revolution [. . .] cited ancient Rome exactly the way fashion cites costumes of the past' (*SW* 4: 395),[24] with the clock evoking one of the great moments of 'world history'. At the same time, however, it belies the politics which it commemorates or exploits through that 'complicity with nothingness, with the petty and the banal', that 'nihilism' which Benjamin diagnoses as 'the innermost core of the bourgeois coziness' (*PW* 216; I2,6). Failing to explode, Liberty flounders in the face of the Hydra's many heads, and we may note *The Eighteenth Brumaire*, written in the very same revolutionary Soho from which the clock emanates, argues the French Revolution a failure insofar as it replaced feudal despotism with a bureaucratic nationalism, perfecting instead of dismantling the state machine, 'this terrifying parasitic body' (Marx 1973: 237). The French Revolution was not cosmopolitan enough. Or rather, succeeding in exploding repeatedly but bathetically, the French Revolution is stuck in eternal return, an event that repeats itself, 'the first time as tragedy, the second time as farce' (Marx 1973: 146). The Dean is convinced that precisely in their continual abortion, these clocks 'should do a great deal of good, as they show that Liberty can't last, but must fall down'. 'Papa says Liberty was invented at the time of the French Revolution', Jane continues: 'How awful it seems!' (*SF* 73).

Returning to the site of Podgers's murder, why did Wilde locate the event at Cleopatra's Needle? The monument images London as a latter-day Egypt, a move which Giovanni Battista Belzoni (1778–1823) had made as early as 1820–1, when he exhibited a facsimile of the tomb of Seti I at the Egyptian Hall, 170–1 Piccadilly, completed in 1812 and designed by Peter Frederick Robinson (1776–1858). In *Dorian Gray*, we learn from Basil that Dorian had lent miniatures to the Egyptian Hall's Dudley Gallery (*DG* 12.293): it not only makes Dorian a collector of curiosities, but allies him with the Egyptian, a thanatic monster, both alive and dead, like Dickens's Jasper. But if the Egyptian Hall gave Regency London the air of cosmopolitanism, hoping to figure itself as the ancient empire reincarnated, then fifty years later, Egypt compared unfavourably to the contemporary power of the British Empire. In *Edwin Drood*, Rosa characterises it as a land suffocated by its subterranean past: 'Tiresome old burying grounds! Isises, and Ibises, and Cheopses, and Pharaohses; who cares about them? And then there was Belzoni or somebody, dragged out by the legs, half choked with bats and dust' (*ED* 3.31). She mummifies Belzoni with his exhibits, with the Egyptian already posthumous by the 1870s, so it was fitting that the Needle would eventually arrive only in 1878, almost sixty years too late. Fitting, too, that Podgers is murdered there: it was a monument that was always already out-of-time, what Benjamin would call, politicising Nietzsche, *unzeitgemäße*.

Having said this, the precise significance of Cleopatra's Needle in Wilde's text is curiously difficult to determine. The site at once evokes both the idea of monumental London and a resistance to this idea. Consider, for a moment, the Obélisque de Louxor, with which Cleopatra's Needle is inevitably compared. Reflecting on the symbolic significance of the Parisian obelisk in 1938, Georges Bataille (1897–1962) comments:

> There was some difficulty in finding an appropriate symbol for the Place de la Concorde, where the images of royalty and the Revolution had proven powerless. [. . .] The apparently meaningless image imposed its calm grandeur and its pacifying power on a location that always threatened to recall the worst. Shadows that could still trouble or weigh upon the conscience were dissipated, and neither God nor time remained. (1985: 221)

As Lefebvre argues, a monument which, by definition, 'embodies and imposes a clearly intelligible message [*une évidence lisible*]', also 'hides a good deal more' (*PS* 143). 'Being political, military, and ultimately fascist in character', monumentality 'mask[s] the will to power [. . .] beneath signs and surfaces which claim to express collective will and collective thought' (*PS* 143). In Dickens's *A Tale of Two Cities* (1859), Sydney Carton, awaiting the guillotine, has a 'prophetic' vision of the Place de la Révolution as though it were what it will become, 'this place – then fair to look upon, without a trace of this day's disfigurement' (2003j: 15.375), recalling Marius's prophetic vision of the Roman Forum in ruins (*ME* 1: 2.12.200). In practice, however, the Place de la Concorde maintained this trace as the Obélisque de Louxor, which figures as a monument to this 'disfigurement', a decapitation both personal and political. Cleopatra's Needle, by contrast, lacks that sort of 'message' which is present, if disingenuously, in Paris: it maintains only a trace, its message endlessly displaced.

How then to place the trace of the presence of the past from this monument-as-text? If the Needle figures monumental London, it suggests political London, its 'imperial bravura' and a sort of bourgeoisie conservatism. Podgers appears to be a sacrificial victim, a lower-class offering to his social superior, presenting himself at the site in the name of 'duty'. But at the same time, through metonymic association with the Obélisque de Louxor, the Needle may remind us of the trace of a revolutionary spirit which resists the 'fascism' of monumentality. It causes a re-situation – albeit temporary – from political London to revolutionary London. It reminds us that the Liberty that was 'invented' during the French Revolution was not radical enough for Marx, or for Wilde, and the trace of this failure is monumentalised by the Needle. Such an idea of Liberty 'must fall down' (*SF* 73), crumbling as all monuments, which in their attempted masking of the will to power aim to resist time eternally. Collapsing, such monuments necessarily leave their own trace as an intrinsic moment in any aesthetics of space.

Dickensian Dream Spaces II: Wilde after Dickens

In chapter 15 of *Dorian Gray*, Dorian leaves Lady Narborough's party, presumably located either in Mayfair or in St James's, and returns home. There, he is possessed by a 'mad craving', and retrieves a 'small Chinese box' from a cabinet, containing opium, its 'odour curiously heavy and persistent' (*DG* 15.322). The adverb links opium to the 'curious' aesthetics 'effects' belonging to the *fin-de-siècle* metropolis, imaging London as a dream city. Dorian dresses 'commonly' (*DG* 15.323), walking east to Bond Street, famous for catering to dandies from the eighteenth century onwards.[25] He hails a hansom, giving the driver an address 'in a low voice' (*DG* 15.323), the journey being recorded in the opening paragraphs of chapter 16, where 'a cold rain began to fall, and the blurred street-lamps looked ghastly in the dripping mist' (*DG* 16.324). The image recalls Clennam in *Little Dorrit* describing the 'street-lamps, blurred by the

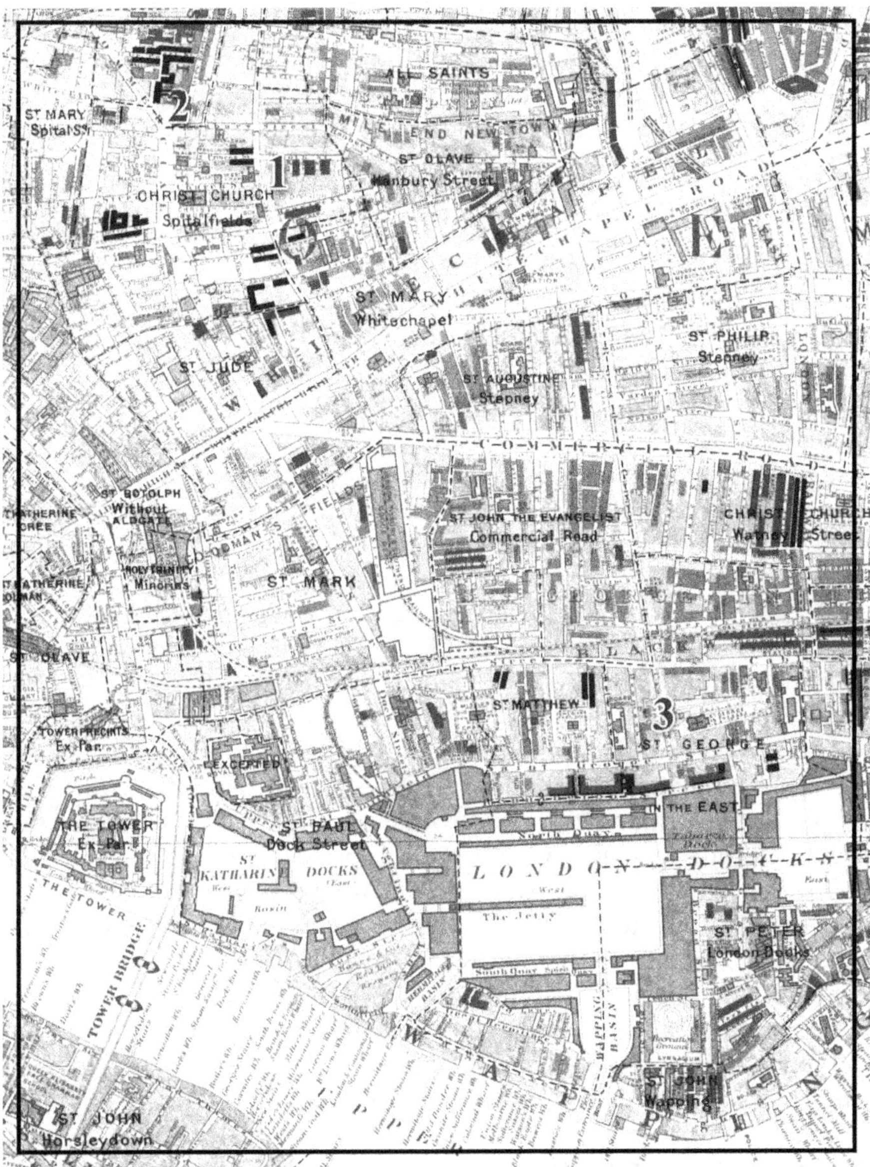

Figure 4.7 The East End

1. Brick Lane; 2. Hanbury Street; 3. Bluegate Fields

foggy air' on the Strand (2012: 2.9.521), through which the hansom presumably passes on the way 'towards the river' (*DG* 15.323), but here they figure as 'ghastly', horrific, a word that came to be ghosted by its orthographic neighbour 'ghostly' (*OED* 'ghastly' *adj.* 2a), so that the connotations become otherworldly. The social topography mapped is reminiscent of Wilde's earlier portrait of St Giles's, with the public houses just closing, and 'dim men and women [. . .] clustering in broken groups round their doors. From some of the bars came the sound of horrible laughter. In others, drunkards brawled and screamed' (*DG* 16.324). Perhaps based on Jerrold's *London: A Pilgrimage* (1872: 142; Carens 1995: 70), the description is thanatic, the moon hanging 'low in the sky like a yellow skull' (*DG* 16.324), imagery recalling *Salomé*. It figures the moon as an emblem of death, at once baroque and allegorical (Benjamin 1998: 166), readable in two ways, both as 'human spirit petrified' and as 'nature in decay' (Buck-Morss 1991: 161). The skull figures as a memento mori that proleptically foreshadows Dorian's end. In this way, the environment becomes an element of Wilde's aesthetics of space, so that 'a huge misshapen cloud stretched a long arm across' to hide the moon. The prosopopoeia functions like a pathetic fallacy, echoing Dorian's own 'misshapen' image in his portrait (*DG* 11.277, 11.286, 14.312, 16.326, 18.339).

As Dorian's journey continues, 'a steam rose from the horse as it splashed up the puddles' (*DG* 16.324). The image recalls the opening paragraphs of *Bleak House* where London is described as 'a great (and dirty) city' (*BH* 1.13). Dickens's parenthesis calls into question the logic of the conjunction, so that the dirtiness may qualify the greatness or suggest that the city's glory is dependent on its night-side. Taking the river route, a distance of just under five miles, Dorian's journey would take approximately an hour. He is consumed by his 'craving', with 'the way seem[ing] interminable, and the streets like the black web of some sprawling spider. The monotony became unbearable' (*DG* 16.325). The syntactic parallel connects the journey with 'monotony', that condition which Jasper attempts to escape by 'scattering' his consciousness through opium in the East End. It also links the 'unbearable' with the 'interminable', the latter comparable with Conrad's use of the word in *Heart of Darkness*, published nine years after *Dorian Gray*. This is another novel that questions of the logic of the conjunction when London is described as 'the biggest, and the greatest, town on earth' (Conrad 2008a: 103). In the opening on the *Nellie*, moored at Greenhithe, twenty miles east down the river from Bluegate Fields, Conrad's narrator looks eastwards past Gravesend, a name doubly connotative of death (graves-end), towards the Empire, with 'the sea-reach of the Thames stretch[ing] before us like beginning of an interminable waterway' (2008a: 103). Here, the 'interminable' opens London up to the Other, a vision 'leading to the uttermost ends of the earth'

(2008a: 104, 187), promising to take both Marlow and the narrator beyond the pleasure principle. In *Dorian Gray*, by contrast, the 'interminable' closes London in on itself in the image of 'the black web of some sprawling spider'. Wilde's phrase, recalling the 'web' of St Giles's in 'Lord Arthur Savile's Crime' (*SF* 60), anticipates Borges in *The Aleph* (1945), his apocalyptic vision of 'a silvery spider-web at the center of a black pyramid' and of 'a broken labyrinth (it was London)' (2004: 130). In Borges's dream space, the labyrinth and spider's web become intertwined, associating Ariadne with Arachne. Like the labyrinth, the web is another 'representational' image in Lefebvrean terms: people will be caught in it. In this sense, Wilde's phrase echoes Augustus Mayhew's *Paved with Gold* (1857), discussing the commercialisation of London and the way in which the increased 'visibility' of abstract space displaced the inhabitants of the slums, envisaging 'the metropolis [. . .] transformed into a huge spider's web' (1858: 41).

Dorian's hansom passes 'lonely brickfields', 'the strange, bottle-shaped kilns with their orange, fanlike tongues of fire' (*DG* 16.325), another Rue d'Enfer and more thanatic imagery, evoking the inferno. The allusion suggests Brick Lane, which passes from Shoreditch south to Whitechapel. The location would have been loaded for Wilde's readers in 1890–1: it was there, between 3 April and 9 November 1888, that Jack the Ripper committed the Whitechapel murders, with one of his victims, Annie Chapman, discovered off 29 Hanbury Street, which intersects with Brick Lane. As the hansom diverts from the main road, it passes houses with 'fantastic shadows [. . .] silhouetted against some lamp-lit blind[s]. He watched them curiously. They moved like monstrous marionettes, and made gestures like live things' (*DG* 16.325), phrasing recalling 'Lord Arthur Savile's Crime' (*SF* 59) and 'The Harlot's House' (l. 24). The simile here is arresting, reversing the reader's expectations, the figures dead, but making 'gestures like live things' (*DG* 16.325). There is nothing 'natural' about the trope, which allegorises the living as dead, the inanimate as animate, as in a fetish. If the language here implies Baudelaire's 'Les sept vieillards', the women as 'monstres disloqués' (l. 5) who totter like 'marionettes' (l. 13), and whose monstrosity troubles gender ('monstres' is masculine),[26] then it also quotes Dickens once more. In *Edwin Drood*, when Puffer tries to light her pipe, her matches 'jump and start, as I cough and cough, like live things' (*ED* 23.257). Such an intertextual echo locates Wilde's aesthetics of space 'after Dickens', the phrase drawn from 'The Dawn Again', set in the same opium dens in Bluegate Fields to which Dorian is travelling. He is now approaching the place, and 'over the low roofs and jagged chimney-stacks of the houses rose the black masts of ships. Wreaths of white mist clung like ghostly sails to the yards' (*DG* 16.326), another ghostly/ghastly image.[27] Dorian pays his driver and walks the last distance. The descriptive prose here is constituted by short, staccato sentences, focusing on chiaroscuro effects: 'Here and there a lantern gleamed at the stern of some huge merchantman. The light shook and splintered in the puddles. A red glare came from an outward-bound steamer that was coaling. The slimy pavement looked like a wet mackintosh' (*DG* 16.326). The 'slimy pavement', added to the 1891 revised edition, perhaps quotes Arthur Conan Doyle's (1859–1930) *The Sign of Four* (1890), published alongside *Dorian Gray* in *Lippincott's Monthly Magazine* in 1890. There, Watson recalls a dreary September evening down the Strand: 'the lamps were but misty splotches of diffused light which threw a feeble circular glimmer upon the slimy pavement' (2014: 16). More broadly, Wilde's image disorientes both Dorian and the reader: the location, defined by darkness, is fractured by light arriving from all directions, the 'red glare' connoting hell, 'splintering' and fragmenting the visible field. Disrupting the gaze, East End space 'scatters' consciousness, as in the late Dickens.

Dorian finally arrives at the opium den, 'a small shabby house that was wedged in between two gaunt factories' (*DG* 16.326). Wilde's depiction is reliant upon Dickens's aesthetics of space, but the location in London's docklands would also have carried another important set of connotations to his readers in 1891, compared to those of *Edwin Drood* in 1869–70. Memories would have been fresh of the London Dock strike of 14 August 1889, the year before Wilde's novel was first serialised, in an event that served to concentrate public attention on the poverty of the area, the 'problem' of the East End, as Lord Henry puts it earlier (*DG* 3.203).[28] Indeed, in the opium den, Wilde describes a very different social space from those mapped elsewhere in the novel, and a very different kind of cosmopolitanism:

> Some Malays were crouching by a little charcoal stove, playing with bone counters and showing their white teeth as they chattered. In one corner, with his head buried in his arms, a sailor sprawled over a table, and by the tawdrily painted bar that ran across one complete side stood two haggard women, mocking an old man who was brushing the sleeves of his coat with an expression of disgust. (*DG* 16.326–7)

The Malaysians are figured as skulls, memento mori once again, allegorical figures, recalling, on the one hand, Holbein's *Gambler* (1547), and, on the other, Baudelaire's 'Le jeu', those skeletal figures characterised synecdochically as 'faces without lips, / Lips without colour over toothless jaws' (ll. 5–6), who prefer 'suffering to death, and Hell to nothingness' (l. 24). As in Dickens, the presence of Malaysians maps the social space not only of the *fin-de-siècle* London docklands, but of the Empire, indicating the colonial triangle that linked India, Malaysia and China, and British interests in the East. It is a different kind of cosmopolis, evoking those 'routes of financial exploitation and moral contamination' that linked London with the world beyond (Agathocleous 2011: 118).[29] This kind of cosmopolitanism is a point reinforced by the figures upstairs in the den, where 'a half-caste, in a ragged turban and a shabby ulster, grinned a hideous greeting' (*DG* 16.328). All the figures seem to be emerging out of a dream, as though that is what is proper to this dream space. They recall de Quincey in the *Confessions*, describing his encounter with a 'Malay', one which produced an 'anxiety', here as much national as personal, which 'fastened afterwards upon my dreams, and brought other Malays with him worse than himself' (2008: 58).

If Wilde is alluding to Holbein's *Danse Macabre* here, as Baudelaire had been, and as Dickens too had in 'A Small Star in the East', then this would be to associate the opium addicts with those 'monstrous marionettes', the prostitutes, discussed a few paragraphs earlier (*DG* 16.325). When Dorian goes upstairs, we have a similar description, the reader being confronted by 'the grotesque things that lay in such fantastic postures on the ragged mattresses. The twisted limbs, the gaping mouths, the staring lustreless eyes, fascinated him. He knew in what strange heavens they were suffering, and what dull hells were teaching them the secret of some new joy' (*DG* 16.327). Parkinson calls opium 'the fascinating drug' (1866: 423), noting the 'lacklustre eyes' (1866: 425) of the intoxicated, and Wilde's phrasing in the passage takes in not only Parkinson and the 'grotesque' of Baudelaire, but also Edward Young's (1683–1765) *Night Thoughts* (1742–5), another allegorical text dealing with melancholy, where saints 'teach dull Hell her own black arts' (9.1813). When Dorian leaves the den, intending to move on to another, he is pursued by James Vane, intent on revenge. Dorian is attacked, a violence which is implicated in the social space, accosted in an archway (*DG* 16.330), a liminal kind of architectural uncanny (Vidler 1992: 3), where all but one (Mary Jane Kelly) of the Ripper's the victims were discovered.

Once again, however, it is important to notice the way in which Wilde, writing after Dickens, has Dickens carefully underwrite the description of these spaces. The 'two haggard women' Dorian meets when he first enters the room evoke the opening descriptions of *Edwin Drood*, where Jasper awakes next to 'a Chinaman, a Lascar, and a haggard woman' (*ED* 1.7), namely Puffer, and where the adjective marks her doppelgängers, Jasper and Neville, with Dorian (or at least his portrait) also 'haggard' (*DG* 8.256). Puffer appears again in Wilde's text, ghosting the figure of the woman Dorian discusses with Adrian Singleton, whom he has met in the den, and whose life, we have been told by Basil, has been 'ruined' by his friendship (*DG* 13.293). Suggesting that he will travel to the 'other place', Adrian replies: 'That mad-cat is sure to be there. They won't have her in this place now' (*DG* 16.327). We can be sure the description is carefully chosen, because the simpler description 'woman' had been deleted by Wilde in favour of 'mad-cat' in the manuscript (*DG* 327n.). It recalls Princess Puffer, but with Wilde's portrait here beginning with the fictional, aesthetic world of *Edwin Drood*, rather than the real figure of Lascar Sal upon whom Dickens based his character. In that novel's final chapter, 'The Dawn Again', Puffer lays her hand on Jasper's chest and moves him back and forth 'as a cat might stimulate a half slain mouse' (*ED* 23.261), seeking to elicit from him information regarding the murder of Edwin. This 'catlike action' is repeated a few paragraphs on, and a third time, where she is described as 'unwinking, catlike, and intent' (23.263). In the context of the opium den, Wilde's allusion to a woman described as a 'mad-cat' takes in the late Dickens, so that Wilde maps one space not only through a geographically real and embodied experience of the East End, but also, and at the same time, through a prior aesthetics of this space.

Bric-à-Brac London

In 'The Critic as Artist', Wilde claims that aestheticism must be understood to be a kind of 'cosmopolitanism' (*CR* 202), but while Julia Prewett Brown (1997) has contextualised Wilde's idea alongside a Kantian heritage, the relationship between his cosmopolitanism and his aesthetics of space has not been widely discussed.[30] This is significant because, as this chapter has demonstrated, Wilde's cosmopolitanism reflects the social conditions of the late nineteenth-century city. For Wilde, 'cosmopolitan' 'criticism will annihilate race-prejudices, by insisting upon the unity of the human mind in the variety of its forms' (*CR* 203). It disintegrates national boundaries, a point that recalls Marx and Engels, for whom the growth of the city produces the proletariat, who, in their turn, would dissolve the idea of 'nationality' (2002: 324).[31] During the late nineteenth century, London was *the* cosmopolitan city, and we have encountered some of those immigrants who produced the social space of this city: the Greeks of Greek Street, the Germans and Russians of Soho, the Jewish immigrants of Holborn, and the Malaysians and Chinese of the East End. But we have also noticed the way in which the higher classes found themselves in close proximity to their lower-class neighbours. As Lady Henry puts it: 'even those who are born in England become foreigners after a time, don't they?' It turned London itself into a work of art that was 'quite cosmopolitan' (*DG* 4.209).

There is something utopian in Wilde's cosmopolitanism, perhaps best illustrated in 'The Soul of Man', a somewhat unrealistic idealism of which Pater's Marius had already been suspicious in the doctrines of both Apuleius and Marcus Aurelius.[32] But if Wilde's cosmopolitanism implies a revolutionary spirit, as the promise of a true *fraternité*, then in practice his writings on London show him to have been divided between cosmopolitan promise and capitalist reality. The *flâneur* is, after all, a consumer of space, representing himself 'as outside the circuits of production and reproduction, consuming the spectacle of the city' (Gagnier 2000: 172).[33] In his 'curious' vision of Piccadilly, treating the space of the city as a kind of arcade (*DG* 4.211), Wilde figures the *fin-de-siècle* city as an aesthetic object that is produced and reproduced through its consumption, in a way that anticipates 'the productive consumption of space' that Lefebvre identifies at work in the later twentieth century (*PS* 359).[34]

At the absent centre of Wilde's aesthetics of space lies Dorian's home, a site that seems deliberately difficult to locate. In chapter 12, Dorian is walking northwards from Lord Henry's house when he comes across Basil 'at the corner of Grosvenor Square and South Audley Street' (*DG* 12.291). In the heart of Mayfair, Grosvenor Square lies just south of Oxford Street and to the east of Hyde Park, next to Park Street, where Lady Jane Wilde (1821–96) would live (no. 116); the location also features as the family residence of the Bracknells (no. 104) in *The Importance of Being Earnest* (3.334). Making his way from Curzon Street, Dorian would probably have walked up South Audley Street, which runs north to meet Grosvenor Square at its south-west point, passing on his way the premises of Mr Hubbard, 'the celebrated frame-maker' (*DG* 10.270). But while Wilde clearly marks the general space where Dorian and Basil meet as Mayfair, precisely where Dorian's home is located remains unclear.

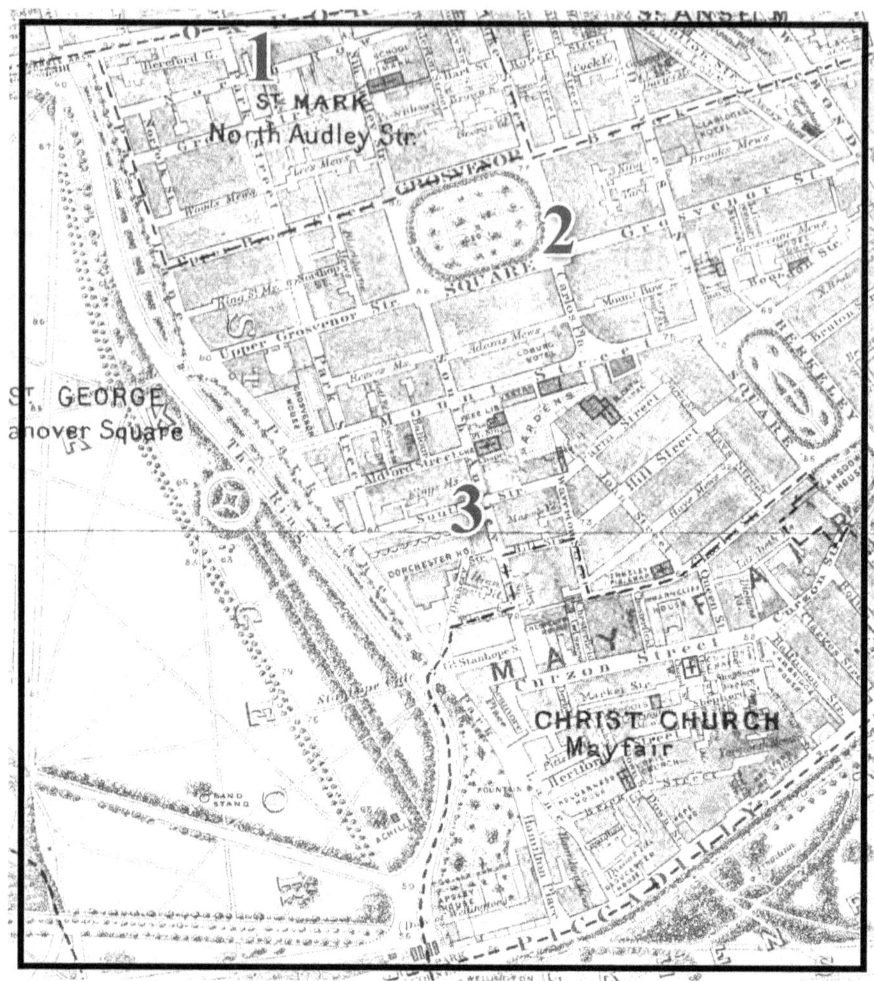

Figure 4.8 Grosvenor Square

1. 116 Park Street, Lady Wilde's home; 2. 104 Grosvenor Square, Lady Bracknell's home in *The Importance of Being Earnest*; 3. South Audley Street

For Lefebvre, representational space always has its 'affective kernel' (*PS* 42), but in *Dorian Gray*, this centre is unlocatable. The difficulties are augmented because of the fog on the night when Dorian and Basil meet, with the former exclaiming 'I can't even recognise Grosvenor Square' (*DG* 12.291). We recall that this particular problem of 'recognition' is precisely a question of the aesthetics of space, with Vivian noting in 'The Decay of Lying' how 'there may have been fogs for centuries in London. [. . .] But no one saw them, and so we do not know anything about them. They did not exist till Art had invented them' (*CR* 95). It is a London in dialogue with Whistler, offering a kind of 'literary version of soft-focus', as Freeman memorably puts it (2007: 118). More specifically, however, Wilde's image of London finds itself again in dialogue with Dickens, be it *Bleak House* with 'fog everywhere' (*BH* 1.13), where this fog serves to obscure any locatable space, or the 'heavy and dark' fog of *Our Mutual Friend*: 'Animate London, with smarting eyes and irritated lungs, was blinking, wheezing, and choking; inanimate London was a sooty spectre, divided in purpose between being visible and invisible, and so being wholly neither' (1997: 3.1.417). The city as 'spectre', as trace. But Dorian's house is also difficult to locate because it seems out of place, or to have no place proper to it. Since representational space embraces 'lived situations', Lefebvre argues that it 'immediately implies time' – a time that monumentalism through its will to power seeks to deny (*PS* 42). But Dorian's home cannot be monumental, since it has no site. Housing his portrait, which is resistant to time, it is out of time, untimely in Benjamin's sense (1998: 166), like Dickens's Curiosity Shop or like the trace, 'the simulacrum of a presence that dislocates itself, displaces itself' (Derrida 1982: 24). Unsurprisingly, the portrait figures explicitly as a 'ruin' (*DG* 8.250), as an allegory of London, recalling Benjamin, for whom 'allegories are, in the realm of thoughts, what ruins are in the realm of things' (1998: 178).

Recalling his trip to Soho, Lord Henry remarks that London 'is like a bric-à-brac shop, all monsters and dust, and everything priced above its proper value' (*DG* 1.178), a city of ruins. After Haussmannisation, Paris figures as an allegorical ruin for Baudelaire in 'Le Cygne', and the modern cosmopolitan city becomes 'jumbled bric-à-brac' (l. 12), a phrase lurking behind Lord Henry's. Rather than think Wilde's London a symptomatic, psycho-textual precipitate, or, by extension, a hack job bolted together out of 'stock' images, it becomes possible to reconceive his aesthetics of space as a kind of collage carefully constructed out of textual bric-à-brac. Certainly, his prose is 'poetic' in the sense that Tambling speaks of Dickens's 'poetry of the city' (2015). Wilde's texts are remarkably literary, densely allusive, and intensely aware of their historical past, so that Wilde reads and writes the city of the London through the texts that preceded it, producing a kind of Benjaminian 'constellation'. In this sense, *Dorian Gray* becomes readable as an allegory of London, of the changing city, and of the ruins that remain. It is a cosmopolitan London, a city becoming-otherwise, a foreign space that maintains the trace of the past in a present that always displaces itself. The reader becomes like Lord Arthur, reading the same city twice over, both as it 'really is' and through the texts which are continually reconstructing the reality and the aesthetics of this space, a critical operation through which Wilde moves past both Arnold and Pater, 'de-realising' space in seeing 'the object as in itself it really is not' (*CR* 159). In other words, this sees Wilde move from the broadly phenomenological position of Pater towards a critical operation that may be instead termed 'phantasmatological', representing a London that is 'unreal', melting into air.[35] Wilde's aestheticism reads the city afresh, in an aesthetics of space that is built through a cosmopolitan sensibility. It is like Lord Arthur's vision of a foreign, phantasmic London, seen through the eyes of another, 'a pallid ghost-like city, a desolate town of tombs' (*SF* 60).

Notes

1. On the Sunday Trading Riots of 1855, see Harrison 1965.
2. Lord Goring rides on Rotten Row in *An Ideal Husband*, as does Mrs Erylnne in *Lady Windermere's Fan* (1.280–1); in *Dorian Gray*, Dorian's 'friendship' means that Lady Gwendolen can no longer show herself there (*DG* 12.294).
3. Wilde met Morris at the latter's lecture on tapestry that Wilde reviewed for the *Pall Mall Gazette*, 2 November 1888 (2013b: 96–8). He would then review Morris's novel *The House of the Wolfings* for the same publication, 2 March 1889 (2013b: 184–7), with the two beginning to correspond (*LOW* 476). Wilde was also friendly with May Morris (1862–1938) (*LOW* 396), an active figure on the London socialist scene.
4. On Wilde and the demonic, see Whiteley 2015: 235–9.
5. As King Schœneus notes in 'Atalanta's Race', 'If thou losest life, then all is lost', but Milanion replies: 'Doubt not that I have counted well the cost. / But say, on what day wilt thou that I gain / Fulfilled delight, or death to end my pain?' (ll. 323, 325–7). Wilde alludes to *The Earthly Paradise* in 'The Critic as Artist' (*CR* 151, 477n.), although in a letter to William Arthur Smith Benson (1854–1924), 16 May 1885, he distances Morris's poem from socialism (*LOW* 260).
6. Although Burlington Arcade was not, as Wilde's narrator suggests, 'low', but on two storeys.
7. The same location returns in chapter 6, set at 'a little private room at the Bristol' (*DG* 6.231) where Lord Henry informs Basil of Dorian's engagement. Joseph Bristow suggests the Bristol is Wilde's 'invention', noting that the word 'Boodles' was deleted here in the manuscript (*DG* 384n.). Boodle's was the notable club that produces Lord Goring (*An Ideal Husband*, 1.231), founded in 1762 at 49–51 Pall Mall, before moving to premises at 28 St James's Street in 1782; adjacent to Boodle's

lay D. R. Harris and Co. (no. 29), opened in 1790, the likely model for the chemist Pestle and Humbey's where Lord Arthur purchases poison (*SF* 64). But Wilde must have changed the reference to designate the Bristol Hotel, which had private rooms, and which was located in Burlington House, the family home of Lord Cavendish.

8. On Wilde and fascination, see Baumbach 2015: 190–208 and Whiteley 2015: 126–32.
9. The phrasing will be recalled in the first draft of *Dorian Gray*, in language which Wilde's editor, J. M. Stoddart (1845–1921), cut from the text: 'even the sinful creatures who prowl the streets at night had cursed him [Dorian] as he passed by, seeing in him a corruption greater than their own, and knowing too well the horror of his real life' (*DG* 120n.).
10. There was a Rich Street in the East End, off West India Dock Road, but not in Marylebone.
11. The Holborn Royal Theatre had a short-lived existence, opening in 1870 only to burn down in 1880: in this context, there is an irony to the reference to the 'great flaring gas-jets' (*DG* 4.211) that illuminated the stage. London's alternative theatres, demolished to make way for Kingsway, which was opened in 1905, are discussed by Sherson 1925.
12. Mr Isaacs, the fictional proprietor of the Holborn Royal Theatre, is figured as a 'hideous Jew' (*DG* 4.211). On Wilde's anti-Semitism, see Nassaar 2003 and Salamensky 2012.
13. Electric bells feature in *Lady Windermere's Fan* (1.481), *An Ideal Husband* (3.645) and *The Importance of Being Earnest* (1.272). Benjamin links advances in lighting and the gradual adoption of gas in Paris to social topography (*PW* 562–70; T).
14. It was there that Lady Henry had first seen Dorian at a performance of Richard Wagner's (1813–83) *Lohengrin* (1850) (*DG* 4.208) and that Lord Henry and Dorian would relax the night after Sybil's death (8.252). The Opera House staged *Lohengrin* in June 1888 (Saint et al. 1982: 97), but the Royal Holborn Theatre, where Sybil works, had been destroyed in 1880: these kinds of discrepancies prevent the dating of the action and mark Wilde's London as a representational space.
15. The *OED* gives Rudyard Kipling's (1865–1936) travelogue on the Yellowstone River, published in the *Pall Mall Gazette*, 24 March 1892, as the first use of 'jade-green'. The essay was actually first published three years earlier in the *Pioneer* in 1889 (1890a: 171, and see also 205). While it is unclear if Wilde had read Kipling's *American Notes*, he would almost certainly have read 'Without Benefit of Clergy', in which 'jade-green' also appears (1890b: 152), published in *Macmillan's Magazine*, June 1890, but by this point the manuscript of *Dorian Gray* was completed.
16. On Wilde and the Anglo-Japanese tradition, see Nunokawa 2003: 41–53.

17. For the cherry's association with the lips, see for instance, Sidney's *Astrophil and Stella*, 82.5–8. The *OED* dates the association of cherries with the hymen and the breaking of virginity to 1889, but the *Oxford Dictionary of Slang* dates 'cherry' for a young attractive woman to the middle of the nineteenth century.
18. A Bayles Court existed further south, off Adam Street, south of the Strand, a location that no longer exists. For the earlier site, see Lockie 1810.
19. The *OED* cites Southey's *Joan of Arc* (1796) (8.156–7) for 'bayle', the 'outer line of fortification', an etymological allusion perhaps lying behind Wilde's name for this revolutionary space.
20. This blurring effect is one also described in the context of Holborn. Leaving the Bristol, Lord Henry and Dorian take the brougham to watch Sybil perform, with Basil following in a hansom. Basil experiences 'a strange sense of loss', feeling that Dorian would 'never again be to him all that he had been in the past': 'Life had come between them. . . . His eyes darkened, and the crowded, flaring streets became blurred to his eyes' (*DG* 6.237). Basil becomes aware that he can never recover Dorian as his aesthetic ideal in reality, an idea to which he is bound, not least homoerotically. The reference here, noted by none of Wilde's editors, is to the Bible, where St Paul (Romans 11: 10) recalls David (Psalms 69: 23), with 'darkened eyes', or blindness: the inability to see what lies in front. Basil has lost his artistic vision at the same time as he loses his muse. This affects his vision of space, with 'the crowded, flaring streets' becoming 'blurred to his eyes', so that, ironically, it is the only true artist of the story who is unable to engage in the aesthetics of space.
21. A few years later, on 10 March 1893, Alfred Taylor would introduce Wilde to Charlie Parker and his brother, William, for dinner in a private room at Kettner's (surviving into the twenty-first century, closing its doors finally on 30 January 2016), 29 Romilly Street, Soho. William's testimony of the affair that followed was used as evidence during Wilde's second trial of 1895.
22. It is worth noting that Dickens's uncommercial traveller considers Trafalgar Square, designed by Nash and opened in 1844, testimony to 'the abortive ugliness' of monumental London, comparing unfavourably with 'the gallant beauty of the Place de la Concorde' (*UT* 279).
23. Wilde borrowed a copy of Flaubert's *Trois Contes* from Pater the year of its publication while an undergraduate at Oxford (*LWP* 26).
24. Benjamin recalls Marx's *Eighteenth Brumaire*: 'the heroes of the old French Revolution, as well as its parties and masses, accomplished the task of their epoch, which was the emancipation and establishment of modern bourgeois society, in Roman costume and with Roman slogans. [. . .] Once the new social formation had been established, the antediluvian colossi disappeared along with the resurrected imitations of Rome – imitations of Brutus, Gracchus, Publicola, the tribunes, the senators and Caesar himself' (Marx 1973: 147).

25. It is on Bond Street that Lord Arthur buys a 'pretty little silver *bonbonnière*' in which he deposits Lady Beauchamp's poison (*SF* 65).
26. On this point, see McLees 1989: 98.
27. This phrasing recalls Henry Wadsworth Longfellow's *The Golden Legend* (1851), another demonic tale, where Prince Henry looks out at the Mediterranean from Genoa, its sublime 'vague immensity' haunted by 'white ships', 'With all their ghostly sails unfurled / As phantoms from another world' (1871: 409). Wilde had met Longfellow shortly before the latter's death in 1882 and held his work in high esteem.
28. For the growth and importance of the docks, see R. Porter 1998: 188–91. On the London Dock strike of 1889, see Steadman Jones 1971: 315–36.
29. On the way in which racialised depictions of opium in Victorian literature relate to Wilde's self-presentation as a colonial subject, see Marez 1997.
30. Brown 1997 mentions London only twice, both times in passing. Treatments of nineteenth-century cosmopolitanism have tended to deal with Wilde peripherally: see Berman 2001: 47, and, more generally, Agathocleous 2011. Late nineteenth- and early twentieth-century cosmopolitanism is a growth area of interest, however: see the special issue of *Comparative Critical Studies* on '*Fin-de-Siècle* Cosmopolitanism', edited by Stefano Evangelista and Richard Hibbitt (2013).
31. And for Marx and Engels on cosmopolitanism, see 2002: 223.
32. On the utopianism of nineteenth-century ideas of cosmopolitanism, read in a French context, see Kerr 2013, and on the links between nineteenth-century utopianism and modernism, see the essays collected in Gregory and Kohlmann 2011.
33. For a similar idea, linking the nineteenth-century dandy with later twentieth-century incarnations, see Feldman 1993. On this consumption of the spectacle proper to Wildean desire, see Nunokawa: 'How wonderful is this world as Wilde sees it, though; all the wonder of the visible world rather than a single "dull gray hue", a gorgeous spectrum in which each episode of color is all the richer for the fact that, at the end of the day, or the night, or the briefest glance, it finally fades into the light of commonness, no more than an instance, a single showing of the social mosaic' (2003: 33–4).
34. Although Lefebvre is guarded on the topic of aestheticism (*PS* 317).
35. On Pater's phenomenological and Wilde's phantasmatological positions, see Whiteley 2010: 22–4 and 2015: 17, 36 respectively.

Chapter 5

Henry James: Modern Space

On 10 August 1894, Henry James wrote to Edmund Gosse (1849–1928), from his home at 34 De Vere Gardens in West London, expressing regret for having missed Walter Pater's funeral. He had been 'deterred by [. . .] my very limited acquaintance with Pater, my non-communication with him for so long, and above all by (what I supposed would be) the compact Oxfordism of it all; in which I seem to feel myself to have no place' (*LHJ* 3: 483). James felt he would have been an alien at both Pater's funeral and Oxford itself, marked as an outsider. Later that winter, having received a copy of Gosse's reminiscences published in *Critical Kit-Kats* (1896), James praised Pater's diaphanous style and life:

> I think he has had – will have had – the most exquisite literary fortune: i.e. to have taken it out all, wholly, with the pen (the style, the genius) and absolutely not at all with the person. He is the mask without the face [. . .] Well, faint, pale, embarrassed, exquisite Pater! [. . .] He shines in the uneasy gloom – vaguely, and has a phosphorescence, not a flame. (*LHJ* 3: 492)

For James, reading Pater in the future perfect, the radical and divisive figure so famous for that hedonistic 'Conclusion' ended up burning with a 'phosphorescent' rather than 'hard gem-like' flame (*SHR* 189).

The careers of James and Pater overlapped in a number of interesting ways.[1] While in Florence in May 1873, James wrote to his brother, William (1842–1910): 'I saw Pater's *Studies* [. . .] in the English bookseller's window: and was inflamed to think of buying it and trying a notice. But I see it treats several things I know nothing about' (*LHJ* 1: 391). This unwritten review constitutes a teasing missed encounter in the history of Pater's reception. But James must have read the *Renaissance*, because he refers to the essay on Botticelli in 'Florentine Notes', published the following year, in which he calls Pater an 'accomplished critic' (*IH* 18.260). Pater, for his part, read *The Europeans* (1878), praising it to Alexander Macmillan (1818–1896), who passed on the compliment through Frederick Macmillan (1851–1936), with James expressing his thanks to 'the exquisite P.' (Moore 1993: 21). The two men would meet a few months later in January 1879 at a 'literary *salon*' in Harley Street, with James wryly noting to his mother that Pater 'is far from being as beautiful as his own prose' (*LHJ* 2: 212). This focus on Pater's 'exquisite' 'style', also noted in the posthumous appreciation quoted above, is significant in understanding James's literary career. As critics such as Jonathan Freedman (1990) and Michèle Mendelssohn (2007) have pointed out, James's early works show him responding to aestheticism from a position divided between ironic detachment and a kind of willing investment in this religion of beauty.[2] In the early novels *Roderick Hudson* (1875) and *The American* (1876–7), James examines critically the aestheticist mode of living, while also allowing himself to participate to a degree through a kind of literary *flâneurie*. But the interest in Pater's beautiful prose was something which stayed with James, even after the huge commercial success of the novels of his so-called middle years, written after he had met Zola and Goncourt in Paris.[3] It manifests, most obviously, in James's shift towards an interest in capturing the 'internal' or 'subjective' drama of the mind in the work of his later years, the 'major phase', as Leon Edel called it (1947), building on earlier work by F. O. Matthiessen (1944). It is also marked by his writing, which, with its convoluted syntax, full of contingent qualifying clauses, may be considered a kind of Paterean 'decadent' style, attempting to capture the nuance and balance of finely wrought thought in finely wrought prose.

Perhaps it is unsurprising in this context to find that James can be considered another practitioner of a post-Ruskinian aesthetics of space. The two men would meet in 1869, with James hearing Ruskin lecture on Greek myth at University College, introduced via their mutual friend Norton (*LHJ* 1: 92). Although he found some of Ruskin's moralising hard work, famously calling him a 'general scold', James was impressed by the older man as an aesthetician, and James's own interest in aesthetic theory dates to the time when Ruskin's ideas regarding 'art, representation, and the relation of each to morality' were dominant on both sides of the Atlantic (Freedman 1990: 91). In an essay from 1868, the year before they met, James shows that he considered Ruskin the central figure of nineteenth-century aesthetic theory, with most later ideas traceable 'back to [their] starting point, on the margins of *Modern Painters*' (1989: 34). Fitting, then, that I propose to read *The American Scene* within the margins of *Modern Painters* in this chapter. Published in 1907, James's travelogue recounts his return to his homeland, 1904–5, undertaken on the heels of the publication of his 'major' novels, *The Wings of the Dove* (1902), *The Ambassadors* (1903) and *The Golden Bowl* (1904). It turns on the problem of how best to represent the new kind of space he encountered on this trip, one that was accentuated by the fact that it was undertaken after twenty years' absence from America. For most of his adult life, James had lived in Europe, briefly in Paris before settling in London, where he made his name as a novelist in the 1880s, socialising with most of the major writers of the period, including Morris, Pater and Ruskin, becoming friends with Whistler, and travelling extensively through Italy. His impressions of that country would be captured in essays later collected as *Italian Hours*, and *The American Scene* is implicitly in dialogue with this volume of Italian impressions, published two years later but many of which were culled from his earlier volumes, *Transatlantic Sketches* (1875) and *Portraits of Places* (1883). The comparison pits a European 'picturesque' against an America that resists such an aesthetic. In 'Summer in France' (1873), written over thirty years before *The American Scene*, James had called himself a 'sentimental tourist', a phrase that recurs throughout *Italian Hours* (*IH* 1.9, 1.18, 6.77, 8.103, 10.145), but the persona of his later travelogue speaks of himself as a 'restless analyst' (*AS* 1.1.9). Whereas the former had treated the bucolic landscapes and old ruins of Europe, the restless analyst would be less reliant on the 'picturesque'. Appearing some 152 times in the course of his *Transatlantic Sketches* (Herford 2016: 157), the word is used only eleven times in *The American Scene*. Ruskin, to recall, had argued that a desire for the picturesque was symptomatic of the 'decadence' of the modern city and its inhabitants, and James had been influenced by Ruskin's idea of the 'noble picturesque' in earlier work (Francescato 2010: 33–7). The *OED* reminds us that the French *pittoresque*, from which the English word derives, relates to the idea of an aesthetic object that is 'worthy of being painted'. But the American city, this 'vast crude democracy of trade', resists this idea, full as it was of 'the new, the simple, the cheap, the common, the commercial, the immediate, and, all too often, the ugly' (*AS* 1.8.53). It is only in the context of the tradition of an aesthetics of space that treats all of life in the spirit of art that 'the particular ugliness' of New York (3.4.107) may become an 'aesthetic' object. As Ruskin had put it in *Modern Painters*, the artist's selection of objects may be conducted more 'for their meaning and character, rather than their beauty', 'using them rather to throw light upon the particular thought he wishes to convey' (*CW* 3: 134). But James seems unable to square such theoretical insight with this ugliness witnessed all around: New York becomes an 'aesthetic wound' (*AS* 3.4.107), registering the sense of modernity as trauma.

As an Anglo-European literary figure, James found himself very much a foreigner on home soil when he returned to America, and it is in this sense that this present study reads *The American Scene* in the context of a British tradition of post-Ruskinian writing on space. The decision to do so may seems slightly surprising: there are plenty of other Jamesian spaces which could have been read here, texts which balance the picturesque alongside a more aestheticist focus on affective 'impressions'. Indeed, the preface to *The Aspern Papers* (1888) written for the New York Edition (1907–9), composed during the same period as *The American Scene*, shows the way in which he came to conceive of Venice as an aesthetic space, building as much on Ruskin as Byron. James considers the city a powerful site of 'impressions' (2009a: xxviii) and 'intensity' (xxxii), promising 'a palpable imaginable *visitable* past' (xxxi), but where the 'haunting presences' (xxviii) of this past mark 'old' Europe apart from 'some vision of, say, "old" New York' (xxxiii). Like many writers such as Swinburne, Wilde and Lee, James became fascinated with Venice's 'decayed monument[s]' (xxxiii), the city's aesthetic pleasures rather than its theoretical import. But there are important reasons for choosing to read *The American Scene* in this chapter, for it is in the space of New York in particular that we find that the impulse to aestheticise space comes upon obstacles that are concurrent with the very project of an aesthetics of space. Indeed, reading *The American Scene* in the light of this post-Ruskinian tradition, what becomes clear is that the travelogue documents what is quintessentially new and different about early twentieth-century America: a new kind of space was being produced, one which challenged the 'aesthetic' vision.

As I have argued, the possibility of being able to write an aesthetics of space is historically situated in the nineteenth century: it is only after Dickens and Ruskin, after the realist novel and the project of reading space 'theoretically', that the division between *aesthesis* and *theoria* comes to be mobilised in such a project. James was consciously aware of his status as writing 'after Dickens'. In his autobiography, he reflected on 'how tremendously it had been laid upon young people of our generation to feel Dickens, down to the souls of our shoes' (2011: 205). London was haunted by the power of the novelist, and shortly after settling in the city in 1869, James made a pilgrimage to Craven Street, Strand, where Mr Brownlow lives in *Oliver Twist* (2003h: 41.387) and where Scrooge is overwhelmed by the phantasmic face of Jacob Marley on a knocker (2003d: 41–2).

There, James found 'the whole Dickens procession marched up and down, the whole Dickens world looked out of its queer, quite sinister windows' (2011: 439). James saw what was left of Craven Street first hand (with its eastern end, where Dickens had worked, having been demolished to make way for the Embankment, 'a mere fact of more oppressive enclosure now, telling all sorts of vague loose stories about it'). 'Packed to blackness with accumulations of suffered experience' (2011: 439), Craven Street served to impress upon him the ways in which modern London problematised a 'theoretical' reading. On 10 March 1869, writing to his sister Alice (1848–92) from his apartment at 7 Half Moon Street, James remarked on the violence of London's 'vast impression':

> I have been crushed under a sense of the mere magnitude of London – its inconceivable immensity – in such a way as to paralyse my mind for any appreciation of details. [. . .] The place sits on you, broods on you, stamps on you. (*LHJ* 1: 90)

It 'broods on you', producing melancholia. Later in his career, when he was approached by Macmillan to write a *Life of Dickens*, he noted that he meant to 'do it on the spot, as much as possible in London' (*LHJ* 2: 295). As John Kimmey (1991) has argued, James must be considered primarily a London writer, and one of his last projects was something of a projected sequel to *The American Scene*, to be titled *London Town*. Work on the latter was abandoned in favour of completing the former, but *London Town* seems likely to have turned on related themes to *The American Scene*, noting melancholically, like Baudelaire's *flâneur* strolling Paris, 'the great demolitions and temporary hoardings: the old houses, few, very few, that survive' (*CNJ* 273).

By the end of the nineteenth century, writing after Dickens also meant coming to terms with the fact that London and Paris had begun to be rivalled in the imagination by the American city. For all its modernisation, the European capital maintained a 'little old-world effect as of a homelier time' (*CNJ* 274). A '*feeling of old London*' survived 'through, and in spite of, everything' (*CNJ* 278), still maintaining respect for 'the precious history of things' (*CNJ* 280). In New York, by comparison, history was everywhere effaced. As such, American space required a different kind of representation: the 'little arts of pathetic [. . .] "realism"' (*AS* 1.5.38) were fundamentally unable to capture the realities of the American scene. While James recognised in New York 'material for the artist, for the painter of life' (*AS* 2.1.63), citing Baudelaire, it is precisely the 'immensity' of the American scene that separates the capital of the nineteenth century from that of the twentieth century. Even the naturalism of Zola, who had so influenced the novels of James's middle years, would have floundered when faced with New York. For James, Zola's 'love of the human aggregation', vast as it was for its time, dealt with 'inferior, [. . .] mere Parisian scale' (*AS* 2.1.64). If realism and naturalism had sought to record reality, faithfully mimetic in their gesture, then New York precisely ruptured the possibilities of any sort of accurate representation of the space of modernity. 'Zola's huge reflector got itself formed', James comments, 'in a far other air; it had hung there, in essence, awaiting the scene that was to play over it, long before the scene really approached it in scale' (2.1.65). In other words, naturalism reflected a human scene it had already on some level anticipated, created and made possible. By contrast, 'the reflecting surfaces, of the ironic, of the epic order, suspended in the New York atmosphere' cannot themselves be adequately reflected. The epic scale here is itself 'ironic', marked by distance, and any reflection would become caught in a feedback loop, a *mise en abyme* of the image. New York, in other words, had 'got ahead of [. . .] any possibility of poetic, of dramatic capture' (*AS* 2.1.65). It is for precisely these reasons that the American city at the turn of the twentieth century resists not simply a 'theoretical' comprehension, but also the impulse of writers to treat its spaces aesthetically, while paradoxically admitting that such spaces could only ever be approached as such. It is this kind of divided image of early twentieth-century American space that this chapter maps, helping us see the ways in which the post-realist response to nineteenth-century spaces augured the modernist moment.

Approaching American Space

James invites his readers to approach *The American Scene* within the context of late nineteenth-century aesthetic theory, as is clear from the very first paragraph of the book. He notes that 'the impressions of the very first hours' of any experience 'have always the value of their intensity' (*AS* 1.1.5), telling choices of terms. The word 'impression' appears no fewer than 190 times in the text (Hannah 2013: 154), and James's preface announces that his avowed aim with the book had been to re-approach America 'vibrat[ing] with [. . .] curiosity', 'tak[ing] my stand on my gathered impressions' (*AS* 3). The phrasing recalls Pater's 'Conclusion' to the *Renaissance*, emphasising the subjectivity of aesthetic appreciation. But as Daniel Hannah (2013) and Adam Parkes (2000) have argued, James's 'impressionism' must also be contextualised alongside his interest in impressionist painting. It always finds itself on the side of *aesthesis* rather than realism, and he compares impressionism's effect 'to the momentary effect of a large slippery sweet inserted, without a warning, between the compressed lips of half-conscious inanition' (*AS* 1.5. 37). Visual pleasure is so saccharine that it invites a forgetting, in a loss that is clearly erotic. But impressionism for James is also haunting, as seen in the moment when he stands before John Singer Sargent's (1856–1925) 1903 portrait of Henry Lee Higginson (1834–1919) at Harvard, an image which carries the traces of the 'lurking ghosts' of the past (*AS* 1.8.48). In this sense, what impresses itself upon the mind of the observer is not simply the phenomenon of the thing itself (*pace* Arnold), but a series of traces which cannot be wholly distinguished from that thing. Nevertheless, the American scene attempts to exorcise that 'haunting presence', to deny the past.

James admits that a space such as New York cannot be known, but can only be discerned in its '"effect"': it is '"felt"' rather than seen. It cannot be viewed by the visual faculty alone, and in his preface, James tells the reader that true 'perception' comes not only from 'freshness of the eye', but also from 'a state of desire' (*AS* 3). In recent years, much has been made of desire in *The American Scene*, with critics reading James's return as a 'queer' one.[4] Certainly, he was drawn to the crowd, in *flâneur* mode, where what attracts him is the '*allure*' – he italicises the word – of the 'monotonous commonness, of the pushing male crowd, moving in its dense mass' (*AS* 2.1.65). These queer readings are astute, and there is a great deal of the sexual in James's experience of America on his return, particularly in the masochism of 'a certain recklessness' of his 'surrender to impressions' (1.1.7). In discovering New York actively obliterating its sense of the past, that which would promote *theoria*, James responds by losing himself in the 'fascination' (3.2.96) of the gaze and the pleasure of sensations, precisely a question of *aesthesis*. He savours with a kind of delicious relish the idea of voiding himself in the crowd, expressing a death-drive, so that experiencing New York becomes a moment of exquisite *jouissance*, 'a welter of objects and sounds in which relief, detachment, dignity, meaning, perished utterly and lost all rights' (2.1.65).

As swiftly becomes clear, James recognises that any engagement with space must be an 'invested' one; that it is both an engagement with a 'real' space, and haunted by the traces of the historical and aesthetic pasts of these spaces. But in New York, this past is only present as an effect of its absence or as a sense of the 'void'. Thus, the presence of the past is everywhere and nowhere in *The American Scene*. Having sailed on the *Kaiser Wilhelm II* from Southampton on 24 August 1904, arriving at Hoboken, New Jersey, on 30 August, James writes that he 'emerg[ed] from the relatively assured order of the great berth of the ship' (*AS* 1.1.5). Perhaps, as Ross Posnock argues, the 'berth' of the ship puns on the idea of being born (1998: 230), but regardless, in being reborn into a new America, James immediately discovers that the country was not what he remembered. He had conceived the trip to America as a chance to reconnect not only with his homeland, but also with his own past. In notebook entries dating to his trip, James shows that he was intensely aware of his age at this time (*CNJ* 235), embarking on what would indeed be the last phase of his life. So when, in the first paragraphs of *The American Scene*, he expresses his Paterean desire that registering the impressions of America might bestow a secure sense of that past, his hope is that a phenomenology of space might help ground the subject and their impressions.[5] He hopes that these 'instant vibrations', where the sensory is affective, might recall an earlier state of things in their 'intensity' (*AS* 1.1.5). Describing another impression of New York in a later chapter (as we shall see, repetition and deferral are quintessential features of American space), he recognises in the 'great' city the 'intensity of life', another Paterean phrase, and notes the overwhelming bodily affect, the 'vibrations' which become a matter difficult to explain (*AS* 2.1.58). As 'impressions', etymologically to impress, crowd upon, crush or imprint, James registers the sense in which American space does mental violence to the subject, in a moment when they are inscribed, marked by the sensation. But in New York, at least, the impressions do not solidify to give a sense of the past as expected. For James, this should be the return of the native (one of his discarded options for a title, Hardy having already made it his own), where he might meet his past made present again precisely through *aesthesis*, registered 'at every turn, in sights, sounds, smells, even in the chaos of confusion and change' (*AS* 1.1.5). It should be possible, but in reality 'recognition *was* difficult', with the verb italicised, not the act of recognition or its difficulty: something gets in the way, blocks the process. The return to New York, both physical and psychic, is never a return to the same space: both the city and the subject are no longer what they were, registering 'gaps [. . .] in one's experience, in one's consciousness, [. . .] muffled spots in one's general vibration' (*AS* 1.6.42). Indeed, since *The American*

Scene is always a double record, both of the self and of the country, such 'gaps' rupture any pretension that either the subject 'James' or his subject 'America' may be able to secure this identity. It turns *The American Scene* into the record of a double failure of the attempt to secure what Peter Collister calls 'The American Self' (2007: 4).

The title tells us much about what James is trying to capture: the scene of America, an impression of the country through some of its 'key notes'. The latter word is peppered throughout the text, with the idea of notation or inscription linked to that of a musical theme. James is searching for that 'peculiar character and a particular pathos' of the scene (*AS* 4.1.120) which would capture an impression of the central qualities of what America means at the turn of the twentieth century. But as 'notes' of America, it also invites comparison with Dickens's *American Notes*, written as he travelled through America in the first half of 1842. When Dickens returned for a second reading tour in 1867 (his plans for an earlier visit having been delayed by the Civil War), James tried but failed to get tickets (*LHJ* 1: 81). However, he met the novelist four days later at the house of Norton (Tucker 1996), writing in his autobiography: 'I saw the master – nothing could be more evident – in the light of an intense emotion, and I trembled, I remember, in every limb' (2011: 205). Indeed, Dickens was certainly on James's mind when he returned to America: his notebooks from his trip to Cambridge show him reminiscing about 'that night of Dickens, and the *emotion*, abiding, that it left with me' (*CNJ* 238). When he came to write *The American Scene*, he referred to the text of *American Notes* in discussing Dickens's 'passionate protest' against Pennsylvania Penitentiary (*AS* 9.4.221; compare Dickens 2003a: 1.7.111–24). But it is important to also note the difference that separates the two works: while the Englishman wrote of an America still in its infancy, the returning native arrived in a country fully grown.

James never really manages to capture successfully the key 'note' of the American scene, giving a series of variations on the theme. It consistently refuses to be adequately conceptualised or written, as too excessive. The point recalls Ruskin, describing the genius of Turner, that sense in which 'the eye [. . .] cannot rest upon, nor cling to, nor entirely understand' modern space (*CW* 3: 323). Perhaps it is for this reason that James is constantly trying to 'frame' the scene, for his readers and for himself, attempting to keep America within the bounds of reason. He uses this idea of 'framing' consistently throughout the text. What lies within the scene arrests the attention, captures it, stops it in its tracks; what lies beyond is unthought or unspoken. Framing, in this sense, becomes an aesthetic operation of 'taste', removing the unseemly from the scene. In this context, it is important to note that James associates 'taste' with Europe rather than America, with old hierarchical social systems rather than new democratic ones, for 'it takes an endless amount of history to make even a little tradition, and an endless amount of tradition to make even a little taste' (*AS* 4.2.127). Psychoanalytically, James's desire to 'frame' America may be read in the terms of a defence mechanism, and within the context of the problem of 'recognising' either himself or the American scene. For Lacan, building on Freud's idea of the unconscious as 'another scene' [*eine andere Schauplatz*] (*SE* 5: 535–6), fantasy is 'scenic', that space where 'all things of the world come to be staged in keeping with the laws of the signifier' (Lacan 2014: 33), and where what lies beyond the frame is the 'real', which is traumatic. But if James's framing operation has a great deal of the aesthetic impulses of such a theatrical staging, he also registers a sense of impatience with his own conceit. At Cape Cod, for instance, the restless analyst finds the 'social question' 'dogging' his steps, wanting 'to get into the picture, to cross, as it were, the threshold of the frame' (*AS* 1.4.29). His desire to read space 'theoretically' finds itself conflicted with the aesthetic operation of framing.

The excessive registers two separate problems: the first is personal and professional, so that it makes recognising either oneself or America itself difficult; the second aesthetic, so that it introduces the problem of how to frame the picture. *Theoria* is precisely unable to adequately conceptualise that quality of excess that characterises modern America. 'The subject was everywhere', James writes, a 'thrilling' experience (*AS* 1.1.7), but where 'there is too much of the whole thing [. . .] for the personal relation with it' (*AS* 3.1.94), so that the encounter becomes disturbing, calling the subject into question. The past, which if registered would give grounding to the subject, is lost behind a kind of façade, as James finds himself struck by 'the sense of "old New York"' as a 'picture now so violently overpainted' (*AS* 1.1.7). For James, the American scene is one that seeks to erase the trace of the past in a simulacrum that testifies to an ideology of democracy and capitalism. He was perhaps only partly right in this, having arrived in New York at the moment when the dominant architectural style had recently shifted, away from the 'Cosmopolitan Era' (1865–90) which followed the Civil War to the 'Composite Era' (1890–1915). The former, borrowing from a wide range of different historical styles, had been replaced by an ordered classicism, in part in response to the ways in which the city was perceived to have lost its identity (McNamara 1993: 127). But for James, such a shift, even had he shown an awareness of it, would have been too little, too late. That there is no real '"old New York"' left is implied by the fact that the phrase appears as a quotation, as through America's past must always be a question of citation, the attempt at making-present a reality no longer accessible except through pastiche or repetition. The entire city becomes a kind of 'stock' image of modernity.

James finds New York founded on an aesthetic of surplus effects, an 'insistent testimony to waste' (*AS* 4.1.120). He is struck by 'the constant shocked sense of houses and rows, of recent expensive construction [. . .] marked for removal, for extinction, in their prime, and awaiting it with their handsome faces so fresh and yet so wan and so anxious' (4.1.119), the prosopopoeia giving pathos. The poetry of the passage recalls Ruskin's Murano, 'a line of miserable houses' recently built, the adjective personifying them, 'yet already tottering to their ruin' (*CW* 10: 37). Indeed, if there is a key 'note' in *The American Scene* it is this: that the size of America, manifested in its growth, is built upon a void. In Boston, James's narrator begins to see America as a vast project of forgetting: 'what was taking place was a perpetual repudiation of the past, so far as there had been a past to repudiate' (*AS* 1.6.43). Regardless of whether 'positive' or 'negative', characterised by 'a shabbiness to disown or a deception to expose', the past had 'become the victim of supersession' (1.6.43). The project then differs from that kind of forgetting which is strategic, either socially or psychologically. This is no selective editing of the past, which Nietzsche diagnoses as the condition of European 'modernity' and calls its 'decadence'. Rather, in America we find that both positive and negative alike are erased in a 'supersession', a word that already in the late nineteenth century had begun to become associated with the philosophy of G. W. F. Hegel (1770–1831) and his teleological dialectic of progression. It leads James's narrator to his own experience of 'pathos' (1.6.43), registering a loss in America.

As Kevin McNamara notes, James's 'preference for Europe's longer tradition required the very forgetting of history that he – rightly – did not allow the American scene' (1993: 145). Still, if New York is a city that lacks a sense of its past, trying to erect itself upon a kind of historical void, then James's comparison between the new skyscrapers which dominated the skyline of New York and the Park Street Church in Boston offers one way through which to approach his attempts to write the American scene. The latter, built in 1809 with its 'dear old delightful Wren-like spire', invoked European models, and compared favourably with the skyscrapers (*AS* 2.2.73). Having not yet been torn down, Park Street Church gives Boston a sense of a past, even if only a recent one, but it also gives a sense of a deeper past, if only faint and deferred, in its architectural citation of Wren, whom James eulogises in his notes for *London Town* (*CNJ* 278–9). As such, Park Street Church's sense of grounding originates in Europe, not America. Likewise, James finds that Boston differs from New York insofar as it is penetrated by the 'warm breath of history', almost forgetting himself, as though he were 'talking about [. . .] old Paris and old London' (*AS* 7.1.169), reading Charles Street through 'far-away Thackeray' (*AS* 7.2.181) and Marlborough Street through the 'long, unlovely [Harley] street' (*AS* 7.3.183) of Alfred, Lord Tennyson (1809–92). In the context of the British tradition which this book has traced, the comparison between the skyscraper as a symbol of American modernity and Boston's evocation of a European past suggests that the aesthetics of American space can only be unpacked by James when read through Europe. It reflects James's impulses to read space 'theoretically', but since Boston only cites this past, without truly memorialising it, such a past is itself nothing more than another aesthetic effect.

We have seen throughout this book how later aesthetic spaces are built through an engagement with earlier ones, which, as representations of space, also serve to rewrite spatial practice. We have also seen the tendency for one city to become inscribed with another, so that London can be read through Paris and vice versa, in another kind of cosmopolitanism. Certainly, James's reading of the American scene finds itself in contrast to his earlier portraits of Italy, and as such derives at least a partial inspiration from Ruskin. We can be sure that James read Venice through Ruskin, since in an 1882 essay on the city, James recommends that the reader be guided by their copy of *The Stones of Venice* (*IH* 1.14). Likewise, in an earlier essay dating from 1872, James approvingly discusses the Englishman's dismay at the construction of the new railway bridge leading to the city, a moment of the 'modernization' of space that traumatised Ruskin's eye (*IH* 3.51–2; compare *CW* 4: 40–1). Two important comparisons between New York and Venice, dating from later in his career, demonstrate the extent to which James's approach to American space also finds itself in dialogue with Ruskin's vision. In his 1892 essay on 'The Grand Canal', James describes it as a route of '"rapid transit" in the New York phrase, in everybody's reach, and enabled everybody [. . .] to rush about Venice as furiously as people rush about New York' (*IH* 2.48), a comparison that recalls Ruskin, noting similarities between 'the crowded thoroughfares of Venice' and London (*CW* 10: 271). James's emphasis on speed, associated here with the 'modernity' of America in particular, and on the attendant loss of poise, its citizens 'furious', implies New York as a 'fallen' city in Ruskinian terms. In *The American Scene*, the comparison is even clearer: both New York and Venice are cities born 'of a Republic and of trade' (*AS* 4.4.138), so that the pomp of the American city speaks of its decadence, auguring its fall. Likewise, when James considers New York's dream-like quality, the way in which its space seems to be 'invested' 'with the tone [. . .] of sea-foam' (2.1.60), and where this 'whitening' effect is distinguished from the 'blackened' quality of 'fog and grime' of Britain's industrial ports. The subtle allusion recalls Ruskin's Venice, fancied as being 'at first a dark city – washed white by the sea foam' (*CW* 9: 323). It is precisely in this sense of the effacement of its history that New York so readily becomes a space of 'investments', evoking both the idea of capitalist speculation and psychoanalytic cathexes, so that the city has the 'semblance' of being a 'vast white page' (*AS* 2.1.59), its future yet to be written. But if New York is compared to Venice, then James sees the American city only as a simulacrum, as in Tiffany's on Fifth Avenue. Completed in 1905 and modelled after the Palazzo Grimani di San Luca, Tiffany's only 'dignity' lies in its being 'a more or less pious *pastiche* or reproduction, the copy of a model that sits where Venetian water-steps keep – or used to keep! – vulgar invasion at bay' (*AS* 4.5.139). Tiffany's is a simulacrum of the Venetian palazzo, New York the simulacrum of Venice. In other words, New York is fallen Venice without the history.

Binding the Aesthetic Wound: New Jersey and New England

Arriving in Hoboken, James crossed over to New York, accompanied by his nephew, before travelling to New Jersey to stay with a friend, the publisher George Harvey (1864–1928). If *The American Scene* is a documentary of nostalgia, an attempt to recover a sense of self, then James makes clear from the very beginning of his travelogue that no one is truly at 'home' in America, marking the word with quotation marks when describing the businessmen returning '"home"' to New Jersey on the ferry (*AS* 1.1.8). The Jersey shore is figured as a ghost town, and in this early passage, James gives a preliminary mapping of one way to make sense of the American scene and its aesthetic. It recalls structurally, thematically and aesthetically

Ruskin's portrait of Murano in *The Sea Stories*, 'the smaller palaces of the Venetians, built for pleasure or repose', figuring early visible manifestations of Venice's decadence, the 'outward appearances' of its decay felt 'first at the extremities' (*CW* 10: 36). In New Jersey, James sees the holiday villas that line its shore as a series of 'great white boxes [. . .] standing there with the silvered ghostliness [. . .] of a series of candid new moons' (*AS* 1.1.10), spectral and otherworldly. These 'boxes' have their 'own marks and signs', speaking to the refrain of the American scene writ large:

> The huge new houses, up and down, looked over their smart, short lawns as with a certain familiar prominence in their profiles, which was borne out by the accent, loud, assertive, [. . .] with which they confessed to their extreme expensiveness. (*AS* 1.1.10)

The houses are 'proud' of their costliness, accentuating the prosopopoeia already present in 'their' lawns, an alienation that speaks to the links between the American scene and capitalism. But they are empty, both physically, having no one at home, and spiritually, carrying no meaning in themselves, as well as aesthetically, so that this moment of 'meaning' can be forever deferred. They have

> the odd appearance everywhere as of florid creations waiting, a little bewilderingly, for their justification, waiting for the next clause in the sequence, waiting in short for life, for time, for interest, for character, for identity itself to come to them. (1.1.10)

They are 'waiting', like Rosa's London (*ED* 22.247, 22.253) or like Arnold's scholar gypsy, for that 'spark from heaven' (l. 171) that would provide the sense of meaning that they lack. As is so typical of the major phase, James's syntax here is itself 'florid', replete with isocola and anaphoric clusters, accentuating both the 'waiting' and the prepositional clause. These houses lack 'identity' as something which must 'come to them', not something of which they are prepossessed. Even James's headnotes to the page of the first edition show that what is at stake here is metonymic, a 'Chain of Villas'. It speaks to the question of desire as that which cannot be satisfied, a sense in which the subject finds themselves produced in the space in-between, 'caught in the rails of metonymy', as Lacan puts it, 'eternally extending towards the *desire for something else*' (2007a: 431). This quality links New Jersey to New York, which, like its 'dowered *débutantes* and impatient youths', appears to be 'wait[ing] for something more' (*AS* 4.2.128). The restless analyst finds America characterised by

> the incoherence and volatility of childhood, its living but in the sense of its hour and in the immediacy of its want, its instinctive refusal to be brought to book, its boundless [. . .] incapacity for attention, its ingenuous blankness to-day over the appetites and clamours of yesterday. (*AS* 4.2.128)

James's prose uses anaphora to connote mimetically the idea of a clause yet to come as that which defines the American scene, a consummation devoutly to be wished, but endlessly deferred.

James tells us that the 'marks and signs' of New York are visible on the Jersey shore as 'the immense, in *villeggiatura*' (*AS* 1.1.10). The *OED* gives the Whig politician and author Horace Walpole (1717–94) as first user of this word, dated to 1742 and originating within the moneyed class who drove British capitalist, commercial and imperial expansion. In New Jersey, the trace of New York is present, but at reduced scale. The term derives from the Italian *villa*, to vacation in the countryside, so that New Jersey's *villeggiatura* connotes Italy, and may remind us in the context of tracing the tradition of the aesthetics of space of Pater's description of holidaying Roman citizens in *Marius the Epicurean*. But as Adorno famously argues, capitalism's genius lies in making even 'unproductive' time (rest, leisure) productive, monetising it. So too James, who notes that 'the expensive, for New York in *villeggiatura* [. . .] is like a train covering ground at maximum speed and pushing on, at present, into regions unmeasurable' (*AS* 1.1.11), an analogy at once spatial and temporal, imaging modernity. For James, as for Ruskin and Dickens, it is this idea of speed that defines modernity. But speed here also registers the distance that separates *American Notes* from *The American Scene* and the mid-nineteenth-century Britain of *Dombey and Son* from the America of the early twentieth century. Whereas in the former, the train reterritorialises the older spatial configurations of the British countryside, precipitating new, capitalist constellations, in the latter, it charts a course through 'smooth' space. America is a wilderness, vast and giving itself to the aesthetic imaginary of the pioneers (or a certain pioneering spirit treated as a philosophy of capitalism) as boundless in its expanse ever westwards, so that James can imagine the train 'pushing on [. . .] into regions unmeasurable' (*AS* 1.1.11). Capitalism here operates as the velocious principle of manifest destiny, deterritorialising itself in a manner only looking towards the 'the promise of great future intensity' (*AS* 1.1.11). James's phrase links capitalist expansion to the American dream, its 'promises', and to a certain understanding of 'democracy' as that which is yet 'to come', a clause which, as Derrida would put it (2003: 37–8), indicates not simply a future horizon but a structural dislocation at the heart of the contemporary moment. But the idea of a future 'intensity' also links the American scene to a certain aesthetic, Paterean philosophy of the intensification of life.

The function of New England for James is in 'bind[ing] up the aesthetic wound' (*AS* 3.4.107), an operation that must be fantastical by definition, precisely since the wound implies trauma.[6] Leaving New Jersey, he took a train to Harvard, staying with William, and then with his friend Edith Wharton (1862–1937) at the Mount, Lenox. James calls it 'New England Arcadia', and whereas New York troubles his aesthetic gaze, his response to New England is 'shamelessly "subjective"', resting on 'the beauty of the impression' (*AS* 1.2.14). In a word, although not one he will use here, New England is 'picturesque', which in Ruskinian terms implicitly draws attention to James's modernity. 'When you wander about in Arcadia you ask as few questions as possible', he writes, before adding: 'that', namely the lack of the interrogative, '*is* Arcadia in fact', a place where 'questions drop, or at least get themselves deferred' (*AS* 1.2.14). New England gives itself to the aesthetic imagination as 'the Arcadia of an old tapestry, an old legend' (1.2.14), insofar as it 'shirks' more rigorous questions, any sense of responsibility to the other, in a fantasy which functions as 'the idyllic *type* in its purity'.[7] It is a kind of wish-image that seeks to ground the American scene and give it a sense of 'origin', but as Tambling argues, New England can only be understood as Arcadian insofar as 'it has no history' (2001: 115). The idea recalls the moment later in *The American Scene* when James visits Washington Irving's (1783–1859) home in Sunnyside, Queens, a space which is 'inevitably, to-day, but a qualified Sleepy Hollow' (*AS* 3.6.118), so that the short story (1820) always already aestheticises the place. Considering the Romanticism of the Hudson River School, James ponders on the power of 'Rip van Winckle' (1819) (*AS* 3.6.117), the tale of a man who falls asleep in the Catskill Mountains, only to reawaken having missed the American Revolution. Allegorically, Irving marks both Rip and America as anachronistic, lacking an awareness of their own past, and New England Arcadia is similarly a space that appears to exist out of time. To be sure, history was present to a 'degree', but it is manifested only 'in the form of the classic abandoned farm', the ruin 'of the rude forefather who had lost patience with his fate' (*AS* 1.2.15). James seeks to read a specific history of puritan industriousness into the space, that 'stout human experiment' (*AS* 1.2.19), but this Arcadian fantasy never manages to hang together, with something interrupting the scene:

> These scenes of old, hard New England effort, defeated by the soil and the climate and reclaimed by nature and time [. . .] these seemed the only notes to interfere, in their meagreness, with the queer *other*, the larger, eloquence that one kept reading into the picture. (*AS* 1.2.15)

That 'queer *other*', in James's overdetermined phrasing, registers the disjunction between the eye and the gaze in Lacanian terms (1998b: 103–4), between what James wants to see and what the picture shows. It is only a 'restless analyst' rather than a 'sentimental tourist' who can register that it was 'the eliminated thing *par excellence* [that] was the thing most absent to sight' (*AS* 1.2.22).

As an Arcadian scene, New England is written by James as another late Romantic, his eye alighting on 'the high places of the hills and deep places of the woods'. But the pleonasms give no sense of the reality of these spaces, full of 'vague, empty, rock-roughened pastures' (*AS* 1.2.15). The natural world seems to promise a sense sublime in 'the great boulders in the woods, the pulpit stones, [. . .] the isolated cliffs and lichened cathedrals' (*AS* 1.2.16), but never quite delivers. By 'pulpit stones', James may be subtly recalling Wilde's quip on Romanticism and desire, with Wordsworth finding 'in the stones the sermons he had already hid there' (*CR* 83), but if so, he gains little spiritual revelation from the scene, New England being purely aesthetic. Indeed, as a 'gorgeous blur' (*AS* 1.5.33), the Massachusetts Berkshires become almost as hard to read as the rest of the American scene. Arcadian New England is a question of what James calls 'type', a quality common not only to its landscape but to its towns. James's narrator notes that the 'charm' resides in the fact 'that the scene is everywhere the same', the 'white paint, on wooden walls, amid open dooryards, reaffirm[ing] itself eternally', producing an '"amusing" vagueness; while the great verdurous vista [. . .] has the air of consciously playing the trick and carrying off the picture' (*AS* 1.5.33). If one of the fundamental truths of space for Ruskin is that it cannot be 'vague' (*CW* 3: 335), New England's 'vagueness', mirroring a wider vagueness in the American scene writ large, shows the limits of *theoria*. Instead, these 'verdurous vistas' connote through their alliterative, sensual ease the sense in which the differences between things are erased, a phrase repeated verbatim in the following paragraph, as though the repetition itself will be enough to paint America. But the 'type' here is also '"amusing"', with James's quotation marks inscribing an irony which reminds us that the 'restless analyst' is attuned to the aesthetics of these spaces, whereas a 'sentimental tourist' might be played by them. James sees that New England Arcadia, like the American scene more broadly, is only 'carried off' precisely because so much is missing.

The Violence of New York: Reading the Void

Travelling from Boston by train, James took a barge to Harlem, experiencing 'the breadth of effect' of seeing 'the great face of New York' (*AS* 2.1.57), 'the vast bristling promontory from the water' (2.1.58). *The American Scene* 'bristles', with the word appearing as either a verb or a noun some twenty-three times, and etymologically 'bristle' signifies a 'point, prong, edge', both inscription and violence. These passages are tours de force of the aesthetics of space. James tells us that the city has 'the sense' of being a 'scene', with the effect of being staged as a 'picture'. More specifically, the scene carries 'an expression of things lately and currently *done*, done on a large impersonal stage and on the basis of inordinate gain' (*AS* 2.1.58). This emphasis on the staging of the drama of capitalist speculation is one of the key notes of James's restless analysis of the New York scene. He sees in the New York skyline '*the will to grow* [. . .] everywhere written large' (*AS* 1.6.43), a fittingly Nietzschean phrase (Tambling 2001: 117), an expression of a will to power, growth 'at no matter what or whose expense' (*AS* 1.6.43). It differs from those ideologies of expansion that he had witnessed 'on the other side of the world', chiefly in London and Paris, precisely because capitalism in America had met with no pre-existing structures which could contain its growth. What is at stake is the texture of American space itself, what marks it as different from Europe. 'It was a question of scale and space and chance, margin and elbow-room', James writes, 'above all, [of] the permitting medium' (*AS* 1.6.43). In other words, the will to grow is precisely a question of deterritorialisation, with nothing 'within the great frame of the picture' of America there 'to prevent or to prescribe' this movement (1.6.43).

For James, the 'real appeal' of the scene lies in the 'impression' this aesthetics gives of 'dauntless power' (*AS* 2.1.59). As 'dauntless', New York cannot be tamed or subdued, with the effect also an affect – the city is both an expression of this power, and one that exercises its dauntless power on the subject:

> It is the power of the most extravagant of cities, rejoicing, as with the voice of the morning, in its might, its fortune, its unsurpassable conditions, and imparting to every object and element, to the motion and expression of every floating, hurrying, panting thing, to the throb of ferries and tugs, to the plash of waves and the play of winds and the glint of lights and the shrill of whistles and the quality and authority of breeze-borne cries [. . .] something of its sharp free accent. (*AS* 2.1.59)

The passage is Dickensian in its effects: the superlatives, the prosopopoeia of the city, which seems to be expressing its power as the force of its own personality. The syntax, full of subordinating clauses and parallel structures, built in layers, also recalls Ruskin. But the passage differs, if subtly, from comparable passages from the realist tradition, precisely since this is a space which is not grounded in historical reality. It figures New York as newborn, ahistorical, as though beginning at the dawn of the twentieth century without a past. 'Rejoicing [. . .] with the voice of the morning', it is mythological, as James's subtle quotation from Ossian (James Macpherson, 1736–96), suggests (1996: 134). The scene stages the sense of New York as the site of the forging of the nation, an expression of its 'might', its will to grow, with the repetitive possessives highlighting the sense of ownership it claims over that future which it will create. This will to grow is expressed throughout in its speed, a giant erotic tumult of 'pants', 'throbs' and 'cries'. James's polysyndetonic style captures this incessant movement in the 'bigness and bravery and insolence' (*AS* 2.1.59) which join things together in the city. New York constitutes a body without organs (Deleuze and Guattari 2004b: 165–84):

> The bold lacing-together, across the waters, of the scattered members of the monstrous organism – lacing as by the ceaseless play of an enormous system of steam-shuttles or electric bobbins [. . .], commensurate in form with their infinite work [. . .] give[s] the pitch of the vision of energy. One has the sense that the monster grows and grows, flinging abroad its loose limbs [. . .], and that the binding stitches must for ever fly further and faster and draw harder; the future complexity of the web, all under the sky and over the sea, becoming thus that of some colossal set of clockworks, some steel-souled machine-room of brandished arms and hammering fists and opening and closing jaws. (*AS* 2.1.59)

Again, the repetition and repetitive syntactic structures, which show the 'web' entangling the subjects. But this is not the labyrinthine web of Wilde's East End: it is a planar web, operating 'under the sky and over the sea'. More precisely, New York is envisaged as a Deleuzo-Guattarian plane of consistency, 'scrambling forms by dint of speed [. . .], breaking down functions by means of assemblages' (2004b: 298), where the city is at once an organism and a machine that has neither beginning nor end. This image of a city is precisely an example of the 'productive consumption of space' in Lefebvrean terms, defined by speed (*PS* 374–5). The 'monster' is 'Democracy' itself, as James notes earlier (1.6.44), and New York its 'miscellaneous' expression (1.5.40). Lacking an origin, writing itself upon the void, in a moment mythologising its power, as though the city and the nation emerge fully fledged from the head of Zeus, New York is a new kind of 'monstrous' city.

New York refuses to bow down to the older gods or ways of life, the ones rooted in what Lefebvre would term an 'abstract' spatiality. It worships capital, democracy and a 'vast, costly, empty newness' (*AS* 4.4.137). It expresses a 'universal will to move', another Nietzschean formulation, that palilogical demand 'to move, move, move, as an end in itself, an appetite at any price' (2.1.65), riding roughshod over the city's history. Movement for movement's sake becomes a topographical principle in New York, which operates simultaneously on two planes. To the vertical plane of its skyscrapers is added the horizontal plane of its streets, its 'original sin' and 'primal topographical curse', marking it forever as fallen. Structured by 'the longitudinal avenues [. . .] perpetually, yet meanly intersected' (2.3.77), New York, 'of all great cities, [is] the least endowed [. . .] with any happy accident or surprise, any fortunate nook or casual corner, any deviation, in fine, into the liberal or the charming' (2.3.78). These sorts of 'fortunate nooks' are found throughout London, as in the Staples Inn of *Edwin Drood* (*ED* 11.112), the kinds of spaces which Dickens's uncommercial traveller 'haunts' (*UT* 262). In his notes for *London Town*, James records encountering them by surprise time and again while walking London: 'nooks' which becomes a '*retreat*' from the trauma of modernity, cushioning the subject from 'the vague city hum outside', precipitating 'the ghostly sense, the disembodied presences' of the past (*CNJ* 275). But such nooks are absent in New York, which marries a rationalised and 'visible' topography in Lefebvrean terms to 'the great religion of the Elevator' (*AS* 4.5.139).[8] A product of the skyscraper's law of 'lateral development', it is height for height's sake. But more than that, the elevator introduces a new form of spatiality: no longer is verticality the sole dominion of the monumental or the cathedral, producing the space of the surrounding countryside and dominating that space. Instead, the elevator's Icarian dreams aim to reterritorialise the sky itself, so those spaces too may be harnessed by the capitalist mode of production.

Comparing the aesthetics of the skyscraper to Giotto's (1266–1337) Campanile in Florence, James muses about the fate of Trinity Church, dating from 1846 and located at the intersection of Broadway and Wall Street. Built in Gothic Revival style, its spire soared over the city. At the time when James left for Europe, it was the tallest building in New York, visible from the harbour, and remained so until 1869, when the Brooklyn Bridge overtook it. But on his return, its spire is 'cruelly overtopped and so barely distinguishable [. . .] in its abject helpless humility' (2.1.61). The verb recalls Isabel Archer in *The Portrait of a Lady* (1880–1), who hopes for the 'immense pleasure' of seeing her husband Gilbert Osmond 'overtopped' (2009b: 43.445, 51.532). James waxes Ruskinian on the beauty of Trinity Church, asking 'where, for the eye, is the felicity of simplified Gothic, of noble pre-eminence, that once made of this highly-pleasing edifice the pride of the town?' 'Deprived' of its prominence, the church's Gothic lacks 'theoretical' impact in the context of the early twentieth century, its 'smothered visibility' felt as something that 'aches and throbs [. . .] in its caged and dishonoured condition' (2.1.61). James notes 'the growing invisibility of churches, their everywhere reduced or abolished *presence*' (2.1.65). It parallels his notes for *London Town*, which, for all its modernity, comes to recall Dickens's 'City of London Churches', a melancholic itinerary of those spaces which were gradually being lost to the forces of progress (*CNJ* 277–80). This 'growing invisible' is New York's 'inexorable law' (*AS* 2.1.65), James writes, as though the city itself is 'inexorable', an idea that recalls Baudrillard, writing of a later America, and noting that 'the word "inexorable" is itself inexorable' (2007: 58).

Viewing the scene from the water between Jersey City and 23rd Street, James finds that 'the multitudinous sky-scrapers' strike him 'like extravagant pins in a cushion already overplanted, and stuck in as in the dark, anywhere and anyhow' (*AS* 2.1.60). He sees 'the pincushion' again when passing the southern tip of Manhattan, looking over the Battery, from which vantage the city looks like a 'plantation' (2.1.60). If skyscrapers cannot compare to the 'builded majestics' of earlier civilisations, 'towers or temples or fortresses or palaces' (2.1.61), all sites of very specific spatial practice, they nevertheless become 'monumental' structures. Rewriting the New York skyline into an encomium on the American dream, they also recall the sense in which Lefebvre links monumentalism to fascism, the desire to overwrite rather than memorialise the past. The link between the monumental and power was one which James understood. Considering Augustus Saint-Gaudens's (1848–1907) *Standing Lincoln* (1887) in Chicago, James was impressed by 'the combination of intensity of effect' with a sense of 'dissimulation' and the monument's 'deep disavowal' of the past (*AS* 4.2.129). Likewise, in reading the skyscrapers of the New York scene, the connotations of the 'plantation' recall the history of American trauma that these monuments seek to overwrite. James's use of the word marks the fact that America cannot erase the country's colonial past or memories of the Civil War, in which his younger brothers Wilky and Roberston had fought. In his book on *Nathaniel Hawthorne* (1879), James speaks of the Civil War as marking 'an era in the history of the American mind' which 'introduced into the national consciousness a certain sense of proportion and relation'. It figures as the fall, 'the tree of knowledge', a dividing line in the American consciousness, so that those who come thereafter are postlapsarian (1984: 427–8). New York's architecture of power seeks to efface this history, but the new 'plantations' of its skyline imply older ones, that economic history upon which America's capitalist domination would be founded.

It is in moments such as these that the traumatic past of America slips into view, precisely in a kind of anamorphosis (Lacan 1998b: 79–90), where what is 'real' is only visible when the subject takes a specific vantage point. But America does not invite or welcome such a reading, as testified to by the 'violence' of the skyscrapers. Its power lies in its ability to convince its subjects that the American dream is more than smoke and mirrors. The aesthetic phantasmagoria that is America itself is materialised in the Waldorf-Astoria, opened in 1893, and designed by Henry Hardenbergh (1847–1918) in German Renaissance style (and demolished in 1929 to make space for the Empire State Building). The Waldorf-Astoria gives the American scene in microcosm, playing a similar role for James to that the Bonaventure Hotel, Los Angeles, played in Jameson's reading of postmodernity. Dating to 1974–6, designed by John Calvin Portman Jr (1924–2017), 'the Bonaventurre aspires to being a total space, a complete world, a kind of miniature city' (Jameson 1991: 40). So too the Waldorf-Astoria, where 'the air swarms, to intensity' with 'the characteristic condensed and accumulated' (*AS* 2.3.78). This 'characteristic' is a brash and bristling loudness, a putting of oneself front and centre, in an endless promotion, a desire to move and grow, to speculate and expand, in which James registers a residual 'effect of violence' (2.3.78). McNamara usefully compares James's description with a later incarnation of a specifically American imaginary, Disneyland (1993: 135). The point recalls Baudrillard, who famously reads Disneyland as a model of simulacra which restages in miniature the American scene as a theatre of desire (2004: 12). The same is true of the Waldorf-Astoria in James's New York: it is a space that claims itself to be both 'an æsthetic ideal' and a 'synonym for civilization' (*AS* 2.3.78–9). It is all surface effect, society glimpsed as forever on the move, where the idea of being-at-home is only ever performed by 'the hundreds and hundreds of people in circulation, the innumerable huge-hatted ladies in especial, with their air of finding in the gilded and storied labyrinth the very firesides and pathways of home' (2.3.80–1). The phrasing reminds us that these figures are the products of the Gilded Age of late nineteenth-century America. The guests, however, only have the 'air' of finding their way or themselves at 'home'. Always moving, the Waldorf-Astoria, functioning as an aesthetic 'synonym' of American 'civilization', only exists 'in order to hide the fact that it is the "real"' America itself that is simulacral (Baudrillard 2004: 12). It images New York and the American scene as 'a gorgeous golden blur' (*AS* 3.2.81), recalling New England Arcadia (1.5.33), suggesting the hotel as a site of forgetfulness. It is 'a paradise peopled with unmistakable American shapes, yet in which, the general and the particular, [. . .] melted together' (3.2.81).

The void here is precisely what the fantastic image seeks to mask, a point to which James returns frequently. America gives 'a particular impression of this interesting struggle in the void' (*AS* 4.1.122), and the smooth space which it striates is 'a void', its 'pecuniary power' beating 'its wings in the void' (4.1.120). Visible in New York and its expansive movement west, capital becomes 'a power by itself, a power unguided, undirected, practically unapplied, really exerting itself in a void that could make it no response, that had nothing [. . .] to offer in return' (1.1.11). The repeated prefixes highlight the negation, suggesting that behind the 'expensive' façade, there is nothing left. James is deeply unsettled by the imagery, telling himself that the 'void' must only be an 'apparent' one, since without such a qualification, 'there would be neither comedy nor tragedy' (1.1.13). But the city seems to treat itself as 'provisional', which is also 'the very sign its energy is that it doesn't believe in itself': 'its mission would appear to be, exactly, gild the temporary, with its gold, as many inches thick a may be, and then, with a fresh shrug, [. . .] give up its actual work [. . .] as the merest of stop-gaps' (2.3.84–5). In this remarkable passage, James suggests not simply that an American aesthetics of the surface stands for a void where history should be, but that it comes to stand in for itself, and badly. But the temporary and the contingent become the capitalist motor that prevents the American scene from standing still. New York suffers from the

> constant inability to convince; to convince ever [. . .] that she is serious, [. . .] about anything but that perpetual passionate pecuniary purpose which plays with all forms, which derides and devours them, though it may pile up the cost of them in order to rest a while, spent and haggard, in the illusion of their finality. (2.3.85)

James's prose here is mimetic, a glittering surface, echoing Ruskin's failed attempt to separate *aesthesis* and *theoria* in reading Venice. The alliteration of the voiceless stops in the 'perpetual passionate pecuniary purpose', which themselves 'pile up' as the sentence progresses, diverts the attention through a pleasurable excess of the materiality of the signifier. If these chapters of *The American Scene* are ostensibly about James's attempt to adequately capture and transcribe his impressions of the 'effects' of New York, then what he comes to realise is the 'general insincerity' of these effects (2.3.85). Moreover, he finds himself precisely lost in an aesthetics of these spaces, and submits to its pleasures in his writing.

Other Spaces: Greenwich Village, Central Park and the East Side

James arrived in New York during the decade of the greatest immigration to the city. An early passage in *The American Scene* describes Ellis Island as a bureaucratic space. In a way that anticipates Kafka, the immigrants stand before the Law, 'appealing and waiting, marshalled, herded, divided, subdivided, sorted, sifted, searched, fumigated, for longer or shorter periods' (*AS* 2.1.66). The asyndeton gives a sense of the bewilderingly staccato experience of being bureaucratically 'processed'. James considers the ways in which 'this visible act of ingurgitation on the part of our body politics and social' (2.1.66) dehumanises the immigrants, in the precise act of attempting to incorporate them into society. It 'ingurgitates' them, swallowing them up in the American 'machine' (3.2.95), with the nation understood as a 'great assimilative organism' (3.2.97). It leads James to consider the sense in which the American citizen, by definition an immigrant, is always an alien (2.1.66). As with the 'England' of Dickens's *Edwin*

Drood, James comes to see 'America' as a master-signifier, so that it becomes difficult to attach any 'meaning [. . .] to such a term as the "American" character' (*AS* 3.1.92).

James's response to New York's immigrants is as divided as his response to America's aesthetics of space more generally. While critics such as Peter Buitenhuis (1970: 84–6) have attempted to find points through which to rehabilitate James in *The American Scene*, the text is openly racist and anti-Semitic (Haviland 1997: 150–7). As McNamara has argued, there are always two New Yorks in James's reading, dividing his response: 'he wanted to produce from the "aliens" an oppositional culture, but one with which he would not, finally, identify himself' (1993: 124). James is clearly repulsed by many of the immigrants he meets, the 'aliens in the first grossness of their alienism' (*AS* 3.1.92), but he also displays sympathy for some of their lives, and particularly those who refuse to be fully incorporated (3.2.98–9). He enjoys spending time in these alien spaces precisely since they have not been homogenised, a residuum which cannot be fully introjected by the psychic force of the American 'machine'. They give character to the space which the 'American' aesthetic cannot, resisting the 'vagueness' characteristic of so much of New York.

James's divided response to the city's 'alien' presence registers a 'sense of dispossession' (*AS* 2.1.67) that splits the American subject.[9] His impression of these immigrants gives James the sense of having 'seen a ghost in his supposedly safe old house' (*AS* 2.1.66): they got there first, as it were, so that the spaces of James's own past are no longer sites of security, but always already haunted by the other. To be 'dispossessed' means to have lost something that was once yours, here a kind of identity in the psychic, spatial and social senses. The term, introduced in chapter 2, insists in chapter 3 where James speaks of the Lower East Side and Fifth and Madison as spaces where 'the alien was [. . .] truly in possession' (3.1.90). James is struck by the fact that the Italian-American immigrants, 'foreign as they might be, [. . .] were *at home*' (3.2.96), whereas James was not, dispossessed of his American heritage. And if dispossession splits the subject, so too does the aesthetic 'impression' of America, which is alienating. This is seen when James finds himself 'up to his neck in what I have called his "subject"' at Gramercy Park (1.1.8), where he writes at once in the third and first person, and where the idea of the '"subject"' is one which is always provisional, another citation.

James's dispossession is not only aesthetic, but also theoretical, insofar as it lacks the stability of appealing to a recognisable past that would ground the subject. He had been born at 2 Washington Place on 15 April 1843, and as he arrives in 'precious' Greenwich, James hopes to recapture a sense of some 'earlier vibrations' (*AS* 2.2.68). The space recalls 'a pleasanter, easier, hazier past' (2.2.68), 'the unquenchable intensity of the impressions of childhood' (2.2.69). It is a topic that we have seen concern Pater and which will in turn concern Proust. But it is precisely the disjunction between the past and the modern reality which produces James's discomfort. Coming to Washington Square, which he immortalised in his 1880 novel of the same name (although it was a novel he did not rate highly, cutting it from the New York Edition), he found himself in the 'presence, so to speak, of [. . .] the ruthlessly suppressed birth-house on the other side of the Square' (*AS* 2.2.69) – 'so to speak', because it is the presence of absence. In its stead stood 'a high, square, impersonal structure', impersonal in both senses of the word, which 'blocks [. . .] the view of the past' (2.2.69–70). The 'effect' of the scene was to 'amputate' James 'of half my history' (2.2.70), producing 'melancholia' (2.2.68). In one sense, James knows the lost object of his cathexis, the home; but since, like Marius's *White-nights*, the house also stands for a stable relationship with the past, as such it eludes him. Indeed, James's only real connection with the New York of his childhood is aesthetic, taking place in the Church of the Ascension on Fifth Avenue, built 1840–1, where he sits in front of the 1887 stained glass windows created by his childhood friend John La Farge (1835–1910) (*AS* 2.2.72). Faced by this new Greenwich, James confesses to 'a horrible, hateful sense of personal antiquity' (2.1.63). Both the American scene and *The American Scene* can be read as melancholic: in each case, it is precisely the subject's identity that is lost. This melancholia links the subject 'James' with his subject 'New York'.

Perhaps this may partially explain the ways in which James's encounter with 'other' spaces is marked by anxiety and disgust (Rawlings 2004). As he walks eastwards towards Rutgers Street, he senses 'a great swarming, a swarming that had begun to thicken, infinitely', with the scene 'bristl[ing], at every step, with the signs and sounds, immitigable, unmistakable, of a Jewry that had burst all bounds' (*AS* 3.3.100). James had used 'swarming' beforehand to describe New York more generally (2.1.64), and will shortly use it again to discuss its Jewish spaces (3.3.102). The term maps an entire aesthetics of nineteenth-century city space: it cites Baudelaire's Paris of 'Les sept vieillards' (l. 26) (Tambling 2001: 135), but equally well Wordsworth, Dickens or Huysmans. Likewise, Manchester's inhabitants are also 'swarming' their way through 'filth, debris, and offal heaps' (2009: 65) for Engels. In Marxist terms, 'swarming' registers a question of class, that classic nineteenth-century fear of the 'masses' as something which 'culture' must keep in check. Bursting its bounds in the Jewish quarter, this 'swarming' is linked with sexual reproduction, for as James notes, 'the children swarmed above all – here was multiplication with a vengeance' (*AS* 3.3.100), speaking to an anxiety on behalf of James and his fellow Anglo-Protestants, those who imagine that they were 'there' first. New York's East Side has become a site of 'overflow', suggesting the idea of effluence, another image of waste. If capitalism relies on a kind of 'excessive' expenditure, as Bataille has shown (1985: 126), these passages remind us of the material costs of the modern city.

James's description of the people 'swarming' suggests a becoming-animal, and he compares the Jewish immigrants to 'snakes or worms', 'innumerable fish' (*AS* 3.3.100) and 'an ant-like population' (3.3.102). At Rutgers Street, this becoming-animal is described in spatial terms when commenting on the 'fire-escapes with which each house-front bristles' (3.3.101), that verb again, and which he calls a 'spaciously organized cage for the nimbler class of animals in some great zoological garden' (3.3.102). The racist analogy is 'irresistible' he says, coming immediately to him as a psychic response, with the apartments at Rutgers Street 'a little world of bars and perches and swings for human squirrels and monkeys' (3.3.102). This becoming-animal turns the 'heart of New York' (3.3.102), the 'cauldron' (3.1.92) of America, into a 'whirlpool' (3.3.102), dissolving identity. But of course, New York is precisely a city which has no 'heart' (1.5.40), and James considers this absent 'heart' to be the void of capitalism itself, associating the 'whirlpool' with the 'thrill of Wall Street' (2.1.63). The imagery of the 'whirlpool', picking up Pater's conclusion to the *Renaissance*, also suggests the vicarious thrill James feels when losing his own identity in the American scene. It gives another, Wildean connotation to the idea of a cosmopolitanism which calls into question the subject's identity and which is experienced as a moment of aesthetic pleasure (*CR* 176–7).

Central Park seemingly offers the balm for this wounded soul, a 'picturesque' retreat from the violence of the modern city. In terms of spatial practice, witnessed on 'a splendid Sunday afternoon of early summer', Central Park becomes another 'alien' space where 'the variety of accents with which the air swarmed seemed to make it a question whether the Park itself or its visitors were most polyglot' (*AS* 4.4.133). The Park 'hums' with a 'babel of tongues' (3.1.90), and the 'impression' it gives is of a 'tour of the little globe' (4.4.133).

James calls the scene the best of all the 'impressions' he had caught of New York, but this potential revaluation of the 'alien' in the American scene is built on an aesthetic rather than a political appreciation of the other. It involves 'placing' the other (4.4.132), which also suggests putting them in their place.

Whereas the great European cities had developed public spaces organically as they grew, Central Park was planned from the outset with a 'democratising' motivation. Established in 1857 and landscaped by Frederick Law Olmsted (1822–1903) and Calvert Vaux (1824–95), the majority of the park was laid between 1860 and 1873, differing from its European points of comparison as being a space that had been 'directly prescribed [. . .] from its origin, to "do", officially, on behalf of the City' (*AS* 4.4.131). This 'doing' is precisely an 'aesthetic' question, with Central Park designed from the outset to cater to 'the æsthetic appetite' (4.4.131):

> It has had to have something for everybody, since everybody arrives famished; it has had to multiply itself to extravagance, [. . .] to be, breathlessly, everywhere and everything at once, and produce on the spot the particular romantic object demanded, lake or river or cataract, wild woodland or teeming garden, boundless vista or bosky nook, noble eminence or smiling valley. (4.4.132)

The Park is thus a space of representation in the most rigorous Lefebvrean sense. The demand to 'have something for everybody', to always have the ability to produce the object of desire for the casual observer, is precisely its social function. It institutes a sense of repose, charming them as a 'pleasure-ground'; it is for this reason that the Park, above all, must be remarkable, 'to have feature at any price, the clamour of its customers being inevitably for feature' (4.4.132). Not a specific feature (although that also), but 'feature' understood as a prize in itself: Central Park exists only as a 'picturesque' fantasy that exists to attempt to bind the aesthetic wound of the otherwise monologic 'vagueness' of the American scene.

America's 'Multiplied Apertures': A Thought from the Outside

For James, the problem of New York, and of America more broadly, read both socially and aesthetically, is the confusion of categories, and the deconstruction of the boundaries between what lies within and without. Or rather, the problem of the American scene is that there is nothing within: all is surface. This is precisely what makes New York a quintessential aesthetic space. In Central Park, James notes 'the air of hard prosperity, the ruthlessly pushed-up and promoted look worn by men, women and children alike' (*AS* 4.4.133). In part, the passage reveals how hopelessly occluded James can be to the 'social question', for 'in that particular light, [. . .] such grossnesses as want or tatters or gin, as the unwashed face or the ill-shod, and still less the unshod, foot, or the mendicant hand, became strange, unhappy, far-off things' (4.4.134). James seems to be sailing along in Dickens's 'ark', lost in an aesthetic dream blind to social reality. But at the same time, the passage reveals the extent to which James himself has become a part of the American scene, obsessed with the conspicuous presentation of the surface.

This is another sense in which James is a divided subject, torn between *theoria* and *aesthesis*. Reading New York theoretically leads James to criticise the city as 'all formidable foreground' (*AS* 3.3.99), and marks him apart from the decadence of a Wilde, which privileged an aesthetics of the surface.[10] If Lord Henry admonishes that 'only shallow people [. . .] do not judge by appearances' (*DG* 4.212), James is troubled by the void which lies beneath those glittering aesthetic surfaces that make up the American scene. Considering the American Club, James writes that the 'universal custom of the house' in America is that 'almost no one of its indoor parts [is] distinguishable from any other' (*AS* 4.2.125). There is a 'diffused vagueness of separation between apartments, between hall and room, between one room and another, between the one you are in and the one you are not in, between place of passage and place of privacy' (4.2.125). Having lived so long in Europe, his 'spirit attuned to different practice', James considers this a 'strange perversity' of the American scene. Its spatial 'instinct' lies in seeking to 'minimiz[e], for any "interior", the guilt or odium or responsibility, whatever these may appear, of its being an interior' (4.2.125). James's unrelentingly puritan image, associating the interior with the soul, sees America as lacking depth. It has to be so, for America has cast aside that history, the recess of its past, seeking to exteriorise everything onto the surface, 'like a conspiracy for nipping the interior in the bud, for denying its right to exist':

> Thus we have the law fulfilled that every part of every house shall be, as nearly as may be, visible, visitable, penetrable, not only from every other part, but from as many parts of as many other houses as possible, if they only be near enough. Thus we see systematized the indefinite extension

> of all spaces and the definite merging of all functions; the enlargement of every opening, the exaggeration of every passage, the substitution of gaping arches and far perspectives and resounding voids for enclosing walls, for practicable doors, for controllable windows, for all the rest of the essence of the room-character. (4.2.125–6)

The idea recalls Benjamin, who argues that 'the shattering of the interior occurs [. . .] around the turn of the century' (*SW* 3: 38). The 'effacement' of differences becomes the new principle of American space. Character is lost, and with it the marks of the social itself, since James associates the division of rooms conservatively with the gendered and, in his opinion, 'proper' division of society: interior space belongs to the woman, an idea which Ruskin forcibly defends in *Sesame and Lilies* (1865).[11] The effect of this 'effacement' is another dispossession: in America, modern man is exposed, becoming 'a homeless wanderer', like Lear on the heath, speaking to an existential crisis, and differing from that 'state of homelessness on earth' which Ruskin identified in the architecture of Torcello (*CW* 10: 21), since there is no womb-like kernel to retreat to (*SE* 17: 243). Post-industrial mental life becomes empty, its essence deferred, its openings showing 'other apertures, corridors, staircases, yawning, expanding, ascending, descending, and all as for the purpose of giving his presence "away"' (*AS* 4.2.126). 'Giving his presence "away"' also gives him away, revealing him precisely as a subject without qualities.

Whether on the grand scale of the limitless will to grow and expand, vertically in the 'bristling' skyscrapers, horizontally westwards across the country, or on the local scale of the interior of the houses themselves, American space seeks to forget the past, overwrite the history, in a capitalist orgy of limitless expenditure. If Dickens's Jasper reads London as a libidinal economy, mobilising desire as the truth of modern space, then in America, space is simply one more commodity that exists only to be consumed endlessly. The experience is precisely one of *aesthesis*, and James's New York, for all his desire to read the city theoretically, becomes one of the most radical, if unsatisfying, exercises in the aesthetics of space inaugurated by Ruskin. In America, space is not simply produced or consumed, but '*productively consumed*', where the process of consuming itself produces new spatial formations as its surplus effect (*PS* 349), dissolving the boundaries between inside and outside. James's point is Adornian: in America, 'private' space is consumed only to be reterriorialised by the capitalist mode of production. What is lost is precisely a sense of history, which may 'ground' the subject in their past, stabilising the identity of either James or the American scene. It is in James's New York, more than any of the other spaces that we have encountered in the course of the book, that we see the condition of modernity as the law of a new mode of the production of space: all that is solid melts into air. In this sense, *The American Scene* documents James's troubled relationship with the British tradition of the aesthetics of space – troubled precisely insofar as the space of early twentieth-century America resists both *theoria* and *aesthesis*. James, a returning native who is also by this point of his career something of an Anglo-European in temperament, tries to read New York both from the vantage point of nineteenth-century historicism and informed by nineteenth-century aesthetic theory, but finds neither a sufficient resource through which to better understand or represent America. It is precisely in this inability to bind the aesthetic wound that his work augurs modernism.

Notes

1. On Pater and James, see Freedman 1990: 133–66.
2. See also the essays collected by Izzo and O'Hara 2006.
3. On James in Paris, see Brooks 2007 and Wrenn 2008.
4. For a queer reading of *The American Scene*, see Buelens 2002, and more generally, on James and sexuality, see Stevens 1998 and Ohi 2011.
5. On Pater's phenomenological reduction, and the way in which he considers the moment of appreciation a kind of transcendental apperception of the aesthetic subject, see Whiteley 2010: 23–4.
6. On trauma and *The American Scene*, see in particular Tambling 2001: 101–11. I am indebted throughout this chapter to Tambling's psychoanalytic approach to James's travelogue.
7. Joel Porte 1990: 12 argues that James's vision of New England Arcadia may also imply Pater, who had used the Latin phrase 'Et Ego in Arcadia Fui' as an epigram to his essay on Johann Joachim Winckelmann (1717–78) (*SHR* 141).
8. James's interest in the reification of the elevator and in the elevator as the reification of the 'stroll' anticipates Jameson on the postmodern elevator as the 'dialectical intensification of the autoreferentiality of all modern culture' (1991: 42).
9. See Buelens 2002 for a reading *The American Scene* as a document of dispossession.
10. On Wilde's surface effects, see Whiteley 2015: 265–8. James had little time for 'the repulsive and fatuous Oscar', whom he had seen in Washington in January 1882 (*LHJ* 2: 372). Later in his career, antipathy would mix with jealousy when James tried his hand at playwriting:

his play *Guy Domville* (1895) folded at the St James's Theatre, succeeded by *The Importance of Being Earnest*. Earlier, James had written disparagingly of *Lady Windermere's Fan* as having 'absolutely no characterization and all the people talk equally strained Oscar' (*LHJ* 3: 373). Lacking 'character' is, of course, precisely what characterises the American scene.

11. On James's gendering of space, although without reference to Ruskin, see McNamara 1993: 128–30.

Conclusion

Unreal Cities – Towards Modernism

In writing *The Waste Land* (1922), T. S. Eliot (1888–1965) first considered as a title *He do the Police in Different Voices*, drawn from Dickens's Betty Higden (1997: 1.16.198). It invites comparison between *Our Mutual Friend* and *The Waste Land*, the realist and modernist cities. Noting this resonance, Karl Smith (2008) reads Dickens's London as a precursor of Eliot's 'Unreal City'. But, of course, Eliot's London is not the same as Dickens's, even if, written 'after Dickens', it necessarily incorporates the former as an intrinsic element of its own. Indeed, Eliot's London owes as much to Baudelaire's Paris as to Dickens. In his notes to the poem (2005: 81), Eliot glosses his famous image of London by reference to 'Les sept vieillards'.

> Unreal City,
> Under the brown fog of a winter,
> A crowd flowed over London Bridge, so many,
> I had not thought death had undone so many. (ll. 60–3)

In 'Les sept vieillards', the modern city is a 'swarming [*fourmillante*] city, city full of dreams' (l. 1), haunted by 'ghosts in daylight' (l. 2). It is 'swarming', that term which we have encountered repeatedly throughout this study, from Wordsworth to Dickens to James. In this version of Paris, 'a dirty yellow fog filled all the space' (l. 9), where Baudelaire's poetic persona encounters seven 'monstrous' old men (l. 42). Horrified, he seems unable to differentiate reality from waking nightmare, uncertain whether the seven are doppelgängers of one another or one subject multiplying itself (l. 36). As 'baroque spectres' (l. 31), they become allegorical figures of the space of the city and modern life. In suggesting that Baudelaire's image of the city lies somewhere behind that of *The Waste Land*, alongside numerous other allusions, Eliot links modernism with decadence, speaking to the melancholia of the modern subject.[1] The modernism of this 'Unreal City' lies precisely in this overwhelming sense of prior aesthetic traces that inscribe any attempt to read the city, this cacophany of precedent voices, as much as in the sense of social fragmentation that alienates the subject. The reality of modern space has become 'unreal', if not – as in the late Dickens – 'for the first time' (*ED* 23.261),[2] yet in a manner which the earlier tradition of the aesthetics of space could necessarily only anticipate, still to fully realise.

'Modernism' is another of those contested words, like 'realism' or the 'aesthetic', which have been difficult to define. Broadly speaking, modernist art seems to encompass two distinct strands. On the one hand, we have the sense of historical rupture, a traumatic break with those teleological, progressive, idealist theories of history and culture of the nineteenth century, a sense of resignation, manifested aesthetically in the break with traditional forms and the privileging of the fragment. If the millenarianism of the *fin de siècle* was one formative moment in the production of the intellectual conditions which would foster this modernism, it was fuelled philosophically by Nietzsche, psychologically by Freud's discovery of the unconscious, and scientifically by Albert Einstein's (1879–1955) theories of relativity and *Raumzeit* [spacetime]. Henri Bergson (1859–1941) problematised the ways in which time had traditionally been reduced to spatial metaphors in *L'évolution créatrice* [*Creative Evolution*] (1907), in which he introduced the idea of the subjective experience of time, *durée* [duration]. In this sense, not only was the stable Enlightenment subject of the Cartesian tradition under assault from seemingly all sides, but so too was that subject's relationship with space and time. More broadly, the sense of pessimism and negativity that penetrates a great deal of modernist art was registered historically in the seismic events of the First World War. On the other hand, many works of modernism also manifested a synthetic desire to reforge out of the fragments a new image of totality, one that possessed at least the potential of an aesthetics of hope for the future. Eliot's 'Unreal City' expresses both sides of modernism: his London is fragmented, a palimpsest built out of 'a heap of broken images' (l. 24), but one in which spiritual resurrection may yet be possible, giving subtle indications of 'something further to come' (*ME* 2: 4.28.220).

Indeed, these two faces of modernism – fragmentary and messianic – may be also understood through Ruskin's distinction between the aesthetic and theoretical gazes. *Theoria*, in its pretention to see through the sensuous surface, through the housetops and into the moral heart of things, seems to offer the promise of an 'inspired' image of the 'truth of space'. But these claims, based on Ruskin's reading of the Gothic and rooted in a historical idea of society which was swiftly being demolished, came to be viewed with some degree of suspicion by the 'aesthetic' writers that followed him. Indeed, when read today, Ruskin's own claims to modernism may be seen to rest on his proto-post-industrialism in work such as 'Fiction, Fair and Foul', and the tradition of the aesthetics of space anticipates modernism precisely in its privileging of an aesthetics of the fragment. From Jasper's ecstatic vision of Cloisterham Cathedral, a moment at once anachronistic and anatopic, to Lord Henry's encounter with a *fin-de-siècle* London 'rich in curious effects' (*DG* 19.350), writers in this tradition recognised the limits of the 'theoretical' appreciation of modern space, in which, as in James's New York, all that is solid melts into air. James's work is doubly important, since it also registers the ways in which modernist space was no longer a tale of two cities: Paris and London, the capitals of the nineteenth century, were joined by New York as a third centripetal point in the modernist imaginary. As in the cities captured by F. Scott Fitzgerald (1896–1940) and John Dos Passos (1896–1970), such a re-situation also served to register the ways in which the historical links that grounded the subject in the past had been ruptured. The modernism of James's New York lies in his sense of American space as an 'aesthetic wound' that evades attempted mediation, resists the impulse to totality.

Traditionally, it is the movements of 'impressionism' and 'symbolism', in both art and literature, which have been seen as the transitional signals that carried nineteenth-century realism into modernism. As Clark has shown (1984), late nineteenth-century impressionist artists like Monet, Edgar Degas (1834–1917) (who rejected the title, preferring to call himself a realist) and Auguste Renoir (1841–1919), as well as post-impressionists like Georges Seurat (1859–91), created a Baudelairean aesthetics of Parisian space that competed with the city anatomised by naturalists like Zola. So too in Britain, where the 'empiricist' London of Gissing (to use Freeman's term) competed with the fragmentary city imaged by Symons. Influenced above all by Paul Verlaine (1844–96), Symons revels in the aesthetics of *fin-de-siècle* metropolitan space, personifying the streets, its 'fingers' ('City Nights I. In the Train' l. 3) and 'flashing eyes' (l. 6), accentuating the visual, the subject overwhelmed by 'the dazzling vista' of London space (l. 12). Symons's style, which Pater was to praise for capturing 'the spectacle of modern life' in English poetry rather than poetic prose (Symons 2017: 181), is quintessentially 'decadent'. The influence of Verlaine, invoked in the 'Fêtes galantes' sequence of *Silhouettes* (1892), was perhaps even more marked in *London Nights* (1895), in which the figure of the ballet dancer, which had also fascinated Mallamé, stands as a symbol for the modern city, a 'spice-laden atmosphere, / Where only nature is a thing unreal' ('Lilian I. Proem', ll. 13–14). As Symons wrote in *London: A Book of Aspects* (1909), he was trying to capture a sense of the 'real London', rejecting the empiricist approach of the naturalists in favour of a fragmented, asyndetonic aesthetic composed out of 'a continual sequence of pictures' (1909: 2).

Symons was drawn to the capital, taking up bachelor's lodgings in 1891 at Fountain's Court, Temple, where he lived until 1900, writing his most important poetry. But if Symons's London, just like Wilde's, owes much to symbolist and 'decadent' Paris, as Verlaine himself noted (Symons 2017: 189), it had a presence of its own. 'There is in the aspect of London a certain magnificence', he wrote, 'the magnificence of weight, solidity, energy, imperturbability, and an unconquered continuance. It is alive from border to border' (1909: 1). It is this sense of the enervating pleasure of modern metropolitan space that we find registered, if somewhat against himself, in Wordsworth's London, a shifting, fleeting series of bright images and sensations, an 'emporium' of commodities offered to the gaze, as well as in Dickens, enjoyed a little less ambiguously and expressed in his urban phenomenology. But it is precisely after Ruskin as much as after Dickens that the city and its pleasures could become the object of an explicitly 'aesthetic' gaze. No longer would the aim be to produce a representation of space in order to know, control or dominate it; rather, in this burgeoning tradition, the representational space of the modern metropolis could be appreciated in the spirit of art. Throughout the tradition of the aesthetics of space, we find the decadent city of a Symons anticipated and made possible, precisely through that shift of emphasis from *theoria* to *aesthesis*. And just as Symons did, so too the aesthetics of space influences modernism in privileging this fragmentary experience of modern space as one of aesthetic pleasure.

'Cityful' Aesthetics in Virginia Woolf and James Joyce

One of the most obvious heirs to the tradition of the aesthetics of space was Virginia Woolf. Tutored by Pater's sister, Clara (1840–1920), Woolf acknowledged her debt to the aesthete in the preface to *Orlando* (1928) (2015: 5), her own kind of imaginary portrait. Like Pater and Proust, Woolf reflected on the 'contradiction[s]' of Ruskin, in whom 'the colour and warmth of Italy fought with his English puritanical love of order, method and cleanliness' (1994: 503), *aesthesis* against *theoria*. While Auerbach considers *To the Lighthouse* (1927) the pinnacle of the 'realist' tradition (2003: 525–53), Woolf distanced herself from the novels of the nineteenth and early twentieth century. In her famous essay 'Mr. Bennett and Mrs. Brown' (1924), she criticises the 'reality effects' of realism, seeking to 'observe every detail with immense care' (1988: 511), and particularly the way in which this tradition uses space to define character. Surveying realism, 'one strange fact is immediately apparent': while every sort of space was represented, 'in all this vast conglomeration of printed pages, in all this congeries of streets and houses, there is not a single man or woman whom we know' (1988: 508). Whether the spaces be interior, loaded with that bourgeois bric-à-brac which stands in for character, or exterior, 'swarming' with lost souls, Woolf charges 'this appalling narrative business of the realists' with being 'false, unreal, merely conventional' (1980: 209). Realism failed to represent the reality of the everyday life of the subject, their consciousness, memories, hopes and dreams.

Not so Clarissa Dalloway. If the London of *Mrs Dalloway* (1925) invites comparison with the earlier Dickens, it also demonstrates the distance between realism and modernism, and the ways in which Woolf learnt lessons from those who foreshadowed her aesthetics of space. Set on one summer's day, 13 June 1923, Woolf's novel follows her characters as they walk through London, specifically Westminster, rather than around 46 Gordon Square, Bloomsbury, where she lived.[3] Her city is full of beauty, 'not the crude beauty of the eye', to be sure, but *aesthesis* nonetheless, 'a sense of pleasure-making' (*MD* 138), 'absorbing, mysterious, of infinite richness, this life' (*MD* 139). As Lisbeth Larsson notes, Woolf's writing of London differs from that of Dickens, for whereas he is at pains to describe the spaces of the city in which his characters find themselves, Woolf is content to simply indicate the location by mentioning addresses and locations (2017: 7–8). In keeping with her argument in 'Mr. Bennett and Mrs. Brown', Woolf shifts the focus from a description of space to a post-industrialist emphasis on the effects of spaces on the individual consciousness. These effects are aesthetic and often euphoric, the city 'like the pulse of a perfect heart, life struck straight through the streets' (*MD* 43).

For Robert Alter, *Mrs Dalloway* constitutes what he calls 'urban pastoral', in which the city provides a 'sense of invigoration, harmony with one's surroundings, and enrapturing aesthetic revelation' (2005: 105). Although Alter passes over the significance of the post-Ruskinian tradition that is my own focus, his important work on the urban modernism of Woolf, and particularly Joyce's *Ulysses*

(1922), influences my analysis of their aesthetics of space in this section, which deals with a number of the same passages. But while acknowledging the presence of trauma both explicit in the figure of Septimus Warren Smith, who is suffering from shell shock and will commit suicide, and implicit, looming as historical background, Alter's idea of Woolf's 'urban pastoral' is ultimately affirmative, and contrasts with the reading of *Mrs Dalloway* put forward by Tambling, for whom the novel is marked by repression. Tambling notes throughout *Mrs Dalloway* the presence of the state (1989: 138–40), which affects the subject through the newly renovated architecture of Westminster and in those monuments which Peter Walsh encounters as he walks up Whitehall. First, he 'glared at the statue of the Duke of Cambridge' (*MD* 43), Prince George (1819–1904), Commander-in-Chief of the Forces, 1856–95, causing Walsh to reflect upon having been sent down from Oxford in 1893, perhaps in part owing to his youthful socialism. He meets some 'boys in uniform, carrying guns', who 'marched with their eyes ahead of them, [. . .] on their faces an expression like the letters of a legend written round the base of a statue praising duty, gratitude, fidelity, love of England' (*MD* 43); they are carrying a wreath to be laid at the 'empty tomb', The Cenotaph, erected in 1920 and designed by Edwin Lutyens (1869–1944). Continuing to Trafalgar Square, Peter is confronted by 'all the exalted statues, Nelson, Gordon, Havelock, [. . .] the spectacular images of great soldiers' standing proud, images of ascetic 'renunciation' and 'discipline' (*MD* 44). But in spite of his resentment, which leads to resistance, Peter is ultimately a subject of the space, considering London 'a splendid achievement in its own way'. 'Coming as he did from a respectable Anglo-Indian family which for at least three generations had administered the affairs of a continent', Peter hails from a line of state functionaries, finding his meaning in the nation, with 'civilisation [. . .] dear to him as a personal possession' (*MD* 44). 'Possession', of course, was one of the things that eluded James on his return to America, its lack wounding him: unlike Peter Walsh, James could no longer find his place. For Tambling, 'the very "invention of tradition" is in progress (1989: 140), witnessed in the patriarchal imagery of militarism and power which had reconstructed London from the 1880s, a process which was only accentuated in the years following the Great War. *Mrs Dalloway* witnesses the ways in which new spaces are produced, where the repressed returns not only through Septimus and his 'double' Clarissa (Woolf 1994: 549), but also in the space of London.

No doubt, both Tambling and Alter are right to a degree. But for our purposes, it is the city of pleasure rather than repression which most obviously manifests Woolf's indebtedness to the tradition of the aesthetics of space. Take the moment early in the novel when Clarissa first hears the sound of Big Ben:

> There! Out it boomed. First a warning, musical; then the hour, irrevocable. The leaden circles dissolved in the air. Such fools we are, she thought, crossing Victoria Street. For Heaven only knows why one loves it so, how one sees it so, making it up, building it round one, tumbling it, creating it every moment afresh; but the veriest frumps, the most dejected of miseries sitting on doorsteps (drink their downfall) do the same; can't be dealt with, she felt positive, by Acts of Parliament for that very reason: they love life. In people's eyes, in the swing, tramp, and trudge; in the bellow and the uproar; the carriages, motor cars, omnibuses, vans, sandwich men shuffling and swinging; brass bands; barrel organs; in the triumph and the jingle and the strange high singing of some aeroplane overhead was what she loved; life; London; this moment of June. (*MD* 4)

As in Symons, we find a genuine excitement transmitted through the passage, recognising techniques drawn from Dickens and Ruskin in the rhythm and the repetition, the swift transitions between asyndeton and polysyndeton, the use of semi-colons to simultaneously link and divide. In this passage Woolf's modernist stream of consciousness, an idea rooted in Pater's 'Conclusion' (*SHR* 188) as much as in William James's psychology, creates a synaesthetic aesthetics of space. In Big Ben's 'boom', sound becomes meaning, in an ephemeral 'instant' of vibration. As she crosses Victoria Street (opened in 1851, another project of 'visibility', clearing the slums of 'Devil's Acre'), Clarissa seems to be waxing Shakespearean, 'such fools we are, she thought', recalling, consciously or not, Rosalind in *As You Like It* (3.5.53). The subtle allusion anticipates the ways in which she comes back time and again to the lines of the song of *Cymbeline*, 'Fear no more the heat o' the sun, / Nor the furious winter's rages' (4.2.257–8), first encountered in an open book lying in the window of Hatchard's, 187 Piccadilly (*MD* 8, 25, 34, 158). Aesthetic traces are part of the fabric of Clarissa's engagement with the city; its space is created by the subject through their *aesthesis* 'every moment afresh' (*MD* 4), phrasing recalling Pater. But Woolf reverses Pater's operation, for whereas the 'Conclusion' images a world 'contracting' from the exterior to the interior, the subject 'a solitary prisoner' in 'its own dream of a world' (*SHR* 188) – a metaphor which Woolf is well aware of (*MD* 163) – then Clarissa moves in the other direction, as manifested in her sympathetic identification with her 'double' Septimus. Likewise, when she reflects on how she experiences life in the modern city: 'somehow in the streets of London, on the ebb and flow of things, here, there', she and Peter could find themselves 'liv[ing] in each other', and becoming 'part of people she had never met' (*MD* 8).

In *Mrs Dalloway*, it is the characters themselves who create the space they live in, but their contingency and potential absence are always implied, with death a constant presence in the novel. When she hears of Septimus's suicide, Clarissa thinks herself 'somehow very like him'. At this precise moment, the aesthetic experience of the city enters into her consciousness, 'insinuates' itself as another thought of the outside: 'The clock was striking. The leaden circles dissolved in the air. He made her feel the beauty; made her feel the fun' (*MD* 158). The repetition of the opening scene serves three functions. Expressing compulsion, it is linked to the death-drive, and associates 'clock time' – Big Ben as a symbol of the state and the will to power – with death, as in 'Lord Arthur Savile's Crime'. Likewise, it associates the ephemeral aesthetic instant of vibration with iteration and citation, as well as linking Septimus's suicide with the will to life. As in Pater, for whom beauty and death are locked in a chiastic structure (*IP* 141), Clarissa finds beauty in the vibrancy of modern metropolitan space, in a moment of affirmation. Earlier in the novel, Woolf reflects on a time when 'curious antiquaries, sifting the ruins of time' might find London 'a grass-grown path and all those hurrying along the pavement this Wednesday morning [. . .] but bones with a few wedding rings mixed up in their dust and the gold stoppings of innumerable decayed teeth' (*MD* 14). The imagery, another memento mori, recalls Marius's vision of a fallen Rome (*ME* 1: 2.12.200), but lacks that sense of melancholia encountered in Pater.

Woolf's aesthetics of space has learnt a great deal from the nineteenth-century tradition that has been the subject of this book, but *Mrs Dalloway* also highlights the limitations of this tradition. The aesthetics of space of Ruskin, Dickens, Pater, Wilde and James is gendered male, so that women, if and when they feature in these works, are figures who must be accompanied, as when Sybil walks with James in *The Picture of Dorian Gray*, or ones who are under threat, as when Rosa arrives in London, alone and scared, in *The Mystery of Edwin Drood*. Alternatively, women are simply presented to the male gaze as aesthetic objects, as in the ballet of umbrella and skirt of Huysmans's *À rebours*, or in the figure of the prostitute, whose commodified body is reduced to a 'clockwork puppet' in 'The Harlot's House' (l. 19), eviscerated of agency and substance. Indeed, it is Ruskin who emblematises this aesthetic and social division in *Sesame and Lilies*, and against whom Woolf writes in *A Room of One's Own* (1929), the title of which asserts a woman's right to her 'possession and control of personal space' (Neverow 2010: 96). Susan Merrill Squier (1985) has shown the ways in which Woolf's city navigates gender, balancing Woolf's own love of walking London – shared with Clarissa Dalloway (*MD* 5) – with an awareness of the dangers metropolitan spaces posed for women (Larsson 2017: 10). These dangers are dramatised by Peter's pursuit of the woman with the 'red carnation'. Following his symbolic castration in front of the monuments of Whitehall and Trafalgar Square, he catches sight of a 'young woman', and follows her through 'the random uproar of the traffic' (*MD* 45), aroused by 'excitement', asserting his masculinity precisely through his aesthetic consumption of her body. But Peter is less *flâneur* than predator, all the while 'stealthily fingering his pocket-knife' (*MD* 45). He does not recognise this sexual violence within, however, romanticising himself as 'an adventurer, reckless, [. . .] swift, daring, [. . .] a romantic buccaneer' (*MD* 45–6), repeating the point for emphasis, or as though trying to convince himself: 'He was a buccaneer' (*MD* 46). He stalks her through the city: 'On and on she went, across Piccadilly, and up Regent Street, ahead of him, her cloak, her gloves, her shoulders combining with the fringes and the laces and the feather boas in the windows' (*MD* 46). She is fetishised, fragmented into a series of partial objects, inanimate and corporal treated alike, the focus on the fringes and lace signifying her body as eroticised zones of transition, sensuous sites of texture, and where the girl merges into the consumer fetishes in the shop windows, passing into simulacrum. The passage shows another, less palatable, misogynistic side to the ways in which the modern subject, treating life in the spirit of art, but under the auspices of the male gaze, may create the aesthetics of those spaces that surround them.

Alter (2005: 108) suggests that the passage may have found partial inspiration in Leopold Bloom's pursuit of the girl in the silk stockings in *Ulysses*, which Woolf was reading when she wrote *Mrs Dalloway*. Joyce is another figure who developed insights drawn from the tradition of the aesthetics of space. He chose to immortalise Dublin, a city which had 'been a capital for thousands of years, [. . .] the "second" city of the British Empire', and was 'nearly three times as big as Venice' (1975: 78). The fact that Venice is named here by Joyce makes clear the nineteenth-century tradition of the aesthetics of space underwriting his Dublin. If the city's population was only around 300,000 in 1904 when *Ulysses* is set (also on a single day, 6 June), and by this point it was no longer Britain's second city but its fifth (Harding 2003: 20–1), Dublin nevertheless came to rival London, Paris and New York as a modernist city precisely through Joyce's contribution to literary history. As he famously put it, his aim in *Ulysses* was 'to give a picture of Dublin so complete that if the city suddenly disappeared from the earth it could be reconstructed out of my book' (Budgen 1989: 69). In so doing, Joyce gave an image of the 'multiple variations that make up the social life of a city – its degradations and its exultations' (Ehrlich 2002: 14). In his earlier stories collected in *Dubliners* (1914), Joyce had developed a more realist style, with Dublin marked by the aesthetic of his fellow Irishman Wilde, as in the spectral effects of 'The Dead', discussed in Chapter 4, or as when he productively mobilises the ambiguity of an adjective to personify space. Thus, 'Araby' (1905) opens with an image of North Richmond Street 'being blind', the 'houses of the street, conscious of the decent lives within them, gaz[ing] at one another with brown imperturbable faces' (2008a: 19). Connoting the panoptic sense of Catholic Dublin as a space where the neighbour's gaze regulates social interaction, the physical cul-de-sac also speaks to the protagonist's spiritual blindness, where the epiphanic moment of insight lays him bare 'as a creature driven and derided by vanity' (2008a: 24).

But by the time of writing *Ulysses*, the mimetic features of realist prose, while not wholly discarded, give way to a city of affect. As Stephen Dedalus puts it in 'Aeolus', 'Dublin. I have much, much to learn' (*U* 7.139), and the resultant voyage of discovery leads Joyce's Dublin to become, in practice, far more radically aesthetic than Woolf's London. His city is a chaotic 'whirlpool' of images (*U* 9.188), with Pater rubbing proverbial shoulders with Homer in the National Museum on Kildare Street, and where stray images caught on advertising hoardings (Leopold Bloom's profession) mingle with half-remembered songs, lines of poetry and the prodigious sensorium of modern space, the 'ineluctable modality of the visible' (*U* 3.37). Once again, we have a city navigated through prior aesthetic traces, most obviously in 'Oxen of the Sun', where Dublin is represented through a series of styles drawn from the history of English literature, including those of Dickens's *David Copperfield* (*U* 14.399), Ruskin's *The Stones of Venice* (*U* 14.401) and Pater's 'The Child in the House' (*U* 14.401).[4] Take 'Scylla and Charybdis', in which Stephen does not simply navigate the city through the text of *Hamlet*, but seems to become Hamlet, incorporating Hamlet's words as his own, living through them, in a Nietzschean moment where the subject passes into 'every name in history' (Nietzsche 1996: 347), or like Wilde's Gilbert, whose 'imagination' allows him to live 'countless lives' (*CR* 178). Influenced by Pater, Stephen compares 'the artist who weave[s] and unweave[s] his image' to the physical body, weaving and unweaving itself, 'their molecules shuttl[ing] too and fro' (*U* 9.186).

More broadly, in the idea of the subject multiplying itself in space through the experience of *aesthesis*, Joyce's Dublin is Paterean insofar as his city is one of 'perpetual motion' (*SHR* 186), as in Bloom's pursuit of the silk-stockinged girl in 'Lotus Eaters'. This chapter, mapping onto the *Odyssey*, sees the city traversed by desire, taking up the sense of intoxication and forgetting borrowed from Homer, and implying both *jouissance* and the death-drive, connoting the loss of the subject in the pleasure of the gaze. This is an idea which we have seen anticipated in James's 'queer' spaces of New York, but unlike James, whose prose is still married to nineteenth-century realist traditions, Joyce frees the signifier from the referent, showing instead how the subject simultaneously registers and creates space, *aesthesis* passing through the prism of the stream of consciousness. All the while maintaining an unrelated conversation with M'Coy, Bloom simultaneously follows the girl with his eyes, moving slightly to one side to 'Watch! Watch! Silk flash stockings white. Watch!', losing her as a tram passes – 'Lost it. Curse your noisy pugnose' – before catching sight of her again: 'Flicker, flicker: the laceflare of her hat in the sun: flicker, flick' (*U* 5.71). The juxtaposition of alveolars and plosives in the repeated 'flicker', the former picked up in the sound of the 'laceflare', gives the line not only a visual impression of Paterean aesthetic 'flickering' (*SHR* 187) but, in its lyrical materiality, an erotic charge. Arresting the sequence in the concluding 'flick' mimes the flaring of the lace, in an image that skirts the orgasmic. 'Flick' suggests a kind of flirtatiousness, imagined on Bloom's part, a delicious sense of physical collision (*OED n.*[1] 1), his desire rewriting the aesthetics of the space (Alter 2005: 125). Colloquially, 'flicker' (*OED v.* 2a) means to fondle, kiss or caress, so that the aesthetic impression codes her body as available for more than the pleasure of the eye. Moreover, the final apocope prevents resolution or closure, allowing desire to remain suspended as a promise of the aesthetic instant.

The modern space of Dublin allows such chance and charged encounters to redistribute the sensible. Thus, the infamous moment in 'Nausicaa' when Bloom brings himself to climax at the hitching up of Gerty MacDowell's skirt, coinciding with a fireworks display at Sandymount Strand:

> And then a rocket sprang and bang shot blind blank and O! then the Roman candle burst and it was like a sigh of O! and everyone cried O! O! in raptures and it gushed out of it a stream of rain gold hair threads and they shed and ah! they were all greeny dewy stars falling with golden, O so lovely, O, soft, sweet, soft! (*U* 13.350)

Constituting not simply a moment in which space is rewritten through desire, the scene also seems to recall aesthetically Whistler's infamous *Nocturne in Black and Gold: The Falling Rocket*. Sandymount Strand becomes a pleasure garden, like those in Cremorne, London, the location captured in Whistler's painting, which had a reputation for prostitution (Acton 1867: 103–5). In such intermedial echoes, real and imagined pleasures, the carnivalesque potential of modern urban reality and impressionist art come together to create Joyce's aesthetics of space.

Transition defines the modern city, to one thing constant never. The past is constantly being paved over, but maintains hidden traces that the consciousness mobilises as intrinsic moments of the aesthetics of space. At the conclusion of *The Great Gatsby* (1925), Fitzgerald imagines 'the old island [. . .] that flowered once for Dutch sailor's eyes – a fresh, green breast of the new world' (2008: 143). It is a sense of the past that James suggests New York can no longer see. The topic is a recurrent one in modernist works, at once nostalgic and an uncanny reminder of the lived realities of modern space. In *Mrs Dalloway*, Rezia, standing in Regent's Park, imagines the scene 'at midnight, when all boundaries are lost', when 'the country reverts to its ancient shape, as the Romans saw it, lying cloudy, when they landed, and the hills had no names and rivers wound they knew not where – such was her darkness' (*MD* 20–1). This specific image of the ancient Romans in London, as well as the allusion to 'her darkness', recalls Conrad's Marlow thinking back to 'very old times, when the Romans first came here, nineteen hundred years ago' (2008a: 105). In *Heart of Darkness*, Marlow juxtaposes London as the supposedly 'civilized' centre of a worldwide empire with the 'marshes, forests, savages' encountered by the Romans:

> Land in a swamp, march through the woods, and in some inland post feel the savagery, the utter savagery, had closed round him – all that mysterious life of the wilderness that stirs in the forest, in the jungles, in the hearts of wild men. (2008a: 106)

Those Romans were forced to 'live in the midst of the incomprehensible', 'fascinated' by the darkness which 'goes to work upon him. The fascination of the abomination – [. . .] the powerless disgust, the surrender, the hate' (2008a: 106). The comparison sees Conrad's *fin-de-siècle* apocalypticism read contemporary London as much as the Congo as the heart of darkness, rotten to its core and spreading its disease as an infection from its 'venerable stream' out to the 'uttermost ends of the earth'. In this, it reverses the imagery of *Edwin Drood*, where the infection moves from the 'darkness' of the East End and the Empire back into the heart of England. Conrad's phrase 'fascination of the abomination' implies the death-drive and recalls Dickens's 'attraction of repulsion' (*UT* 263). Both authors remind us in different fashions of the ways in which the realities of modernity traumatise the subject. But they also remind us that this trauma implies history, if only as reconstructed through what Freud calls *Nachträglichkeit* (*SE* 17: 44–5), that 'deferral' which implies the sense of being 'late', as well as a rupturing of the 'ordering' of the 'civilized' values of the past.

In 'Nestor', Stephen, seeing a vision of excess prompted by a recollection of William Blake (1757–1827), hears 'the ruin of all space, shattered glass and toppling masonry' (*U* 2.24), seemingly apocalyptic imagery. But such connotations are undercut when the phrase is repeated in 'Circe', there as stage directions reflecting Stephen smashing a chandelier, to which the gas jet replies: 'Pwfungg!' (15.542). Nevertheless, humour notwithstanding, *Ulysses* is intensely aware of Dublin's past: if it is history's absence that traumatises James in New York, marking its modernity, then in *Ulysses* history is 'a nightmare' from which Joyce is 'trying to wake' (*U* 2.34). We have seen throughout this book that the aesthetics of space is aware of politics, even when, as in Pater's Rome, it treats it at an aesthetic remove. Joyce's Dublin is also political, but mobilises this politics in a different manner from that of Wilde, who identified himself as a socialist but who arguably managed to maintain aesthetic distance precisely by writing London rather than Dublin, where he was born.[5] In 'Lestrygonians', Bloom reflects on Ireland's imperial subjugation, and on what he considers the futility of political violence (Manganiello 1980: 3–5), thinking of the nationalist politician Charles Stewart Parnell (1846–91), whose memory carries a 'certain fascination' (*U* 8.156), and passing by chance 'the brother', John Howard (1843–1900): 'Image of him. Haunting Face. Now that's a coincidence' (*U* 8.157). Bloom had just been considering the city's routine: 'Things go on same, day after day: squads of police marching out, back: trams in, out.' The presence of the police, registered parenthetically in Bloom's mind, caught between homely philosophising and the movement of the trams, is foreshadowed a few moments earlier. 'A squad of constables debouched from College street, marching in Indian file. Goosestep. Foodheated faces, sweating helmets, patting their truncheons' (*U* 8.154), images of Empire and patriarchal power, but also somewhat farcical, the 'patting' of their 'truncheons' at once a threat of colonial violence and at the same time suggesting the impotence of their power. Following this, as Bloom sees, 'a squad of others, marching irregularly, rounded Trinity railings making for the station' (*U* 8.155). The police are part of this rhythmic texture of city space, like the shunting trams, and like the marching boy soldiers whom Peter Walsh encounters in Whitehall. Bloom is walking along Westmoreland Street, registering both the architecture of the space and the economic history that makes it possible. Property is continually 'changing hands. This owner, that', linking the buildings of modern Dublin, like 'Kerwan's mushroom houses built of breeze' – referring to low-cost housing built by Michael Kirwan (not 'Kerwan') for Dublin Artisans' Dwellings Company (Gifford and Seidman 2008: 171–2) – with marvels of the architectural past: 'Pyramids in sand. [. . .] Slaves Chinese wall. Babylon' (*U* 8.157). Dublin is also built on its Celtic past, 'Big stones left. Round towers' (*U* 8.157), its Bronze Age burial sites and pre-Norman monastery towers, so that, in combination with the modernity of the scene, Joyce images the city in historical flux: 'Cityful passing away, other cityful coming, passing away too: other coming on, passing on. Houses, lines of houses, streets, miles of pavements, piledup bricks, stones' (*U* 8.156–7). Joyce's 'syncopated' style in this passage has been beautifully analysed by Alter (2005: 127); it is a technique we may recognise both from the realism of Dickens and as it was developed in the 'impressionism' of Wilde, James and Symons. Modern space itself is itself 'piledup' (compare *AS* 2.3.85), carried from the houses to the blocks to the streets, the miles of pavement stretching out into the future. But most arresting in the passage is another related neologism, 'cityful'. As an adjectival form, the word implies the ways in which the space of Dublin possesses an abundance of the character of the city, which is itself 'piledup'. But 'cityful' here becomes a noun, both registering the sense in which quality produces substance (precisely a question of *aesthesis*) and signifying the 'characteristic', as James might say, of the modern city's excess. One space passing away as another comes into being: 'cityful' expresses the plenitude of the modernist city in both Joyce and Woolf, the aesthetic representation of an experience of prodigal bounty. In this, and for all the traces of its traumatic history, Joyce's Dublin becomes another site of affirmation, a 'cityful' space of pleasure and a riotously 'piledep' *aesthesis* – 'and yes I said yes I will Yes' (*U* 18.732).

Marcel Proust, *Mémoire Involontaire* and the Aesthetics of Space

As with Dickens's Crisparkle who finds Milton coming 'unbidden to his ear' (*ED* 16.144), Joyce and Woolf's aesthetics of space are constructed in part out of the memories that impress themselves involuntarily onto the conscious mind. This impression affects a subject's relationship with both time and space: it ruptures the chronological demands of 'clock time', with its attendant rationalisation and ordering of space, in a moment of *durée* that also serves to expand both space and the world of the subject. The point recalls Joyce, writing in echo of Pater's 'The Child in the House': there is the sense in which 'a scene disengages itself in the observer's memory, evoked, it would seem, by a word of so natural a homeliness as if those days were really present there [. . .] with their immediate pleasures' (*U* 14.401). By the time of writing 'Oxen of the Sun', Joyce had read 'a little' Proust, although precisely how much is unclear (Joyce 1975: 273), but like his French contemporary, his summary of Pater's aesthetics of space anticipates the modernist preoccupation with memory as that which 'de-realises' time and space, or rather, which shows that space and time are always already de-realised.

The topic of space is central to Georges Poulet's (1902–90) phenomenological reading of *L'espace proustien* [*Proustian Space*] (1963). For Poulet, the narrator's memories produce not only his childhood, but 'also a room, a church, a town, a solid topographical whole' (1977: 16). Proust's novel constitutes 'a collection of images, which, if brought together, furnishes a place and forms *an illustrated space*' (1977: 105), but one which does not constitute a totality.[6] Rather, Proust gives the reader a subjective experience of space, registered in a moment of *aesthesis*. As Deleuze puts it, time has 'the strange power to affirm simultaneously fragments that do not constitute a whole in space, any more than they form a whole by succession in time'. De-realising space multiplies it, so that in Proust, 'time is precisely the transversal of all possible spaces, including the space of time' (Deleuze 2008: 84). As Proust writes in the final sentence of

Le temps retrouvé [*Finding Time Again*] (1927), the final volume of *À la recherche du temps perdu*, a 'real' portrait of any given character would see them

> occupying a place far larger than the very limited one reserved for them in space, a place in fact almost infinitely extended, since they are in simultaneous contact [. . .] with such distant periods of their lives, between which so many days have taken up their place – in Time. (*RTP* 4: 625; 6: 358)

In Proust's masterpiece we see perhaps the most important way in which the nineteenth-century tradition of the aesthetics of space came to influence modernism. Explicitly a quality of 'visual memory' (*RTP* 1: 45; 1: 49), *mémoire involontaire* constitutes an aesthetics of space.[7]

Proust considers the experience of *mémoire involontaire* one that realism cannot fully capture. In *Du côté de chez Swann* [*The Way by Swann's*] (1913), Marcel remarks of the novel that 'a real human being, however profoundly we sympathize with him, in large part is perceived by our senses, that is to say, remains opaque to us' (*RTP* 1: 84; 1: 87). On the other hand, Proust compares *mémoire involontaire* to an experience of reading that goes beyond the 'reality' that the text supposedly seeks to represent. This is particularly true of our experience of space, a point of importance given that, as we have seen, the tradition of the aesthetics of space represents those spaces as aesthetic constructs which are traced throughout by prior literary representations. As Marcel comments, in the literary text, landscapes, 'already less interior to my body than the lives of these characters', become 'half projected in front of me' (*RTP* 1: 85; 1: 87). So too in our dreams, in which 'an image [. . .] remains for ever stamped, is adorned and enriched, by the glimmer of the colours not its own that may happen to surround it in our daydream' (*RTP* 1: 85; 1: 88). We have seen this kind of effect repeated throughout the course of this book, as in Ruskin's Byronesque Venice and Wilde's Dickensian London. This adornment and enrichment expand real space in the aesthetic instant, rupturing 'clock time' and simultaneously rewriting our experiences of those spaces, as dramatised in Jasper's ecstatic dream vision of Cloisterham Cathedral, a trace which can no longer be shaken from any moment in which this space is engaged with in the 'reality' of the narrative. For Proust, these aesthetic interpenetrations of space become 'an actual part of Nature itself' to be 'explored' (*RTP* 1: 85; 1: 88). Indeed, these Proustian reflections on the power of literature are clearly composed in dialogue with Pater. Proust, like Woolf, challenges the potential solipsism of the 'Conclusion'. 'For even if we have the sensation of being always surrounded by our own soul, it is not as though by a motionless prison', Marcel reflects: 'rather, we are in some sense borne along with a perpetual leap to go beyond it, to reach the outside, [. . . through] the resounding of an internal vibration' (*RTP* 1: 85–6; 1: 88).

The influences of Ruskin and Pater are felt everywhere in Proust's masterpiece – or, to be more precise, the influence of Ruskin and the covert presence of Pater. While Douglas Ainslee (1865–1948) recalled that Proust often discussed with him the relative merits of the two English aestheticians (Eells 2004: 95–6), Proust apparently preferred Ruskin, a point perhaps indicated by his relegation of Pater's name to the footnotes of his translations. While Ruskin is named in the pages of *À la recherche du temps perdu* (*RTP* 2: 9, 4: 224, 413; 2: 228, 5: 609, 6: 141), even if he is occasionally lampooned as 'a moping monomaniac' (*RTP* 1: 99; 2: 319), Pater is not. Nevertheless, as the famous incident with the *petites madeleines* clearly dramatises, *mémoire involontaire* is accessed precisely through a moment of sensuous *aesthesis*, where a chance encounter with a 'material object' (*RTP* 1: 44; 1: 47) prompts the power of recollection. This recalls Pater's 'The Child in the House', which Proust seems likely to have read (Eells 2002: 151–4). Likewise, Marcel's description of his childhood home in Combray (*RTP* 1: 43; 1: 46), where, ascending the staircase, he was fascinated by the 'aesthetic effects' that impressed themselves upon the mind, suggests the influence of Pater's imaginary portrait (*IP* 134–5). *À la recherche du temps perdu* charts the ways in which the aesthetic sensibility is formed firstly in childhood, and in particular by the formative ways in which the child is impressed by and engages with the sensory experience of space.

The recollection of the town of Combray and the surrounding countryside has a power over Marcel that both is the product of *aesthesis* and prompts his aesthetic sensibility. The topography is divided into two ways, Swann's and Guermantes (*RTP* 1: 132–3; 1: 135), with geographical space signifying more than simply physical location. To Marcel they become 'much more than their distances in kilometres', rather 'the distance that lay between two parts of my brain where I thought about them, one of those distances of the mind which not only moves things away from each other, but separates them and puts them on different planes' (*RTP* 1: 133; 1: 136). Indeed, as becomes clear, the aesthetics of these two ways 'formed for me for all time the countrysides where I would like to live' (*RTP* 1: 182; 1: 185), a projection that also served to rewrite Marcel's later encounters with other spaces, precisely through these hidden tributaries of recollection. Thus, Marcel finds that when encountering certain natural objects afresh – 'the cornflowers, the hawthorns, the apple trees' – they 'communicate immediately with my heart', 'because they are situated at the same depth, on the level of my past' (*RTP* 1: 182; 1: 185).

Combray itself is a space that is clearly written after Ruskin, 'its church summing up the town, representing it, speaking of it and for it into the distance' (*RTP* 1: 47; 1: 51), and in the Gothic of Saint-Hilaire 'the steeple [. . .] seemed to become aware of itself' (*RTP* 1: 62; 1: 66). Proust returns to this interest in the Gothic in the final part of *Du côté de chez Swann*, 'Place-names: the Name'. The young Marcel reflects on the power of the name and the ways in which prior aesthetic renditions of spaces impact their experienced 'reality', focusing on three Gothic towns: Balbec (Cabourg, Normandy), Florence and Venice. For instance, Marcel imagines a Florence that constitutes, 'in its essence, the spirit of Giotto' (*RTP* 1: 382; 1: 393), recalling an earlier passage in which he had reflected on 'the startling strangeness, the special beauty' of Giotto, whose 'symbolism' represented ideas 'as real, as actually experienced or physically handled' (*RTP* 1: 81; 1: 84). As Hillis Miller suggests (1976: 109), this brief consideration of the power of allegory, influential on both Benjamin and Paul de Man (1919–83), seems to have been itself influenced by Pater's development of Ruskin.[8] But it is most obviously Venice, once again, which shows this proleptic power of the aesthetics of space, and just as Ruskin's Venice is foreshadowed for him by Byron, so too Marcel's Venice is anticipated through Ruskin. Proust quotes Ruskin on Venice as '"the school of Giorgione, Titian's home"' (*RTP* 1: 384; 1: 395; compare *CW* 7: 375); its architecture '"bossed with jasper and paved with Emeralds"' (*RTP* 1: 385; 1: 395; compare *CW* 11: 244); the men of Venice '"majestic and terrible as the sea, bearing armour that gleamed with bronze beneath the folds of their blood-red cloaks"' (*RTP* 1: 385; 1: 395; compare *CW* 11: 244); the city's streets framed by 'those "rocks of amethyst"' which are '"like a reef in the Indian Ocean"' (*RTP* 1: 386; 1: 395; compare *CW* 10: 6). These passages, anticipating the aesthetics of Venice drawn in *Albertine disparue* [*The Fugitive*] (1925), show that Ruskin's most powerful Proustian legacy lay in the ways in which his descriptive prose created an aesthetics of space, that volcanic style, erupting with opulent imagery. In other words, what Proust, the greatest of his modernist heirs, learnt most from Ruskin was a question not of *theoria* but of *aesthesis*.

Like those writers of the tradition of the aesthetics of space that preceded him, Proust is less concerned by the apparent 'contradiction of wanting to look at and touch with the organs of my senses what I had created in a day-dream and not perceived with my senses' (*RTP* 1: 383; 1: 394). Rather, he welcomes the ways in which imagination and fantasy construct both his recollections of and engagements with space. In Venice in particular, that city that arguably inaugurated the tradition of the aesthetic of space, reality combines with 'the atmosphere of dreams' (*RTP* 1: 386; 1: 395). Proust invests space with the accumulated power of desire as expressed through the faculty of *aesthesis*. 'As my imagination drew strength from contact with my sensuality, as my sensuality spread throughout all the domains of my imagination, my desire grew boundless', Marcel comments, so that the object of his desire becomes localised as 'a necessary and natural product' of a particular space (*RTP* 1: 154–5; 1: 157). This serves both to create this space in the mind and to mark the aesthetics of these spaces off from 'reality', so that the space becomes 'raised a little above itself', as Pater puts it (*IP* 133). 'It was only by transforming' the image of any given place, Proust writes, 'by subjecting its reappearance in me to their own laws', that spaces become 'more beautiful', but also 'different' from what might be possible 'in reality' (*RTP* 1: 380; 1: 391). On the one hand, 'by increasing the arbitrary joys of my imagination', these aesthetic images also 'aggravated the future disappointments of my travels' (*RTP* 1: 380; 1: 391), with Marcel sounding like Huysmans's des Esseintes. On the other hand, however, these spaces become 'more particular' through this process, so that they also become 'more real' (*RTP* 1: 380; 1: 391). Place names become 'a store of dreams' that 'magnetized' his 'desires' (*RTP* 1: 382; 1: 393).

In this sense, *mémoire involontaire* is not simply the recollection of the past *aesthesis* of space, but, like Jasper's dream vision, a recollection of the history of the subject's desire in space. 'The reality I had known no longer existed' (*RTP* 1: 419; 1: 430), Marcel comments in the final paragraph of *Du côté de chez Swann*, the 'memory's picture' never amounting to an accurate synthesis of the impressions of the past:

> The places we have known do not belong solely to the world of space [. . .] They were only a thin slice among contiguous impressions that

> formed our life at that time; the memory of a certain image is only regret for a certain moment; and houses, roads, avenues are as fleeting, alas, as the years. (*RTP* 1: 419–20; 1: 430)

Proust's aesthetics of space crowns the tradition that this book has mapped. In Proust, we find that space, the subject and the process of *aesthesis* are brought together, documenting the ways in which all three are interlinked in that process which Pater had so memorably described as the 'continual vanishing away, that strange, perpetual, weaving and unweaving of ourselves' (*SHR* 188).

Notes

1. Including the melancholic Pater, whose ecstatic description of *La Gioconda* (*SHR* 99) is invoked in Eliot's 'Belladonna, the Lady of the Rocks' (l. 49). Eliot, however, was often dismissive of Pater, precisely on grounds of style (2005: 162, 163), and in 'Arnold and Pater' (1930), he famously charged the aesthete as being 'not wholly irresponsible for some untidy lives' (1932: 442). On modernism and decadence, see in particular Sherry 2015.
2. Perhaps surprisingly in this context and given our discussion in Chapter 2, Smith's study of Dickens's 'Unreal City' (2008) makes no reference to *Edwin Drood*.
3. On Woolf's London, see Brewster 1960 and Larsson 2017. See also Beja 1977 for a useful map of *Mrs Dalloway*.
4. Of course, not only English literature but other traditions as well, fittingly for a novel written in exile, the postscript beneath 'Penelope' reading '*Trieste–Zurich–Paris, 1914–1921*' (*U* 732). Jackson Cope (1981) has written illuminatingly on the debts Joyce owed to Italian decadence in the form of Gabrielle D'Annunzio (1863–1938), and Joyce's debt to French realism is well established. See also Ehrlich 2002 on the influence of French symbolism on Joyce's writing the city. On the Dublin of *Ulysses* as a world-city, and compared to Dos Passos's New York, see Harding 2003: 95–132.
5. On Wilde, Ireland and his politics, see Killeen 2005.
6. For a reading of Poulet's reading of Proust, see Malpas 1999: 159–74.
7. On Proust and the visual, see Carbone 2010.
8. In letter 7 of *Fors*, July 1871, Ruskin considers Giotto 'quite literal in his meaning, as well as figurative' (*CW* 27: 130). Pater expands the point in 'The Myth of Demeter and Persephone' (1875): 'The personification of abstract ideas by modern painters [. . .] shocks [. . .] the aesthetic sense [. . .] as a mere transparent allegory [. . .] On the other hand, such symbolical representations, under the form of human

persons, as Giotto's Virtues and Vices at Padua, [. . .] are profoundly poetical and impressive. They seem to be something more than mere symbolism, and to be connected with some peculiarly sympathetic penetration, on the part of the artist, into the subjects he intended to depict. Symbolism intense as this, is the creation of a special temper, in which a certain simplicity, taking all things literally, *au pied de la lettre*, is united to a vivid pre-occupation with the aesthetic beauty of the image itself, the *figured* side of figurative expression, the *form* of the metaphor' (1910c: 98–9).

Works Cited

Acton, William. *Prostitution, Considered in Its Moral, Social, and Sanitary Aspects*. London: John Churchill, 1867.

Adorno, Theodor. *Prisms*. Trans. Samuel and Shierry Weber. Cambridge, MA: MIT Press, 1967.

—. *Notes to Literature, Vol. 2*. Trans. Shierry Weber Nicholson. New York: Columbia University Press, 1992.

—. *Essays on Music*. Trans. Susan H. Gillespie. Berkeley: University of California Press, 2002.

—. *Aesthetic Theory*. Trans. Robert Hullot-Kentor. London: Continuum, 2004.

Agathocleous, Tanya. *Urban Realism and the Cosmopolitan Imagination in the Nineteenth Century*. Cambridge: Cambridge University Press, 2011.

Aji, Hélène. *Ezra Pound and Referentiality*. Paris: Presses de l'université de Paris-Sorbonne, 2003.

Alexander, Edward. *Matthew Arnold, John Ruskin, and the Modern Temper*. Columbus: Ohio State University Press, 1973.

Alter, Robert. *Imagined Cities: Urban Experience and the Language of the Novel*. New Haven: Yale University Press, 2005.

Althusser, Louis. *For Marx*. Trans. Ben Brewster. London: Verso, 2005.

—. *On Ideology*. Trans. Ben Brewster. London: Verso, 2008.

Amiel, Henri-Frédéric. *Amiel's Journal*. Trans. Mrs Humphry Ward. London: Macmillan, 1885.

Anderson, Mark M. *Kafka's Clothes: Ornament and Aestheticism in the Habsburg* Fin de Siècle. Oxford: Oxford University Press, 1992.

Anon. *Handbook for Travellers in Southern Germany: Being a Guide to Würtemberg, Bavaria, Austria, Tyrol, Salzburg, Styria, &c., the Austrian and Bavarian Alps, and the Danube from Ulm to the Black Sea*, 11th edn. London: John Murray, 1871.

—. 'Curiomania.' *Pall Mall Gazette* (13 January 1886). Pp. 4–5.

Anstruther-Thomson, C. *Art and Man*. London: John Lane, 1924.

Anthony, P. D. *John Ruskin's Labour: A Study of Ruskin's Social Theory*. Cambridge: Cambridge University Press, 1983.

Aristotle. *Nicomachean Ethics*. Trans. W. D. Ross. In *The Complete Works of Aristotle*. Ed. Jonathan Barnes. 2 vols. Princeton: Princeton University Press, 1984. 2: 1729–1867.

Arnold, Matthew. *The Complete Prose Works of Matthew Arnold, Vol. 1*. Ed. R. H. Super. Ann Arbor: University of Michigan Press, 1960.

—. *Selected Poems*. Ed. Timothy Peltason. Harmondsworth: Penguin, 1994.

Auerbach, Erich. *Mimesis*. Trans. Willard R. Trask. Princeton: Princeton University Press, 2003.

Austin, Linda M. 'Reading and the Romantics: Ruskin's "Fiction Fair and Foul".' *Studies in Romanticism*, 29:4 (1990). Pp. 583–601.

Bachelard, Gaston. *The Poetics of Space*. Trans. Maria Jolas. Boston: Beacon Press, 1994.

Bakhtin, Mikhail. *The Dialogic Imagination*. Trans. Caryl Emerson and Michael Holquist. Austen: University of Texas Press, 1981.

—. *Problems of Dostoevsky's Poetics*. Trans. Caryl Emerson. Minneapolis: University of Minnesota Press, 1984.

Baldick, Robert. *The Life of J.-K. Huysmans*. Oxford: Clarendon Press, 1955.

Barthes, Roland. *The Rustle of Language*. Trans. Richard Howard. Berkeley: University of California Press, 1989.

Bataille, Georges. *Visions of Excess: Selected Writings, 1927–1939*. Trans. Alan Stoekl. Minneapolis: University of Minnesota Press, 1985.

Baudelaire, Charles. *Œuvres complètes*. Ed. Claude Pichois. Paris: Gallimard, 1961.

—. *The Painter of Modern Life and Other Essays*. Trans. Jonathan Mayne. London: Phaidon, 1964.

—. *Selected Writings on Art and Literature*. Trans. P. E. Charvet. Harmondsworth: Penguin, 2006.

—. *The Flowers of Evil*. Trans. James McGowan. Oxford: Oxford University Press, 2008.

—. *Paris Spleen: Little Poems in Prose*. Trans. Keith Waldrop. Middletown, CT: Wesleyan University Press, 2010.

Baudrillard, Jean. *Simulacra and Simulation*. Trans. Sheila Faria Glaser. Ann Arbor: University of Michigan Press, 2004.

—. *Fragments: Cool Memories III, 1990–1995*. Trans. Emily Agar. London: Verso, 2007.

Baumbach, Sibylle. *Literature and Fascination*. London: Palgrave Macmillan, 2015.

Baumgarten, Alexander Gottlieb. *Aesthetica*. Frankfurt: Ioannis Christiani Kleyb, 1750.

Beaumont, Matthew, ed. *Adventures in Realism*. London: Blackwell, 2007.

—. *Nightwalking: A Nocturnal History of London*. London: Verso, 2016.

Becker, George J. *Documents of Modern Literary Realism*. Princeton: Princeton University Press, 1963.

Beckson, Karl. *London in the 1890s: A Cultural History*. New York: Norton, 1992.

—. ed. *Oscar Wilde: The Critical Heritage*. London: Routledge, 1998.

Beja, Morris. 'The London of Mrs. Dalloway.' *Virginia Woolf Miscellany*, 7 (1977). P. 4.

Benjamin, Walter. *Selected Writings*. Ed. Michael William Jennings, Howard Eiland and Gary Smith. 4 vols. Cambridge, MA: Harvard University Press, 1996–2003.

—. *The Origin of German Tragic Drama*. Trans. John Osborne. London: Verso, 1998.

—. *The Arcades Project*. Trans. Howard Eiland and Kevin McLaughlin. Cambridge, MA: Harvard University Press, 1999.

Bergson, Henri. *Creative Evolution*. Trans. A. Mitchell. London: Palgrave Macmillan, 2007.

Berman, Jessica. *Modernist Fiction, Cosmopolitanism, and the Politics of Community*. Cambridge: Cambridge University Press, 2001.

Berman, Marshall. *All That Is Solid Melts into Air: The Experience of Modernity*. London: Verso, 1988.

Berridge, Virginia, and Griffith Edwards. *Opium and the People: Opiate Use in Nineteenth-Century England*. London: Allen Lane, 1981.

Blanchot, Maurice. *The Space of Literature*. Trans. Ann Smock. Lincoln: University of Nebraska Press, 1982.

—. *The Step Not Beyond*. Trans. Lycette Nelson. Albany: State University of New York Press, 1992.

—. *The Instant of My Death*. Trans. Elizabeth Rottenberg. Stanford: Stanford University Press, 2000.

Bloom, Harold. 'Water Pater: The Intoxication of Belatedness.' *Yale French Studies*, 50 (1974). Pp. 163–89.

Booth, Charles. *Life and Labour of the People*. London: Williams and Norgate, 1889.

Borges, Jorges Luis. *The Aleph and Other Stories*. Trans. Andrew Hurley. Harmondsworth: Penguin, 2004.

Bowen, John. *Other Dickens: Pickwick to Chuzzlewit*. Oxford: Oxford University Press, 2000.

Boyiopoulos, Kostas. *The Decadent Image: The Poetry of Wilde, Symons, and Dowson*. Edinburgh: Edinburgh University Press, 2015.

Brewster, Dorothy. *Virginia Woolf's London*. New York: New York University Press, 1960.

Bridgham, Elizabeth A. *Spaces of the Sacred and Profane: Dickens, Trollope and the Victorian Cathedral Town*. London: Routledge, 2008.

Briggs, Asa. *Victorian Cities*. London: Odhams, 1963.

Brooks, Peter. *Realist Vision*. New Haven: Yale University Press, 2005.

—. *Henry James Goes to Paris*. Princeton: Princeton University Press, 2007.

Brown, Julia Prewett. *Cosmopolitan Criticism: Oscar Wilde's Philosophy of Art*. Charlottesville: University Press of Virginia, 1997.

Browning, Robert. *Selected Writings*. Ed. Richard Cronin and Dorothy McMillan. Oxford: Oxford University Press, 2015.

Buck-Morss, Susan. *The Dialectics of Seeing: Walter Benjamin and the Arcades Project*. Cambridge, MA: MIT Press, 1991.

Budgen, Frank. *James Joyce and the Making of 'Ulysses'*. Oxford: Oxford University Press, 1989.

Buelens, Gert. *Henry James and the 'Aliens' in Possession of the American Scene*. Amsterdam: Rodolpi, 2002.

Buitenhuis, Peter. *The Grasping Imagination: The American Writings of Henry James*. Toronto: University of Toronto Press, 1970.

Bürger, Peter. *Theory of the Avant-Garde*. Trans. Michael Shaw. Minneapolis: University of Minnesota Press, 1984.

Byerly, Alison. *Realism, Representation, and the Arts in Nineteenth-Century Literature*. Cambridge: Cambridge University Press, 1997.

Byron, Lord George Gordon. *The Complete Poetical Works*. Ed. Jerome J. McGann and Barry Weller. 7 vols. Oxford: Oxford University Press, 1980–93.

Carbone, Mauro. *An Unprecedented Deformation: Marcel Proust and the Sensible Ideas*. Trans. Niall Keane. Albany: State University of New York Press, 2010.

Carens, Timothy L. 'Restyling the Secret of the Opium Den.' In *Reading Wilde: Querying Spaces*. Ed. Carolyn Dever and Martin J. Taylor. New York: Fales Library, 1995. Pp. 65–76.

Carlyle, Thomas. *The Complete Works of Thomas Carlyle*. Ed. Henry Duff Traill. 30 vols. New York: P. F. Collier & Sons, 1897.

—. *Sartor Resartus*. Ed. Kerry McSweeney and Peter Sabor. Oxford: Oxford University Press, 2008.

Casanova, Pascale. *The World Republic of Letters*. Trans. M. B. DeBevoise. Cambridge, MA: Harvard University Press, 2004.

Cawston, Arthur. *A Comprehensive Scheme for Street Improvements in London Accompanied by Maps and Sketches*. London: E. Stanford, 1893.

Certeau, Michel de. *The Practice of Everyday Life*. Trans. Steven Rendall. Berkeley: University of California Press, 2002.

Chappell, Patrick. 'Paper Routes: *Bleak House*, Rubbish Theory, and the Character Economy of Realism.' *ELH*, 80:3 (2013). Pp. 783–810.

Cianci, Giovanni, and Peter Nicholls, eds. *Ruskin and Modernism*. London: Palgrave, 2001.

Clark, T. J. *The Painting of Modern Life: Paris in the Art of Manet and His Followers*. New York: Random House, 1984.

Clements, Patricia. *Baudelaire and the English Tradition*. Princeton: Princeton University Press, 1985.

Cockshut, A. O. J. '*Edwin Drood*: Early and Late Dickens Reconciled.' In *Dickens and the Twentieth Century*. Ed. John Gross and Gabriel Pearson. London: Routledge and Kegan Paul, 1962. Pp. 227–38.

Cohen, Jane R. *Charles Dickens and His Original Illustrators*. Columbus: Ohio State University Press, 1980.

Collins, Philip. 'Dickens and London.' In *The Victorian City: Ideas in the Air*. Ed. Harold J. Dyos and Michael Wolff. London: Routledge and Kegan Paul, 1973. Pp. 537–57.

—. 'Dickens and the City.' In *Visions of the Modern City*. Ed. William Sharpe and Leonard Wallock. New York: Columbia University Press, 1983. Pp. 97–117.

Collins, Wilkie. *The Moonstone*. Ed. John Sutherland. Oxford: Oxford University Press, 2008.

Collister, Peter. *Writing the Self: Henry James and America*, London: Pickering & Chatto, 2007.

Conrad, Joseph. *Heart of Darkness*. Ed. Cedric Watts. Oxford: Oxford University Press, 2008a.

—. *The Secret Agent*. Ed. John Lyon. Oxford: Oxford University Press, 2008b.

Cook, Matt. *London and the Culture of Homosexuality, 1885–1914*. Cambridge: Cambridge University Press, 2003.

—. 'Wilde's London.' In *Oscar Wilde in Context*. Ed. Kerry Powell and Peter Raby. Cambridge: Cambridge University Press, 2013. Pp. 49–59.

Cope, Jackson I. *Joyce's Cities: Archaeologies of the Soul*. Baltimore: Johns Hopkins University Press, 1981.

Crook, J. Mordaunt. *Brasenose: The Biography of an Oxford College*. Oxford: Oxford University Press, 2008.

Daley, Kenneth. *The Rescue of Romanticism: Walter Pater and John Ruskin*. Athens: Ohio University Press, 2001.

Dearden, James S. *The Library of John Ruskin*. Oxford: Oxford Bibliographic Society, 2012.

Defoe, Daniel. *A Tour Through the Whole Island of Great Britain*. Ed. Pat Rogers. Harmondsworth: Penguin, 1986.

Deleuze, Gilles. *The Logic of Sense*. Trans. Mark Seem. London: Continuum, 2004.

—. *Nietzsche and Philosophy*. Trans. Hugh Tomlinson. London: Continuum, 2006.

—. *Proust and Signs*. Trans. Richard Howard. London: Continuum, 2008.

—. and Félix Guattari. *Anti-Oedipus: Capitalism and Schizophrenia*. Trans. Robert Hurley, Mark Seem and Helen R. Lane. London: Continuum, 2004a.

—. and Félix Guattari. *A Thousand Plateaus: Capitalism and Schizophrenia*. Trans. Brian Massumi. London: Continuum, 2004b.

De Quincey, Thomas. *Confessions of an English Opium-Eater*. Ed. Robert Morrison. Oxford: Oxford University Press, 2008.

Derrida, Jacques. *Margins of Philosophy*. Trans. Alan Bass. Chicago: University of Chicago Press, 1982.

—. *The Truth in Painting*. Trans. Geoffrey Bennington and Ian McLeod. Chicago: University of Chicago Press, 1987.

—. *Rogues: Two Essays on Reason*. Trans. Pascale-Anne Brault and Michael Naas. Stanford: Stanford University Press, 2003.

—. *On Touching – Jean-Luc Nancy*. Trans. Christine Irizarry. Stanford: Stanford University Press, 2005.

Dickens, Charles. *The Pilgrim Edition of the Letters of Charles Dickens*. Ed. Madeline House et al. 12 vols. Oxford: Clarendon Press, 1965–2002.

—. *Sketches by Boz*. Ed. Dennis Walder. Harmondsworth: Penguin, 1995.

—. *Our Mutual Friend*. Ed. Adrian Poole. Harmondsworth: Penguin, 1997.

—. *'Gone Astray' and Other Papers from* Household Words, *1851–59*. Ed. Michael Slater. London: Dent, 1998.

—. *Martin Chuzzlewit*. Ed. Patricia Ingham. Harmondsworth: Penguin, 1999.

—. *The Old Curiosity Shop*. Ed. Norman Page. Harmondsworth: Penguin, 2000a.

—. *'The Uncommercial Traveller' and Other Papers, 1859–70*. Ed. Michael Slater and John Drew. London: Dent, 2000b.

—. *Dombey and Son*. Ed. Andrew Sanders. Harmondsworth: Penguin, 2002a.

—. *The Mystery of Edwin Drood*. Ed. David Paroissien. Harmondsworth: Penguin, 2002b.

—. *American Notes: For General Circulation*. Ed. Patricia Ingham. Harmondsworth: Penguin, 2003a.

—. *Bleak House*. Ed. Nicola Bradbury. Harmondsworth: Penguin, 2003b.

—. *Barnaby Rudge*. Ed. John Bowen. Harmondsworth: Penguin, 2003c.

—. *A Christmas Carol and Other Christmas Writings*. Ed. Michael Slater. Harmondsworth: Penguin, 2003d.

—. *Great Expectations*. Ed. Charlotte Mitchell. Harmondsworth: Penguin, 2003e.

—. *Hard Times*. Ed. Kate Flint. Harmondsworth: Penguin, 2003f.

—. *Nicholas Nickleby*. Ed. Mark Ford. Harmondsworth: Penguin, 2003g.

—. *Oliver Twist*. Ed. Philip Horne. Harmondsworth: Penguin, 2003h.

—. *Pictures from Italy*. Ed. Patricia Ingham. Harmondsworth: Penguin, 2003i.

—. *A Tale of Two Cities*. Ed. Richard Maxwell. Harmondsworth: Penguin, 2003j.
—. *The Pickwick Papers*. Ed. Mark Wormald. Harmondsworth: Penguin, 2003k.
—. *David Copperfield*. Ed. Jeremy Tambling. Harmondsworth: Penguin, 2004.
—. *Little Dorrit*. Ed. Dennis Walder. Oxford: Oxford University Press, 2012.
Dowling, Linda. *Language and Decadence in the Victorian Fin de Siècle*. Princeton: Princeton University Press, 1986.
—. 'Walter Pater and Archaeology: The Reconciliation with the Earth.' *Victorian Studies*, 31:2 (1988). Pp. 209–31.
—. *Hellenism and Homosexuality in Victorian Oxford*. Ithaca: Cornell University Press, 1994.
Doyle, Arthur Conan. *Sherlock Holmes: Selected Stories*. Ed. Barry McCrea. Oxford: Oxford University Press, 2014.
Drayton, Michael. *Works: Vol. 1*. London: W. Reeve, 1753.
Dryden, Linda. *The Modern Gothic and Literary Doubles: Stevenson, Wilde and Wells*. London: Palgrave Macmillan, 2003.
Eagles, Stuart. *After Ruskin: The Social and Political Legacies of a Victorian Prophet, 1870–1920*. Oxford: Oxford University Press, 2011.
Eastlake, Laura. *Ancient Rome and Victorian Masculinity*. Oxford: Oxford University Press, 2019.
Edel, Leon. 'The Major Phase of Henry James.' *University of Toronoto Quarterly*, 16:4 (1947). Pp. 424–8.
Eells, Emily. *Proust's Cup of Tea: Homoeroticism and Victorian Culture*. London: Ashgate, 2002.
—. '"Influence Occulte": The Reception of Pater's Works in France before 1922.' In *The Reception of Walter Pater in Europe*. Ed. Stephen Bann. London: Continuum, 2004. Pp. 87–116.
Ehrlich, Heyward. 'James Joyce's Four-Gated City of Modernisms.' In *Joyce and the City: The Significance of Place*. Ed. Michael Begnal. New York: Syracuse University Press, 2002. Pp. 1–17.
Eliot, George. *Middlemarch*. Ed. Rosmary Ashton. Harmondsworth: Penguin, 2003.
Eliot, T. S. *Selected Essays*. London: Faber & Faber, 1932.
—. *The Annotated Wasteland*. Ed. Lawrence Rainey. New Haven: Yale University Press, 2005.
Ellmann, Richard. *Oscar Wilde*. Harmondsworth: Penguin, 1988.
Engels, Friedrich. *The Condition of the Working Class in England*. Ed. David McLellan. Oxford: Oxford University Press, 2009.
Evangelista, Stefano. 'Rome and the Romantic Heritage in Walter Pater's *Marius the Epicurean*.' In *Romans and Romantics*. Ed. Timothy Saunders,

Charles Martindale, Ralph Pite and Mathilde Skoie. Oxford: Oxford University Press, 2012. Pp. 305–26.

—. and Richard Hibbitt, eds. '*Fin-de-Siècle* Cosmopolitanism.' *Comparative Critical Studies*, 10:2 (2013).

'F.' 'In Pater's Rooms.' *The Speaker* (26 August 1899). Pp. 207–8.

Feldman, Jessica. *Gender on the Divide: The Dandy in Modernist Literature.* Ithaca: Cornell University Press, 1993.

—. *Victorian Modernism: Pragmatism and the Varieties of Aesthetic Experience.* Cambridge: Cambridge University Press, 2002.

Ferguson, Priscilla Parkhurst. *Paris as Revolution: Writing the Nineteenth-Century City.* Berkeley: University of California Press, 1997.

Fields, James T. *In and Out of Doors with Charles Dickens.* Boston: James Osgood, 1876.

Fitzgerald, F. Scott. *The Great Gatsby*. Ed. Ruth Prigozy. Oxford: Oxford University Press, 2008.

Flaubert, Gustave. *Œuvres: Tome II.* Ed. A. Thibaudet and R. Dumesnil. Paris: Gallimard, 1952.

—. *Three Tales.* Trans. Roger Whitehouse. Harmondsworth: Penguin, 2005.

Ford, Jane, Kim Edward Keates and Patricia Pulham, eds. *Economies of Desire at the Victorian Fin de Siècle: Libidinal Lives.* London: Routledge, 2015.

Forster, E. M. *A Room with a View*. Ed. Oliver Stallybrass. Harmondsworth: Penguin, 1986.

Forster, John. *The Life of Charles Dickens.* Ed. A. J. Hoppé. 2 vols. London: Dent, 1966.

Foucault, Michel. *Discipline and Punish: The Birth of the Prison.* Trans. Alan Sheridan. Harmondsworth: Penguin, 1991.

—. *The Use of Pleasure: The History of Sexuality, Vol. 2.* Trans. Robert Hurley. Harmondsworth: Penguin, 1992.

—. 'Different Spaces.' Trans. Robert Hurley. In *Aesthetics, Method and Epistemology: Essential Works of Foucault, 1954–1984, Vol. 2.* Ed. James D. Faubion. Harmondsworth: Penguin, 2000a. Pp. 175–85.

—. 'The Thought of the Outside.' Trans. Brian Massumi. In *Aesthetics, Method and Epistemology: Essential Works of Foucault, 1954–1984, Vol. 2.* Ed. James D. Faubion. Harmondsworth: Penguin, 2000b. Pp. 147–69.

—. *The Birth of the Clinic: An Archaeology of Medical Perception.* Trans. Alan Sheridan. London: Routledge, 2003.

—. *History of Madness.* Trans. Jonathan Murphy and Jean Khalfa. London: Routledge, 2009.

Francescato, Simone. *Collecting and Appreciating: Henry James and the Transformation of Aesthetics in the Age of Consumption.* Bern: Peter Lang, 2010.

Frank, Ellen Eve. *Literary Architecture: Essays Toward a Tradition*. Berkeley: University of California Press, 1979.

Freedman, Jonathan. *Professions of Taste: Henry James, British Aestheticism and Commodity Culture*. Stanford: Stanford University Press, 1990.

Freeman, Edward Augustus. *An Essay on the Origin and Development of Window Tracery in England*. Oxford: John Henry Parker, 1851.

Freeman, Nicholas. *Conceiving the City: London, Literature, and Art, 1870–1914*. Oxford: Oxford University Press, 2007.

Freud, Sigmund. *The Standard Edition of the Complete Psychological Works of Sigmund Freud*. Trans. James Strachey. 24 vols. London: Vintage, 2001.

Frichot, Hélène, Catharina Gabrielsson and Jonathan Metzger, eds. *Deleuze and the City*. Edinburgh: Edinburgh University Press, 2016.

Fronto. *Correspondence, Vol. I*. Trans. C. R. Haines. Cambridge, MA: Harvard University Press, 1919.

Fuller, Peter. *Theoria: Art, and the Absence of Grace*. London: Chatto & Windus, 1988.

Gagnier, Regenia. *The Insatiability of Human Wants: Economics and Aesthetics in Market Society*. Chicago: University of Chicago Press, 2000.

Garbett, Edward Lacy. *Rudimentary Treatise on the Principles of Design in Architecture as Deducible from Nature and Exemplified in the Works of the Greek and Gothic Architects*. London: John Weale, 1850.

Gifford, Don, and Robert J. Seidman. *Ulysses Annotated*. Berkeley: University of California Press, 2008.

Gissing, George. *Charles Dickens: A Critical Study*. London: Blackie, 1898.

Gomel, Elana. '"Part of the Dreadful Thing": The Urban Chronotope of *Bleak House*.' *Partial Answers*, 9:2 (2011). Pp. 297–309.

Goncourt, Edmond, and Jules Goncourt. *Journal: Mémoires de la vie littéraire, Tome 1: 1851–1856*. Ed. Robert Ricatte. Monaco: Éditions de l'imprimerie nationale, 1956.

Gosse, Edmund. *Critical Kit-Kats*. London: Heinemann, 1896.

Gregory, Rosalyn, and Benjamin Kohlmann, eds. *Utopian Spaces of Modernism: British Literature and Culture, 1885–1945*. London: Palgrave Macmillan, 2011.

Hales, Shelley. 'A Search for Home: The Representation of the Domestic in *Marius the Epicurean*.' In *Pater the Classicist*. Ed. Stefano Evangelista, Charles Martindale and Elisabeth Prettlejohn. Oxford: Oxford University Press, 2017. Pp. 135–48.

Hannah, Daniel. *Henry James, Impressionism and the Public*. London: Ashgate, 2013.

Harding, Desmond. *Writing the City: Urban Visions and Literary Modernism*. London: Routledge, 2003.

Hardy, Thomas. *The Woodlanders*. Ed. Dale Kramer. Oxford: Oxford University Press, 2009.

Harrison, Brian. 'The Sunday Trading Riots of 1855.' *Historical Journal*, 8 (1965). Pp. 219–45.

Harrison, John Smith. 'Pater, Heine, and the Old Gods of Greece.' *PMLA*, 39:3 (1924). Pp. 655–86.

Harvey, David. *Social Justice and the City*. Baltimore: Johns Hopkins University Press, 1973.

—. *Paris, Capital of Modernity*. London: Routledge, 2006.

Haviland, Beverly. *Henry James's Last Romance*. Cambridge: Cambridge University Press, 1997.

Hegel, G. W. F. *The Letters*. Trans. Clark Butler and Christine Seiler. Bloomington: Indiana University Press, 1984.

Heidegger, Martin. *Poetry, Language, Thought*. Trans. Albert Hofstadter. New York: Harper & Row, 1977a.

—. *The Question Concerning Technology and Other Essays*. Trans. William Lovitt. New York: Harper & Row, 1977b.

Herford, Oliver. *Henry James's Style of Retrospect: Late Personal Writings, 1890–1915*. Oxford: Oxford University Press, 2016.

Hewison, Robert. *John Ruskin: The Argument of the Eye*. London: Thames & Hudson, 1976.

—. *Ruskin on Venice: The Paradise of Cities*. New Haven: Yale University Press, 2009.

Hillis Miller, J. *Charles Dickens: The World of his Novels*. Cambridge, MA: Harvard University Press, 1958.

—. 'Walter Pater: A Partial Portrait.' *Daedalus*, 105:1 (1976). Pp. 97–113.

Hilton, Tim. *John Ruskin: The Early Years*. New Haven: Yale University Press, 1985.

—. *John Ruskin: The Later Years*. New Haven: Yale University Press, 2000.

Holland, Eugene. *Baudelaire and Schizoanalysis: The Sociopoetics of Modernism*. Cambridge: Cambridge University Press, 1993.

Holleran, Claire. *Shopping in Ancient Rome: The Retail Trade in the Late Republic and the Principate*. Oxford: Oxford University Press, 2012.

Hollington, Michael. 'Dickens the Flâneur.' *The Dickensian*, 77 (1981). Pp. 71–87.

—. *Dickens and the Grotesque*. Totowa: Barnes and Noble, 1984.

—. 'Adorno, Benjamin and *The Old Curiosity Shop*.' *Dickens Quarterly*, 6:3 (1989). Pp. 87–95.

Holmes, Charles John. *Self and Partners (Mostly Self)*. London: Macmillan, 1936.

Horace. *Satires. Epistles. The Art of Poetry*. Trans. H. Rushton Fairclough. Cambridge, MA: Harvard University Press, 1926.

Hugo, Victor. *Les Misérables*. Ed. Maurice Allem. Paris: Gallimard, 1951.

—. *Les Misérables*. Trans. Norman Denny. Harmondsworth: Penguin, 1982.

Husserl, Edmund. *The Crisis of European Sciences and Transcendental Phenomenology*. Trans. D. Carr. Evanston: Northwestern University Press, 1970.

Hutchinson, Ben. *Lateness and Modern European Literature*. Oxford: Oxford University Press, 2016.

Huysmans, Joris-Karl. *À vau-l'eau*. Brussels: Henry Kistemaeckers, 1882.

—. *La cathédrale*. Paris: Tresse & Stock, 1898.

—. *À rebours*. Ed. Rose Fortassier. Paris: Imprimerie nationale, 1981.

—. *Là-Bas*. Ed. Yves Hersant. Paris: Gallimard, 1985.

—. *The Cathedral*. Trans. Clara Bell. Sawtry: Dedalus, 1989.

—. *The Damned*. Trans. Terry Hale. Harmondsworth: Penguin, 2001.

—. *Against Nature*. Trans. Robert Baldick. Harmondsworth: Penguin, 2003.

—. *Downstream*. Trans. Robert Baldick. New York: Turtle Point, 2005.

—. *Écrits sur l'art: 1867–1905*. Ed. Patrice Locmant. Paris: Bartillat, 2006.

Inman, Billie Andrew. *Walter Pater's Reading: A Bibliography of his Library Borrowings and Literary References, 1858–1873*. New York: Garland, 1981.

—. *Walter Pater and His Reading: With a Bibliography of His Library Borrowings, 1874–1877*. New York: Garland, 1990.

—. 'Estrangement and Connection: Walter Pater, Benjamin Jowett, and William M. Hardinge.' In *Pater in the 1990s*. Ed. Laurel Brake and Ian Small. Greensboro: ELT Press, 1991. Pp. 1–20.

Izzo, David Garratt, and Daniel T. O'Hara, eds. *Henry James Against the Aesthetic Movement: Essays on the Middle and Late Fiction*. Jefferson: McFarland, 2006.

James, Henry. *The Letters of Henry James*. Ed. Leon Edel. 4 vols. Cambridge, MA: Harvard University Press, 1974–84.

—. *Literary Criticism, Vol. 1: Essays on Literature, American Writers, English Writers*. Ed. Leon Edel and Mark Wilson. New York: Library of America, 1984.

—. *The Complete Notebooks*. Ed. Leon Edel and Lyall H. Powers. Oxford: Oxford University Press, 1987.

—. *The Painter's Eye: Notes and Essays on the Pictorial Arts*. Ed. John L. Sweeney. Madison: University of Wisconsin Press, 1989.

—. *Italian Hours*. Ed. John Auchard. Harmondsworth: Penguin, 1995.

—. *The American Scene*. Ed. John F. Sears. Harmondsworth: Penguin, 2003.

—. *The Aspern Papers and Other Stories*. Ed. Adrian Poole. Oxford: Oxford University Press, 2009a.

—. *The Portrait of a Lady*. Ed. Roger Luckhurst. Oxford: Oxford University Press, 2009b.

—. *Notes of a Son and Brother and the Middle Years: A Critical Edition*. Ed. Peter Collister. Charlottesville: University of Pennsylvania Press, 2011.

Jameson, Fredric. 'The Realist Floor-Plan.' In *On Signs*. Ed. Marshall Blonsky. Baltimore: Johns Hopkins University Press, 1986. Pp. 373–83.

—. *Postmodernism, or the Cultural Logic of Late Capitalism*. Durham, NC. Duke University Press, 1991.

—. *The Political Unconscious: Narrative as a Socially Symbolic Act*. London: Routledge, 2002.

—. *Late Marxism: Adorno or the Persistence of the Dialectic*. London: Verso, 2007.

—. *The Antinomies of Realism*. London: Verso, 2013.

Jenkyns, Richard. *The Victorians and Ancient Greece*. Oxford: Blackwell, 1980.

Jerrold, Blanchard. 'Charles Dickens: In Memoriam.' *Gentleman's Magazine*, 5 (1870). Pp. 228–41.

—. *London: A Pilgrimage*. London: Grant, 1872.

Johnson, Edgar. *Charles Dickens: His Tragedy and Triumph*. Boston: Little, Brown, 1952.

Joyce, James. *Selected Letters*. Ed. Richard Ellmann. London: Faber & Faber, 1975.

—. *Dubliners*. Ed. Jeri Johnson. Oxford: Oxford University Press, 2008a.

—. *Ulysses*. Ed. Jeri Johnson. Oxford: Oxford University Press, 2008b.

Jung, C. G. *Memories, Dreams, Reflections*. Trans. Richard and Clara Wilson. New York: Vintage, 1989.

Kafka, Franz. *The Metamorphosis and Other Stories*. Trans. Joyce Crick. Oxford: Oxford University Press, 2009.

Kant, Immanuel. *Critique of the Power of Judgment*. Trans. Paul Guyer and Eric Matthew. Cambridge: Cambridge University Press, 2000.

Karlin, Daniel. *Proust's English*. Oxford: Oxford University Press, 2005.

Keefe, Robert. '"Apollo in Picardy": Pater's Monk and Ruskin's Madness.' *ELT*, 29:4 (1986). Pp. 361–70.

Kerr, Greg. *Dream Cities: Utopia and Prose by Poets in Nineteenth-Century France*. Cambridge: Legenda, 2013.

Killeen, Jarlath. *The Faiths of Oscar Wilde: Catholicism, Folklore and Ireland*. London: Palgrave Macmillan, 2005.

Kimmey, John. *Henry James and London: The City in his Fiction*. Bern: Peter Lang, 1991.

Kipling, Rudyard. *American Notes*. New York: Manhattan Press, 1890a.

—. 'Without Benefit of Clergy.' *Macmillan's Magazine*, 62 (1890b). Pp. 148–60.

Kirwan, Daniel Joseph. *Palace and Hovel: Phases of London Life*. Hartford, CT: Belknap & Bliss, 1870.

Kite, Stephen. *Building Ruskin's Italy: Watching Architecture*. London: Ashgate, 2012.

Lacan, Jacques. *Freud's Papers on Technique*. Trans. John Forrester. New York: Norton, 1991.

—. *On Feminine Sexuality*. Trans. Bruce Fink. New York: Norton, 1998a.

—. *The Four Fundamental Concepts of Psychoanalysis*. Trans. Alan Sheridan. New York: Norton, 1998b.

—. *Écrits*. Trans. Bruce Fink. New York: Norton, 2007a.

—. *The Other Side of Psychoanalysis*. Trans. Russell Grigg. New York: Norton, 2007b.

—. *Anxiety*. Trans. A. R. Price. Cambridge: Polity, 2014.

—. 'On a Reform in its Hole.' Trans. John Holland. *S: Journal of the Circle for Lacanian Ideology Critique*, 8 (2015). Pp. 14–21.

Lamb, Charles. *The Letters of Charles and Mary Anne Lamb, Vol. 1: 1796–1801*. Ed. Edwin W. Marrs. Ithaca: Cornell University Press, 1975.

Landow, George P. *The Aesthetic and Critical Theories of John Ruskin*. Princeton: Princeton University Press, 1971.

Larsson, Lisbeth. *Walking Virginia Woolf's London: An Investigation in Literary Geography*. Trans. David Jones. London: Palgrave Macmillan, 2017.

Laver, James. *The First Decadent*. London: Faber & Faber, 1954.

Lefebvre, Henri. *The Production of Space*. Trans. Donald Nicholson-Smith. London: Blackwell, 1991.

—. *Rhythmanalysis*. Trans. Stuart Elden and Gerald Moore. London: Bloomsbury, 2013.

Levenson, Michael. '*Fin-de-Siècle* London.' In *Henry James in Context*. Ed. David McWhirter. Cambridge: Cambridge University Press, 2010. Pp. 37–46.

Lindsay, Jack. *The Monster City: Defoe's London, 1688–1730*. London: Hart-Davis MacGibbon, 1976.

Livi, François. *J.-K. Huysmans: À rebours et l'espirit decadent*. Paris: La renaissance du livre, 1972.

Lockie, John. *Topography of London*. London: G. & L. Nichol, 1810.

Longfellow, Henry Wadsworth. *The Poetical Works*. Ed. William Michael Rossetti. London: E. Moxon, 1871.

Lukács, Georg. *The Historical Novel*. Trans. Hannah and Stanley Mitchell. Lincoln: University of Nebraska Press, 1983.

Lynch, Kevin. *The Image of the City*. Cambridge, MA: MIT Press, 1960.

MacCarthy, Fiona. *William Morris: A Life for Our Time*. London: Faber & Faber, 1994.

McKee, Patricia. *Reading Constellations: Urban Modernity in Victorian Fiction*. Oxford: Oxford University Press, 2014.

McKnight, Natalie. "'A Little Humoring of Pussy's Points!'; or, Sex – the *Real* Unsolved Mystery of *Edwin Drood*." *Dickens Quarterly*, 30:1 (2013). Pp. 55–63.

McLees, Ainslie Armstrong. *Baudelaire's Argot Plastique: Poetic Caricature and Modernism*. Athens: University of Georgia Press, 1989.

McNamara, Kevin R. 'Building Culture: The Two New Yorks of Henry James's *The American Scene*.' *Prospects*, 18 (1993). Pp. 121–51.

Macpherson, James. *The Poems of Ossian and Related Works*. Ed. Howard Gaskill. Edinburgh: Edinburgh University Press, 1996.

Mallarmé, Stéphane. *Correspondance, Tome I: 1862–1871*. Ed. Henri Mondor and Lloyd James Austin. Paris: Gallimard, 1959.

—. *Correspondance, Tome III: 1886–1889*. Ed. Henri Mondor and Lloyd James Austin. Paris: Gallimard, 1969.

Mallett, Philip. 'The City and the Self.' In *Ruskin and the Environment: The Storm-Cloud of the Nineteenth Century*. Ed. Michael Wheeler. Manchester: Manchester University Press, 1995. Pp. 38–75.

Malpas, J. E. *Place and Experience: A Philosophical Topography*. Cambridge: Cambridge University Press, 1999.

Manganiello, Dominic. *Joyce's Politics*. London: Routledge, 1980.

Marez, Curtis. 'The Other Addict: Reflections on Colonialism and Oscar Wilde's Opium Smoke Screen.' *ELH*, 64:1 (1997). Pp. 257–87.

Marlowe, Christopher. *The Complete Works, Vol. 1*. Ed. Fredson Bowers. 2nd edn. Cambridge: Cambridge University Press, 1981.

Martindale, Charles, Stefano Evangelista and Elisabeth Prettlejohn, eds. *Pater the Classicist*. Oxford: Oxford University Press, 2017.

Marx, Karl. *Surveys from Exile*. Trans. David Fernbach. Harmondsworth: Penguin, 1973.

—. *Capital, Vol. I*. Trans. Ben Fowkes. Harmondsworth: Penguin, 1990.

—. *Early Writings*. Trans. Rodney Livingstone and Gregor Benton. Harmondsworth: Penguin, 1992.

—. and Friedrich Engels. *Collected Works, Vol. 4: Marx and Engels: 1844–1845*. London: Lawrence and Wishart, 1975.

—. and Friedrich Engels. *Collected Works, Vol. 5: Marx and Engels: 1845–1847*. London: Lawrence and Wishart, 1976.

—. and Friedrich Engels. *Collected Works, Vol. 48: Engels: 1887–1890*. London: Lawrence and Wishart, 2001.

—. and Friedrich Engels. *The Communist Manifesto*. Trans. Samuel Moore. Harmondsworth: Penguin, 2002.

Matthiessen, F. O. *Henry James: The Major Phase*. Oxford: Oxford University Press, 1944.

Maxwell, Catherine. 'Whistlerian Impressionism and the Venetian Variations of Vernon Lee, John Addington Symonds, and Arthur Symons.' *The Yearbook of English Studies*, 40 (2010). Pp. 217–45.

—. *Scents and Sensibility: Perfume in Victorian Literary Culture*. Oxford: Oxford University Press, 2017.

Mayhew, Augustus. *Paved with Gold or, The Romance and Reality of the London Streets*. London: Chapman and Hall, 1858.

Meckier, Jerome. *Hidden Rivalries in Victorian Fiction: Dickens, Realism, and Revaluation*. Lexington: University Press of Kentucky, 1987.

Mendelssohn, Michèle. *Henry James, Oscar Wilde and Aesthetic Culture*. Edinburgh: Edinburgh University Press, 2007.

Merrill, Susan. *A Pot of Paint: Whistler v. Ruskin*. Washington: Smithsonian Institution Press, 1992.

Mighall, Robert. *A Geography of Victorian Gothic Fiction: Mapping History's Nightmares*. Oxford: Oxford University Press, 2003.

Miller, John. 'Rebellious Tigers, a Patriotic Elephant and an Urdu-Speaking Cockatoo: Animals in "Mutiny" Fiction.' *Journal of Victorian Culture*, 17:4 (2012). Pp. 480–91.

Milton, John. *The Major Works*. Ed. Stephen Orgel and Jonathan Goldberg. Oxford: Oxford University Press, 1991.

Monsman, Gerald. *Walter Pater's Art of Autobiography*. New Haven: Yale University Press, 1980.

Moore, Rayburn S. *The Correspondence of Henry James and the House of Macmillan, 1877–1914*. London: Macmillan, 1993.

Moretti, Franco. *Atlas of the European Novel, 1800–1900*. London: Verso, 1998.

—. 'Graphs, Maps, Trees: Abstract Models for Literary History – 2.' *New Left Review*, 26 (2004). Pp. 79–103.

Morris, William. *The Earthly Paradise*. Ed. Florence S. Boos. 2 vols. London: Routledge, 2002.

Morton, Timothy. *Ecology without Nature*. Cambridge, MA: Harvard University Press, 2007.

Murray, Alex. *Landscapes of Decadence: Literature and Place at the Fin de Siècle*. Cambridge: Cambridge University Press, 2016a.

—. '"The London Sunday Faded Slow": Time to Spend in the Victorian City.' In *The Oxford Handbook of Victorian Literary Culture*. Ed. Juliet John. Oxford: Oxford University Press, 2016b. Pp. 310–26.

Nassaar, Christopher S. 'The Problem of the Jewish Manager in *The Picture of Dorian Gray*.' *The Wildean*, 22 (2003). Pp. 29–36.

Neverow, Vara S. 'Virginia Woolf and City Aesthetics.' In *The Edinburgh Companion to Virginia Woolf and the Arts*. Ed. Maggie Humm. Edinburgh: Edinburgh University Press, 2010. Pp. 88–103.

Nietzsche, Friedrich. *Selected Letters of Friedrich Nietzsche*. Trans. Christopher Middleton. Indianapolis: Hackett, 1996.

—. *The Anti-Christ, Ecce Homo, Twilight of the Idols: And Other Writings*. Trans. Judith Norman. Cambridge: Cambridge University Press, 2005.

—. *Thus Spoke Zarathustra*. Trans. Adrian Del Caro. Cambridge: Cambridge University Press, 2006.

Nightingale, Andrea Wilson. *Spectacles of Truth in Classical Greek Philosophy: 'Theoria' in its Cultural Context*. Cambridge: Cambridge University Press, 2004.

Norwich, John Julius. *A History of Venice*. Harmondsworth: Penguin, 2003.

Nunokawa, Jeff. *Tame Passions of Wilde: The Styles of Manageable Desire*. Princeton: Princeton University Press, 2003.

Ohi, Kevin. *Henry James and the Queerness of Style*. Minneapolis: University of Minnesota Press, 2011.

Panofsky, Erwin. *Gothic Architecture and Scholasticism*. Latrobe: Archabbey Press, 1951.

Park, Hyungji. '"Going to Wake Up Egypt": Exhibiting Empire in "Edwin Drood".' *Victorian Literature and Culture*, 30:2 (2002). Pp. 529–50.

Parkes, Adam. 'A Sense of Justice: Whistler, Ruskin, James, Impressionism.' *Victorian Studies*, 42:4 (2000). Pp. 593–629.

Parkinson, Joseph Charles. 'Lazarus, Lotus-Eating.' *All The Year Round*, 15:368 (1866). Pp. 421–5.

Parsons, Deborah L. *Streetwalking the Metropolis: Women, the City and Modernity*. Oxford: Oxford University Press, 2000.

Pater, Walter. 'Thistle.' bMS Eng 1150 (31). Unpublished manuscript. Houghton Library, Harvard University. [n.d.]

—. *Appreciations, With an Essay on Style*. London: Macmillan, 1910a.

—. *Essays from 'The Guardian'*. London: Macmillan, 1910b.

—. *Greek Studies*. London: Macmillan, 1910c.

—. *Marius the Epicurean: His Sensations and Ideas*. 2 vols. London: Macmillan, 1910d.

—. *Miscellaneous Studies*. London: Macmillan, 1910e.

—. *Plato and Platonism*. London: Macmillan, 1910f.

—. *The Letters of Walter Pater*. Ed. Lawrence Evans. Oxford: Oxford University Press, 1970.

—. *Studies in the History of the Renaissance*. Ed. Donald L. Hill. Berkeley: University of California Press, 1980.

—. *Gaston de Latour*. Ed. Gerald Monsman. Oxford: Oxford University Press, 2019a.

—. *Imaginary Portraits*. Ed. Lene Østermark-Johansen. Oxford: Oxford University Press, 2019b.

Pennant, Thomas. *Account of London*. London: Robert Faulder, 1790.

Piggott, Gillian. *Dickens and Benjamin: Moments of Revelation, Fragments of Modernity*. London: Routledge, 2012.

Pile, Steve. *The Body and the City: Psychoanalysis, Space and Subjectivity*. London: Routledge, 1996.

Plato. *Republic*. Trans. Paul Shorey. In *The Collected Dialogues*. Ed. Edith Hamilton and Huntington Cairns. Princeton: Princeton University Press, 1989a. Pp. 575–844.

—. *Symposium*. Trans. Michael Joyce. In *The Collected Dialogues*. Ed. Edith Hamilton and Huntington Cairns. Princeton: Princeton University Press, 1989b. Pp. 526–74.

Porte, Joel, ed. *New Essays on 'The Portrait of a Lady'*. Cambridge: Cambridge University Press, 1990.

Porter, Dale H. *The Thames Embankment: Environment, Technology and Society in Victorian London*. Akron, OH: University of Akron Press, 1998.

Porter, James I. 'Reception, Receptivity, and Anachronism in *Marius the Epicurean*'. In *Pater the Classicist*. Ed. Stefano Evangelista, Charles Martindale and Elisabeth Prettlejohn. Oxford: Oxford University Press, 2017. Pp. 149–62.

Porter, Roy. *London: A Social History*. Cambridge, MA: Harvard University Press, 1998.

Posnock, Ross. 'Affirming the Alien: The Pragmatic Pluralism of *The American Scene*.' In *The Cambridge Companion to Henry James*. Ed. Jonathan Freedman. Cambridge: Cambridge University Press, 1998. Pp. 224–46.

Poulet, Georges. *Proustian Space*. Trans. Elliott Coleman. Baltimore: Johns Hopkins University Press, 1977.

Pound, Ezra. *The Cantos*. New York: New Directions, 1970.

Proust, Marcel. *À la recherche du temps perdu*. Ed. Jean-Yves Tadié. 4 vols. Paris: Gallimard, 1987–9.

—. *On Reading Ruskin*. Trans. Jean Autret, William Burford and Phillip J. Wolfe. New Haven: Yale University Press, 1987.

—. *In Search of Lost Time, Vol. 1: The Way by Swann's*. Ed. Christopher Prendergast. Trans. Lydia Davis. Harmondsworth: Penguin, 2003a.

—. *In Search of Lost Time, Vol. 2: In the Shadow of Young Girls in Flower*. Ed. Christopher Prendergast. Trans. James Grieve. Harmondsworth: Penguin, 2003b.

—. *In Search of Lost Time, Vol. 5: The Prisoner and The Fugitive*. Ed. Christopher Prendergast. Trans. Carol Clark and Peter Collier. Harmondsworth: Penguin, 2003c.

—. *In Search of Lost Time, Vol. 6: Finding Time Again*. Ed. Christopher Prendergast. Trans. Ian Patterson. Harmondsworth: Penguin, 2003d.

Przyboś, Julia. *Zoom sur les décadents*. Paris: Corti, 2002.

Raven, Robert. 'Some Observations on Charles Collins's Sketches for "Edwin Drood".' *The Dickensian*, 96 (2000). Pp. 118–26.

Rawlings, Peter. 'Grotesque Encounters in the Travel Writing of Henry James.' *The Yearbook of English Studies*, 34 (2004). Pp. 171–85.

Robinson, Alan. *Imagining London, 1770–1900*. London: Palgrave Macmillan, 2004.

Rose, Gillian. *Feminism and Geography: The Limits of Geographical Knowledge*. Minneapolis: University of Minnesota Press, 1993.

Ross, Iain. *Oscar Wilde and Ancient Greece*. Cambridge: Cambridge University Press, 2013.

Ross, Kristen. *The Emergence of Social Space: Rimbaud and the Paris Commune*. London: Verso, 2008.

Ruskin, John. *The Complete Works of John Ruskin*. Ed. E. T. Cook and Alexander Wedderburn. 39 vols. London: George Allen, 1903–12.

—. *La Bible d'Amiens*. Trans. Marcel Proust. Paris: Mercure de Paris, 1926.

Rutledge, Steven. *Ancient Rome as a Museum: Power, Identity, and the Culture of Collecting*. Oxford: Oxford University Press, 2012.

Rutherford, Richard. 'Marcus the Stoic in *Marius the Epicurean*'. In *Pater the Classicist*. Ed. Stefano Evangelista, Charles Martindale and Elisabeth Prettlejohn. Oxford: Oxford University Press, 2017. Pp. 121–34.

Said, Edward. *On Late Style: Music and Literature against the Grain*. London: Bloomsbury, 2017.

Saint, Andrew, et al. *A History of the Royal Opera House, Covent Garden, 1732–1982*. London: Royal Opera House, 1982.

Salamensky, S. I. 'Oscar Wilde's "Jewish Problem": Salomé, the Ancient Hebrew and the Modern Jewess.' *Modern Drama*, 55:2 (2012). Pp. 197–215.

Sartre, Jean-Paul. *Baudelaire*. Trans. Martin Turnell. New York: New Directions, 1967.

Schaffer, Talia. *The Forgotten Female Aesthetes: Literary Culture in Late-Victorian England*. Charlottesville: University of Virginia Press, 2000.

Schor, Naomi. 'Agape and Anorexia: Decadent Fast and Democratic Feast.' In *French Food: On the Table, on the Page, and in French Culture*. Ed. Lawrence R. Schehr and Allen S. Weiss. London: Routledge, 2001. Pp. 90–8.

Schwartz, Vanessa. *Spectacular Realities: Early Mass Culture in Fin-de-Siècle Paris*. Berkeley: University of California Press, 1999.

Schwarzbach, F. S. *Dickens and the City*. London: Athlone Press, 1979.

Shakespeare, William. *Anthony and Cleopatra*. Ed. John Wilders. London: Bloomsbury, 1995.

—. *As You Like It*. Ed. Juliet Dusinberre. London: Bloomsbury, 2006.

—. *Macbeth*. Ed. Sandra Clark and Pamela Mason. London: Bloomsbury, 2015.

—. *Othello*. Ed. E. A. J. Honingmann. London: Bloomsbury, 2016.

—. *Cymbeline*. Ed. Valerie Wayne. London: Bloomsbury, 2017.

Shatto, Susan. "Dickens's *Edwin Drood* and Southey's 'Jaspar.'" *Notes and Queries*, 32:3 (1985). Pp. 359–60.

Shelley, Percy Bysshe. *The Poems of Shelley, Vol. 1: 1804–1817*. Ed. Geoffrey Matthews and Kelvin Everest. London: Routledge, 2014.

Sherry, Vincent. *Modernism and the Reinvention of Decadence*. Cambridge: Cambridge University Press, 2015.

Sherson, Errol. *London's Lost Theatres of the Nineteenth Century*. London: John Lane, 1925.

Shrimpton, Nicholas. '"Rust and Dust": Ruskin's Pivotal Work.' In *New Approaches to Ruskin*. Ed. Robert Hewison. London: Routledge, 1981. Pp. 51–68.

—. 'Ruskin and the Aesthetes.' In *Ruskin and the Dawn of the Modern*. Ed. Dinah Birch. Oxford: Oxford University Press, 1999. Pp. 131–52.

Shuter, William. *Rereading Walter Pater*. Cambridge: Cambridge University Press, 1997.

—. 'Pater's "Grudge against Apollo": Mythology and Pathology in "Apollo in Picardy".' *ELT*, 44:2 (2001). Pp. 181–98.

Sidney, Philip. *The Major Works*. Ed. Katherine Duncan-Jones. Oxford: Oxford University Press, 2002.

Simmel, Georg. *The Sociology of Georg Simmel*. Trans. Kurt H. Wollf. London: Macmillan, 1950.

Smith, Karl A. *Dickens and the Unreal City: Searching for Spiritual Significance in Nineteenth-Century London*. London: Palgrave Macmillan, 2008.

Smollett, Tobias. *The Expedition of Humphry Clinker*. Ed. Lewis M. Knapp. Oxford: Oxford University Press, 2009.

Soja, Edward W. *Postmodern Geographies: The Reassertion of Space in Critical Social Theory*. London: Verso, 2010.

Southey, Robert. *Joan of Arc*. Ed. Lynda Pratt. London: Pickering & Chatto, 2004a.

—. *The Curse of Kehama*. Ed. Daniel Sanjiv Roberts. London: Pickering & Chatto, 2004b.

Spencer, Robert. 'Lateness and Modernity in Theodor Adorno.' In *Late Style and its Discontents*. Ed. Gordon McMullan and Sam Smiles. Oxford: Oxford University Press, 2016. Pp. 220–34.

Squier, Susan Merrill. *Virginia Woolf and London: Sexual Politics of the City*. Chapel Hill: University of North Carolina Press, 1985.

Steadman Jones, Gareth. *Outcast London: A Study in the Relationship Between Classes in Victorian Society*. Oxford: Clarendon Press, 1971.

Stevens, Hugh. *Henry James and Sexuality*. Cambridge: Cambridge University Press, 1998.

Stokes, John. 'Wilde's Paris.' In *Oscar Wilde in Context*. Ed. Kerry Powell and Peter Raby. Cambridge: Cambridge University Press, 2013. Pp. 60–71.

Stonehouse, J. H. *Catalogue of the Library of Charles Dickens at Gad's-hill*. London: Piccadilly Fountain Press, 1935.

Swann, Charles. 'Dickens, Ruskin and the City: Parallels or Influence?' *The Dickensian*, 82 (1986). Pp. 66–81.

Symons, Arthur. *London: A Book of Aspects*. Minneapolis: Edmund D. Brooks, 1909.

—. *The Symbolist Movement in Literature*. New York: Dutton, 1919.

—. *Selected Early Poetry*. Ed. Jane Desmarais and Chris Baldick. Cambridge: MHRA, 2017.

Tambling, Jeremy. 'Repression in Mrs Dalloway's London.' *Essays in Criticism*, 39:2 (1989). Pp. 137–55.

—. *Dickens, Violence, and the Modern State: Dreams of the Scaffold*. London: Macmillan, 1995.

—. *Lost in the American City: Dickens, James, and Kafka*. London: Palgrave Macmillan, 2001.

—. *Going Astray: Dickens and London*. London: Pearson, 2009.

—. *On Anachronism*. Manchester: Manchester University Press, 2010.

—. *Dickens' Novels as Poetry: Allegory and Literature of the City*. London: Routledge, 2015.

Tanner, Tony. *Venice Desired*. Oxford: Blackwell, 1992.

Thomas, Ronald R. 'Dickens's Sublime Artefact.' *Browning Institute Studies*, 14 (1986). Pp. 71–95.

Thompson, James. *City of Dreadful Night*. Ed. Edwin Morgan. Edinburgh: Canongate, 1993.

Tucker, Edward L. 'James and Charles Dickens.' *The Henry James Review*, 17:2 (1996). Pp. 208–9.

Tucker, Paul. '"Reanimate Greek": Pater and Ruskin on Botticelli.' In *Walter Pater: Transparencies of Desire*. Ed. Laurel Brake, Lesley Higgins and Carolyn Williams. Greensboro: ELT Press, 2002. Pp. 119–32.

Turner, Frank M. *The Greek Heritage in Victorian Britain*. New Haven: Yale University Press, 1981.

Vance, Norman. *The Victorians and Ancient Rome*. London: Blackwell, 1997.

Vidler, Anthony. *The Architectural Uncanny: Essays in the Modern Unhomely*. Cambridge, MA: MIT Press, 1992.

Villanueva, Darió. *Theories of Literary Realism*. Trans. Mihai I. Spariosu and Santiago García-Castañón. Albany: State University of New York Press, 1997.

Vita, Paul. 'Returning the Look: Victorian Writers and the Paris Morgue.' *Nineteenth-Century Contexts*, 25:3 (2003). Pp. 241–56.

von Eckardt, Wolf, Sander L. Gilman and J. Edward Chamberlin. *Oscar Wilde's London: A Scrapbook of Vices and Virtues, 1880–1900*. Garden City, NJ: Anchor Press, 1987.

Walker, Alexander. *Beauty; Illustrated by an Analysis and Classification of Beauty in Woman*. London: Effingham Wilson, 1836.

Walkowitz, Judith R. *Nights Out: Life in Cosmopolitan London*. New Haven: Yale University Press, 2012.

Walkowitz, Rebecca L. *Cosmopolitan Style: Modernism Beyond the Nation*. New York: Columbia University Press, 2006.

Ward, Anthony. *Walter Pater: The Idea in Nature*. London: Macgibbon and Kee, 1966.

Ward, Mrs Humphry. *A Writer's Recollections*. 2 vols. New York: Harper and Brothers, 1918.

Watt, Ian. *The Rise of the Novel*. Berkeley: University of California Press, 2001.

Wells, H. G. 'Zoological Retrogression.' *Gentleman's Magazine*, 271 (1891). Pp. 246–53.

Welsh, Alexander. *The City of Dickens*. Oxford: Clarendon Press, 1971.

Westphal, Bertrand. *Geocriticism: Real and Fictional Spaces*. Trans. Robert T. Tally Jr. London: Palgrave Macmillan, 2011.

Wettlaufer, Alexandra. *In the Mind's Eye: The Visual Impulse in Diderot, Baudelaire and Ruskin*. Amsterdam: Rodopi, 2003.

Wheeler, Michael. *Ruskin's God*. Cambridge: Cambridge University Press, 1999.

Whiteley, Giles. *Aestheticism and the Philosophy of Death: Walter Pater and Post-Hegelianism*. Cambridge: Legenda, 2010.

—. 'Pater's *Parerga*: Framing the Imaginary Portraits.' *Victoriographies*, 3:2 (2013). Pp. 119–35.

—. *Oscar Wilde and the Simulacrum*. Cambridge: Legenda, 2015.

—. 'Cosmopolitan Space: Political Topographies in Oscar Wilde's London.' *Victoriographies*, 7:2 (2017a). Pp. 124–42.

—. 'An Unnoted Quotation from Pater in Wilde's Review of William Morris.' *Notes and Queries*, 64:4 (2017b). Pp. 640–1.

—. 'Dickens and Southey: *The Mystery of Edwin Drood* and *The Curse of Kehama*.' *Dickens Quarterly*, 35:3 (2018a). Pp. 262–6.

—. *Schelling's Reception in Nineteenth-Century British Literature*. London: Palgrave Macmillan, 2018b.

—. 'A Swine from Epicurus's Herd: The Culinary, Aesthetic, and Erotic in Wilde and Huysmans.' In *Modernism and Food Studies: Politics, Aesthetics and the Avant-Garde*. Ed. Jessica Martell, Adam Fajardo and Philip Keel Geheber. Gainesville: University Press of Florida, 2019. Pp. 19–38.

Wilde, Oscar. *The Complete Letters of Oscar Wilde*. Ed. Merlin Holland and Rupert Hart-Davis. London: Fourth Estate, 2000a.

—. *The Picture of Dorian Gray*. Ed. Robert Mighall. Harmondsworth: Penguin, 2000b.

—. *Poems and Poems in Prose*. Ed. Bobby Fong and Karl Beckson. Oxford: Oxford University Press, 2000c.

—. *De Profundis; Epistola: In Carcere et Vinculis*. Ed. Ian Small. Oxford: Oxford University Press, 2005a.

—. *The Picture of Dorian Gray: The 1890 and 1891 Texts*. Ed. Joseph Bristow. Oxford: Oxford University Press, 2005b.

—. *Criticism: Historical Criticism, Intentions, The Soul of Man*. Ed. Josephine M. Guy. Oxford: Oxford University Press, 2007.

—. *The Importance of Being Earnest and Other Plays*. Ed. Peter Raby. Oxford: Oxford University Press, 2008.

—. *Journalism I*. Ed. John Stokes and Mark Turner. Oxford: Oxford University Press, 2013a.

—. *Journalism II*. Ed. John Stokes and Mark Turner. Oxford: Oxford University Press, 2013b.

—. *The Short Fiction*. Ed. Ian Small. Oxford: Oxford University Press, 2018.

Williams, Raymond. *The Country and the City*. London: Chatto & Windus, 1973.

Wolff, Janet. 'The Invisible *Flâneuse*: Women and the Literature of Modernity.' *Theory, Culture and Society*, 2:3 (1985). Pp. 37–46.

Wolfreys, Julian. *Writing London: The Trace of the Urban Text from Blake to Dickens*. London: Palgrave Macmillan, 1998.

—. *Dickens' London: Perception, Subjectivity and Urban Multiplicity*. Edinburgh: Edinburgh University Press, 2012.

Woolf, Virginia. *The Diary of Virginia Woolf, Vol. 3: 1925–1930*. Ed. Anne Oliver Bell. London: Hogarth, 1980.

—. *The Essays of Virginia Woolf, Vol. 3: 1919–1924*. Ed. Andrew McNeillie. London: Hogarth, 1988.

—. *The Essays of Virginia Woolf, Vol. 4: 1925–1928*. Ed. Andrew McNeillie. London: Hogarth, 1994.

—. *Mrs Dalloway*. Ed. David Bradshaw. Oxford: Oxford University Press, 2009a.

—. *The Voyage Out*. Ed. Lorna Sage. Oxford: Oxford University Press, 2009b.

—. *Orlando*. Ed. Michael H. Whitworth. Oxford: Oxford University Press, 2015.

Wordsworth, William. *The Major Works*. Ed. Stephen Gill. Oxford: Oxford University Press, 2008.

Wrenn, Angus. *Henry James and the Second Empire*. Cambridge: Legenda, 2008.

Wright, Thomas. *The Life of Walter Pater*. 2 vols. London: Everett, 1907.

Xu, Weinying. 'The Opium Trade and *Little Dorrit*: A Case of Reading Silences.' *Victorian Literature and Culture*, 25:1 (1997). Pp. 53–66.

Young, Edward. *Night Thoughts*. Ed. Stephen Cornford. Cambridge: Cambridge University Press, 1989.

Žižek, Slavoj. *The Metastases of Enjoyment*. London: Verso, 2005.

Zola, Émile. *Lettres de Paris, Notes parisiennes: Le sémaphore de Marseille, 1871–1877*. Ed. M. E. Leozappa. Lecce: Milella, 1981.

—. *Thérèse Raquin*. Ed. Auguste Dezalay. Paris: Fasquelle, 1984.

—. *Thérèse Raquin*. Trans. Andrew Rothwell. Oxford: Oxford University Press, 2008.

Index